FIREWALK

A NOVEL

CHRIS ROBERSON

NIGHT SHADE BOOKS
NEW YORK

Night Shade books may be purchased in bulk at special discounts for sales promotion, corporate gifts, fund-raising, or educational purposes. Special editions can also be created to specifications. For details, contact the Special Sales Department, Night Shade Books, 307 West 36th Street, 11th Floor, New York, NY 10018 or info@skyhorsepublishing.com.

Night Shade Books® is a registered trademark of Skyhorse Publishing, Inc.®, a Delaware corporation.

Visit our website at www.nightshadebooks.com.

10 9 8 7 6 5 4 3 2 1

Library of Congress Cataloging-in-Publication Data is available on file.

Print ISBN: 978-1-59780-879-8

Cover design by Claudia Noble

Printed in the United States of America

PROLOGUE

FIVE YEARS AGO . . .

The killer wouldn't stop apologizing as he dismembered the corpse.

"I'm so sorry. I never meant for anyone to get hurt. One more and I'll be done."

Special Agent Isabel Lefevre lay on the rusted metal plates that formed the floor of the lantern room at the top of the lighthouse. It felt like there was a seam of burning ice on her leg where the killer's blade had bit into her flesh, which only burned colder when Izzie tried unsuccessfully to stand.

"I'm sorry." The killer's voice was muffled behind the silver skull mask he wore and sounded labored as he wrenched the corpse's left arm free of its socket. "It's too late to stop now."

Izzie had fired two rounds before the killer slashed the pistol from her grasp. The downward arc of the killer's forward-curving blade had continued, cutting deeply into her leg, and he had kicked her gun away from her when Izzie had collapsed on the floor. She pressed her right palm hard against the cut on the back of her left hand, trying to stanch the flow of blood, but without much success. Her radio was smashed to bits on the floor beside her. She hoped that Detective Tevake and the others had heard the shots, but with the rain pelting hard against the windows outside and the discordant speed metal blaring from the speakers at the bottom of the stairs, it didn't seem likely. She considered calling out for him, but there was the killer's blade to consider.

"You don't have to do this." Izzie's voice cracked as she spoke, and she tried again louder to be heard over the din. "You don't have to do this, Nicholas. You've won."

At the sound of his name the killer paused, and his eyes shifted behind the mask as he looked in her direction. "What did you say?"

"You've won, Nicholas. Whatever your disagreement with the others was about, it's over now. You got what you wanted. There aren't any left." Izzie made herself move her gaze to the mutilated corpse, the wide cut across the abdomen, the organs and intestines strewn across the floor, the severed limbs stacked like firewood. "Francis Zhao was the last one."

Holding the handle of his curved blade with his right hand, the killer used his left to push the skull mask up onto his forehead. Izzie saw tired, haunted eyes in the face of the man the news reporters had dubbed "The Recondito Reaper," but who she and the rest of the task force knew to be Nicholas Fuller, former researcher at Ross University. The dead man lying in pieces on the floor in front of him had been a coworker, years before.

"You think I *wanted* this?" There was a desperate edge to the killer's voice. If he was surprised that Izzie knew his name, it didn't show. "I *warned* them!"

"I know. The university administrators told us all about it." She decided to try a different tack. "You have the power here."

"The *power*?!" The killer stood up, gestured to the windows with the long, forward-curving blade, and then pointed to the floor. "The power is what I'm *worried* about! You think *these* will protect me for long?"

Intricate patterns had been inscribed on the thick glass with a black marker, a riot of mathematical formulae, tight blocks of text, strange sigils. On the floor a ring of salt surrounded pentagrams, hexagrams, spirals, and a confusion of other occult symbols etched in chalk, including a veve for protection that Izzie recognized from her childhood.

"They are *out* there in the dark. More of them. *Waiting*." The killer pulled the skull mask back down over his face. "And I have to stop the ones that are already here."

For a confused moment, Izzie thought that he meant the other police who were already on scene. Detective Tevake was downstairs and the other two Recondito police officers were searching the living quarters next door with Supervisory Special Agent Henderson. But the killer couldn't have known about any of them. He was talking about something else. Something that had him terrified.

"I want to understand." Izzie tried to shift into a sitting position, then slammed back hard on her shoulder when the cut on her leg objected. She was light-headed from the blood loss, and having trouble focusing. She just needed to keep him occupied until the others came looking for her. "Explain it to me."

The killer knelt back down and grabbed the dead man's hair with one hand, and started sawing at his neck with the other.

"Gravity leaks into other spaces, but doors swing both ways. They went down into the dark, and the dark came back with them. Ridden. Passengers. I saw it, even if no one else did. I didn't understand it myself, until the old daykeeper gave me the key. He showed me how to walk through the fire, and see the shadows for what they are. But now he's gone, and there's just me. I only have one more to go and my work is finished. Just one more."

The killer seemed to have forgotten she was there. His voice was little more than a murmur as he sawed and hacked at the dead man's neck, and she struggled to hear him over the music blaring downstairs.

"One more what, Nicholas?" Had he targeted another victim? Was there a member of the university's Undersight team that the task force had failed to identify?

The killer stood up, holding the dead man's severed head by the hair.

"The student. I have to find him, and then I will—"

"Freeze!"

Detective Patrick Tevake stood on the top step of the spiral staircase, aiming his pistol at the killer's back.

The killer turned, severed head in one hand, blade in the other. When Izzie had entered the lantern room he had been behind the door, catching her off guard, but now he was too far away for his blade to be of much use against the police officer's semi-automatic.

"I said don't move!"

"You can't stop me now." The killer took a step forward, bringing him closer to where Izzie lay on the floor. "It's almost over—"

Five rounds slammed into the killer's torso. As he staggered back, his blade fell and clattered on the metal plates while the severed head rolled across the floor, coming to rest at Izzie's side.

"Almost—" The killer's voice gurgled as blood welled at the corners of his mouth.

The killer fell backwards, shattering the window on impact. Broken symbols and ruined formulae rained down as he fell through.

Izzie looked over at the severed head on the floor beside her. The dead man's eyes were closed, and his expression seemed strangely tranquil. She couldn't help but gasp.

"Now it's over." Detective Tevake had crossed the floor to look down at the killer's body on the white rocks below. He glanced over his shoulder at Izzie. "Agent Lefevre, you hanging in there?"

Izzie could hear her pulse pounding in her ears. Her head swam. Darkness crawled at the edges of her vision.

"Agent Lefevre?" The detective was coming towards her now, holstering his pistol. "Izzie?"

The dead man had opened his eyes and was looking directly into hers. Now his mouth began to move, lips clearly forming words, though with no lungs to push air through his larynx he made no sound. Then the darkness closed in around her.

"Izzie, can you hear me?"

NOW . . .

"**C**an you hear me?"

Special Agent Isabel Lefevre sat at her desk in the Behavioral Analysis Unit at Quantico, holding the cold plastic of her phone against her ear, listening to a voice she'd not heard in five years.

"Yes," she finally managed. "I can hear you."

"You have to come back to Recondito, Izzie." Patrick Tevake sounded stricken. "It isn't over."

CHAPTER ONE

"Business or pleasure?"

Izzie stifled a sigh, and immediately regretting taking the earbuds from her ears as the plane began its descent. From the window seat, she could see the skyline of Recondito coming into view below, the swirling waters of the estuary bay separated from the expanse of the Pacific Ocean by the narrow isthmus.

She turned to the passenger in the middle seat and managed a wan smile. "Business."

"What kind of work are you in?"

He was middle aged, dressed in business casual, and was probably in management or sales at some big corporation. Since finishing the paperback novel that had kept him occupied since they boarded the connecting flight in Chicago, he'd been leafing through the inflight magazine that he'd borrowed from Izzie somewhere over Utah. The cover story was about Martin Zotovic, who'd gone from college dropout to self-made millionaire in the last few years after his software company, Parasol, released a series of killer apps for the mobile market. Izzie had several of the company's apps installed on her own phone but had never heard of the Recondito-based entrepreneur until she read the inflight magazine herself before giving it to her fellow passenger. That bit of trivia and the fact that Parasol had recently finished renovating Recondito's landmark Pinnacle Tower were the only points of interest in the article, which was only marginally more diverting than the crossword puzzle that had been left half-solved by some previous passenger, so she hadn't minded giving it up when the man had failed to find his own copy in the seatback in front of him.

Izzie had been grateful that he didn't seem to be the chatty type, preferring to sit in silence with her own thoughts. But apparently he was instead the sort to wait until the safety of the final moments of a flight to engage with the passengers around him. Normally she might have hidden behind a book or magazine herself, but he had taken away her sole defense. The only reading material she'd brought were case files, but she didn't feel comfortable bringing those out into the open where prying eyes might see things the public probably shouldn't, and so the files remained safely stored away in her bag along with her FBI credentials and badge.

"I'm an analyst." Like many Bureau agents, Izzie was usually less than forthcoming about her employment when talking to strangers. It was easier in most situations to let a half-truth suffice than to be drawn into a conversation about sensitive matters with people who might ask questions that she couldn't answer.

"What, like a psychologist?"

"Something like that." Izzie's faint smile made a brief, flickering return, and then she broke eye contact to shift her gaze back out at the city spreading out below them. As the pilot banked to the south towards the airport situated at the bay's southern edge, she spotted the lighthouse that rose above the white rocks of Ivory Point. It was low tide, and the tiny island was connected to the isthmus by the muddy land bridge.

"First time in Recondito?"

Izzie's sigh was harder to suppress this time. Having ridden in silence since O'Hare, he was clearly intent on getting as much social engagement out of the flight's final moments as he could manage. She answered without looking away from the window. "No, I was here once before, but it's been a while." The scar on the side of Izzie's leg itched, and she resisted the temptation to bend down and scratch. "Five years."

"Five years, that's all we've got." He chuckled. "Earth is really dying."

Izzie's head snapped around and she narrowed her eyes suspiciously.

He smiled. "Like the David Bowie song, right? The one about the end of the world?"

Izzie realized that her hands were tightened into fists in her lap. She concentrated on relaxing them. "Oh. Right." She knew her smile had to be even less convincing this time than before.

A flight attendant appeared in the aisle, her hand brushing the man's shoulder. "Sir, can you return your seat to the upright position?"

While he fiddled with the seat controls, Izzie slipped her earbuds back in, and by the time he turned back around she was busy acting as if she were engrossed in a stupid game on her phone. He tried once more to get her attention, but when she pretended not to hear, he turned and began pestering the passenger in the aisle seat, instead.

Izzie absently poked and swiped at the phone's screen, but her mind was elsewhere. Five years . . .

Izzie had only been with the FBI's Behavioral Analysis Unit for a short while when she first traveled to Recondito. What little she knew about the city, outside of what she'd read in the case files on the ongoing investigation, she'd gleaned from popular culture. When she was in high school she'd been a regular viewer of *Behind the Lines,* a primetime sitcom about a cartoonist that was set in the city, though all but the exterior establishing shots were clearly filmed on a soundstage in Hollywood. In college she'd seen an old made-for-TV movie about the Eschaton Center on the outskirts of town that had been popular among film stars and rock musicians until a notorious mass murder-suicide closed its doors forever. Izzie knew a little about the city's music scene in the nineties, from listening to every CD that Ciren had ever recorded, over and over again, and had briefly considered a road trip to see the singer-songwriter perform live on the very stage where she'd begun her career, but in the end Izzie decided she couldn't afford the expense on a student's budget.

All of this served to give her a vague notion of what the city would be like when she first arrived: a small coastal city, with picturesque fish markets and streetcars and museums like she'd seen in the opening credits of the *Behind the Lines* sitcom, coffee shops and theaters and gardens like Ciren had sung about, and maybe even a few leftover hippies and counter-culture types who had orbited the Eschaton crowd. Row houses and Mission Revival architecture and gleaming towers of glass and steel, the Pinnacle Tower and the docks, and the Hyde Park green.

And she'd found all of those things, just as she'd expected. But that was just surface, and the city was so much more.

The locals sometimes called it the "Hidden City," in part because of the bay around which Recondito was built, where the freshwaters of the Varada River mixed with the salty waters of the ocean. Early explorers had named the estuary the "Hidden Bay" when they nearly failed to notice it as they sailed along the coast, the narrow entrance almost completely obscured by the rocky white cliffs that rose on either side. But residents considered Recondito to be hidden in another sense, as well. Bound by hills on one side and the ocean on the other, with the bay in between, there were limits on how large the city could grow, which could have served to make the city quaint and insular, but Izzie found that the opposite was true. If anything, it boasted a richer and more varied culture than cities ten times its size.

The hidden bay had been home to a community of pre-Colombian hunter-gatherers in the days of the pharaohs, and in the millennia since then, visitors to the area had included Spanish explorers, British sailors, New England whalers, Russian missionaries, and more. After a brief gold run in the nineteenth century, Recondito had become a home for immigrants, welcoming waves of newcomers from Ireland, France, the South Pacific, and elsewhere, all of them infusing elements of their own cultures into the city.

Izzie saw evidence of that long history of cultural mixing and melding everywhere. The food was the first and most noticeable feature: espresso in the sidewalk cafés along Rue

Des Livres, so strong that after one sip Izzie thought she would stay awake for a week; savory pirozhki from the bakeries in the Kiev; rashers of bacon at an Irish pub in Ross Village that refused to serve stouts at anything colder than room temperature; mouth-watering Polynesian pork and rice at a hole in the wall in Oceanview that she'd ducked into just to get out of the rain; taquerias and sushi bars and Thai restaurants and pizza joints and on and on. If not for her habit of running three miles every day at dawn, she was sure she'd have gained thirty pounds by the time she left.

But the city's cultural heritage ran far deeper than items on a menu. During the months she was in the city as part of the Reaper task force, Izzie had interacted with any number of people who were Recondito natives: police officers and criminals, millionaires and vagrants, cab drivers, shopkeepers, college professors and construction workers. Each of them clearly had a unique experience with the Hidden City, shaped in their own particular way by the place. The bookseller who still proudly displayed the spiraling tattoos on her face and neck that she'd inked in her troubled youth as a gang member, the same tribal marks that her seafaring Polynesian ancestors would have worn. The scientist whose family had lived in the city when it was little more than a collection of rude huts around a Franciscan mission, who spent his days investigating the mysteries of the universe.

Though she was there for months, Izzie always felt like a visitor to the city, and not simply because she slept in a hotel room and drove a rented car. It was because the longer she stayed in Recondito, the more she discovered about the place, and the more she realized there was left to discover. It was like one of those fractal images that revealed an ever-increasing amount of detail the closer you looked at them. When she finally left, she could navigate the city's streets with ease, knew the best places to eat and the best bars for a late-night drink, but still felt as though she was only beginning to scratch the surface of the city.

She hadn't expected ever to return, and after the way her last visit had ended she was not entirely sanguine about returning now. But Patrick had insisted that he had something that she needed to see. Something about the Reaper case that only she would understand.

So here she was, back in the Hidden City again after all this time.

CHAPTER TWO

The junior agent from the Resident Agency was waiting in baggage claim with a sign on which she'd written "LEFEVRE" in neat block letters, and was dressed in a white shirt, dark pantsuit, and low-heeled boots. She had graduated from the FBI Academy at Quantico so she couldn't be any younger than her mid-twenties, but Izzie couldn't help thinking that she looked like she should still be in middle school. Had Izzie ever been that young?

"Agent Lefevre?" she said as Izzie approached, holding the sign in both hands. Her voice had a tentative edge to it, like a fan approaching a pop star to ask for an autograph.

"That's me," Izzie answered. In her suede jacket, T-shirt, and jeans, she might have passed for an academic on vacation, or a session musician between gigs.

"Special Agent Daphne Richardson." She lowered the sign and stuck out a hand to shake. "It's an honor, ma'am."

"Please, call me Izzie." Daphne was probably only a year or two younger than Izzie had been when she'd first come to Recondito, and here she was treating her like a grand dame. Maybe she did want an autograph, after all.

"Do you have any . . . ?" Daphne glanced over at the baggage carousels. "We're not in any hurry if we need to wait."

"This is it." Izzie hiked the strap of her go-bag higher on her shoulder. "Ready when you are."

Daphne was absentmindedly folding the sign into a tight bundle, the corners neat and precise. "My bureau car is parked in short term." She started walking towards the exit, glancing over her shoulder as Izzie followed. "We've already got you checked in at the extended stay hotel across the street from the R.A. offices, if you want to stop in and freshen up."

"No need." Izzie ran a hand through her braids. Her grandmother would have scolded her for letting them get so fuzzy, she was sure, but Izzie had more important matters to worry about. Like why she had abruptly returned to Recondito in the first place, and whether she would be getting any static from the Senior Resident Agent for the somewhat-flimsy justification for her presence. "I'd rather check in with the SRA sooner rather than later, and get to work."

"Agent Gutierrez is meeting with the chief of the Recondito police at the moment, but he said he would probably be back at the office by the time we got there."

Izzie tried not to see that as a red flag. From what she'd gathered from talking with Patrick Tevake, he hadn't been entirely forthcoming with his superiors about the connections he'd found between his present investigations and the Reaper case, for fear that they'd order him to undergo a psych evaluation at best, and put him on suspension at worst. If the Bureau suspected that there was more to Izzie's visit to the city than she'd let on, that could prove problematic for both of them.

And it was still entirely possible that Patrick was mistaken, after all. Maybe a psych evaluation wasn't the worst idea. But she wanted to see for herself first, and then decide what to do when she had all of the facts at her disposal. It had taken a long medical leave and months of counseling for her to get back into fighting trim after she left Recondito the last time. Until Patrick had called the day before, Izzie had been convinced that the party line on Nicholas Fuller was the correct answer. But if what Patrick had told her was true. . . .

"This is me." Daphne pulled a key ring from her pocket, and turned off the car alarm with a short pair of beeps. Her bureau-issued "bucar" was a late-model compact hybrid with government plates. She popped the trunk for Izzie to toss in her go-bag, and then settled into the driver's seat while Izzie buckled up on the passenger side. When she turned the key in the ignition, nothing happened. She rolled her eyes. "I really need to get this thing serviced. I think it's a problem with the battery, but I'm not sure." She turned the key back to the starting position, then tried again.

The engine started, but the sound of it was all but completely drowned out by cumbia music that blared from the speakers at a deafening volume.

"Sorry!" Daphne said sheepishly, blushing, and quickly stabbed the off button on the car stereo. "I did a stint at the field office in San Antonio and picked up a taste for it."

"Doesn't hurt my feelings." Izzie grinned. "Though I prefer zydeco, myself."

Daphne eased the car out of the parking spot and navigated through the garage. "Maybe we should go dancing
some night while you're in town." She laughed, half-joking
and clearly half-serious. "There's a great little club down in
Oceanview I go to sometimes."

"Maybe," Izzie allowed, though it didn't seem likely.

It had been late spring when last Izzie was in Recondito,
with clear blue skies occasionally punctuated by pouring
rain. Now it was coming on winter, with slate gray skies and
days that seemed to end before they even began. It was only
late afternoon and already the sun was starting to disappear
over the Pacific, and the light that managed to reach down
the concrete and steel canyons of the Financial District was
ruddy and weak. In the drive from the airport in the South
Bay Daphne had kept up a steady stream of pleasantries,
pointing out new construction that had gone up in the last
few years, recommending taquerias and food carts that had
recently opened for business, inoffensive observations about
the ways she suspected the city had changed since last Izzie
had visited. It was when they were just a few blocks away
from the Resident Agency offices that she finally got around
to asking the question that Izzie had been expecting from
the start.

"So what was it really like, that night in the lighthouse?"

Daphne had her eyes on the traffic ahead, both hands on
the wheel, but her attention was on Izzie.

"I read all of the reports when I was still at the Academy,"
Daphne went on. "Everyone did, of course. It was required

course reading, but still . . . I would have read them anyway."
Daphne cut her eyes to the side for an instance, tentatively.
"You're kind of a hero of mine."

Izzie shifted a little in her seat, uncomfortably. "We were
just doing the job."

"Henderson's book had more detail of course," Daphne said.
"But I thought your field reports had more cogent observations."

Thomas Henderson had retired from the Bureau a year
after they wrapped up the investigation in Recondito. He
was on the lecture circuit now, and Izzie had lost track of the
number of times she'd switched on the TV to find Henderson
appearing as a talking head on some cable news show. He'd
made his name with a series of books about his experiences
hunting serial killers for the BAU, starting with a best seller
about the Reaper case. Having read his field reports in the
time that they worked together, Izzie strongly suspected that
he'd hired someone else to ghostwrite the book for him. She
doubted whether Henderson even knew what phrases like
"languid torpor" or "charnel-house smell" even meant. His
diction and attitude had never strayed far from the Baltimore
streets where he'd started out as a beat cop, no matter where
his subsequent career in the Bureau had taken him.

"Thanks?" Izzie hadn't meant it to sound like a question,
but knew that it did.

Daphne turned off of Prospect Avenue onto Hauser, and
Izzie recognized the building that housed the FBI's Recondito
Resident Agency a few blocks up the street. "So?" Daphne said.
"What was it really like?"

Izzie sighed, and forced a smile. "It was a rough night, I'll
admit, but it worked out all right in the end."

Assuming, of course, that it really did end. . . .

The offices of the Resident Agency were pretty much as Izzie had remembered them from the months that she spent there five years before. The computers had been upgraded and the phone system replaced, but otherwise the desks and cubicles of the small bullpen were the same as they'd been when she'd been assigned to the Reaper task force. She was pretty sure that all of the tongue-in-cheek motivational posters and comic strips clipped from newspapers pinned to the corkboard were the same ones that had already been yellowing when last she had been there.

Recondito wasn't large enough of a city to merit more than a two-person Resident Agency on a regular basis, and though the nearest field office was in San Francisco, due to workload requirements the Recondito office actually reported to the Portland field office. Aside from Daphne and Senior Resident Agent Gutierrez, who were the only two FBI agents on permanent assignment in Recondito, there was a small staff of support personnel who worked in the office on a part-time basis—file clerks, computer technicians, translators— and a custodial crew that serviced the entire building. When Daphne and Izzie arrived, though, the place was empty.

After signing in, Izzie checked out a few clips worth of ammunition for her semiautomatic from the gun vault, just as a matter of course. She charged a clip into her pistol's magazine and, after returning it to the hip holster that rode slightly behind her right hipbone, slipped the rest of the clips into an inner pocket of her suede jacket.

"You can use this desk while you're here. The phone extension is 214." Daphne indicated a cubicle along the north wall of the bullpen, opposite the door to the Senior Resident Agent's office. "Dial '9' to get an outside line, and—"

"I remember." Izzie dropped her go-bag onto the desk. "Spent a lot of time on these phones."

"Oh." Daphne seemed a little embarrassed. "Of course."

"I'll probably be using my mobile most of the time." Izzie patted her right pants pocket. The touch of the smartphone through the fabric of her jeans was strangely comforting, and Izzie resisted the urge to pat her other pockets in sequence, as she did every morning. Like most agents, she could be pretty ritualistic about her equipment, making her own sign of the cross every day before leaving her apartment: phone, FBI credentials, firearm, ammunition, handcuffs.

Almost every morning, Izzie couldn't help but remember her grandmother checking her gris-gris bag and charms each day before leaving her house in the Ninth Ward. Mawmaw Jean wouldn't go out into the world without her defenses, even if there was no reason to suspect that she'd have need of them. It was no different for Izzie, though she was concerned with real-world threats and not superstitious nonsense. A mojo hand might have given an old woman a feeling of security when facing imaginary threats like haints and conjure men, but a sack full of charms, roots, and bits of bone wouldn't be much use against a sociopath with a gun.

Of course, Izzie's pistol and badge hadn't been much use against a drug-addled schizophrenic with a blade, so it occurred to her that perhaps she shouldn't be too judgmental.

Izzie was about to call Patrick Tevake to see when he could meet her at the morgue when the door to the office banged against the wall and a storm came blowing in. The storm was a Latino man in his early forties wearing a dark suit and tie, but the pressure in the room dropped as surely as if a tornado were on its way.

"Agent Gutierrez," Daphne said, standing a little straighter. "This is Special Agent Isabel—"

"I know who she is." Senior Resident Agent Manuel Gutierrez glowered as he stomped towards the door of his office. "Agent Lefevre, if you wouldn't mind . . . ?" He gestured gruffly for Izzie to follow as he stepped inside.

Izzie exchanged a glance with Daphne, and from her sympathetic expression it seemed as though the junior agent had found herself in the path of a Gutierrez storm front before.

"Don't mind at all." Izzie closed the door to the senior agent's office behind her.

When Agent Gutierrez nodded toward the straight-back chair that was positioned across the desk from his own upholstered seat, Izzie sat, crossing one leg over the other casually. "I know that you received my request, but if anything was out of order or there are any points that require clarification I'd be happy to—"

Agent Gutierrez raised a hand to silence her. "Please. This is not my first rodeo. I go on record as saying that the BAU of course has this office's complete cooperation in any operational matters." He lowered his hand and leaned forward, looking at Izzie from under his brows. "Off the record, I'm forced to wonder just what the hell you're playing at."

Izzie kept her expression neutral. "Sir?"

Agent Gutierrez sat back and put his hands palm down on the desk in front of him, elbows straight. "I've been getting an earful all morning from the chief of police and the mayor's office. This vice cop of yours followed procedure in requesting Bureau assistance in his investigation, but when his captain informed the chief that we were reopening the highest profile murder case this town has seen in forty years, there was understandable cause for concern." He lifted his hands from the desk, balled them into fists, slowly unclenched them again, repeated the procedure twice and then put his hands back on the desk, palms down and fingers splayed. Izzie recognized an obvious relaxation technique when she saw one, but from the SRA's posture it was less obvious whether it was working.

"I'm not suggesting that we reopen the file on Nicholas Fuller," Izzie said, keeping her voice level. "But Tevake's findings do suggest that there might be more to the Reaper case that's left to be uncovered."

Again the senior agent's hands clenched, unclenched, then fingers splayed. "And how exactly would a cop in the narcotics division be in a position to find whatever it is you think he's found? Your request indicated that it was something in line with the profile that you used to identify Fuller in the first place?"

Izzie considered her response before answering. "I'm forming a theory, sir. I'll need to have a look at the material evidence myself before I can say with any certainty."

Agent Gutierrez sat back with a ragged sigh. "Okay, Agent Lefevre, have it your way. I've assured the police chief and the mayor's office that the Bureau has no interest in drawing any undue attention to this investigation. My hope is that this is simply a case of an overzealous cop tilting at windmills, and that when you examine the material evidence you'll find that there's nothing of interest there. Then you can fly back to Quantico and close the books on this one, once and for all."

"Believe me, sir," Izzie said, "nothing would please me more."

Agent Gutierrez nodded a dismissal, and Izzie rose to leave. When she reached the door, the senior agent cleared his throat for her attention. "When I took this post over from Jim Willoughby, it wasn't long after you and Tom Henderson were here."

"Willoughby was a good agent," Izzie answered.

"He was a mediocre agent who left this office a total disaster." Agent Gutierrez grimaced. "His grasp on department organization was tenuous at best, and a dyslexic monkey could have done a better job of filing reports."

Izzie flashed a tight, controlled smile. She'd been trying to be polite.

"But he always spoke very highly of the work you and Henderson did on the Fuller case. He might not have been the best agent, but he knew a good agent when he saw one."

"Thank you, sir." Izzie nodded. "I appreciate you saying that."

"Good luck, Lefevre. But I hope to god you don't find anything."

"In all honesty, sir," she answered, stepping out the door, "I sincerely hope there's nothing to be found."

CHAPTER THREE

When Izzie exited the building, go-bag slung over her shoulder and a room key for the extended-stay hotel across the street in her pocket, she found Patrick Tevake leaning against an unmarked car parked at the curb, dressed in a suit and tie. Izzie knew that he was only in his late thirties, but he looked like he'd aged at least a decade in the last five years, worry lines already forming at the corners of his eyes, flecks of silver in his dark brown hair. He was still muscular and lean, though the years had softened the line of his jaw.

"Detective Tevake." Izzie nodded a greeting, one hand on her hip, the other holding the strap of her bag.

"Agent Lefevre." Patrick tapped the shield hanging on a chain around his neck. "But it's lieutenant now. I got promoted."

"Well, congratulations."

He stuck out his hand, a half-smile tugging the corners of his mouth. "It's good to see you again, Izzie."

Izzie hummed a noncommittal response as she shook his hand. "I thought we were meeting at the morgue."

"I was on my way and figured you could use a lift." Patrick dropped her hand and pulled a smartphone out of his coat pocket. "And I still had your number active in the 'Find Friends' app, so I knew where to find you."

Izzie reflexively glanced down and patted her pocket, then met his eyes and grinned. "That almost seems creepy, Patrick. Spend a lot of lonely nights tracking my movements, do you?"

"A boy's got to have a hobby," he answered with a shrug. "But no, I save my stalking for work hours." His smile broadened fractionally. "And somehow I suspect if I had kept track, I'd have found you most often in your office working on a case."

"Probably," Izzie allowed. "Or at my apartment doing a jigsaw puzzle or sitting on the couch eating Thai takeout and binge-watching some stupid sitcom."

"With a cat, presumably."

"Too much trouble." Izzie shook her head. "I've got a ficus. Not as much fun to pet, but at least it doesn't scratch up the furniture."

Patrick's smile held for a moment, accompanying a brief chuckle, but then a shadow passed over his features and a serious expression settled in. "Thanks for coming so quickly."

Izzie tightened her grip on her bag's strap, her lips drawn straight. "So you really think there's a connection?"

"Yes." He let out a ragged sigh. "Maybe. I'm not sure. It seems crazy but . . ."

"We both know that just because something is crazy doesn't make it impossible." She paused, and then added, "Just improbable."

"Right." He nodded. "But we also both know that the improbable is kind of what Recondito is known for."

A momentary silence stretched between them, as things not necessary to speak aloud passed unuttered.

"Well . . . " Izzie took a deep breath. "Should we be going?"

"Do you need to check in to your hotel first?"

Izzie glanced down at the bag slung over her shoulder. "Not if you've got space in the backseat for this. The Resident Agency already got me set up with a room across the street, but it's not like I've got an urgent need to unpack."

Patrick pulled a key ring out of his pocket and unlocked the car with a click of a button. He yanked open the passenger side door. "Allow me."

"So gallant," Izzie said, sliding into the seat after tossing her bag into the back. Patrick kept the interior of the car as neat and clean as a rental, though she noticed scratches in the fabric of the backseat that might have been made by finger-nails. There was a file folder resting on the seat beside her bag, but Izzie couldn't read the label from her vantage point.

"Force of habit." Patrick settled into the driver's seat. "Of course, I'm usually opening the door for someone in hand-cuffs after reading them their Miranda rights, but I guess I don't mind if you sit up front."

"Just drive, Patrick. I want to see what you've found for myself."

The city morgue was located in the basement of the Hall of Justice, a dozen blocks north and east of the Resident Agency at the heart of City Center. Typically a short drive, with rush hour traffic it was taking longer than Izzie had expected.

"Might be faster to get out and walk." She looked at the unbroken line of cars that stretched up Prospect Avenue before them, inching along at a snail's pace.

"Lots of construction in town these days, roads being torn up and repaved." Patrick craned his neck in an attempt to look past the obstruction ahead, drumming his fingers on the steering wheel impatiently. "Close one lane of traffic and the rest come to a standstill, apparently."

"So . . . Vice, huh?"

Patrick left off drumming and glanced in her direction. "Yeah, four years now. Narcotics, mainly." He turned back to face the road ahead.

"I thought you'd worked pretty hard to get transferred into Homicide. When we first met, you said it was your dream job."

Patrick winced. "I thought it was. But after everything, I just . . . I needed a change, that's all. I put in a transfer request not long after we closed the Fuller case."

"Was that before or after they hung the Medal of Valor on you?"

He let out a mirthless chuckle. "The captain sat on my transfer request until after the medal ceremony. Said it might send the wrong message to the public." He glanced back in her direction. "The Director of the FBI gave you a letter of commendation, right?"

"Yeah." Izzie shrugged. "I've got it in a drawer somewhere. They weren't thrilled that we didn't take Fuller alive, though."

Patrick shot her a look. "I thought he was going after *you* with that sword of his."

"I know, I know. Believe me, I appreciate the impulse. And it all went in my report." Izzie found that she was scratching the scar at the back of her hand, and forced herself to stop.

"The Bureau understands that it's sometimes necessary to use lethal force, but it's not high on the list of 'desirable outcomes.' Quote, unquote."

Patrick honked the horn when a merging car came too near to his own bumper, narrowly avoiding a collision.

"Speaking of Narcotics . . . ?" Izzie went on as the horn's bleat faded. "'Ink'? Is that what it's called?"

He nodded. "It's a new street drug. Started turning up early this year. At first we thought it was just another designer amphetamine like Molly or Eve, but it's something else entirely." He paused, and then added. "The lab has designated it as a 'synthetic opiate,' but that just means that they don't really understand what it is yet."

"And the dead man?"

"Tyler Campbell. Low-level dealer. We had surveillance footage of him making a deal, but by the time we took him into custody he wasn't in possession. We brought him in for questioning, but he wouldn't give up his supplier. We held him overnight to let him stew a bit, but never had a chance to take him in front of a judge."

"Why not?"

"He died in his cell that night."

"Cause of death?"

He turned and briefly made eye contact. "That's the real question, isn't it?"

The car had finally made it through the intersection at Prospect and 12th, and the Hall of Justice loomed into view just ahead. A towering block of gray stone that covered an entire city block, it was stark and utilitarian in contrast with the Spanish Colonial style of the older city offices that surrounded it.

Patrick pulled the car into a reserved spot on the east side of the building, among a small fleet of patrol cars and other service vehicles.

"Come on," he said, switching off the engine and popping open the door. He reached into the backseat and grabbed the file folder. "We don't want to keep the goddess of the under-world waiting."

CHAPTER FOUR

Izzie zipped her jacket up tighter as they stepped off the elevator into the biting cold air of the cavernous, low-ceilinged space. Autopsy tables were neatly arranged, the metal doors of the refrigerators that lined the back wall were polished mirror bright, and the sinks and workstations were spotless and clean. Bright lights overhead reflected off the white tiles underfoot. Had she seen it in a photo, Izzie could easily believe that it was the picture of sterility. But her nostrils stung with the strong ammonia smell of antiseptic cleaning products that couldn't quite mask the underlying stench of corruption and decay.

And a photo would not have conveyed the teeth-rattling sound of goth rock blaring from the open door of the medical examiner's office.

"A little on the nose, isn't it?" Izzie wrinkled her nose in distaste.

"I think she does it for effect," Patrick answered. "I'm half-convinced she listens to disco music when she's alone down here, and only switches on Bauhaus or Sisters of Mercy when she hears the elevator chime." He stepped further into the morgue, and raised his voice, calling out, "Hello? Anybody home?"

The music suddenly stopped, and a diminutive woman in a white lab coat leaning heavily on a cane appeared in the open doorway. Her jet black hair was cut in an asymmetrical under-cut bob, and the thick-soled black boots she wore boasted an impressive number of buckles and straps.

"You're late, Tevake." Her cane tonked against the tiles as she walked across the floor.

"Aren't most people when they come here?" Patrick gestured towards the sheet-covered body on the nearest autopsy table. "Late one way or another, I mean."

"You make that joke every time." She leaned both hands on her cane, smirking. "Keep trying, though. It's bound to get funny eventually."

"Dr. Nguyen?" He looked from the woman to Izzie. "Allow me to introduce Special Agent Isabel Lefevre." He gestured to the woman. "Izzie, this is Dr. Joyce Nguyen, Recondito's Chief Medical Examiner."

"*Only* medical examiner at the moment, though I keep putting in requests for the city manager to find room in the budget to hire me an assistant." She stepped forward and held her hand out to Izzie. "Please, Agent Lefevre, call me Joyce."

"'Izzie' will do fine." They shook hands. "And it's nice to meet you."

"Actually, we met briefly when you were here last," Joyce said. "I don't blame you for not remembering, though. I was interning with the old M.E., and I was still a mousy little thing in floral prints and sensible shoes with my hair in a ponytail."

"Oh, sure, I remember. You were here when we brought in the Reaper victim who the fishing boat had trawled out of the bay."

"That was me, all right." She paused, smiling a little wistfully. "You don't get remains like that every day."

Izzie remembered those particular remains all too well. The only thing more unsettling that the smell had been the squelching sound that the body parts had made as the M.E. pulled them apart in the course of the examination. That they had once belonged to a human body was a fact that only an expert could recognize readily.

"Speaking of remains . . . ?" Patrick indicated the sheet-covered cadaver on the autopsy bench. "Is that our guy?"

Joyce nodded. "I pulled him out of the fridge this morning when I got your message."

The medical examiner started towards the table, and glanced in Izzie's direction. "I suppose that Tevake has filled you in on the basics?"

Izzie nodded. "Low-level drug dealer, found dead in a holding cell."

"That's the bumper sticker version." She picked up a clipboard that was resting at the foot of the table, and flipped open the chart clipped to it. "Adult white male, well developed, somewhat undernourished and appearing the stated age of twenty-nine years. Head normocephalic. Irises discolored by decompositional changes, but the pupils were equal in diameter. No contact lenses present, no conjunctival petechiae. Nose normal, with purging hemolyzed fluid in the nares and mouth. Teeth present, with evidence of good oral hygiene that had recently been neglected. Left ear pierced but the hole has healed over. Yadda yadda."

She flipped the chart closed, tucked the clipboard under her arm, and began pulling on a pair of blue nitrile surgical gloves.

"I did a thorough external, internal, *and* microscopic investigation, and only found two things of real interest."

Joyce lifted one corner of the covering sheet and took hold of the dead man's left hand, holding it up. She pointed at the fingertips, where the nails had been cut to the quick during the autopsy. "I found trace amounts of an unknown substance beneath the fingernails on both hands. I've sent it to the lab to be analyzed, but I'm still waiting to hear the results."

"Could it be this drug?" Izzie asked. "Ink?"

Joyce glanced at Patrick, who nodded. "That's our working hypothesis," she answered, looking back to Izzie. "Unfortunately, we are largely working in the dark."

"We've had a *lot* of trouble laying our hands on samples of the drug," Patrick added.

Izzie looked at the dead man on the table. "Was he a user as well as a dealer?"

"Maybe." Patrick scowled. "Maybe not. I wish we knew."

"As I understand it," Joyce explained, "determining whether a subject has ingested Ink is based entirely on behavioral and anecdotal factors. In advanced cases there is often a mottled discoloration of the user's skin, but the drug itself doesn't appear to remain in the system after use, and so far we haven't found an effective physical test for it."

"What kind of behavioral factors?" Izzie asked.

"Mood swings," Joyce replied. "Personality changes. Memory loss."

"Whether someone witnessed them taking it," Patrick offered, his scowl deepening.

"As I said." The medical examiner pursed her lips. "Anecdotal factors."

She let the dead man's hand fall back to the autopsy table and covered the arm with the sheet once more.

"You said you found two things of interest?" Izzie asked. "I'm guessing that you didn't mean both hands."

Joyce walked around to the other end of the table, and folded back the sheet covering the dead man's head. "It was the brain."

Izzie could clearly see where the scalp had been cut and folded back, and then stitched back up again after the examination was complete.

"Honestly, I don't know how he was able to function at all, given the state of degeneration, but at the moment it seems the most likely cause of death."

She pulled the clipboard out from under her arm and flipped open to a series of photos, and held one out for Izzie to examine.

"What am I seeing?" Izzie finally asked.

"More importantly, what are you *not* seeing?" Joyce flipped to another page of the report and pulled out what Izzie at first thought was an X-ray, but then realized she was looking at soft tissue and not bone. "I had an MRI done on the organ once I realized how widespread the degradation was, and decided that continuing the physical examination would be counterproductive."

It was a human brain in profile, but dotted throughout with tiny black shadows.

"Is that . . . ?" Izzie looked up and met Joyce's eyes, and then shot a glance at Patrick, but his expression was closed and unreadable.

Joyce nodded. "The man's brain was riddled with vacuoles. Little pockets of nothing, like bubbles in Swiss cheese. My first thought was that it might be variant Creutzfeldt-Jakob disease . . ."

"Mad cow," Izzie said in a voice that was barely a whisper.

"The same agent is responsible for both vCJD in humans and bovine spongiform encephalopathy in cows, yes. But there was no indication of the prions associated with vCJD and BSE in the subject's cerebral tissue. And the degree of degradation was beyond that typically found in even the most advanced cases of prion disease. In fact, I hadn't seen anything like this since . . ."

"Five years ago." Izzie couldn't look away from the face of the dead man on the table.

Patrick opened the file folder that he'd brought from the car, and pulled out a sheaf of MRI printouts.

"The one common factor in Nicholas Fuller's victims." He fanned the printouts on an empty instrument table. "A fact that was never released to the public."

Patrick took the MRI printout from Izzie's hands and laid it on the instrument table with the others. The same dark shadows could be seen on all of them, though none with so many and so large as the latest one.

"I thought that was chalked up to a coincidence. Unrelated to their causes of death." Izzie turned back to Joyce. "That was in the official report that the medical examiner provided."

"*Well* . . ." Joyce rubbed her lower lip with her index finger, considering her answer. "The old M.E. was a . . . shall we say, 'pragmatic' individual. Yes, the degradation in the brains of the murder victims was not a result of the manner of their deaths, which was ruled in every case to be either homicide by cutting instrument or blunt force trauma, followed by post-mortem dismemberment. And so, *technically*, it was unrelated to the causes of death."

"Technically?" Izzie raised an eyebrow.

"Well, the odd thing was that we were completely unable to develop any kind of workable explanation for *why* each of them showed exactly the same type of brain degradation. As in the present case, no prions were found in the cerebral tissue of the murder victims. But assuming for the moment that the pathology was similar to prion-related diseases, it was extremely unlikely that there was a common cause, considering that vCJD and related disease can incubate for up to fifty years. And given the diverse ages, ethnic and geographic backgrounds of the victims . . ." Joyce trailed off.

"It was the *pragmatic* choice simply to dismiss it as a coincidence." Izzie scowled, angrily scratching the scar on the back of her hand.

"It's not Joyce's fault," Patrick said. "She was just an intern at the time. Besides, the killer was dead. There wasn't any pressure from my superiors for a more detailed explanation, *or* from the FBI as I recall. They were all happy to jump on the simplest solution that presented itself."

"To his credit, the M.E. *was* concerned about the potential health risks presented by the victims' remains, so they were properly disposed of, even though we found no evidence that the condition was transmissible. Either post-mortem or in living tissue. And with the absence of any common cause that we could point to—"

"Undersight." Izzie's head was down, her eyes squeezed tightly shut.

"Excuse me?" Joyce was momentarily confused.

"The other fact about the Fuller case that was never released to the public," Patrick explained. "The old M.E. was informed, but perhaps he never told you?"

Joyce shook her head.

"It was a research project headed up by scientists from Ross University. It ran for several years, and all of the victims were involved in one capacity or another, sometimes months or even years apart." Patrick sucked air in through his teeth. "And Nicholas Fuller was one of the head researchers and chief architects of the project, before he left the university."

Joyce's eyes widened. "And this was all at the university here in town? If the agent was on campus, the potential exposure could have been . . ."

Patrick shook his head. "No, not on the campus. The Undersight experiment was located a mile underground in an old mine shaft out in the hills a few miles outside of town."

The medical examiner breathed a sigh of relief, but it was short-lived. "Still, if they were exposed to something down there that caused this condition, then others could still be at risk."

"They went down into the dark." Izzie raised her head and opened her eyes. "And the dark came back with them."

The other two turned to her.

"Was that . . . ?" Joyce began, but Patrick remained silent, studying Izzie's face while his own expression remained closed and unreadable.

"Something that Fuller said, right before the end." Izzie took a deep breath and let it out slowly through her nostrils. "He wasn't simply targeting former colleagues over some workplace grievance. Each of them fit some particular criteria."

She pointed at the spread of MRI printouts.

"These . . . these *things* aren't unrelated to the cause of death." She picked up the newest printout and jabbed a finger at the riot of shadows riddling the dead man's brain. "He targeted them *because* they had these . . . these . . ."

"Vacuoles," Joyce offered.

"These *shadows* in their heads." Izzie realized that she was on the ragged edge of shouting, and didn't care.

Patrick pointed to the printout that she held. "But that's not the brain of one of Nicholas Fuller's victims. That's the brain of a drug dealer who died the day before yesterday. And so far as I know, Tyler Campbell was a high school dropout who never stepped foot on the Ross University campus, much less climbed a mile down an old mine shaft up in the hills."

"So perhaps the condition is transmittable after all?" Joyce scratched the short stubble at the side of her head beneath the undercut bob. "If something down in the mine shaft causes the degradation, but this subject never went down into the mine shaft, what other explanation could there be?"

Patrick looked back to Izzie, waiting for her to answer, clearly having come to a conclusion of his own already.

"It means . . ." Izzie took another deep breath, steadying herself. "It means that it isn't over."

CHAPTER FIVE

The night was fully dark by the time Izzie and Patrick returned to the car. Clouds overhead threatened rain, but for the moment the air was dry and cool. Traffic on the streets had lightened, and the work crews on the roadworks had gone home for the day.

Izzie's hands twitched at her sides, and she found herself craving a cigarette, though she hadn't smoked since college. Her thoughts were racing, running in tight circles around big ideas that fit uncomfortably inside her head.

"You hungry?" Patrick jiggled his keys. "I'm guessing you haven't eaten since you got to town."

It took Izzie a moment. "I haven't eaten since eight o'clock this morning, Eastern time. And that was just an airport bagel."

Patrick pocketed the keys and took hold of Izzie's elbow, steering her away from the car. "Come on, there's a decent Thai place a couple of blocks from here. We'll walk."

As they crossed the street at the light, Patrick pulled the neck chain over his head and tucked his badge in an inner pocket of his suit coat.

"I'm sorry I didn't prepare you for that when we talked on the phone," he said, "but I wanted you to see it for yourself before you made up your mind."

Izzie's stomach growled, as if the thought of eating had awakened her sleeping appetite. She shook her head. "No. Food first. Then questions." She paused, and then added, "*Many* questions."

He nodded, his expression sympathetic, and they walked the rest of the way in silence.

I zzie devoured her chicken Pad Thai without once looking up from the plate, and then finished off half of the Laab Nua that proved too spicy for Patrick's taste. It was nothing compared to the eye-watering jambalaya that her grandmother used to make, but Izzie was too preoccupied to mock Patrick's delicate palate.

"Better?" he asked when she put down her fork and raised her eyes from the table.

Izzie quaffed the rest of her glass of water in one big swig, holding up an index finger to request a moment. Then she wiped her mouth with the back of her hand and nodded. "Yes. Much. I was clearly hungrier than I thought."

"Obviously. Trips to the morgue don't normally do much for one's appetite. Not accounting for Joyce, of course. I went down there once and found her eating a ham sandwich with one hand while dissecting a body with the other." He shuddered. "Anyway . . . questions?"

"Plenty." Izzie pushed her plate away and leaned her elbows on the table. "Let's start with a simple one. Why call me in on this?" She paused. "I mean, I understand why you'd want to request Bureau assistance, but why me specifically?"

Patrick gave her a sidelong glance. "You know why."

"I think I do. But I want to hear you say it."

He opened his mouth, then closed it without speaking, considering his words. "Because you're the only one who would understand."

"Understand what?" Izzie knew, but made him say it anyway.

Patrick sighed. He leaned forward, lowering his voice conspiratorially. "It's like I said on the phone. That night in the lighthouse, when it was just you and me waiting for the EMTs to arrive? The things we talked about . . . ?"

Izzie sat back from the table, defensively. "I was half out of my mind from blood loss, hallucinating and talking nonsense."

He shook his head. "That's what I thought at the time, too. I figured you were in shock, and I needed to keep you talking. But when Joyce told me about Campbell, I kept going back to what you'd said about your grandmother—"

"It's just a bunch of silly superstitions," Izzie interrupted.

"—what you said about your grandmother," Patrick repeated, with emphasis. "And what I told you about my great-uncle. The symbols Fuller had drawn on the floor and the walls. The things we found in his apartment."

Izzie felt as though, were she to close her eyes, she would be back in that lantern room still, hearing the rain pelt on the metal floor through the broken window, Patrick crouched beside her holding her hand, the two of them sharing the things they'd been taught as children.

But her eyes were open.

"Nicholas Fuller was a drug addict who'd had a psychotic break, Patrick. He cobbled together a jumbled mishmash of nonsense to prop up his delusional belief system, and used it to justify killing a dozen of his former colleagues in bloodthirsty rituals. The fact that he borrowed a few tidbits that my superstitious grandmother happened to believe is immaterial."

"And from my great-uncle's beliefs too, don't forget."

"Your *superstitious* great-uncle."

"Well . . ." Patrick paused, titling his head to one side. "Maybe they weren't just superstitions."

Izzie's eyes narrowed. "You can't be serious."

"Like hell I can't." He pulled out his wallet and dropped a few bills on the table. Then he pushed back his chair, standing. "Come on, there's something else I want to show you."

They drove out of City Center, headed west through Ross Village past the coffee shops, boutiques, and bookstores that crowded around the university, then turned south on Mission Avenue towards the Oceanview neighborhood. The narrow isthmus was just a dozen blocks across at its widest, bound by Bayfront Drive on the east and Shoreline Boulevard on the west, both streets angling slightly inwards as they traveled south until finally they met just above Ivory Point where the old lighthouse still stood.

Izzie felt a cold ache in the pit of her stomach.

"Where are we going, exactly?" she asked, impatiently.

"Almost there."

Izzie looked out the window at the taquerias and dive bars that were still serving, the storefront churches and shops that had closed for the night. She wondered if the dance club they passed was the one that Agent Richards had told her about, and whether Daphne might be there right now, shimmying to a cumbia beat. Izzie hadn't gone out dancing herself since she left college. There just didn't seem to be a space for that kind of thing in her life these days. And of course, dancing was always more fun if you had someone to dance with, and Izzie hadn't been on a date in years.

Unless visiting a city morgue with a cop counted as a date, which she didn't think it did. Especially a cop who might just be losing his grip on reality. Besides, he wasn't exactly her type.

"Okay, we're here."

Patrick angled the car into a spot near the corner of Almeria and Mission, not far from the Church of the Holy Saint Anthony. It was quieter here than the busier blocks with the nightlife they'd passed. Izzie supposed it might have been due to the cemetery that stretched behind the church. There were more dead residents than living ones near here.

"You feeling religious?" Izzie nodded towards the church as she climbed out of the car. "Or is it bingo night?"

"Neither," Patrick said, heading in the other direction. "What I want to show you is over here."

He pointed towards the mouth of an alleyway across the street that ran between two Victorian row houses. Lights shone in the upper windows on either side, but at street level the alleyway itself was wreathed in dark shadows. Izzie shrugged and followed Patrick until he was halfway down the alley and stopped.

"Here." He pulled his phone out of his pocket, tapped on the flashlight app, and bright light bathed the brick side of one of the houses. With his free hand, Patrick indicated a spot just overhead.

Izzie saw an intricate design etched into the brick itself, spirals and whorls that looped and curved back on themselves almost like a fingerprint, but with mathematical precision, all bound in a precise circle. It reminded her somewhat of tattoos she'd seen on men and women of Polynesian descent who lived in Recondito. She wondered if Patrick had one himself, hidden beneath his suit coat.

"My great-uncle Alf Tevake carved that for a family that moved here from Kensington Island back in the seventies." He turned, and the light from his phone shone on the opposite wall, revealing another etched design on the next house, as well. "He carved that for a family of islanders that moved in next door when I was eight years old. All of them etched into the brick, and then filled with white paint mixed with sea salt."

"Some kind of blessing, then?" Izzie thought of steps scrubbed with the dust of shattered red bricks, and holy water sprinkled on hardwood floors. "Or protection?"

Patrick nodded. "Like I told you five years ago, my great-uncle was a kind of spiritual leader back on Kensington Island. And he did the same thing for the islanders who moved here." He pointed up at the symbol. "He believed that symbol would act as a ward, a barrier to keep unseen evils at bay."

He lowered the phone, switched off the light, and started to walk back towards the street.

"The first families who came to Recondito from the island settled here in the Oceanview. And so the others who came later tended to move here, as well. Used to be a predominantly Latino neighborhood, and Irish before that, but since before I was born the southwestern corner of the neighborhood has been a Te'Maroan enclave."

"Te'Maroan?" Izzie asked.

"Our name for ourselves. British sailors in the South Pacific gave it the name Kensington Island back during the Napoleonic wars, but to us it was always Kovoko-ko-Te'Maroa." Patrick gestured to the buildings around them. "They used to call this part of the Oceanview 'Little Kovoko.' I'd bet that nearly three out of every five houses on these blocks has one of those symbols carved somewhere on its walls. And I should know." He pointed down a side street. "I grew up just a few doors down that way with my cousins, and my great-uncle used to put us all to work on weekends, making sure that his marks were clean and vines or moss hadn't grown over any parts of them. Paid us a quarter for every one that we cleaned."

"My grandmother had me scrub red brick dust into the wood of her house's front steps. Was supposed to protect against unwanted intruders, humans and spirits alike," Izzie said, and rubbed the back of her neck. She remembered the muggy afternoons on her hands and knees, the grit of the dust rasping against her skin. "She didn't pay me anything, though. You were lucky."

Patrick shrugged. "To be honest, I would have probably done it for free. I think I just liked feeling useful."

"Speaking of useful . . . why are you showing me this, again?"

He tapped at his phone's screen, bringing up a photo gallery. He swiped through until he found the one he was looking for, and then showed it to Izzie. It was a map of Recondito with red and blue dots scattered throughout.

"The red dots are locations where we've verified that Ink deals have gone down. The blue dots are where we've picked up people who we believe were on Ink at the time."

There were dots of both colors all over the map, in Ross Village near the university, in Oceanview near the docks, from the high rises of the Financial District to the municipal buildings of City Center, from the middle class neighborhoods like Hyde Park to the mini-mansions that sprawled up the hills of Northside.

But there was a gap in the coverage that was impossible to miss.

"That's where we are right now." Patrick pointed at the southwestern end of the Oceanview isthmus, which was completely free of dots of either hue. "There hasn't been a single instance of Ink use *or* sale in a six block radius of this spot."

"Nice neighborhood?"

"Better than some, worse than others." A look flickered in Patrick's face, then faded. "But it's not as if there aren't other narcotics-related arrests that happen here. They do, with alarming regularity. I picked up a couple of meth heads a hundred feet from this spot just last week. People here consume illicit drugs at roughly the same rate as they do everywhere else in the city." He paused. "But not Ink."

"Maybe it's a question of territory? Or supply?"

Patrick shook his head. "We've arrested people who lived here who had taken Ink, but they didn't take it *here*. One straight-A high school student from the neighborhood was given a dose by a friend at a party up in Northside, and she never came home. Picked her up sleeping in a park two weeks later. Her parents thought she'd been kidnapped. My partner thought she'd just run away. But it didn't seem right to me. So I did some checking into the other arrests we've made. Turns out that there have been any number of people from this neighborhood who we've arrested for using the stuff, but every one of them was in a different part of the city, and didn't come back here after they started using."

Izzie narrowed her eyes with suspicion. "So what are you saying?"

"I'm saying . . ." He took a deep breath, then let it out slowly. "I think that they *can't* use it here. I think that my great-uncle Alfred's wards are keeping it away somehow."

He stopped, searching her face for any reaction.

"You know how crazy that sounds, right?" she finally said.

He flung his hands in the air and paced a few steps away and then back. "Of *course* I know how crazy it sounds. That's why I called you in."

"Gee, *thanks*." Izzie rolled her eyes.

"Not because *you're* crazy, but because I'm *not*. If I went into my captain's office and told him I thought that magic symbols drawn decades ago by an old man were keeping Ink traffic out of the neighborhood I grew up . . ."

"The psych evals would never end."

"Exactly. But considering what we know about Fuller's victims, and the state of Campbell's brain, and now *this* . . ." He gestured to the buildings around them. "I think it's all connected. It all means something."

Izzie crossed her arms. "So a sword-wielding psycho killer hacks up the bodies of people who already had holes in their brains, and a guy dealing this new street drug has the same kinds of holes in *his* brain, and the one area of town where people aren't buying or using that street drug is covered with magic symbols a Polynesian witch doctor drew years and years ago. And all of that somehow *means* something?"

"*Tohuna*," Patrick corrected. "Shaman, basically, or priest. Not witch doctor. But yeah, otherwise that's it entirely." He paused, catching her eye. "And as for what it means, well . . . I figured as the granddaughter of a . . . what did you call it? A voodoo priestess, right?"

"Mambo," Izzie supplied.

"A *mambo's* granddaughter might be the only one who could help a tohuna's nephew figure out just what was going on. We were both taught how to protect against spirits and stuff like that when we were kids, so maybe—"

"Jesus, Patrick, are you hearing yourself?!" Now it was Izzie's turn to flap her arms and pace back and forth. "Spirits and demons, hexes and hoodoo . . . it's all fairy tales. There's no such thing as magic."

"I didn't say that there was. But maybe . . . maybe there's something else. Maybe the things that my great-uncle said he believed, the things that *your* grandmother believed . . . maybe they were just different ways of understanding something that was too big and too weird for them to fit into words otherwise." He rubbed the bridge of his nose, gathering himself. "Look, I'm a complete agnostic, okay. I don't believe in *their* god"—he gestured at the cross atop the church spire behind them—"and I don't believe in the Great God Te'a either, or Capten Kole the Sky Navigator for that matter. But that doesn't mean—"

"'Sky Navigator,'" Izzie interrupted, quirking an eyebrow.

"Cargo cult on Kensington Island after World War II. Never had more than a dozen followers, but there are still one or two of them around. Nutty belief system, lovely people. But that's beside the point. The *point* is that just because I don't believe in a magic Santa in the sky who throws lightning bolts down at the unbelievers, doesn't mean that I think I know everything about everything. Just because I can't see something doesn't mean it doesn't exist. I don't understand quantum physics but that doesn't keep it from being real, does it?"

Izzie scratched the back of her hand, absently.

"But I *do* believe that something really is going on here. Maybe those symbols that my great-uncle carved on all those walls actually do *something*, and maybe it has something to do with whatever is causing holes to form in people's heads, and maybe *that* has something to do with this new street drug."

"That's a lot of somethings. And a lot of maybes," Izzie said.

"Like you said earlier: *many* questions." He sighed. "It sounds crazy, but if *I* were crazy I'd think it made perfect sense, right?"

"I'm pretty sure that's what crazy people tell themselves."

"So? Are you going to tell my captain that he should order a psych eval, or . . . ?" He let the question hang in the air, waiting expectantly for her to answer.

Izzie rubbed the inside corners of her eyes with her thumb and forefinger. It had been far too long since she last slept, and she was beginning to feel it.

"I'm going to . . ." she began, then broke off, shaking her head. "Let me think about it, okay?"

She met his gaze, and could see the tension on his face.

"It's the best I can do for now," she said.

For a moment it seemed like Patrick was going to press the issue, but then nodded slowly. "How about I give you a ride back to your hotel?"

An awkward silence filled the car as they made their way north through Oceanview, like the drive home after a first date that had gone horribly wrong. The restaurants had all closed down for the night, and the bars had been taken over by the serious drinkers. Izzie was tempted to stop in for a few stiff drinks herself, but an agent getting drunk with their service weapon on them was seriously frowned on at the Bureau. Besides, she was having enough trouble wrapping her head around all of this mess while she was in complete control of her faculties. Cocktails wouldn't help there.

When they passed through Ross Village, only a handful of late-night cafés were still open, but Izzie knew that coffee was the last thing she needed. Sleep wouldn't come easily, if experience was any guide, but at least her body could rest in the bed while her thoughts raced.

Finally they reached City Center, and Patrick pulled up to the curb on Hauser Avenue in front of the hotel across from the FBI offices.

"Sleep well," Patrick said as Izzie reached into the backseat to grab her go-bag, then opened the door to climb out.

With the door still open, she fished in her pocket until she found her room key. Then she began to close the door, but paused, thinking. She leaned down and looked through the open door at Patrick behind the wheel.

Izzie sighed. "Okay. I'll report back to Quantico that we think that there's a connection between this new street drug and the Fuller case, and that I think it merits further investigation. Which is *true*, to a point. But we aren't going to tell *anyone* what we really suspect is going on until we *know* what is really going on. Is that clear?"

Patrick blinked a few times, then nodded eagerly. "Of course. I'm not crazy, remember?"

"Maybe, maybe not," Izzie answered with a wan smile. "But maybe I'm crazy, too." She hiked the strap of her bag higher on her shoulder. "Meet me back here in the morning?"

He grinned. "There's a great donut place around the corner."

"You spend a lot of time thinking about food, don't you?"

"What can I tell you?" He shrugged. "I'm a cop."

"Tomorrow, then." She closed the door then pounded on the top of the car.

Patrick gave her a thumbs-up and then pulled away from the curb.

As she walked in the hotel's front door, Izzie noticed that the retaining wall had a red brick façade. It wasn't her grandmother's red brick dust, but it would have to do.

CHAPTER SIX

The hotel that the Resident Agency had arranged was decent, the bed was comfortable, and with the heavy curtains closed the room was plunged into almost total darkness. The sibilant hiss of the white noise app on her phone completely masked the sounds of people passing by her door out in the hallway, or the faint creak and rumble of the elevators ascending and descending at odd intervals. Only by floating in a sensory deprivation tank would Izzie be more completely undistracted.

And yet still, as she'd anticipated, she found it nearly impossible to sleep.

The time change was partly to blame, of course. Shifting three hours in the course of a single day would confuse anyone's internal rhythms. Izzie hadn't laid down to sleep until it was already deep into the middle of the night back home. And spending most of the day sitting in a cramped airplane was somehow more physically exhausting than being active and mobile, so her muscles were sore and aching, keeping her from completely relaxing.

But the real problem was in her head. Even if her body was exhausted and ready to rest, her mind was racing, thinking about her conversation tonight with Patrick, with the things he had shown her, and the things he had said. Those thoughts kept sparking off memories of days and nights from five years earlier, and the things she had seen and heard then. And underneath it all, moving just beneath the surface of conscious thought, were dim memories from childhood.

And still she tried to sleep. She lay completely immobile on her back, willing her body to relax; first the muscles of her feet, then her calves, and then her thighs, feeling the still-ness creep up her body. Her arms were at her sides beneath the thin covers, palms down and fingers spread. Her head was cushioned by the spongy pillow, eyes closed against the darkness.

As her muscles relaxed, sensation faded. The feeling of her body pressing down into the mattress, the weight of the covers over her, the texture of the sheets against her skin . . . these all became a kind of tactile white noise, and just like her ears eventually tuned out the hiss from the phone on the bedside table, so her skin tuned out the feeling of the bed.

So while her thoughts still looped and swerved, her body seemed to fade away into the darkness, until she was just a disembodied consciousness, alone in the darkness with her thoughts.

And then the voices started.

She'd entered this type of hypnagogic state before, on other nights when she was too exhausted to stay awake but too keyed up to sleep. She'd slip into a kind of middle ground between wakefulness and sleep, still conscious but in a dream-like state. At first, she simply imagined what Patrick would have said had their conversation continued, but in time it seemed like they were having that conversation, as if he were sitting in the corner of her room, there in the darkness, saying to her the things she imagined he would say.

At first, Izzie's mind just replayed things that Patrick had said earlier in the evening, and Izzie knew that she was simply remembering. But as she slipped deeper and deeper into the hypnagogic state, she began answering in her thoughts, saying things that hadn't occurred to her before, asking questions she hadn't thought to ask, and then the conversation went from remembrance into new territory.

It was very important to Izzie in that moment that Patrick understand that she was not defined by her upbringing. She loved and respected the woman who had raised her, but Izzie had struck out into the world and made a place for herself. It had not always been easy for a black girl from the wrong side of the tracks in New Orleans to put herself through college and build a career in the FBI, but she had done it. She was a respected professional, and no conjure man or haint or petro was going to take that away from her.

But loa, like the petro, have to be invited to possess a body and walk the Earth. Izzie had no reason to worry about that, right? It wasn't as if she was going to offer herself up. Of course, it could help with their investigation, to have eyes on the other side. Izzie wasn't a two-headed woman like Mawmaw, and couldn't see the spirit world on her own. But she remembered the rites and rituals from when she was a little girl, and maybe Patrick would be willing to help. Perhaps Marinette-Dry-Arms or Ti Jean or . . .

"Girl, you best wake up."

Izzie sat bolt upright in the bed, wide awake and gasping.

She'd heard that. Hadn't she? Not in her thoughts, but out loud?

She lurched to the side of the bed, fumbling for the lamp switch.

"You got work to do."

Izzie turned to look back over her shoulder into the darkness, hands still grasping for the lamp. "Mawmaw?"

Her fingers finally found the switch, and warm light filled the room.

There was nobody there.

A sweeper truck groaned through the intersection while Izzie jogged in place at the corner, waiting for the Walk sign to light up. The temperature had dropped hard and fast in the last few hours, and the clouds of steam that billowed out with Izzie's every exhalation rose up to the bright streetlamps overhead, dissipating as they rose.

The running shoes that the hotel had lent her were a little tight, and didn't offer the same support as the ones that she normally wore back home, and the hoodie and sweatpants smelled of bleach and other people's perspiration, but Izzie couldn't complain. She'd left home so quickly that she hadn't packed a proper suitcase, just her overnight go-bag, and there wasn't room in it for her exercise gear, even if it weren't gathering dust in the back of the bedroom closet in her apartment. She was just grateful that the hotel had workout clothes and shoes for guests to borrow. Trying to jog in her jeans and boots wouldn't have been much use.

The light changed after the truck had passed, and Izzie continued across the street, past the looming shadow of the Pinnacle Tower and up towards Northside beyond. Her plan was to get to the bottom of the hills before returning to the hotel, and then try sleeping one last time.

She couldn't run like she did before, of course. Not since the silver blade had sliced open her leg. Jogging was the best that she could manage, and even then only for shorter distances and durations than she used to run. Not that jogging was really the goal tonight. It was the movement itself she was after, really. That, and the hope that exertion would clear her head and tire her out.

It was at least three hours until dawn, and Izzie hoped to sleep for at least a short while. In her experience, even one hour of sleep was better than none. But after her last attempt had ended so badly, she needed to try something else.

She had been so certain that she heard the voice of her grandmother speaking to her out of the darkness. Not imagined that she was hearing it, like the chattering voices that echoed silently in her hypnagogic brain, but an actual audible sound.

Which was impossible, of course. And yet . . .

What had she been thinking about? Or dreaming about? She remembered something to the effect that her professional reputation would be damaged if her colleagues thought that she believed in the supernatural, but then somehow she reached a point in the train of thought where she forgot that she didn't believe, and started making plans as if she did. . . .

And what was that about the loa? Where had that come from?

Over the course of her long life, Izzie's grandmother had incorporated bits of other Creole faiths like Cuban Santeria and Gullah Hoodoo and Brazilian Candomblé into her own brand of Voodoo. In Mawmaw's eyes, they were all simply different roads to the same destination. A *mambo asogwe* from Port-au-Prince had taught her about the loa, and instructed her in the rites through which the intermediary spirits could be summoned to possess the bodies of the faithful like a rider mounting a horse, with the ridden bodies remaining under their complete control until the loa withdrew.

Izzie had seen a few loa ceremonies when she was young, and they had unnerved her. She knew now that it was a simply a matter of fervent believers whipping themselves into a state of ecstasy, like Pentecostals speaking in tongues and handling snakes or firewalkers dancing themselves into an ecstatic trance so their feet didn't register the heat of the burning coals. But hearing strange voices coming out of neighbors and family friends, seeing the strange ways their bodies moved across the floor until her grandmother "enticed the spirits to depart" with one last swig of alcohol or one final drag on a cigarette . . . it had been disconcerting for an impressionable young girl to watch.

But Izzie hadn't thought about those evenings in years. What had brought them to mind now, as she lay on the edge of consciousness, half a lifetime and half a continent away from the last time she'd seen her grandmother in this world?

"Girl, you best wake up," she had imagined her grandmother saying in the darkness.

There seemed a sort of bitter irony in the thought of her grandmother trying to wake her, when going to sleep was the one thing she most wanted in this world right now.

"Thanks for nothing, Mawmaw," Izzie said aloud, glancing up at the sky. The moon hung overhead, waxing and almost full, shining in the midst of a golden halo as it passed through the thin layer of clouds. It looked almost like an eye gazing down, maybe watching over her in protection, maybe looking down in judgment. "And I *do* have work to do, thanks very much. But if I don't get some sleep I'm going to be useless in the morning."

She had already gone halfway up the Northside hills, lost in thought. If she didn't head back soon, it would be dawn before she got back. So she turned a corner and headed back towards the hotel.

Izzie had managed to get turned around in the side streets that wound their way up the Northside hills on her jog back down, and didn't realize that she was heading back in the wrong direction until she hit Prospect Avenue. If she'd been heading towards City Center as she thought she was, she would have passed her hotel on Hauser before reaching the businesses and shops along Prospect, but here she was still on residential blocks surrounded by homes.

The lampposts on this stretch of Prospect were spaced farther apart than she was used to, and when she pulled her phone out of her borrowed hoodie's pocket, the screen seemed blindingly bright. She squinted against the glare as she brought up a GPS map, and discovered that she was in the Hyde Park neighborhood, a good dozen blocks to the east of her hotel and half a block south.

Izzie swore under her breath. At this rate, sleep seemed like an ever-diminishing possibility.

She slipped the phone back into her pocket, and turned right to continue west down the sidewalk. The houses that lined this stretch of Prospect were older than the mini-mansions that stacked up the hills of Northside, relatively modest one- or two-story Craftsman bungalows dating back to the 1920s, and while most of the homes Izzie was jogging past were in good repair, there was the occasional exception showing signs of neglect. But even with the odd moss-covered sagging roof or broken shutter hanging off its hinges, this was still a solidly middle class neighborhood, the flower gardens and well-tended shrubs that could be seen in many of the postage-stamp front yards a clear indicator of the care with which most of the residents kept up their homes.

This was a residential area, and unlike Oceanview or even Ross Village where there might be a few stragglers heading home from the bar or frequenting twenty-four-hour coffee shops, Izzie didn't expect to see any other pedestrians out and about at this late pre-dawn hour. The bus lines had stopped for the night long hours before and wouldn't begin again until shortly before sunrise, and there were hardly any cars out on the road, either. A produce truck rumbled by, probably heading to make a delivery at some hotel or restaurant in City Center, and as its headlights shone along the sidewalk ahead of Izzie, she was surprised to see a pair of figures coming towards her. And though her breath fogged in the chill air, the two men approaching her weren't wearing jackets or coats, just long-sleeved patterned shirts and jeans.

She thought at first that they were simply drunk or possibly on drugs, as they lurched forward one staggering step at a time. But the two men didn't seem to have the loose-jointed listing sway of people who had had too much to drink, or the

jittery twitches of meth users. These two moved like marionettes whose strings were being pulled by a first-time puppeteer, or human-shaped robots being piloted by tiny aliens who
hadn't quite gotten the hang of how to drive yet.

As the distance between Izzie and the staggering pair closed,
she began to tense up defensively, and couldn't help but wish
that she had her firearm with her. She'd left the pistol in a locked
safe back in her hotel room along with her handcuffs and badge,
when the weight of her hip holster proved too heavy for the
waistband of the borrowed sweatpants to support. And while she
was well-trained in hand-to-hand combat and confident of her
abilities to protect herself if things went south, she knew that just
the simple act of brandishing a gun might serve to keep things
from getting that far.

She pulled her hands out of the hoodie's pockets and let
her arms fall to her sides, loose and limber. The two were staggering directly towards her now, showing no indication that
they planned to step aside and let her pass. Had they even seen
her? Or were they so far gone on whatever it was they smoked
or swallowed or shot up that they didn't notice she was there?

When they were maybe a half-dozen steps away, Izzie saw
that what she had taken to be two men were actually a man
and a woman. And she suddenly wondered whether their
awkward movements weren't due to intoxication, but were
instead the result of injury. What had appeared at a distance
to be the long sleeves of patterned shirts were actually bare
arms covered in large black bruises or lesions that continued
above the collars of their ragged T-shirts, and bloomed on
their necks and faces as well.

"Are you two okay?" Izzie raised her voice as they closed
the distance between them. "Do you need any help?" She felt

suddenly queasy, as if something she'd eaten was disagreeing with her.

The pair didn't speak as they continued to stagger forward, and instead drew raspy breaths through their open mouths, jaws hanging slack. They didn't meet her gaze, and instead their half-lidded eyes continued to stare vacantly into the middle distance, the expression on their bruised faces blank and impassive.

"Are you sure I can't—?" Izzie said, then stepped aside just in time to avoid colliding with the pair. They continued past her without a word or a second glance.

Izzie watched their retreating backs as they lurched on down the sidewalk. She considered going after them and insisting that they obviously required some kind of assistance, but decided against it in the end. They were clearly adults, and capable of making their own mistakes. And since they were ambulatory and didn't seem to be breaking any laws, she had no reason to contact the authorities. Besides, there was the sense of nausea that had swept over her, and she didn't want to be caught out in the open if she were getting sick.

She shrugged, turned back to the west, and continued jogging towards City Center. Her hotel was only a few blocks away, and with any luck she might get some sleep this time. She might open the curtains a bit when she got back to the room, before turning off the light. She wasn't really in the mood for total darkness again.

CHAPTER SEVEN

When Patrick's call woke her, Izzie had only been asleep a little over an hour, but she still felt immeasurably better than she had a few hours before. She'd fallen asleep in the borrowed workout clothes, and found the smell of them far more noisome now that she was fully awake. She stripped out of them, wrinkling her nose, and left them in a pile on the bed. Then she grabbed a quick shower, brushed her teeth vigorously, and dressed in yesterday's jeans and a fresh shirt. She caught sight of herself in the mirror as she pulled on her jacket, and knew that she would have to address her ratty braids before too much longer, but they would have to wait for the moment.

She went through her personal sign of the cross before opening the door, patting her pockets in sequence. Phone? Check. Credentials? Check. Firearm? Ammunition? Handcuffs? Check, check, and check.

She pulled the Do Not Disturb sign off the outside handle, tossed it into the room, and the door sighed shut behind her. As she headed down the hall, she wondered whether a gris-gris bag might not be more fitting for the day, after all. In for a penny with superstitious nonsense, in for a pound.

Patrick was right about one thing, at least. The donuts *were* delicious.

"Oh my god, these are amazing," Izzie said around a giant mouthful. They were flaky and tender, and sweeter than their plain golden color would suggest, even without any added icing. And huge. One of them alone practically filled the plate, and Izzie had already had three.

"These are island-style donuts," Patrick explained, taking a sip of his steaming hot coffee. He gestured towards the counter and the kitchen beyond. "The owners were neighbors of mine growing up. They graduated from high school with my cousin Susan. We go way back." He leaned forward, lowering his voice conspiratorially. "They set aside the best ones for me."

Izzie rolled her eyes. "Patrick, do you honestly think you're the only cop who gets preferential treatment in a *donut* place?"

Patrick sat back, feigning mock offense. "I'm shocked, *shocked* to find that gambling is going on in here!"

She chuckled and held up the plate holding the last of the enormous pastries. "Your winnings, sir."

When he reached for the last donut, she quickly snatched it up and took a huge bite, chewing with exaggerated bliss. "Mmmm."

Patrick gulped the last of his coffee and slammed the cup down on the table. "Everybody out at once!"

Izzie pushed back from the table, patting her stomach. "Okay, I clearly needed that. Thanks." She stood up, checking to make sure her holster was still in the correct position behind her hip.

Patrick grinned. "So when's lunch?"

"Come on." Izzie headed towards the door. "We've got work to do."

"Where would you like to start?" Patrick said as he followed her outside.

"I want to revisit the physical evidence from the Fuller investigation." Izzie headed towards the curb where Patrick's car was parked. "In particular, the stuff we seized from his apartment. It's possible that we missed something important the first time around."

"For example?" Patrick jingled the keys in his hand as he approached the driver's side door.

"Like what he thought he was accomplishing by killing all of those people."

During the course of the Reaper investigation five years before, the materials that the task force collected had been kept in the Property Room at the 12th Precinct Station House on Odessa Avenue. After the investigation concluded with the death of Nicholas Fuller, everything had been moved to a warehouse that the Property and Evidence division of the Recondito police department maintained in the South Bay's industrial park for long-term storage.

As Patrick navigated his car through the morning traffic heading south along the bay's eastern shore, Izzie mentioned her run-in with the staggering pair the night before.

"Oh, yeah," Patrick said, wincing. "They must have been pretty far gone."

"Far gone on what?"

"Ink. I've only seen a few cases that had gotten that bad, but I guess we'll be seeing more and more of it unless we're able to figure out where the supply is coming from." He signaled to change lanes as they approached South Bay. "I'm sure you've seen photos of people who use crystal meth regularly, right?"

"Sure. 'Faces of meth.' That kind of thing." Izzie cringed, remembering images of sunken cheeks and rotting teeth, slack skin covered in acne and sores, people seeming to age years in a matter of months, decades in a matter of years. "Gruesome."

"Well, Ink is just as bad, maybe even worse. At first it just affects the user's behavior—mood swings, personality changes, memory loss. It's the loss of memory that's the draw for some people that use Ink. Maybe they've had some trauma they'd rather not remember, or a bad breakup they'd rather forget. With enough doses of Ink, all that is washed away. But with continued use it starts to affect them physically, too. There's usually dramatic weight loss, probably due to a loss of appetite. I've even heard of some kids who start using because they've got body image issues and think it'll help them lose weight. But nobody tells them that they might drop a few pounds, but they'll pick up lesions in the bargain."

"Yikes."

"Yeah, they're nasty. I don't know what causes it, exactly. Bruising, maybe? Or maybe Ink jacks up the body's immune system somehow? But however it happens, they start forming these dark patches on their skin, just a few at first, and the longer they keep on using the more they get, bigger and darker. Like nasty black welts all over the place."

"Sounds horrible." Izzie glanced out the window at the hike and bike trails that threaded between the road and the eastern shores of the bay. Couples strolling along, people out running or jogging, young parents pushing strollers. "I guess that means the problem could be worse though, right? I mean, you don't see too many people walking around covered in big black bruises."

Patrick shook his head, and scowled. "Oh, they're out there. But they tend to keep out of sight. Prolonged use of the stuff seems to make them . . . what's the technical term for being sensitive to light?"

Izzie thought for a moment. "Photophobic?"

"Right. Photophobic. They stay holed up indoors during the day, and at night avoid the parts of town that are brightest lit. But if you go looking in the shadows, you'll always find a few blots skulking around."

"Blots?" Izzie echoed.

"That's what some of the vice cops have started calling them." He gestured vaguely at his face and neck. "Because of the lesions."

Patrick shot a look over at Izzie, a somewhat guilty expression on his face.

"I don't care for the term much, myself," he explained. "These kids don't know what they're getting into when they start taking this stuff, and it seems a little heartless to reduce what's happening with them to a dismissive slur."

"You almost sound more like a social worker than a cop."

Patrick shrugged. "I just don't want anyone to get hurt. Even if it's somebody hurting themselves. Protect and serve, right?"

"Makes sense to me."

You guys are lucky," the sergeant behind the desk said, as he flipped through their requisition form. "This material is slated to be purged at the end of the quarter. We keep evidence related to homicide cases longer than most felonies, of course, but we've got to free up that space eventually. Most of it was digitized, though, so you'll always be able to find it in the system. But this stuff . . . ?"

He glanced over at the small collection of file boxes that a clerk was transferring from a handcart to the counter next to him.

"These are headed for the incinerator."

Patrick nodded. "Well, glad we got to them in time."

While the clerk scanned bar codes on the file boxes with a handheld scanner, the sergeant consulted the requisition form again, and then checked the inventory display on his computer's monitor.

"Actually, it looks like the crime scene photos you've requested have already been digitized and purged, but you can refer to the case file number to find them on the departmental database. And . . ." he tapped at his computer's keyboard, checked the form, and then looked back over the counter at Patrick and Izzie. "There's just two more items in the inventory associated with that case number that you didn't include in your list. Do you want those, too?"

Patrick glanced over at Izzie, who raised an eyebrow. "What are they?" he asked, turning back to the sergeant.

The sergeant pushed his glasses up higher on the bridge of his nose and leaned in closer to the monitor screen. "They were listed as 'One face mask—metal' and 'One sword with twenty-inch blade.' They're boxed up separately and packed in plastic, but they were stored along with the rest of the material."

"I'm not sure that we need—" Patrick began, but then Izzie laid a hand on his arm, silencing him.

"Can you add those to the requisition?" Izzie said, addressing the sergeant. "The authorization that Lieutenant Tevake got from his captain should cover that, right?"

"Sure." The sergeant consulted the forms. "This authorizes the lieutenant to requisition any and all physical material associated with that case number. You want 'em, you got 'em." He tapped a few keys on the keyboard, then nodded to the clerk.

A page clattered out of a printer behind the sergeant. He turned to retrieve it, stapled it to the requisition forms, and then slid it to Patrick.

"You'll have to sign an additional statement for the narcotics. New regulation."

Izzie was momentarily confused as Patrick signed the form, then remembered the vials of crystallized powder that had been found among Fuller's effects.

The clerk returned with two additional boxes, one under either arm. The first was half the size of the file boxes on the counter, and the other was three feet long and six inches square.

"I think that does it," the sergeant said, accepting the signed forms from Patrick. "You two need a hand with those?"

Patrick was already hefting a small tower of file boxes, straining only slightly under their weight, while Izzie picked up another. "No, I think we've got it."

The sergeant offered a mirthless smile. "Pleasure doing business with you."

Patrick's vice squad worked out of the 10th Precinct station house, at the corner of Howard and Albion in the northwestern part of the Oceanview. He'd reserved the precinct's community room for their use, and when he and Izzie arrived from the warehouse they began moving the boxes up from Patrick's car in the underground garage beneath the station.

The room was usually used for departmental training or general meetings with community members, but Patrick had moved most of the upholstered chairs to one side of the room, the casters clattering across the well-worn carpet. The room smelled of coffee and age to Izzie, and the humming fluorescents in the fixtures overhead that flickered slightly cast a wan light that made her think of hospital waiting rooms and long lines at the DMV.

It had taken a couple of trips to shift the boxes from the station house's garage up the elevator to the community room on the second floor. Now that all of the boxes were in, they began sorting and unloading them on the long wooden table that dominated the room.

It had been fairly late in the Reaper investigation that the task force had managed to identity the most likely subject who fit the profile Izzie and her partner Thomas Henderson had worked up: Nicholas Fuller. Captain Travers of the Recondito PD had gotten a warrant expedited, but by the time they arrived at Fuller's last known address, he had already vacated the premises. But he had evidently left in a hurry, given the number of personal possessions that remained in his ramshackle apartment. Perhaps he intended to return when his "work" was complete, or maybe he suspected that the authorities were on his scent and had gone into hiding. It was only when they traced his connection with the deceased owner of the inoperative lighthouse on Ivory Point that they knew where to search next, and after that fatal confrontation in the lantern room Fuller was in no condition to account for his movements.

Nor was he around to explain the significance of the things that the crime scene investigators had recovered from his apartment, which left Izzie and Patrick attempting to make sense of the confusing mess that lay before them, five years on.

Spread out on the table was an entire landscape: mountain ranges of piled books and magazines; foothills of stacked memo pads and journals and spiral-bound notebooks; forests of folders stuffed with newspaper clippings and Xeroxes and photographs; vast plains of street maps and topographical surveys marked with pencil and pen; and a sea of technical schematics and architectural blueprints, beyond which an assortment of scientific apparatus and occult amulets had been scattered like calving icebergs.

"Where to even *start* with all of this?" Izzie picked up a book from the top of one of the piles. *Hidden City: Recondito from 1849–1900.* Many pages had been dog-eared, and Post-it page markers bristled like a porcupine's quills. She opened to one of the marked pages, and saw a grainy reproduction of a daguerreotype, showing miners digging in the hills. Someone, Fuller presumably, had circled and marked the faces of each of the miners, with names scrawled near each in a crabbed hand. *Marston. Aldrich. Swan. O'Malley. Chang.* "This all has to mean *something*, right?"

She dropped the book onto the table and picked up another. *The Guildhall: The Rise and Fall of the Recondito Robber Barons*, from which entire pages had been torn out. Beneath it was a paperback reprint of a pulp novel from the 1930s featuring a grinning skull face on the cover, and flipping through it Izzie found that huge blocks of text had been underlined or highlighted or furiously crossed out, sometimes with remarks like "Lies!" or "Possible?" scribbled in the margins in that same crabbed hand.

Izzie noticed that Fuller's handwriting seemed to grow more crabbed and erratic as he went along, with the oldest examples being so neat and orderly that they looked like they were written by a different person than the most recent ones. Izzie thought of studies she'd seen on the effects of drugs and psychosis on an individual's ability to draw accurate representations of what they saw or to correctly form letters and symbols, and wondered if narcotics were to blame for Fuller's apparent degeneration.

The next book in the stack was *In Search of Emanant Truth*, a self-help mass-market paperback from the 1960s written by Jeremiah Standfast Parrish, the founder of the Eschaton Center. The book had an author photo printed on the back cover, which was defaced with the eyes gouged out and the mouth covered with a tight row of Xs in black ink. Beneath that book were translations of the Mayan *Popol Vuh* and *The Tibetan Book of the Dead*, collections of Babylonian myths and Native American folktales, an introduction to the Kabbalistic text *Sefer Yetzirah*, Aleister Crowley and MacGregor Mathers's edition of the *Ars Goetia*, superhero comics, horror novels, and trashy conspiracy theory paperbacks. At the bottom of the pile were scientific journals featuring articles like "Observable Effects of Extra Dimensions" and "Dark Matter in Multidimensional Cosmological Models" and "Brane-World Gravity," but beyond the titles Izzie couldn't make heads or tails of the contents, or of the commentary that Fuller had neatly written in the margins.

The only other thing of note that Izzie gleaned from her quick perusal was that Fuller had scribbled strange symbols on the flyleaves, title pages, and margins of most of the books, but whether these were scientific formulae or mathematical notation or some kind of cyphered writing, she had no way of knowing. And even if she knew which the symbols were, she'd be no closer to understanding their significance.

"Ungh!" Izzie sent a science journal flapping back down to the table like a wounded bird. "This is hopeless."

Patrick looked up from the maps that he was studying on the far side of the table. "I don't know, I think you were right the first time. This meant *something* to Fuller. Here, look." He lifted the map, which showed Recondito and the surrounding areas in topographical relief. It was covered with bits of writing and symbols, circles and lines, that at first glance seemed to Izzie to be completely haphazard. "See that?" He pointed at the mouth of the Hidden Bay, where a neat spiral had been carefully drawn in red permanent marker.

"Ivory Point," Izzie said thoughtfully.

"Exactly. The lighthouse. And see this?"

Above and to one side of the spiral that covered the lighthouse were grouped a collection of larger, more loosely-drawn curves that spiraled and looped through the southwestern corner of the Oceanview.

"That's my old neighborhood," Patrick said. "Little Kovoko." He pulled out his phone, and swiped until it displayed the map of the city that he had shown Izzie the night before. "Fuller drew these symbols at least five years before Ink first appeared on the streets. But look!" The spiraling loops on Fuller's map corresponded exactly to the area where Ink traffic and use had never been reported.

Izzie remained skeptical. "Could be a coincidence . . ." she said without much conviction.

"And this?" Patrick indicated a point a few miles northeast of the city on Fuller's map, where a complex geometric figure of angles and jagged lines was inscribed in black ink. "That's the old mine shaft where the researchers from Ross University did the Undersight experiment."

"Okay, okay." Izzie rubbed her lower lip, looking around the room. "Maybe it's more than a coincidence. And clearly all of this meant something to *Fuller*. But it's like a jigsaw puzzle without the box, so you don't know what picture it's supposed to form." She waved an arm at the mess sprawling out over the table. "Just a bunch of tiny little pieces, and us with no way of knowing how they're meant to fit together."

Patrick dropped the map back onto the table. "I don't know, maybe we just find two pieces that fit and then start from there?"

Izzie took a deep breath and let out a ragged sigh. She leaned forward, palms resting on the edge of the table, and glowered at the confusing mess.

"Well, Fuller was a scientist, right? And a respected one, at least until he wigged out and got fired." She picked up one of the scientific journals. "And based on the legibility of his handwriting, I think all of this"—she nodded, indicating the table—"started with these." She held the journal up beside her head and pointed at it with her free hand.

"What do you have in mind?" Patrick rested his knuckles on the table.

Izzie leafed through the journal, looking at the impenetrable printed text and Fuller's neatly handwritten commentary. References to hidden dimensions and other spaces, dark matter and negative energy, membranes and Planck scale . . . all of which were equally incomprehensible to her, but which Fuller referred back to again and again in his notations in the margins of different books as his writing became increasingly crabbed and erratic.

"We don't know what any of this means. But I'm guessing a scientist would." A slight grin tugged at the corners of her mouth. "So why don't we find a scientist and ask them?"

CHAPTER EIGHT

Walking onto the campus of Ross University was almost like entering a nature preserve. The blocks of Ross Village that surrounded it on all sides were filled with coffee shops and bars, bookstores and boutiques, and the roads were rivers of cyclists and cars ebbing and flowing while crowds of pedestrians jostled on the sidewalks or periodically flooded the intersections at diagonal crosswalks. But the university campus itself was tranquil and serene, white limestone buildings connected by a network of paved paths, dotted here and there with fountains and monuments to past luminaries. After the bustle of the surrounding streets, it was as quiet and still as a garden. Or a cemetery.

It had been springtime when last Izzie visited the university, and the well-tended lawns of the campus had been brilliant green, vibrant, and alive. Now in the last days of fall, the grass had gone to sleep for the winter, tawny brown accented here and there with the last remaining tufts of emerald, crisscrossed with muddy scars left by students too impatient to use the paved walkways. The whiteness of the Oregon limestone from which the buildings were constructed had seemed gleaming and bright against the lively springtime hues, but the autumnal drear instead brought to mind headstones marking a grave.

In the northeastern corner of the campus was a Brutalist bunker of glass and steel and concrete the color of onyx, a relatively recent addition dating from the mid-seventies. In contrast to the ivory white of the older buildings it was a rotten tooth, joyless and stark against the slate gray sky. Metal letters affixed to the black stone above the entrance spelled out the words "Department of Physics," surmounting an abstract bas-relief vaguely suggestive of electrons orbiting a nucleus.

As cheerless as the exterior of the building might have been, though, the man who was approaching the reception desk was as bright as a sunbeam.

"Margaret, you said there was someone here to see me?" He smiled broadly, snowy white hair falling just past the collar of his Oxford shirt, sleeves rolled up to the elbow revealing a faded tattoo on his forearm. He wore a university ID clipped to his breast pocket, and cartoon characters cavorted on the silkscreened fabric of his necktie.

The receptionist covered the mouth of the phone that she was speaking into and nodded. "They said they had some questions for someone in your department, Dr. Kono, and you were the only faculty member whose calendar was free."

"For the thousandth time, Margaret, there's no need to be so formal." He turned to Patrick and Izzie and, glancing at their badges, raised an eyebrow quizzically. "So, is there some problem, officers?"

"Dr. Kono? I'm Lieutenant Tevake, Recondito PD."

"Please, call me Hayao," he answered, still smiling, eyes twinkling in his lined face. Then he turned to Izzie. "And you are?"

"Special Agent Isabel Lefevre, FBI." She shook his hand.

"*Special agent*? How official." He leaned forward, lowering his voice. "A little intimidating, even." Then he laughed.

His smile was infectious. "You can call me Izzie, if that helps," she answered with a slight grin.

"I think it might!" The professor clapped his hands once, then rubbed his palms together as if to warm them. "So, to what do I owe the pleasure of your visit?"

Izzie glanced at Patrick, and he nodded, indicating that she should take the lead.

"We're investigating a case that is potentially connected to a man who used to be on the faculty here." She paused, reaching for the folder tucked under her arm. "His name was Nicholas Fuller?"

The professor's smile evaporated like a snowflake in the summer sun.

"Oh. My."

Izzie searched his face. His reaction was not that of someone who had simply heard the name before. "Did you know him?"

"Yes." Dark memories clouded the professor's expression. "Yes, I did."

"Would you be willing to answer a few questions?" Patrick asked.

The professor seemed to be staring at something in the middle distance, lost in thought and unspeaking.

"It could potentially be a big help to our investigation," Izzie added.

The professor gathered himself again, returning to the present moment. He blinked a few times, then nodded. "Yes, yes, of course. I'd be happy to help."

He turned and gestured for them to follow as he headed down the hallway.

"We'll talk in my office."

Patrick and Izzie exchanged a glance as they trailed after him. She knew that he was thinking the same thing she was. They'd come seeking insight into the things that Fuller had written, but now it appeared they might be getting insight into the man himself, as well.

Hayao Kono's windowless office was cramped but comfortable, with three monitors arranged like changing room mirrors atop a standing desk, shelves along two adjoining walls stuffed to the brim with textbooks and scientific journals, and on the third wall a long, low display case in which vintage tin toys were carefully arranged—rocket ships, ray guns, wind-up robots, and more. Above the display case was mounted an antique brass astrolabe, around which were hung framed prints of cosmological majesties like nebulae and swirling galaxies and other more puzzling mundanities like Romanesco broccoli and ammonite shells. And along the fourth wall near the door was the only item of furniture in the room other than the desk, a love seat upholstered in a floral print that looked like it would be more at home in the parlor of an old-fashioned spinster aunt than in the office of a physicist.

"Please, sit." Hayao motioned towards the narrow couch. "Make yourselves comfortable."

Izzie sat, though she wasn't sure comfort was a viable option. The florid embroidery of the love seat's upholstery rasped against her skin when she touched it, and the couch cushions were thin and unforgiving. She perched awkwardly on the edge of the seat, the folder she'd brought with her resting on her knees.

"Thanks for agreeing to speak with us," said Patrick, who didn't seem to be faring any better on the couch than she was.

The professor nodded, distractedly, and flickered a smile that faded as quickly as it had appeared. It was as though his usual genial demeanor was a shell beneath which darker thoughts were now bubbling up and threatening to break through.

"Such a promising young mind." Hayao had a faraway look on his face. "Such a terrible waste."

He trailed off, looking over at the wall of framed prints surrounding the astrolabe.

"This is Nicholas Fuller you're referring to?" Patrick pulled a small notebook and pen out of the inner pocket of his suit coat.

The professor glanced over at him. "Nicholas was a graduate student of mine and later, when he'd finished his postdoctoral studies overseas and returned to Recondito as a member of the faculty, we were colleagues." He paused, remembering. "I would have even said that we were friends, once upon a time. Of course that was before . . . before . . ."

A pained look clouded his face for a moment and then passed.

Izzie opened the folder on her lap and pulled out one of the scientific journals. "These were found among Fuller's possession after his death, and we believe that he was responsible for the notes written in the margins." She held the journal out to the professor. "We were hoping someone here might be able to explain their significance?"

Hayao stepped forward and took the journal, then opened it and began to flip through. "Oh, certainly, I remember this paper." He chuckled slightly, idly turning the pages. "Chilton's conjecture caused a considerable amount of controversy at the time, but later findings refuted what he . . ."

The professor paused, narrowing his gaze. He ran a finger along a line of handwritten commentary, intently. Then he continued on, reading the notations on the next page, and the page after, the lines on his face deepening in concentration.

"But he couldn't possibly have . . ." He turned another page. "Could he?" Then he kept on reading.

"Dr. Kono?" Izzie said after nearly a minute had passed in complete silence, the professor completely absorbed. "Hayao?"

The professor seemed not to hear, but instead stopped short on the last page, disappointment in his face. "Oh, Nicholas." He slapped the journal shut with annoyance, and looked back to Izzie and Patrick. "It's just nonsense, plain and simple. I thought maybe that he'd worked out a solution . . . but no, it turned out to just be more of the same pseudoscientific gibberish he was spouting when he was last here. Before . . . you know . . ."

He trailed off and gave Izzie and Patrick a meaningful look, as though there were no need for him to go on.

"What solution did you think he'd worked out, professor?" Patrick's pen hovered above his notebook.

Hayao sighed wearily. "Nicholas possessed a brilliant mind and a keen sense of curiosity, but he was a little too eager to find answers, I always thought. A little too willing to accept correlation as causation, or to cherry-pick data that supported a hypothesis he preferred while dismissing anything that didn't." His tone became somewhat professorial. "You can regard any hypothesis as a question, and the scientific process as a way of testing out potential answers." He held up the journal. "Nicholas was sure that he had the answer to this particular question, even if the evidence didn't always agree with him."

"And these?" Izzie handed the professor the other journals.

"Mmm." Hayao rifled through the others, nodding as he went. "These are all different aspects of the same question, really. It was Nicholas's primary obsession throughout his career. A mania, really, in the technical sense of the term." He handed the journals back to Izzie. "Ultimately, I think that obsession was the thing that pushed him over the edge."

"So what *is* the question?" Izzie asked.

"In layman's terms," Patrick added a little sheepishly. "If you don't mind."

"Not at all." The professor chuckled. "It's pretty simple, actually. It all starts with the problem of gravity. Namely, why is it so weak?"

He clearly could read the confusion in their faces.

"There are four fundamental forces that govern the universe: gravity, electromagnetism, the strong nuclear force, and the weak nuclear force. Everything from the energy levels in a single hydrogen atom's electron to the orbital movements of entire galaxies is governed by the interplay of those four things. Out of all four, gravity is by far the weakest, by orders of magnitude, but we're not sure exactly why. It's sometimes called the 'hierarchy problem,' and there have been any number of possible explanations put forward that . . ."

Patrick had his hand up like a student in a classroom.

"Yes?" Hayao defaulted to professorial mode.

"What do you mean, gravity is weak? Like, on the moon? Or weightless in space?"

"No, not really." The professor shook his head. "Although that's certainly an illustration of one of gravity's limitations, in a way. It takes an enormous amount of matter to begin to exhibit significant gravitational effects—like a moon or a planet for instance—but compared to gravity we see a disproportionately larger effect produced by the interactions of individual electromagnetic particles, and the same is true of the nuclear forces, as well. Gravity is the outlier, and one possible explanation is that it isn't entirely here. Maybe part of is *missing*. That's one of the hypotheses that the Undersight project was designed to test."

Izzie and Patrick both perked up at the mention of the name.

"You see, Undersight was primarily intended to function as a detector for dark matter, which might be composed of non-baryonic matter or WIMPs."

"Wimps?" Izzie quirked an eyebrow.

"Weakly Interacting Massive Particles," Hayao explained. "Stuff that has mass but doesn't interact the same way that normal matter does, but which could help account for discrepancies in calculations about how much stuff we *should* see in the universe based on our best models of how things work, and how much *visible* stuff there is out there to see. In much the same way, 'dark energy' has been proposed to account for similar discrepancies in the amount of energy that has been calculated to exist based on things like the rate the universe is expanding, and the amount of energy that we can actually detect." He paused, clearly in his comfort zone discussing such matters, even in such simplified terms. "That 'missing' matter and energy are really out there, we just can't detect them. So maybe they're down here with us, too, and we just don't realize it."

"And how did Undersight figure into this?" Izzie asked.

"Well, people have put detectors deep underground to search for various things that are hard to detect on the surface of the Earth, like neutrinos. And the Undersight team adapted a similar strategy to search for dark matter and dark energy, instead. But it was Nicholas who suggested that the apparatus could be tasked with searching for something else, as well. Namely, that missing gravity."

The professor had started to pace slowly back and forth across the small space, punctuating his words with broad sweeps of his arms and precise gestures with hands, depending on the circumstance.

"There are a number of theories that account for the hierarchy problem by proposing that there are extra spatial dimensions beyond those we perceive, and that gravity is in essence 'leaking' into one or more of these additional dimensions. The force itself is operating on the same scale as the other three fundamental forces, but the effects are not noticeable since most of the effect is occurring elsewhere."

Izzie could not help but be reminded about what Fuller had said towards the end, that night in the lighthouse's lantern room, about gravity leaking into other spaces. And what was it he had said about doors? That they "swing both ways"?

"There are similar hypotheses that account for dark energy in much the same way, using additional spatial dimensions to account for that discrepancy. Nicholas felt that all of these—dark matter, dark energy, the hierarchy problem and the weakness of gravity—are all the result of our universe existing in a higher-dimensional space, but further of our universe interacting with *other* universes that are also part of that higher-dimensional space, though ones in which the relative strengths of the fundamental forces are different. And like water finding its own level between two containers, the forces ebb and flow until the strengths are equalized between two or more universes that are in contact."

Hayao sighed a little wistfully.

"An elegant hypothesis in a lot of ways, and one that accounted for a great many unanswered questions. But Nicholas took it even further, and suggested that the different universes 'orbit' through higher-dimensional space just like planets or galaxies. From time to time, he argued, connections between two or more universes can be broken and other new connections form. And when that happens, he was convinced, the relative strengths of the fundamental forces could undergo rapid change."

Now it was Izzie's turn to raise her hand. "You mean gravity itself could get even weaker?"

"Possibly." Hayao shrugged. "Or grow stronger. Or effectively disappear entirely." He paused, shaking his head. "The possible ramifications were profound. But again, it was still an untested hypothesis, not backed up by data or verified through experimentation. But Nicholas would not be deterred. He was *convinced* that the findings from Undersight would prove him right."

"So what went wrong?" Patrick asked.

Tension crept back into the professor's posture as his face closed off. "He never even tested his hypothesis. There were three other teams who were scheduled to run experiments using the Undersight apparatus before Nicholas, and so once the technicians and engineers had finished setting up the equipment down in the mine shaft, the teams started to go down to calibrate the sensors for their needs. Since everything would need to be completely reset in order for Nicholas's tests to run, he didn't even go down into the shaft for the first eighteen months of operation, but instead stayed in his office working on his calculations when he wasn't teaching a class."

Hayao began pacing again, but with an urgency to his step now, not a breezy stroll but more like the anxious steps of a caged animal.

"It was around that time that I left the university on a year-long sabbatical to perform a series of experiments with the Large Hadron Collider at CERN, so much of what I know about what happened next came to me secondhand." He gritted his teeth. "Maybe if I'd been here at the time, I could have been able to do something to help. Maybe Nicholas would have listened to me when he ignored the others. But . . ."

He broke off, shaking his head as though to shake something loose.

"In any event, as I understand the sequence of events, Nicholas began having . . . difficulties with some of the other researchers. At first everyone just assumed it was nerves, or that he was simply eager to take his turn, but as time went on his clashes with the teams that were conducting experiments with the equipment became increasingly hostile, even violent. He began acting paranoid, insisting that other researchers had hidden agendas that they were keeping from the rest of us. No one was allowed to enter the shaft while an experiment was in progress, for fear of interfering with the measurements, but several times Nicholas had to be physically barred from going down there, anyway. And all the while, his claims about his own hypothesis continued to get more grandiose."

"Sounds almost like schizophrenic delusions," Izzie observed.

"Or the paranoia of a meth head," Patrick added.

"All such explanations were considered at the time, believe me," Hayao answered, sadly. "What choice did we have? And from what I've been told, I believe that Nicholas *had* started taking some kind of psychotropic by the end."

Izzie remembered the vials of powder that were in the evidence boxes back in the 10th Precinct community room.

"But his behavior got even worse when he became obsessed with the history of Recondito. Nicholas had first come to the city as a graduate student, having done his undergraduate work at the University of Texas, and in all the time I'd known him he'd never displayed even a passing interest in anything to do with his present surroundings beyond which numbered parking spot was his and where he could find the best chicken fried rice near campus. But I was told that when he was denied entry into the mine shaft for the last time, he started pestering the geology department, interested in anything they knew about the hills and the surrounding countryside. And then the history department, and archaeology, and comparative religious studies, driven by a seemingly insatiable curiosity about the land and uses to which people had put it. Then he happened to meet the family of one of our colleagues. They had lived in this area for centuries, since it was still part of New Spain . . ."

"Aguilar," Izzie interrupted.

The professor looked at her with mild surprise.

"He was one of the staff members I interviewed when I was part of the F—" she paused, then said, "part of the *Reaper* task force five years ago. He was one of our principle sources of information about Fuller's behavior leading up to the . . . incidents."

"Yes, well," Hayao answered, "if anyone were to know, it would be Ricardo Aguilar. His grandfather Roberto was still alive at the time, and somehow Ricardo got it into his head that it might help satisfy Nicholas's burning curiosity if he could talk to someone who could answer more of his questions about the city's history. So Ricardo introduced them, though his relationship with his grandfather had always been somewhat strained, as I understood it. And from that point onwards, until the old man passed away some months later, he and Nicholas were virtually inseparable. The elder Aguilar owned a considerable amount of property in the city—"

"Including the Ivory Point Lighthouse." Izzie could not help interrupting.

"Yes, including that." Hayao's expression was grim. "And as Ricardo told the story, when they weren't holed up in the old man's private library, his grandfather and Nicholas could be found walking the city streets together, visiting various apartment buildings or offices or even mausoleums in the cemetery, as though they were searching for something. Or for someone."

"Did they find it?" Patrick asked.

The professor shrugged. "Who can say? The elder Aguilar had a stroke shortly afterwards and never regained consciousness. And Nicholas . . ." He sighed, a pained look on his face. "Nicholas isn't around to explain himself."

"And it was after the old man died that Nicholas attacked Tompkins and got fired?" Izzie asked.

"Within a few days of the old man's passing, as I recall," Hayao answered. "The way it was described to me, Alice Tompkins and Francis Zhao were interviewing Martin Something-or-other, an undergraduate student who had applied to assist them in recalibrating the Undersight equipment for the next Undersight experiment, when Nicholas burst into the conference room, shouting like a madman, and proceeded to attack poor Alice with a hammer. Thankfully she only suffered a few broken bones in her hand before Francis and the student were able to restrain Nicholas. Campus security came and took him away, screaming and ranting the whole way."

Hayao shook his head sadly.

"Alice graciously decided not to press charges for the assault, but the scandal was such that the administration had no choice but to pursue disciplinary action of its own, and terminated his employment. By the time I came back to the university at the end of the year, Nicholas had broken off contact with the entire department. I tried to reach out to him, but he refused my calls and my letters were returned unanswered. And none of us ever saw him again." He winced. "Well, I suppose that Francis and Alice . . . and all of the others . . . they saw him before he . . . he . . ."

Izzie knew that each of them had indeed seen Fuller one last time, and then had never seen anything else, ever again.

Hayao had one hand held across his eyes, head tilted back slightly.

"I'm sorry . . ." he said, his voice strained. He took a deep breath, collecting himself. "Hm."

He lowered his hand, and Izzie could see that his eyes were red-rimmed and welling with fresh tears.

"In any event, the Undersight program continued for several more years, though many of the chief researchers ended up leaving the university for the private sector once their own projects were complete. I had plans to conduct some experiments of my own, but after . . . after the killings . . ."

He blinked rapidly.

"The university decided to shutter the Undersight project afterwards. There were simply too many painful memories for everyone involved, with so many colleagues lost and . . . and . . ."

He gulped a breath awkwardly, tears rolling down his cheeks. He raised both hands to his face and pressed the heels of his palms against his eyes.

"I'm sorry. . . . It's just very difficult to . . ."

Izzie and Patrick exchanged a glance, and she could see that he was thinking the same thing that he was. They would not be getting any additional useful intelligence out of the professor in his present emotional state, and it was clearly time for them to leave.

"We appreciate your assistance, sir," Patrick said. "I think we have what we need."

The professor wiped his eyes, struggling to regain his composure. "Are you sure? I'm not normally so . . . so . . ." He flapped his hand. "You know."

"We completely understand," Izzie assured him as she collected the scientific journals back into the folder, and she and Patrick started towards the door.

"Well, if there's anything else that you need, you know where to find me."

Izzie paused at the door as Patrick stepped out into the hallway. She looked back at the professor. "Actually, there is one thing. Would you happen to know if Dr. Aguilar is available? We may have a few follow-up questions for him."

"Let me check the departmental calendar."

Hayao turned to the standing desk and tapped the keys of his computers' keyboard. As a window unfurled in the middle of the three monitors, Izzie saw that the simple acting of engaging in such a mundane task seemed to give the professor something to hang on to, an anchor in the present moment to keep his mind from drifting back into the past. When he spoke again, his voice still sounded somewhat strained, but he was pushing through it, moving past the darkness behind him into something beyond.

"It looks . . . looks like he's still in New Mexico today, but his return flight is scheduled for late tonight." The professor swallowed hard, blinking, and when he continued his voice was a little clearer still, less strained. "I'm not sure whether he'll be back here tomorrow or if he plans to take the day off, but he has office hours posted for the day after tomorrow and the rest of the week, so I'm sure you won't have any trouble catching him." He glanced over his shoulder at her, a fragile smile on his face. "He's doing some very interesting work at the Very Large Array out there. You should ask him about it. Fascinating stuff."

"I'll definitely do that."

The fragile smile widened slightly, and then almost immediately began to fade once more. It was as if she could see the dark memories surfacing in his mind, shadowing his expression.

"Thank you again, sir. I appreciate you taking the time to talk with us."

He nodded a cursory goodbye and then looked away, staring into the past.

Izzie couldn't think of anything to say that might help, and so she turned and walked through the door, leaving the professor alone with his memories, and followed Patrick down the hallway and out into the light.

CHAPTER NINE

"**W**ell, that happened," Patrick said as they walked back across the university campus to the lot where he'd parked the car. "Wasn't quite how I expected that conversation to go."

"But maybe that was a conversation that would have been more useful five years ago." Izzie scowled, and couldn't help but feel a burning shame of self-recrimination. "It's clear that Kono was close to Fuller, and probably knew personal details about his life that the rest of their colleagues might not have shared."

"Possibly." Patrick glanced over, searching her face. "What of it?"

"So I should have talked to him back then." Izzie gestured angrily at the black bunker behind them. "Sure, Ricardo Aguilar gave us the evidence we needed to find where Fuller was hiding, but we only approached him in the first place because he was the head of the department. My focus was *entirely* on the people who had been directly associated with Undersight."

Patrick nodded, and answered in a conciliatory tone. "Which made sense, once we realized that all of the victims had worked on the project at some point, even if they weren't at the university anymore. That's how we identified Fuller as the primary suspect in the first place."

"Okay, sure." She was exasperated, in no mood to be patronized. "But if I'd done a more thorough job, if I'd asked the right questions . . ."

She stopped short. When Patrick turned to her, she had a stricken look on her face.

"Could we have found Fuller sooner?" There was a pleading edge to her voice. "Maybe Francis Zhao would still be alive if I had known to talk to Kono first . . ."

Patrick put his hand on her shoulder. "Look, you did everything right."

"But if only I'd—"

"No," he interrupted, his hand squeezing her shoulder a little tighter in a comforting gesture. "You did everything right. You couldn't just interview everyone at the university on the off chance they remembered a guy who had been fired from a job there years before."

"Kono would have remembered him, obviously."

Patrick nodded, grudgingly. "But it was Aguilar who gave you the list of Undersight staffers to interview, remember? There was no reason to think that you needed to talk to anyone else, especially once we made the connection between Fuller and Aguilar's grandfather and the lighthouse. We knew where to look, and doing any additional digging would just have been an unnecessary delay. You, me, Henderson,

Ramirez, and Johnson went straight from the 12th Precinct house out to Ivory Point as soon as the judge signed off on the no-knock warrant. We couldn't have gotten there any sooner than we did."

Izzie sighed. "Maybe you're right. But that doesn't make it any easier to accept."

A moment stretched out as they stood in silence, then Patrick dropped his hand from her shoulder.

"We should get going," he said, his tone serious. "There's something really important that we need to address."

"What is it?" asked Izzie. As Patrick turned and continued walking towards the parking lot, Izzie raised an eyebrow, curious. "Did I miss something?"

"Yes," he answered with a smile as he glanced back over his shoulder at her. "We missed lunch, and I'm *starving*."

For many years the south side of Prospect Avenue between Argent and Gold Streets had been a vacant lot, ever since a notorious fire in the 1940s completely destroyed the Guildhall building that had once stood on that spot. It was notorious in one respect because so many notable city leaders and captains of industry had perished in the fire, and notorious in another because the blaze had weakened the structural integrity not only of the building itself but of several levels of subbasements below, causing the whole affair to subside into a massive make-shift landfill. Surveyors and engineers determined that in order for any new structure to be built on the spot, the whole block would need to be excavated and refilled and graded before the ground there would be stable enough to safely support a building of any significant size. And when that effort was decided to be prohibitively expensive, no investors were willing to risk the capital necessary to rehabilitate the lot, and so the city took possession and simply had the landfill bulldozed flat, dumped a thin layer of soil on top, and designated it a city park. It was a park in name only, though, just a couple of acres worth of patchy grass bordered by sidewalks on all four sides, the only notable feature being the stone archway that stood at the corner of Prospect and Gold Street, which had once been part of the main Guildhall entrance, and was all that remained of the building after the fire.

But while it stood vacant for decades, real estate was at too high a premium in Recondito for the lot to be unused forever. As the local economy began to shift from flagging concerns like shipping and fishing to more lucrative industries like technology and telecommunications, there was increasing pressure on the city to put the lot to productive use. The ground was too unstable to support a permanent structure, but it was strong enough that cars and small trucks could be safely parked on it, provided the trucks were not too heavily laden, and so local businesses petitioned the city to sell the block for parking. A vote from the city council was required to change the lot's designation as a city park, but many councilmembers were reluctant to pave over yet another midtown block for a parking lot, and so the issue was stalled until a compromise was proposed. The site of the former Guildhall building could be paved for parking, the city council declared, but only if a percentage of the space was leased to food cart vendors. Available seats at restaurants in City Center and the Financial District, which were separated by Gold Street and bordered by Prospect Avenue and Northside Boulevard, had increasingly become a problem as more and more businesses moved into Recondito's midtown, and food trucks and carts had recently begun to offer a solution. But parking in midtown was always an issue, and many local business owners balked at having trucks and carts stationed for weeks at a time in front of their storefronts. Designating the empty lot as a home for food carts and visitor parking alike solved more than one problem, and support for the proposal was enthusiastic and virtually unanimous.

None of which Izzie had known fifteen minutes before, but which Patrick had decided to explain at length as they walked the perimeter of the food cart pod, trying to decide what to eat. As she dithered between bratwurst on the one hand and pho on the other, Patrick put in an order for grilled cheese at one cart and poutine fries at another, all the while enthusiastically declaiming his love for the idea of food carts and trucks in general.

In the end, Izzie settled on Korean barbeque tacos and a sparkling Italian limeade, and she and Patrick retreated up the street to lean against a wall while they ate.

"It's good, right?" Patrick said around a mouthful of cheese curds and gravy.

Izzie chased a spicy mouthful of chicken and kimchi with a swig of fizzing limeade and then nodded, eyes watering slightly. "Though I'll admit that I kind of prefer to sit when I'm eating." She set the bottle of limeade back on top of the mailbox that they were using as a makeshift table.

Patrick shrugged. "Variety is the spice of life." He bit off a hunk of his grilled cheese, and then gave a little moan of delight as he chewed.

"You really do think about food an awful lot, don't you?"

He took a sip of root beer and grinned. "It's hard not to, living in Recondito. This is a fantastic town for eating."

Izzie finished off the last of her taco, and used a paper napkin to wipe the corners of her mouth and clean off her hands. "I strongly suspect that you brought me here and gave me the living history tour of the food cart lot in an attempt to distract me from my feelings of guilt about not questioning Kono sooner."

"Well?" He swallowed the last bite of his poutine fries. "Did it work?"

"Maybe. A little." A faint smile played across her face. "Thanks for trying, either way."

"My pleasure." He stuffed wrappers and napkins into a Styrofoam container and tossed it in the trash. "It wasn't the Izzie Lefevre Show back then, you know. It was a joint task force, and a lot of people shared those responsibilities. You did your bit, and so did the rest of us."

"And this Ink investigation? Is that the Patrick Tevake Show? I don't see you bringing anybody else from your vice squad into this yet."

Patrick drew a ragged breath. "I'm not the only one assigned to the Ink problem, no. There are a few other detectives who have been trying to locate informants who could help us identify the source. But I'm the only one working this particular line of inquiry . . . for obvious reasons." They started walking up the street. "Besides, it's not like Ink is the only drug we're dealing with out here."

That sparked a thought for Izzie. "Speaking of which, Kono mentioned that Fuller may have started taking some kind of psychotropic."

"Yeah?"

"I'm wondering what the lab techs had to say about those vials of white powder that CSI found in Fuller's apartment."

Patrick rubbed his palms together. "Let's go find out, shall we?"

CHAPTER TEN

Back in the community room at the 10th Precinct station house, Patrick pulled up the Reaper investigation case files on a laptop computer while Izzie dug through the few remaining unpacked file boxes in search of the vials. She had to lift the three-foot-long narrow box to get at a stack underneath, and was struck by the weight of it. The label read simply "One (1) sword with 20-inch blade" along with an inventory control number and a bar code. A prosaic description for a deadly weapon that had been used to murder and dismember a dozen men and women. Izzie felt her skin crawl, and set the box aside.

"Looks like the CSI team used a narcotics identification field kit on the vials when they initially searched the apartment," Patrick said, not looking up from the laptop's screen. "But their findings were inconclusive and so a sample was sent to the Recondito PD's Office of Forensic Science for analysis."

Izzie opened another box, which contained some personal effects that the crime scene investigators had considered worthy of interest: receipts from hardware stores and outdoor supply companies, bank statements, a photo album, and so on. But no glass vials. She was sure that she had seen them in one of these boxes when they were sorting through them that morning, though.

"Aren't narcotics normally destroyed after an investigation?" she wondered aloud as she opened the next box.

"After the trial is over, yeah," Patrick answered. "But procedure is also to keep any seized narcotics in evidence until the lab results are in. And since the lab was still testing the samples when all of this was shifted over to long-term storage, the one procedure canceled out the other and . . ." He sat up, his expression brightening. "Ah, here we go."

He scrolled down the page with the arrow keys, reading intently.

"Huh . . ." he said after a moment, a somewhat perplexed look on his face.

"Do you have something you'd like to share with the class?"

"Yeah, it's just . . ." He sat back, scratching the raspy stubble of his five o'clock shadow. "Weird."

Izzie put down the lid of the box, and fixed him with a look. "What? Spit it out."

"The lab reports were fairly inconclusive. The chemical composition of the powder didn't quite match anything on the USC's schedule of controlled substances, but . . . here, I'll read what they said. 'The chemical compound in the provided sample is a methylated indoleamine derivative (indole alkaloid derived from the shikimate pathway) with a structure homologous to that of Dimethyltryptamine, most probably originating in a plant species of unknown origin, and there is a high probability that it functions as a serotonergic hallucinogen, acting as an agonist or antagonist of certain serotonin receptors.' End quote."

"That's a mouthful," Izzie said. "What does it mean?"

"Dimethyltryptamine is more commonly known as DMT," Patrick explained.

"Oh, right." She looked up from the box. "I read a book about it once. That's the stuff that makes people see angels or machine elves or whatever, right?"

Patrick cocked an eyebrow. "Just what kind of books have you been reading, Izzie?"

She put her hands on her hips. "I'm serious. Look it up."

He rolled his eyes, but brought up a browser window and tapped out a search string. Scanning the results, he clicked through to a few pages and read. "I'll be damned. I thought it was just some synthetic drug that old hippies and rave kids took. But it says here that it occurs naturally in all sorts of different plants *and* in the human body."

"Right," Izzie said. "There's a brew made from one of those plants that's used in religious ceremonies in South America. My grandmother knew an Ialorixá from Brazil—a Candomblé priestess—who talked about it all the time. It's called . . ." She looked up at the ceiling as she rifled back through old memories. "Ayahuasca."

"That's it." Patrick nodded, still looking at the laptop screen. "There's all kinds of results here about it being offered as part of 'shamanic retreats' in Central and South America, along with vision quests, firewalking, that kind of thing. And there's . . . hang on a second." He clicked a link. "It's used in the States, too. I'm looking at an exemption on the Schedule I list for a church that includes it in their sacraments." He sat back, thoughtfully. "Huh. My great-uncle used to brew up a foul-smelling sludge for his rites sometimes, using kawa roots."

"Kawa?"

He looked over in Izzie's direction. "That's the Te'maroan word for it. I'm not actually sure what the name in English is, but the plant grows all over the western Pacific. My great-uncle brought some seeds with him when he came to the States and used to grow it in his backyard. The whole block would stink to high heaven when he cooked up that brew, but he always said it was a vital part of his work. That he needed it to see what was hidden."

Izzie moved the small box labeled "One (1) Face mask— metal" to one side and opened the last of the file boxes.

"I wonder . . ." Patrick broke off, musing.

"What?" Izzie reached into the box and pulled out a sealed evidence bag containing a pair of small glass vials, with an inventory control number and bar code on a white label on the outside. "You wonder . . . ?"

He pushed his chair back from the table, the casters rattling on the thin carpet, and then stood up with a weary sigh. "Just . . . what if Fuller was taking this stuff for the same reason? As part of some kind of religious ritual?"

"I don't know, the image of him that I got from talking to Kono was that he was a pretty straitlaced science guy." She paused, and then added, "At the beginning at least."

He walked down the table, glancing at the confusion of items scattered there.

"Exactly. You said that the earliest examples of him writing notes in the margins were all scientific texts, right? But later there's all of this occult stuff." He picked up a book at random, Kenneth Grant's *The Magical Revival*. "And Kono said that he was getting obsessed with comparative religion and history and that kind of thing. So maybe he picked up the idea along the way?"

"Possibly. Or maybe he started taking the DMT or whatever it was on a whim, and then had some kind of experience that piqued his interest in religion and the supernatural? I'm sure that vivid hallucinations of machine elves could do that to a person. But no." She shook her head, a skeptical expression on her face. "It can't just be that. The professor also said that Fuller became obsessed with geology and archeology towards the end, remember, but only in direct relation with Recondito."

Patrick dropped the book back onto the stack. "But whether he took the drug and then turned religious or got religion and then started taking the drug, the question remains: where did he get it?"

Izzie held up the evidence bag with the vials to the light, looking intently at the contents as if the answer might be hidden inside. "I'm guessing you don't get a lot of people tripping on 'methylated indoleamine derivatives' on the streets of Recondito? No handy nicknames for kids who wander around zonked on jungle plants seeing angels? I mean, if you've got *one* street drug that hasn't shown up anywhere else in the world yet, there's bound to be more, right?"

Patrick chuckled mirthlessly. "No, thank god. Aside from Ink, it's just your garden-variety meth and crack and heroin and such." He reached out and took the evidence bag from her. "Four years I've been working vice, and this is the only instance of this kind of stuff that I've run into. Like I said . . . it's weird."

Izzie leaned on the table. "But we *are* sure that Fuller was taking this stuff, right? Did the M.E. run a toxicology test when he did the autopsy?"

"That would've been standard procedure." He nodded towards his laptop. "I can look it up, and worst-case scenario we could check with Joyce over at the morgue, see if she remembers anything."

"Might be worth checking. I'm not sure that it would help us much to know one way or the other, but still . . ." Izzie lowered her head and sighed, feeling run-down and weary.

Her gaze fell on the riot of books stacked on the table in front of her, and one in particular caught her eye: *The Guildhall: The Rise and Fall of the Recondito Robber Barons.*

"Huh."

She reached down and picked up the book, then held it up to show Patrick. She pointed at the cover, which featured a sepia-toned photograph of a mammoth building, with a stone archway over the main entrance.

"This is that same building you were telling me about, right?" she asked. "The one that burned down where the food carts are now?"

Patrick nodded. "I think so, yeah."

Izzie took a closer look at the book. It had more dog-eared pages and Post-it markers sticking out from it than any of the other books on the table.

"Fuller clearly spent a lot of time with this one." She opened the book and began flipping through the pages. Nearly every page was so covered in handwritten notes that it was sometimes difficult to make out the original text. And the notes had clearly been written over a long period of time, with later notes furiously scribbled in that crabbed hand on the same pages as older observations carefully written in neatly legible letters. "A *lot* of time. I wonder what he found so fascinating about it?"

In an insert in the middle of the book were photos showing the building in its glory days, with rooms full of important looking men with big mustaches and beards wearing old-fashioned suits, enormous banquets and society gatherings, receptions for presidents and potentates and other visiting dignitaries.

"Who were these guys?" Izzie muttered, turning the book over to look at the copy on the back cover.

"It was a private club of local bigwigs, I think," Patrick answered, uncertain. "Like the Masons or the Elks Club or something like that, right?"

Izzie scanned the description on the back cover.

"Says here that the group presented itself to the public as a private civic organization," she said. "And that legally it was. But that behind closed doors it was actually a cabal of corrupt politicians and crooked businessmen who spent decades rigging elections, monopolizing trade, and generally screwing over everyone in the city of Recondito who wasn't a member." She glanced up at Patrick before continuing. "I'm paraphrasing, of course."

"But why Guildhall?" Patrick asked. "Sounds like something out of a fantasy role-playing game."

"Because because because," Izzie muttered as she turned to the index at the back of the book. "Because . . ." She ran her finger down the list of entries until she found what she was looking for, and then flipped to a page near the front of the book. "Because," she said triumphantly, "quote, *'the organization was initially founded in 1851 as the Recondito Mining Guild to settle disputed mining claims in the hills outside of* town.' Yadda yadda yadda, *'founders included Samuel Marston, Josiah Aldrich, Matthias Swan, Brennan . . .'"*

She lowered the book, head cocked to one side quizzically.

"What?" Patrick asked.

"I know that I just . . ." She folded the book and tucked it under one arm, and then started pawing through the others on the table. "This morning I was looking at another one that . . ."

Her hands closed on another book, *Hidden City: Recondito from 1849–1900*. It had nearly as many dog-eared pages and Post-it markers as *The Guildhall* book. She opened it up, fluttering through the marked pages one after another.

"Here it is." She turned the book around and displayed the page to Patrick. On the page was a grainy reproduction of a daguerreotype depicting a group of miners with picks and shovels, with a printed caption explaining that the men were breaking ground on a new mine shaft in the spot marked on a small inset map of the Recondito hills at the bottom of the page. Fuller had circled the faces of each of the miners and written names beside each in his crabbed hand. *Marston. Aldrich. Swan. O'Malley. Chang.*

Patrick took the book from Izzie to see it more clearly.

"These are the guys who started the Guildhall outfit," Izzie said, "and Fuller was straight-up *obsessed* with them." She pulled the other book from under her arm and fanned through the pages. "Who knows *why* he was obsessed with them, but he clearly was."

"I think I might know." Patrick held the book open in one hand, and with the other starting pushing around the topographical surveys and street maps that were spread out on the far end of the other. He found the one he was looking for, and then pulled it out from under the pile, unfurling it with a shake. Then he sat the book down on top of it. "This mine shaft that they're starting to dig?" He pointed from the book to the topographical map. "It's *this* mine shaft."

Izzie looked where he was pointing on the map, and saw a complex geometric figure of angles and jagged lines that Fuller had drawn in black ink on the spot.

"Undersight," Izzie said, eyes widening.

Patrick nodded.

Izzie picked up the copy of *The Guildhall* again, studying the cover. "So this cabal of robber barons was started by the same guys who dug the hole that all of Fuller's victims went down into."

"Looks like it."

She flipped through the book once more, noting again how many notes Fuller had made on each page, and how much time he'd clearly spent doing it. "So maybe it wasn't the Undersight project he was obsessed with?"

"What do you mean?" Patrick asked.

She looked up and met his gaze. "Maybe it was the mine shaft itself? Or something else down there? Is that crazy?"

"Is that crazy?" He repeated with a snort. "Izzie, remember who we're talking about here. This guy was nuttier than a—"

A knock at the door to the community room interrupted whatever metaphor he was about to employ. "Tevake?"

Izzie turned to see a man in a rumpled suit with a police badge hanging around his neck standing in the open doorway. She wasn't sure if his mustache was meant to be ironic or not, but either way she didn't approve.

"Hey, Harrison," Patrick said, straightening. "What's up?"

"Chavez and I managed to track down the guy that your dead dealer was meeting with in that surveillance footage, and we think we've got a solid lead on the Ink supplier." He leaned against the door frame, casually. "The judge signed a search warrant so we're good to go. We're heading out now to meet with the search team, and then we're hitting it. You want to come with?"

"Yeah, I do," Patrick said, after considering it for a moment. He glanced at Izzie. "Want to tag along?"

"Sure." She shrugged, putting the book back on the table and reaching for her jacket. "Why not?"

Patrick was putting his own suit coat back on as he walked towards the door. "Harrison, this is Special Agent Lefevre with the FBI. She's assisting me with my investigation."

"Pleasure," the detective said, his tone flat, and stuck out his hand.

When Izzie shook it, he squeezed harder than was necessary. She wasn't sure if it was just a macho thing or some kind of intimidation play, but it didn't matter. She just smiled and squeezed back, and her smile broadened when she saw him wince in discomfort. If he thought that Quantico was in the habit of graduating shrinking violets, he was deeply mistaken.

"What's all this mess?" Harrison said, glancing with disdain at the evidence piled on the table.

"Background on our investigation," Patrick said as they stepped out into the hallway, then locked the door to the community room behind them.

As Patrick continued down the hallway, Harrison glanced back past Izzie at the community room. "Just what kind of case are you two working?"

Izzie shrugged. "Honestly, I wish I knew."

CHAPTER ELEVEN

The search team of uniformed officers in tactical gear was waiting in a commandeered storefront when Izzie and the others arrived. While Patrick and his fellow plainclothes officers strapped themselves into bulletproof vests with "POLICE" stenciled on the front and back, Izzie glanced out the window onto the street. They were in Hyde Park, not far from where she had been jogging early that morning. The shop was a neighborhood gardening supply store, and the owners were in the back having coffee and surreptitiously glancing at the unexpected excitement at the front of the shop when they thought no one was looking. The Closed sign on the door deterred the occasional passerby from entering, and the straggling fronds of hanging plants and racks of clay pots obscured the view of the shop's interior from the sidewalk outside.

The police sergeant in command of the search team raised an eybrow at Izzie's nylon jacket with "FBI" printed on it in bright yellow letters. He turned to Harrison, who was going over the latest surveillance photos on a tablet computer with his partner and Patrick. "We're bringing the feds in on this one, sir?"

Harrison shook his head, dismissively. "She's not *my* date."

"Think of it as a ride-along," Patrick said, glancing up from the tablet.

"I'm just here to observe," Izzie offered, while checking that her semiautomatic's magazine was fully charged.

The sergeant shrugged, and Izzie went to join Patrick and the others.

"Speaking of observing, what are we looking at?" she said.

"Harrison and Chavez identified the other man in our surveillance video as this guy." Patrick handed her the tablet, on which was the mugshot of a man in his late thirties with a scowl and a neck tattoo. "Malcolm Price."

"He's got a list of priors, mostly narcotics-related," Chavez explained. "Did time for a felony possession with intent to distribute, got out on parole last year. The commission just terminated his supervision, and the PO said that he was a model parolee."

"That gullible chucklehead." Harrison stroked his mustache with his thumb and forefinger, starting just beneath his nose and smoothing outwards to the corners of his mouth. He had made the same gesture at least four times since they'd left the station house, and Izzie was beginning to think it was a tic. "He thinks that *all* of the skells he's minding are model parolees. He wouldn't know probable cause if it bit him in the ass."

Chavez ignored his partner and continued. "His record is clean since he got out, and he hasn't been associating with any known felons. But he's also still unemployed, to the best of our knowledge, which makes it hard to explain how he's affording this place."

He reached over and swiped the tablet's screen, and brought up a photo taken with a telescopic lens of Malcolm Price unlocking the front door of a two-story bungalow.

"It's a rental," Chavez said. "The landlord says that Price pays his rent every month in cash. When he signed the lease Price listed Pinnacle Tower as his place of employment—said he was doing janitorial work there—but we checked and the placement service that provides that staff doesn't have any record of him."

"Maybe he's working there under a different name?" Izzie looked up from the tablet. "It can be hard for an ex-con to get honest work. An alias might help."

Harrison shook his head. "No dice. We did door duty in the Pinnacle, seeing if anyone there recognized a photo of Price, but came up empty."

Izzie wondered how reliable those findings were. She knew from growing up with aunts who worked as maids that there were many people who couldn't pick out of a lineup the person who emptied their trash and swept their floors every day if their lives depended on it.

"Is there any doubt that he's the man seen meeting with Tyler Campbell in the surveillance video?" Patrick asked.

"None at all," Harrison answered.

"It checks out." Chavez swiped back to the mugshot and pointed out Price's neck tattoo. "The tat is clearly visible in the video."

Patrick seemed satisfied. "So what's the plan?"

"We've had his place under surveillance for the last forty-eight hours, and we've tracked him coming and going with canvas tote bags full of something." Harrison flapped his hand. "You know, the kind the hippies want you to use at the grocery store?"

"We're pretty sure he's trafficking." Chavez took the tablet back from Izzie and powered it down. "And we have reasonable suspicion that there are quantities of Ink inside the house. The judge signed off on a no-knock warrant, so this is a straight-up raid." He nodded towards one of the officers in tactical gear, who was carrying a door ram. "We bust in, secure the place, and see what we find."

"And we know he's home?" Patrick said.

"Yes, sir," the sergeant answered. "We had eyes on him entering two hours ago with an unidentified adult male and female, and none of them have come out yet."

Harrison leered suggestively.

"Any idea who they are?" Patrick turned to Chavez, who shook his head.

"We weren't able to ID them from seeing just the backs of their heads." The sergeant scowled fractionally, and Izzie couldn't tell if he was annoyed at Patrick's question or his own failure to identify the two suspects, or both.

Chavez motioned towards the door. "The house is one block to the west of here. We've got another team standing by in a service van up the street, and when we give the signal they'll approach from the other side. Squad cars will block the intersections on the eastern and western approaches, so there won't be any vehicles passing by. There's entrances on the front and back sides of the house, and we're going in both sides at once. Looks like there's windows big enough for egress on the north side, so we'll need a pair of officers watching those at the same time. There's a dormer window in the attic, but it's about a twenty-five-foot drop from there to the pavement so I don't think they'll be taking that way out."

"Mullins," the sergeant said, glancing at his team, "you and Dobson take the windows on the north side." He nodded to the man carrying the door ram. "Carlson, you're on the front door."

"Okay. Everybody ready?" Chavez scanned the faces of the others. Patrick nodded, and Izzie put her hand on her holstered pistol.

"Let's go already." Harrison rolled his eyes like an impatient teenager.

Chavez thumbed the side of the radio clipped to his bulletproof vest. "Team 2, we are moving out."

"Copy that," buzzed a voice from the speaker.

"Team 3, block off the streets when I give the word."

"On it," another voice buzzed in response.

"Move out!" Chavez shouted, and shouldered open the door.

The moments that followed were a flurry of images and sounds. The flash of the red and blues atop the squad car that blazed past, brilliant in the late afternoon dim. The screech of the tires as the patrol cars swerved and slammed to a halt, blocking the intersections. The rattle of gun belts and the thud of boots on the pavement as the police raced up the sidewalk without saying a word.

Izzie trailed behind the others, pistol held low at her side in a two-handed grip. Patrick was just ahead of her, bringing up the rear of the column as Chavez and Harrison charged ahead.

Further up the street, Izzie could see another black-and-white pulling into position, sealing off the other end of the block from traffic. A panel van had run halfway up the curb in front of the rental house, and a team of officers in tactical gear was leaping out onto the ground.

Izzie couldn't have kept up with the others even if she hadn't been intentionally hanging back. Just running at this pace was enough of a strain, never having fully recovered from the cut that very nearly cost her the use of one leg. By the time she reached the front yard of the rental house, Chavez's team was already in position and one of the uniformed officers was preparing to take down the door with the ram. It was roughly the size and shape of a stovepipe, with handles at the middle and one end, and made of solid steel so it weighed as much as a small child.

At a signal from Chavez, the officer swung the ram back and then slammed it with a massive thud into the door, shattering the wood around the doorknob and lock.

"Go!" Chavez shouted.

The officer with the ram immediately jumped to one side as the sergeant kicked the door the rest of the way in and the others surged inside, weapons aimed and shouting for anyone inside to get down on the floor. Izzie could hear the other team doing the same from around the back of the house, while two officers peeled away from the rest and took up positions beneath the big bay windows on the north side of the building.

Patrick was waiting in the yard and watching the house when Izzie caught up with him.

"You're not going in?" she asked.

He glanced in her direction. "Figured I'd give you a chance to catch up. Besides, this is Chavez and Harrison's party, I'm just along for the ride."

"Are they good cops? How confident are you that this is the—"

Suddenly a quick burst of gunfire erupted from the second floor of the house.

Patrick thumbed on his radio. "Shots fired. Repeat, shots fired!"

Izzie had stepped back to get a better look at the upper part of the house. There was the narrow dormer window that Chavez had mentioned, at least twenty-five feet up. While there was light shining from the broken doorway on the front and the bay windows to one side, the space beyond the dormer window was pitch-black.

When Patrick lowered his hand from the radio, Izzie drew his attention to the high window. "Do you think maybe there's—"

Before she could complete the thought, the window suddenly burst outward as a man hurtled headfirst through the glass. He plummeted to the paved walkway below, wreathed in a cloud of shattered glass. The shards twinkled like stars in the light of a streetlamp as they fell, but the man himself seemed wrapped in shadows.

The man landed on the concrete with a sickening thud and the scraping crunch of breaking bones, just a few steps in front of where Izzie was standing.

"Is . . . ?" Patrick said. "Is that . . . ?"

The man's left shoulder had been forced back by the impact, so that his left arm was almost pressed against his spine, and the whiteness of the bones that had torn through flesh and clothing on his rib cage and right leg were cast in stark contrast to the bright arterial blood that was welling up around them. His head had snapped back at an unnatural angle, broken bones sticking out of the side of his neck, and his eyes were wide open and sightless. There were fresh bullet wounds in his chest, and the condition of the exit wounds on his back indicated that he had been shot at close range by someone right in front of him. The shots would've had to have passed through his lungs and probably his heart as well, possibly shattering his spine.

Izzie crouched down and searched for a pulse on his neck with her left hand, and failed to find one. If the man had been alive when he went through the window, he wasn't anymore.

"Yeah, it's him. Or *was*, at any rate. See the neck tattoo?" Izzie pointed at the dead man's neck as she straightened up. "This is your guy Malcolm Price, all right."

Someone was shouting for an ambulance upstairs, and at first Izzie thought it was just for the dead man on the pavement. She glanced up at the dormer window above. The sergeant was looking down, a stricken expression on his face, and she could hear him say "Holy . . ." He had a hand pressed to the side of his neck above his tactical armor, and Izzie could see blood welling up between his fingers.

"The *late* Malcolm Price, now," Patrick said. "But did he jump, was he thrown, or . . . ?"

He left off when the dead man on the pavement began to climb to his feet, his broken bones making a sickening sound as they ground against each other.

CHAPTER TWELVE

"The hell?!" Patrick shouted, raising his pistol and aiming it at the man who was sprawled dead on the ground the moment before.

Izzie jumped back, raising her own pistol in a two-handed grip. "He didn't have a pulse!"

Malcolm Price stood awkwardly for a moment, his head still lolling far to one side, eyes open but unfocused. His mouth moved, but no sound came out. Izzie found it horribly familiar.

Black welts suddenly began to rise up on the skin of his face, neck, and arms. Small at first, no bigger than a fingerprint, but swelling in size until they were as large as handprints between one blink and the next.

"Patrick?" Izzie said, without taking her eyes off the dead man in front of them. She felt suddenly nauseated, and a foul taste stung her tongue. "Are you seeing this?"

From the corner of her eye she could see Patrick nodding. "Seeing," he said, "but not understanding."

The dead man swayed on his feet, then took a staggering step forward, like a drunken marionette.

"Malcolm Price!" Patrick yelled. "You are under arrest. Get down on your knees and keep your hands where I can see them."

If the dead man heard him, he gave no sign, but instead took another staggering step forward, directly towards Izzie. His mouth continued to move in silence as sightless eyes turned on her.

Izzie felt a familiar dread rising up from the pit of her stomach, as the nausea grew.

"Freeze!" she shouted.

The dead man took another step, now halfway to where Izzie stood.

"Sir, don't make us shoot!" Patrick said, but the dead man continued on, raising his arms towards Izzie.

Suddenly, there was the piercing sound of a shotgun firing from off to the right. The blast hit the dead man square in the back, and he staggered forward for half a step, but stayed on his feet.

Izzie turned to see one of the tactical team members at the corner of the house, his shotgun still at his shoulder.

"Go down, damn it!" the officer shouted, and fired another blast from his shotgun, which hit the dead man in the left leg, shredding his knee.

With a sickening crunch, the dead man pitched forward face-first onto the ground.

"Hold your fire, Tiltson!" Patrick called out to the officer. He turned to Izzie. "You okay?"

"He had already taken at least three shots to the chest before he went through the window," Izzie said, her tone level but with a tension beneath the words. "Then the injuries sustained hitting the pavement. And there was *no* pulse. How was he able to get up and move around?"

As the tactical officer with the shotgun approached slowly, Chavez and several of the other uniformed officers raced out the door, including Officer Carlson, who was still holding the door ram.

"Tevake!" Chavez shouted. "Everything under control?"

"Yeah," Patrick answered, lowering his pistol as he turned to answer. "The suspect was coming for Agent Lefevre, but Officer Tiltson was able to—"

"Patrick!" Izzie shouted as the dead man struggled to climb to his feet again.

"You have got to be *kidding* me," Patrick said.

The black welts had bloomed even larger, until now it was as if the dead man were a walking shadow.

As if he were covered in ink. . . .

Patrick and Izzie jumped back, putting more distance between the dead man and themselves.

"On your hands and knees, now!" Chavez shouted at the dead man, a stabbing gesturing with his pistol punctuating each word.

"Tried that," Patrick deadpanned. "Didn't work."

"Shooting him clearly doesn't seem to work, either," Izzie said.

Once more on his feet, the dead man again began to stagger towards Izzie, hands out and grasping, mouth working.

"He's jacked up on *something*," Chavez said. "I've seen guys on PCP do stuff like this, break half the bones in their bodies and still keep on trucking."

Izzie realized that the others didn't understand what was happening. Patrick might, but not the rest of them. They still thought this was a living thing they were facing. But she knew better.

"You! Carlson!" She pointed at the officer with the door ram. "Get over here!"

Carlson glanced from Izzie to Chavez, who shrugged. "You heard her, get over there."

As Carlson double-timed it over from the front door of the house, Izzie kept backing up, staying a couple of steps out of the dead man's reach as he continued to lurch towards her.

"The door ram!" Izzie shouted, as she sidestepped to lure the dead man away from the others, his back turned towards the approaching Carlson. "Hit him in the head as hard as you can. Try to snap his neck."

Carlson glanced back to Chavez again, who motioned him to hurry up.

Taking the handles of the door ram in either hand, he reared back, then rushed forward as he swung the ram in a wide arc at shoulder level, aiming for the side of the dead man's head.

The steel cylinder connected with a crunch, whipping the dead man's head hard to the other side. Bones audibly snapped and cracked, but the head still remained connected to the body. The impact knocked the dead man off his feet, though, and he went tumbling onto his left side.

His right arm still reached out for Izzie, and he began to try standing once more.

Izzie holstered her pistol, took three quick steps forward, and took hold of the door ram in Carlson's hands.

"Get back," she told him as she took the ram from him.

He took a step away, bewildered.

Izzie planted a foot on the dead man's chest, pinning him to the ground. Then she grunted in exertion as she lifted the door ram high over her head, and brought it crashing down as hard as she could on the dead man's neck.

The bones of the dead man's neck shattered to powder, and his head was only attached to the rest of his body by tattered muscle and the shredded remains of his spinal cord.

She dropped the ram clattering to the ground.

The dead man's mouth had stopped moving. But as Izzie watched, the black welts began to fade, like water drops evaporating on a skillet.

By the time Patrick and the others were at her side, only seconds later, the inky blotches had completely faded.

CHAPTER THIRTEEN

"What the hell *was* that?" Officer Carlson said, looking from the mangled corpse to the bloodied door ram and back. "Some kind of zombie or something?"

Patrick and Izzie shared a glance.

"Don't be an idiot, Carlson," Chavez sneered, holstering his pistol. "Like I said, he was just jacked up on something, probably didn't even realize he'd been shot. I've seen this kind of thing before."

An ambulance siren could be heard Dopplering in from up the street.

"Why were you away from your post, Tiltson?" Chavez went on, wheeling on the officer with the shotgun. "You were supposed to be watching the other side of the house."

"I heard the window breaking," the officer answered, shifting uneasily. He seemed to be the rookie on the squad, and had clearly gotten caught up in the heat of the moment. "I came around the corner, and saw the suspect advancing on

Lieutenant Tevake and Agent Lefevre, and I . . ." He paused, taking a breath. "I saw a shot and I took it."

Chavez shook his head. "Well, just remember to keep the facts straight when we review the incident. The captain will have my ass if he thinks this wasn't a righteous kill." He turned to Izzie. "Will you be available for an interview for the departmental shooting investigation, agent? Might not be necessary, but just in case . . ."

Izzie nodded. But she knew that Chavez and his superiors wouldn't be eager to hear *her* interpretation of the events.

"Look, just what happened in there?" Patrick asked Chavez as he holstered his own pistol.

Chavez turned and headed back towards the front door of the rental house, Patrick and Izzie following close behind.

"We entered the residence, and found an unidentified male and female in the kitchen. Sergeant Jefferson and Officers Dewey and Ramirez continued to the second floor while Harrison and I detained the two suspects. Shots were fired upstairs, and then the third suspect went out the window." Chavez glanced back at Patrick as he entered the house. "We're still piecing together what happened."

Izzie and Patrick followed the detective inside, stepping over the splintered wood of the shattered door.

The living room was about what Izzie would have expected the home of a guy with shady connections who paid his rent in cash would look like. Giant flat-screen TV mounted to the wall, wired to game consoles and media players. Leather couch. Recliner. Glass table. All of it expensive and garish. But also piles of empty pizza boxes and Chinese takeout containers, full ashtrays and beer bottles. Takeout menus and auto magazines.

"We found them through here," Chavez said, continuing down a narrow hallway to the kitchen.

Harrison was in the kitchen with one of the uniformed officers, Mirandizing a man and woman who were kneeling on the floor, their hands cuffed behind them. "Do you understand each of these rights I have explained to you?"

The room had a strange smell to it that Izzie couldn't quite place, and she couldn't quite decide if it was foul or appealing. It called to mind the ozone tang of electric motors and summer rains, the peppery scent of a body that hadn't bathed in weeks, fresh flowers and rotting meat, all mixed together. There was an unpleasant taste on her tongue that she couldn't identify, and a swelling sense of nausea in her gut.

"What's all this?" Izzie looked down at the kitchen table.

On the surface of the table were scattered piles of what Izzie at first took to be ballpoint pens, but on closer inspection were auto-injectors, like EpiPens carried by those with potentially fatal allergies. These didn't carry any kind of labels or branding, though, and were instead jet black. There were also a couple of syringes, a box of disposable medical gloves, and a few empty IV bags.

"Ink," Patrick said, nudging one of the auto-injectors with the tip of a pencil he'd pulled from his pocket. "That's how they sell it. One dose per pen. Looks like these are empty, though."

"Empty as in they've already been used?" Izzie asked. "Or as in they haven't been filled up yet?"

Patrick lifted the edge of one of the clear plastic IV bags. "I'm guessing the latter. Maybe they were using this place as a lab to cook the stuff, or however it's made?" He looked around. "But if that's the case, then where's the stuff? This is all fixings and gear, but I'm not seeing any Ink."

"What does it look like, anyway?"

Patrick met her gaze and shrugged. "Like ink. You know, fountain pens, writing with quills, that kind of thing? But with a thicker consistency, more like motor oil."

"Not going to talk, huh?" Harrison was still addressing the man and woman, who hadn't said a word, but just glared at him in silence.

"We'll take them back to the station house and book them," Chavez said, nodding to a uniformed officer to take them away.

"Sir?" another officer called from the hallway. "You might want to check this out."

Harrison and Chavez left the kitchen, and Izzie and Patrick trailed after.

Izzie could see into the living room at the end of the hallway. The ambulance had arrived and EMTs were entering the house as Sergeant Jefferson was being helped down the stairs by one of the other officers. They'd improvised a compress to stanch the flow of blood from the wound in his neck, but he was looking pretty wan and pale.

"Guy freaking *bit* me . . ." the sergeant was saying as the EMTs rushed to assist, but Izzie's attention was called back to where Harrison and Chavez were standing.

"It's locked, sir," a uniformed officer was explaining, indicating a wooden door on one side of the hallway. It had a keyed entry knob on it, such as an exterior door might have.

Patrick looked down one end of the hall and then the other, considering. "Probably leads to the basement," he guessed.

"Why lock an interior door with a key?" Chavez said.

"To keep somebody out?" Harrison deadpanned, stroking his mustache.

"Or keep something in," Izzie said, in a low voice.

Harrison turned to the others. "Where's the ram?"

Chavez glanced at Izzie before answering. "Forensics may want it in its current condition. Maybe we call for another one?"

"No need." Patrick stepped past them to more closely inspect the door, running his fingertips along the doorjamb, rapping the door itself with a knuckle. "It's an entry doorknob, but it's just set in a hollow-core interior door. Hinges are on the other side, so . . ."

He motioned for the others to step back. Then he turned to one side, bending his right leg and bringing his foot up almost to waist level, using his arms to counterbalance his weight. Then he kicked the door as hard as he could right beside the doorknob . . .

And his foot punched right through the material of the door.

"Aw, crap!" Patrick moaned, his leg stuck in the door, pinwheeling his arms to try to stay upright.

Izzie and Chavez rushed to his side to help steady him, while Harrison held back, chuckling.

"Smooth move, Tevake," he said, stroking his mustache.

"Shut up, Harrison," Chavez shot back, as Patrick awkwardly yanked his foot back out of the door.

While Izzie helped Patrick right himself, Chavez leaned down and inspected the hole in the door.

"The knob didn't budge, but . . ." He stuck his hand through the door, looked up at the ceiling as he felt around blindly on the other side, and then grinned as he heard a click. He pulled his hand back through, and then turned the knob with a flourish, opening the door. "That did the trick. Nice work, Tevake."

Patrick was bending down to massage his bruised ankle, smirking. "Be sure to say flattering things in your report."

Chavez leaned his head through the open door, and felt along the inside wall with his hand. "I don't see a light switch." He pulled a small flashlight from a nylon patch velcroed to his vest, clicked it on, then shined the beam down the dark steps. He turned to the others. "Harrison, get with Jefferson, find out just what the hell happened upstairs. I'm going to go down and check this out."

Harrison shrugged, and headed towards the front room.

"We're coming with," Patrick said, glancing back at Izzie to follow.

"Good god!" Chavez recoiled after he'd taken two steps down.

The stench hit Izzie as she passed through the door, and she covered her nose and mouth with her hand while trying not to gag.

"We've got a body down here," Chavez said, slowly descending the steps.

Patrick had snapped on a flashlight of his own. "More than one."

Izzie reached the bottom of the stairs just after the others, and spotted a cord hanging from a bare lightbulb on the rafters above. She pulled the string, and a stark white light flooded the basement.

"Oh, Christ," Chavez said.

There were canvas army cots stretched over folding wooden frames lining the back wall of the space. On three of them were bodies that were stripped naked, lying facedown on the cots, with their arms hanging down and touching the dirt floor.

Patrick leaned in for a closer look, pinching his nose shut. "They've been dead a while, that's for sure."

There was a rolling surgical stand to one side, on top of which were coils of clear plastic tubing and bits of metal that Izzie couldn't identify.

"I'm guessing this is going to clear up a couple of missing persons cases," Chavez said as he flicked off his flashlight and put it away. "But what the hell are they *doing* down here? Was this some kind of shooting alley or something?"

"Maybe." Patrick straightened up, shaking his head. "If it were, though, and these people OD'ed down here, why leave the bodies?"

Izzie was looking around. "No way. Why come down here to get high when there are couches and stuff upstairs? That doesn't make sense."

"And why was the door locked?" Patrick asked.

Chavez scowled. "We'll have CSI see what they can find out. And we'll call the M.E., let her know she's got her work cut out for her."

"I'm sure Joyce'll *love* that." Patrick looked down at the putrefying corpses. "But you know, having said that . . . she actually *might* enjoy this. Could be a challenge for her."

"I think our friend that went out the window will be more than enough challenge for one day," Chavez said, heading for the steps. "Come on, I want to hear what Jefferson has to say."

As they climbed the steps back to the ground floor, Izzie glanced over her shoulder at the three bodies at the back of the basement. Notions and half-formed theories were beginning to orbit each other in her thoughts, slowly coming into alignment.

An EMT was bandaging Sergeant Jefferson's neck when Izzie and the others returned to the living room. Jefferson was seated on the leather couch, head titled far to one side while the bandage was applied.

"The antibiotics should stave off infection, but this will just be temporary until we can get you to Recondito General." The EMT finished taping the bandage into place. "You're going to need stitches."

"Great," the sergeant said with a sneer. "My wife's going to *love* that."

"So what happened?" Chavez looked from the sergeant to Harrison and back again.

"Dewey, Ramirez, and I proceeded to the second floor to look for the suspect," the sergeant answered. "We cleared two bedrooms and a bathroom, finding nothing. There was a stairway leading to the attic, so we ascended. Found the suspect sitting in the middle of the floor. Like he was meditating or something like that. Room was totally empty, otherwise."

"Meditating?" Patrick asked.

The sergeant began to shrug reflexively, then winced in pain from his injured neck. He blinked hard. "Yeah, you know, legs crossed, like yoga shit." He raised his head, laying a hand tenderly against his bandaged neck. "I told him to lay facedown on the floor, so I could cuff him, and he jumped to his feet and came right at me."

The other two officers, Dewey and Ramirez, were standing a few feet away, stricken looks on their faces.

"I told him to stand down, that I didn't want to shoot, but then he was just . . . on me, you know? Nutjob got his teeth on my neck. Dewey managed to pull him off of me, and then

Ramirez put three in his chest. Thought that'd put him down, but he just shrugged it off like they were bee stings. Turned around and started running. He was headfirst through the window before we could stop him."

"Crazy, right?" Harrison said, but Izzie noticed that both Patrick and Chavez ignored him. They were too focused on what the sergeant had said.

"I'm telling you," Chavez repeated, "jacked up on something, feeling no pain."

Patrick glanced in Izzie's direction, and a look passed between them. "Yeah," Patrick said, "it was probably something like that." She could see that he didn't believe it any more than she did.

Chavez turned to Harrison. "Do we have an ID on the man and woman we found in the kitchen?"

Harrison opened up a notepad. "Ibrahim Fayed and Marissa Keizer. At least that's what their employee badges say. Neither one of them had any kind of other ID on them."

"Employee badges?" Patrick echoed.

Harrison nodded. "Card keys for the Pinnacle Tower."

"So maybe the suspect *did* work there?" Chavez rubbed his chin thoughtfully. "Or used to, anyway. Could be a connection there."

"We'll know more once we interrogate them back at the station house," Harrison said, sounding eager to get to it. Izzie got the impression that he was a guy who enjoyed playing the "bad cop" in interrogation rooms.

"Anything else of note upstairs?" Chavez asked, glancing at the sergeant and the two other officers who had accompanied him.

"Not much," the sergeant answered. "One bedroom with a single bed, dirty laundry, other signs of habitation. The other bedroom was filled with stolen goods, from the looks of it."

Chavez arched an eyebrow. "That a fact?"

The sergeant nodded fractionally, mostly with his eyelids. "Smartphones still in the box, shrink-wrapped. Laptops. Boxes of software. Office equipment. That kind of thing." He snorted slightly. "Cases of printer paper, even."

"Sounds more like a tech startup than a drug operation," Izzie suggested.

"Makes sense, though." Patrick glanced in her direction. "If they had access to an office building after hours, anyway. That kind of stuff is easy to transport, and easy to unload. So long as no one has tracked the serial numbers, you could make good money—fast cash—turning around that kind of stuff." He shrugged. "Or maybe the guy was just planning on going into business for himself."

Chavez shook his head. "Nah, this was a middleman, at best. Somebody at the top of the food chain wouldn't live like this." He looked around the room at the empty pizza boxes and beer bottles, the overflowing ashtrays and trash. "This guy was rank and file, taking orders from someone higher up."

"But there doesn't seem to be any Ink on the premises," Patrick objected. "Just gear and fixings."

"Maybe they were waiting on a delivery?" Chavez sounded unconvinced even as he said it.

"I say we head back to the station house already," Harrison said. "Let CSI and the M.E. deal with this mess."

Chavez nodded slowly. "Okay, okay. We'll see if we can get those two to give us something useful."

Harrison grinned, which Izzie couldn't help but find unsettling. The mustache wasn't helping.

Patrick's car was parked on a side street off Prospect Avenue a few blocks away. It was well past sunset now, and a chill was settling into the air.

"I'm heading back to the station house to help Chavez with the paperwork," he said as he slid behind the driver's wheel. "You want me to drop you somewhere or . . . ?" He let the question trail off, leaving it to her to provide alternatives.

"I should check in at the Resident Agency. Fill them in on our progress, do some paperwork of my own."

Patrick nodded as he steered the car out into traffic. "Sounds good."

They rode in silence for a few blocks, Izzie staring idly out the passenger window, Patrick with his eyes fixed on the road ahead, neither of them saying a word.

It was Patrick who broke the silence.

"That guy was totally dead when he got up from the pavement and came at you," he said, not taking his eyes off the road.

"Yep," Izzie answered without turning, still staring out the window. "Totally."

Another moment stretched out silently between them.

"How the hell did that happen?" Patrick finally said. "A dead guy getting up and running around?"

Izzie didn't answer immediately.

"I'm not sure," she said, her voice low. Then she turned and glanced over at Patrick. "But I'm not sure I want to find out, either."

He nodded slowly.

"Yeeeah," he said, drawing out the word until it tapered off into silence.

They passed another block in silence.

"Maybe Joyce will have something for us tomorrow," he finally added.

Izzie nodded, without much enthusiasm. Maybe she would.

They rode the rest of the way to the building that housed the Resident Agency, and it wasn't until Patrick pulled the car to a stop at the curb that he spoke again.

"You know as well as I do that the stuff going on here . . ." he said as she put her hand on the latch to open the car door. "It's not natural."

She didn't turn around, but didn't open the door.

"It's *super*natural, Izzie. That's why I called you in on this."

She closed her eyes and took a long slow breath in through her nostrils.

"These guys—Chavez, Harrison, the rest of them—they see a guy take three shots to the chest, fall twenty-five feet to the pavement, get up, get shot *again*, get *up* again, and only go down when you bash his head in with a battering ram . . . They see that, and they can convince themselves that it's because he was 'jacked up' on something."

Izzie lowered her hand and turned back around in her seat to face him.

"Maybe it's because of how we were raised," he went on, "I don't know. Maybe we're just more open to the possibility. But tonight *proved* that what's going on in this town is way beyond natural."

She chewed at her lower lip before answering.

"Okay," she finally said. "Yes. You're right. Goddamn it, you're right."

She sighed wearily.

"It was *possible* that it was just a coincidence that there weren't any reported Ink cases in the neighborhood your great-uncle protected, and it was entirely probable that all of the evidence from Fuller's apartment was just proof that he was a manic obsessive who'd had a psychotic break. But *clearly*, there's no rational explanation for how Malcolm Price was still up and moving after all that. And his *mouth* moving, too, without saying a word . . ."

She shuddered.

"Like the head of Francis Zhao that night in the lighthouse," Patrick said.

Izzie nodded slowly. "Exactly like that."

Patrick searched her expression.

"And what about the dead bodies in the basement?" he asked. "What was Price *doing* in that house?"

"I'm not sure," she answered. "But I heard stories when I was a little girl." She paused, taking a deep breath, mustering the courage for what she was about to say. "Stories about zombies."

Patrick drew back, head cocked to one side, a disbelieving smirk on his face. "What? Like *Night of the Living Dead*, George Romero kind of stuff?"

"No, of course not." A hint of annoyance crept into Izzie's voice. "Like old-school Haitian Vodou. The bodies of the dead brought back as slaves by a bokor—a sorcerer of the left hand. No memory of their former lives, no personalities, just bodies that move around and do whatever their masters tell them to do."

Patrick's skepticism was waning. "And you think that's what's happening here? Some kind of voodoo thing?"

"I'm not sure." Izzie scratched the scar on the back of her hand, a nervous tic. "It's not exactly like the stories I heard. But similar enough that I wonder whether there might not be some connection."

Patrick nodded, thoughtfully. "So what do we do next?"

"We continue the investigation, of course," Izzie said, turning and opening the car door.

Stepping out onto the curb, she turned and leaned down to look back through the open door.

"But we keep ourselves open to possibility, and see where that leads us."

Patrick sighed. "I hope that will be good enough."

Izzie stood on the sidewalk and watched as he drove away. Then she turned and started towards the front entrance of the building.

"I hope so, too."

CHAPTER FOURTEEN

Izzie wasn't surprised to find that Special Agent Daphne Richardson was still in the office when she arrived, despite the fact that it was almost nine o'clock in the evening. With only two FBI agents on staff in the Recondito Resident Agency, there were bound to be times when there was more than enough work to go around, and as the junior agent it would likely fall to Daphne to pick up the slack.

"Oh hey, Agent Lefevre," she said, looking up from the stacks of paperwork on her desk. "I was wondering if you were coming by today."

Izzie slipped off her suede jacket and draped it over a chair. "Considering how late it is, I guess I just made it under the wire. And please, it's Izzie."

Daphne smiled. "Sorry."

Izzie rested a hand on the corner of Daphne's desk, looking down at the tidy stacks of documents. "Manuel has you burning the midnight oil, I guess?"

"That slave driver," Daphne answered sarcastically, then shook her head. "No, just kidding. It's by choice. I told Agent Gutierrez that I was taking some time off this afternoon to go apartment hunting, but that I'd make it up when I got back."

"Apartment hunting?" Izzie crossed her arms and leaned her hip against Daphne's desk.

"Yeah," Daphne said with a sigh. "I rented the first place I could find when I got transferred here last year from San Antonio and, well . . . I could have been a little choosier. I mean, the apartment was *okay*, but I could have found somewhere a lot nicer, and in a much better area. My lease runs out next month, and I was planning on renewing, but this morning I got a letter from my landlord informing me the rent would be going up an additional five hundred bucks, and that roach motel is *not* worth two grand a month."

Izzie raised an eyebrow. "That much?"

Daphne nodded. "I mean, my paygrade is still GS-10 but I got bumped up to step 9 last quarter, so with the locality pay I can definitely afford it. But for that much money, I expect to get something a little nicer."

"I mean, why is it going up that much?"

"Oh." Daphne shrugged. "The market is just crazy tight right now, and rents are going up all over the place. There's just so many people moving to town these days."

"Any luck with the apartment hunt?"

"Not yet." Her shoulders slumped. "There was one place that would be perfect, just a few blocks north of here, but it got yanked out from under me by a guy who just moved to town to work for Parasol. It wasn't cheap, either. But all these programmers and tech folks who are moving to Recondito get paid a *lot* more than government scale, so they can afford whatever the going rate is."

Izzie remembered the inflight magazine article about the self-made-millionaire and his killer apps. "Parasol just bought a big building here in town, didn't they?"

"Pinnacle Tower, right?" Izzie nodded, answering her own question. "Yeah, that's definitely it."

Izzie was thoughtful. "That name has come up a few times today."

Now it was Daphne's term to treat Izzie to a quizzical look. "Something to do with your investigation?"

Izzie nodded. "Maybe. The police lieutenant that I'm assisting is working a street drug case, and several of the suspects work at the building, or at least have worked there at some point."

"Parasol employees, then?"

"Maybe? I'm not sure."

"If they work there *now*, then they must be," Daphne said. "Parasol bought the whole building before they started their renovations, and kicked everybody else out. It was a big stink in the local news. A lot of the other tenants of the building— businesses, law firms, medical practices—got eviction notices as soon as Parasol took ownership. They petitioned the mayor's office to step in, but the owner of Parasol—"

"Martin Zotovic?" Izzie asked, dredging the name up from her memory.

"That's him." Daphne nodded. "Well, I read this big exposé on a renter's advocacy site the other day, all about Znth, Zotovic's private equity outfit that's been buying up all kinds of real estate around the city . . . and not just office buildings like the Pinnacle Tower, either, but residential properties, ranches and farms outside of town, old mining claims, all sorts of stuff. . . . Anyway, turns out that Zotovic was one of the principle contributors to the mayor's re-election campaign. So it wasn't that surprising when the mayor sided with him over the tenants." She swiveled in her chair, idly. "So far as I know, it's just Parasol in the building now. And from what the rental agent told me this afternoon, there are a *lot* of people moving to town just to work for them, so they'll probably end up filling the building before too much longer."

"I guess there's a lot of money to be made in phone apps," Izzie said with a shrug.

Daphne picked up her own phone from the desk, and grinned. "They've got my money, anyway. I couldn't live without this thing." She tapped the phone to display the time, then let it clatter back onto the desktop. "Well, it's nine o'clock, so I think I'm done for the day." She pushed her chair back from the desk. "I was thinking about grabbing a drink on the way home. Care to join me?"

Izzie chewed her lip, considering. "Well, I'd planned on filing an update, but . . ." She glanced over at the guest cubicle that had been assigned to her, and discovered that she had absolutely no desire to keep working. "That could wait until morning, I guess."

Daphne stood up, and unclipped her holster from her belt. "I'm locking this up in the gun vault, since I'm planning on having at least a couple of rounds." Federal agents were allowed to carry firearms at all times, off duty or on, but mixing guns and alcohol was another matter entirely. "You planning to stick with soft drinks or . . . ?" She let the question hang expectantly in the air.

Izzie smiled, unclipped her own holstered pistol from her belt, and held it out to Daphne. "I'll get it back when I come in to type up my report. Because, sister, after the day I've had, I deserve to tie one on."

So, where are we drinking?" Izzie shivered slightly as they emerged into the cold night air.

"There's a new craft cocktail bar that just opened up a few blocks that way," Daphne answered, gesturing to the right up Hauser. "I haven't tried it yet, but the Yelp reviews are good."

"Let's give it a shot," Izzie answered.

The after-dinner crowd was out in force, and there was a crowd lining up to get into a live music venue across the street. Izzie had never heard of any of the acts on the marquee, and wasn't sure if that was because they were local musicians who hadn't made it big outside the city, or if she was slowly easing into middle age and growing out of touch, or both. Daphne was familiar with all of them, though her tone suggested that she wasn't impressed with the lineup.

"They're okay, I guess. But not worth standing in line out in the cold for." She pushed her hands deeper into her coat pocket, hunching her shoulders. "To be fair, I stood in that same spot for hours during a torrential downpour to see Ciren play a live set last December, so I'm not really in any position to judge."

Izzie wheeled on her. "You got to see Ciren live?"

Daphne turned and smiled. "Are you a fan?"

"I'm burning with jealousy, is what I am."

"It was her first live performance in a few years," Daphne went on. "A special solstice show. Natalie's Charm was the opening act, and they joined her onstage for the closing number."

"You're kidding. When I was in my twenties I would have straight-up murdered someone for a chance to see Ciren and Natalie's Charm live on the same stage."

Daphne's grin widened. "It *was* pretty awesome. And totally worth getting completely drenched in the rain for." She glanced back at the crowd huddled on the sidewalk in front of the club. "But the Miller Street Rats? Give me a break."

They continued on up the street.

"This is the place." Daphne nodded at a brightly lit storefront bar up ahead.

It was narrow, with a marble bar running along one side and dotted with barstools, a scattering of tables and chairs along the other side. The tables were already all taken by patrons, as were most of the barstools, but it looked like there was room for them to squeeze in at the back.

"I didn't know that kids were still into Ciren," Izzie said as they waited to catch the bartender's eye, having to raise her voice slightly to be heard over the conversational din.

"Are you suggesting that I'm a 'kid,' Agent Lefevre?" Daphne's tone was playfully scolding.

"You're younger than me," Izzie chuckled, "and I refuse to accept that I'm getting older, so that makes you an honorary kid."

"Not *that* much younger, surely." Daphne caught the waiter's eye and he headed their way.

"What'll it be, ladies?"

"Amaretto sour," Daphne answered.

"I'll try this one," Izzie said, pointing to a complicated-sounding signature cocktail on the menu involving small batch gin, bitters, simple syrup, muddled limes, and mint, among other ingredients.

"Can I see some ID?" the bartender asked Daphne.

Izzie laughed as Daphne pulled out her driver's license and showed it to him. "See!" she said, nudging Daphne's shoulder.

Then it was Daphne's turn to laugh when the bartender turned to Izzie. "You too, miss."

Izzie knew she should be flattered, but she wasn't really. "Here," she said, holding out her own license.

Satisfied that they were of age, the bartender moved off down the bar to fix their drinks.

"Ohio?" Izzie said, catching a glimpse of Daphne's driver's license as she put it away.

Daphne shrugged. "Columbus. I grew up there, and that's still technically my permanent address." She sighed. "I inherited the house when my mother died, and couldn't bear to sell it, so I rented it out. The license . . ." She gestured airily. "Well, it's just easier to keep renewing my Ohio license than to go through the rigmarole of getting a new one out here, I guess. I know I should, but . . ." She shrugged. "Where are you from?"

"New Orleans," Izzie said.

"Ah," Daphne sighed. "*N'awlins.*"

"Nuh uh." Izzie shook her head, her expression twisting in a moue of distaste. "That's how *tourists* say it, honey. Not locals."

Daphne grinned sheepishly. "Oh. Sorry. I just went there the one time on spring break, thought that was how it was done." She accepted the Amaretto sour as the bartender slid it across the bar towards her, nodding thanks in his direction. "I loved the city, though," she went on, turning her back to Izzie. "The French Quarter. Jackson Square. All of that stuff."

Izzie muttered polite thanks to the bartender for her cocktail, and swirled the liquid in the glass. It had so many mint leaves in it that it looked more like a salad in a glass than a cocktail. "That stuff is just one tiny sliver of New Orleans. Most tourists never get to learn about the rest of it."

"Well, here's to learning new things," Daphne said, raising her glass.

"*Bon santé*," Izzie toasted as their glasses clinked. And then, seeing Daphne's somewhat perplexed expression, translated, "Good health."

They each took a swig of their drinks. Izzie's was halfway gone after the first sip, it seemed.

"How is it?" Daphne asked, gesturing to Izzie's drink.

"Good," she answered, equivocating. "But with all this foliage in here, there's not much room for the damned drink." She took another sip, and the glass was almost empty. "I think I'll stick with something simple for the next round."

Daphne's expression seemed to brighten. "Oh, so you'll stick around for another?"

Izzie shrugged noncommittally. "Like I said, after the day I had, I think I deserve it."

"The investigation isn't going well?" Daphne asked, looking over the rim of her highball glass.

"It's . . . complicated." She thought back over the events of the day, from the visit to the Property and Evidence warehouse that morning, to the midday visit to Ross University, and then finally the late afternoon drug raid out in Hyde Park. It had been a busy day. No wonder she felt so exhausted.

But she found that she was in no hurry to get back to her hotel room. For one, because she was sure that her sleep schedule was still out of tune, and she didn't relish another long night's attempt to find slumber. And second, because she was enjoying Daphne's company far more than she had anticipated she would. When they'd first met the day before, Izzie had seen her only as the Resident Agency's resident rookie. But the longer they talked, the more she got to know her. . . . Izzie didn't socialize much, as a rule, and dated even less. She was enjoying the novelty of just hanging out and talking with someone new.

That Daphne had confessed to idolizing Izzie the day before was never far from her thoughts, though. She had intentionally avoided the limelight that former agents like Tom Henderson sought, and she wasn't looking for hero worship now.

But Daphne seemed to have relaxed somewhat, now that they were getting to know each other a little better, and was talking to Izzie more like a colleague than as someone she'd idolized from afar.

"Is it anything you can talk about?" Daphne asked. "The investigation, I mean."

Izzie finished the rest of her drink while she considered her answer. Having someone who was willing to act as a sounding board, who didn't have the same prejudices and preconditions as Patrick Tevake, might be useful. But at the same time, she wasn't eager to admit out loud some of her more outlandish theories about what they'd discovered, much less to another Bureau agent. Patrick was concerned about his superiors at the Recondito PD ordering psych evaluations, but Izzie was concerned about losing her security clearance, or worse.

"Like I said," she finally answered. "It's complicated."

"But it has something to do with the Reaper case, right?"

Izzie set her glass back down on the bar, and motioned for the bartender. She ordered a gin gimlet on the rocks when he came within earshot, and Daphne raised a couple of fingers, telling him to make it two.

"Yeah," Izzie replied, turning back to Daphne. "Tangentially, at least."

"Is it a copycat thing? Somebody new out there following the same M.O.?"

"No, nothing like that. It's more to do with the *reasons* behind the Reaper killings. As in, what Nicholas Fuller thought he was accomplishing, why he targeted the victims that he . . ." She paused, and glanced around the room. None of the other patrons seemed to be eavesdropping on their conversation, but it never hurt to be cautious when discussing sensitive matters out in public. "Why he targeted those specific individuals," she continued.

"Mmmm," Daphne hummed, suspiciously. She was a clever woman, and could clearly sense that Izzie was talking around something big without mentioning it. "Okay. But why now, after all this time? What's different now that wasn't the case last year, or five years ago for that matter?"

"Well, Patrick . . . Lieutenant Tevake, that is . . . he is working with Vice, investigating a new street drug."

Daphne sat up a little straighter, raising an eyebrow. "But he was like this superstar of the Homicide squad during the Fuller case, right? I've read all the files, remember. He was the one who was with you that last night . . ." She trailed off, seeming to recognize some flicker of discomfort in Izzie's expression. "I'm sorry if that's insensitive of me to mention."

Izzie laid a hand on her arm. "Not at all. It's all a matter of public record, after all. And you had already told me that you read the files when you were at Quantico, so I knew you were familiar." She smiled. "It's kind of nice not to have to explain what happened that night, actually. I've been in circumstances a few times in the years since then where I'd be talking with someone who *didn't* know, and found it difficult to figure out just how to explain. That night was . . . it was . . .." Even now, she was having difficulty putting it into words.

"Like you said yesterday," Daphne said and laid her hand over Izzie's arm. "It was a rough night, but it worked out okay in the end, right?"

The soft touch of Daphne's fingertips was cool and smooth against the back of her hand, but Izzie felt warmed.

"Yeah." Izzie's smile was weak but sincere, and she met Daphne's unbroken gaze. "I suppose you're right."

The bartender returned with two glass tumblers filled with ice cubes and gin, and sat them down on the bar. Daphne lifted her hand from Izzie's, and that brief moment of connection between them faded.

Izzie reached for her drink, gratified that aside from the slender wedge of lime nestled on the rim, it was otherwise free of plant matter. The first sip was good, icy cold and exactly what she needed.

"Oh, man, that takes me back," Daphne said after taking a sip, putting the tumbler down on the bar, the ice cubes clinking delicately. "I'm not sure I've even *had* gin since college. It was my drink of choice back then." She cast a sly sidelong glance at Izzie. "Of course, I smoked like a fiend back then, so one sip and I'm already craving a cigarette. Sense memory or something, I guess."

Izzie almost sputtered, swallowing a mouthful before reacting. "Oh my god, I was thinking the same thing last night when I left the morgue. Even though I quit smoking *years* ago, I just suddenly was itching for one."

Daphne took another sip, and as she lowered her glass she leaned in and whispered conspiratorially, "We totally *shouldn't* get a pack of cigarettes, right? That would be a horrible idea." She grinned. "Wouldn't it?"

"It's tempting," Izzie admitted. Then she shook her head. "But no, totally shouldn't. That's a horrible idea." She took another sip of her gin gimlet.

"Then we'll just have to have another round, instead." Daphne raised her glass.

"That sounds like an *excellent* idea," Izzie answered with a grin.

Three rounds later they both decided it was time to call it a night. As they listed out the door, Izzie was glad that she had locked her pistol up in the gun vault at the office. Not that she would seriously have shot the guy who catcalled them from a passing car as they stepped outside if she *did* have her gun with her, she was too well trained for that, but the temptation was so strong that she was glad that her training wouldn't be put to the test. The foul things that the guy had shouted as he cruised by . . .

But Daphne wasn't one to let the offense pass unanswered, and so she stepped into the street as the car drove off, hurling invectives at the catcaller. "And besides," she finished off, "you're not our type!"

Izzie stifled a laugh. But Daphne was right, he very much *wasn't* her type.

"That rat bastard," Daphne said, then stumbled as she stepped back onto the curb.

Izzie rushed forward and caught Daphne before she fell, then helped her regain her balance.

"Thanks," Daphne said, still holding onto Izzie's arm, not letting go.

Their faces were close, their breath forming blended clouds of steam that rose into the chilly air like slowly expanding smoke rings.

"I think . . ." Izzie started to say, and then they were kissing.

Afterwards, she wouldn't be able to recall if she had moved in first, or if Daphne had. But she would remember for a long time how good the kiss felt—warm, lasting, and deep.

They finally broke apart, both gasping for air. They remained nose to nose, looking into one another's eyes.

"My place isn't that far from here," Daphne began, suggestively. "Unless you wanted to go back to your . . . ?"

Izzie pulled away, dropping her hands and taking a step back. "No, I can't . . ."

"What's wrong?" Daphne looked stricken. "I thought . . . I mean . . . it seemed like . . ."

Izzie shook her head. "No, it's not you. Hell, it's not even me. I just can't right now."

"Oh." Daphne had a wounded expression on her face. "Okay. That's fine, I guess that . . ." She held her hands up in front of her, opened her mouth to continue then closed it again. She nodded twice, then went on, "This was a mistake. I'm sorry. I misread the situation and . . ."

"No, no," Izzie interrupted. "You read it perfectly. I'm just in a weird place at the moment, and need a little time to figure things out."

Daphne bit her lip as a moment of silence stretched out awkwardly between them. "You okay getting back to your hotel from here?" she finally asked, trying to adopt a casual tone and not quite succeeding.

"Yeah, I'll be fine," Izzie answered.

"Then I guess . . ." she shrugged. "I'll see you later?"

As Daphne turned and walked away, Izzie felt like she should say something. But the words didn't come, and she was left alone on the sidewalk.

CHAPTER FIFTEEN

Sleep came easy, aided by the lingering buzz from the cocktails that Izzie had drunk, but her dreams were meandering and dark. A door she had never noticed in her grandmother's house in the Ninth Ward opened to reveal a basement lined with rotting corpses and severed heads that whispered horrible secrets that she could not hear but somehow understood instinctively. Shadows deepened and with the logic of dreams Izzie knew that she was deep underground, miles of solid rock above her, waiting for robber barons to dig down and discover her, but that she was not alone in the darkness. There was something else shifting unseen around her, carrying with it the ozone tang of summer rains, the scent of fresh flowers, and the offal stench of rotting meat. And with alarm came the sudden realization that the darkness that was all she could see around her was not the blackness that came with the absence of light, but instead a color from no earthly spectrum that her senses could process, that her mind refused to comprehend.

There was a voice that rumbled, but she could not hear it, feeling instead a subaudible tone that vibrated the bones of her rib cage and touched her deep inside. And she knew what the voice was saying but could not bring herself to admit it . . .

When the insistent ringing of her phone roused her from slumber, the knowledge that had seemed so crystal clear and real in the dream evaporated and was gone like an ice cube in a hot skillet. When she scrambled to tap the screen to answer, Izzie realized that she hadn't bothered to turn on her white noise app when going to bed. Clearly, five stiff drinks had been all the white noise she needed.

"Hullo?" she croaked, fumbling to put the phone to her ear.

"Rise and shine, sleepyhead." Patrick sounded impossibly awake and chipper at this unforgiving hour of the day.

"M'kay." Izzie put her other hand over her eyes, which felt desiccated and raw, and there was a hammering behind her forehead.

"You up for breakfast? I know this Mexican joint that does killer migas—"

"No. No, no." Hungover and sweating, Izzie's stomach roiled at the thought of food. "God, no."

"Everything okay?" There was concern in Patrick's tone.

"Just feeling a little rough." Izzie rolled with a sigh into a sitting position on the edge of the bed. "Late night."

Patrick chuckled, not unsympathetically. "Got ya. Well, I'm heading into the station house in a bit, wondered if you needed a ride."

"Um." Izzie had to pause for a moment and consider her options. "Actually, I'll make my way over there in a while. I'm just getting a slow start to the day, looks like."

"Sounds good. But don't be too long, I was thinking about getting sushi for lunch, and you don't want to miss out."

"I'll be there." Izzie rolled her eyes. "See you soon."

She tossed the phone onto the bedsheet, then pushed herself with a groan to her feet.

"Okay, brain," she said out loud to herself, angling towards the shower. "We can do this." But she was only half-convinced.

The long, hot shower did a reasonable job of making her feel human again, and the two complimentary bottles of water that she guzzled helped settle her insides a little. It would be a while before she felt ready to tackle anything more substantial than an antacid, she knew, but at least she would be able to function.

When she was dressed and headed for the door, she did her sign of the cross, patting her pockets in turn, but stalled out halfway through when she reached for the holster that wasn't on her belt.

She remembered the gun vault in the R.A. office across the street, and then the drinks at the bar. The silky touch of Daphne's lips against hers, the spreading warmth inside as they stood nose to nose, looking deep into one another's eyes. And the way things had abruptly come to an end.

"Shit," Izzie hissed under her breath. "This is going to be awkward."

Despite what was often depicted erroneously in movies and television shows, the FBI didn't have a non-fraternization policy when it came to agents and other Bureau employees getting involved with one another. So long as two people didn't work together in a supervisor-subordinate capacity, it wasn't prohibited. That said, Izzie tended to avoid such entanglements as a general rule, just to avoid complicated or awkward situations.

Such as the one she was walking into now.

"Good morning, Agent Lefevre." Senior Resident Agent Manuel Gutierrez was pouring coffee into a World's Best Dad mug from a steaming pot as Izzie came through the front door. "So nice of you to drop by and grace us with your presence."

She knew he intended it to be funny, but there wasn't a trace of humor to his tone. Either he was just chronically humorless, or was in a bad mood for one reason or another. Whatever the case, it was hardly putting Izzie at ease.

"Agent Richardson tells me you stopped by last night." He nodded across the room, where Daphne was sitting at her desk with her back to the door. "I hope your investigation isn't turning up anything that might be a problem here?"

"No," Izzie answered, shaking her head. "No problem. Just following some leads, at the moment."

Agent Gutierrez took a sip of his coffee as he headed towards his private office. "Good. I hope your luck continues."

As the Senior Resident Agent closed his office door behind him, Izzie made her way to Daphne's desk.

"Daphne," was all Izzie said by way of greeting, standing behind her chair.

"Agent," Daphne answered without turning around.

"I . . . uh . . ." Izzie glanced around. There were a couple of file clerks working at other desks nearby, and a computer technician was servicing a printer along the far wall. This was the sort of potentially awkward situation that Izzie always tried to avoid. "I was wondering if you could open up the gun vault for me. I need to get my firearm."

Daphne sighed dramatically, then pushed her chair back, wheels squeaking across the tiled floor. She stood up in a huff and started towards the gun vault door. "Come on, then."

Daphne punched the code into the electronic door lock, and then pushed the door open, holding it for Izzie to step inside.

"Thanks," Izzie muttered as she walked through.

The door closed behind them as Daphne followed her inside, turning on the light. She went over to the locked cages where Izzie's firearm was stored, and pulled out a ring of keys from her pocket.

"Daphne, about last night . . ." Izzie began.

"I'm sorry," Daphne interrupted, turning around. "That was a mistake." Far from being annoyed or angry, as Izzie thought she might be, Daphne's expression was one of embarrassment. "I'd had a lot to drink, and things got out of . . ." She shook her head, a blush rising in her cheeks. "I normally have a strict policy *not* to get involved with other agents. Or with law enforcement in general, to be honest. There was this sheriff's deputy I dated in San Antonio, and it was nice for a while— god, she was a great dancer—but when things went south, and we still had to deal with one another on a professional basis . . ." She trailed off, flapping her hand as if waving away a foul smell that wafted by. "It was a giant mess. And I made it a personal rule that I wouldn't go down that road again."

She paused, searching Izzie's face for a reaction.

"I'm sorry?" Daphne said again.

"Oh my god, no." Izzie reached out and lightly touched Daphne's elbow, then quickly pulled her hand back lest the gesture be misread. "Don't apologize, seriously. I was totally expecting to say almost *exactly* what you just did when I came in today." She shook her head. "Well, except for the part about dating a sheriff's deputy in Texas. Mine was a forensic pathologist in Ohio—she wasn't much of a dancer, but she was very damned cute—but otherwise, same thing. It was great, and then it very much wasn't. So I *never* date coworkers anymore." She smirked. "I don't really date much at *all*, to be honest."

Daphne nodded in sympathy. "It's hard to meet people. Moving around every couple of years, unable to talk much about what we do since so many cases are sensitive or even classified..."

Izzie sighed. "And when most of the people you interact with are other law enforcement, in one capacity or another, or *criminals*, well... it's easier to spend your off-hours at home on the couch watching TV than worrying about your social life."

"I don't even have a cat," Daphne said. "Just a bonsai tree in a Snoopy coffee mug."

"Ficus." Izzie tapped her own sternum, grinning. "Not as much fun to cuddle with as a puppy or kitten, but easier to clean up after."

Daphne smiled. "I really do like you though, Izzie. If not for my personal 'no fraternizing' rule I might..."

Izzie nodded. "Yeah, same here. But hey, I'm glad that I've got someone I enjoy hanging out with here. Makes being in town on my own a little easier to manage."

"Well, happy to be of assistance. Speaking of which..." She unlocked the cage and pulled out Izzie's holstered pistol. "Here you are, and not a scratch on her."

"Maybe we can get together for a drink again while I'm in town." Izzie clipped the holster back onto her belt. "Though maybe not quite so *many* drinks next time."

Daphne nodded ruefully as she headed for the door. "Definitely. And hey, maybe we can even go out dancing."

Izzie grinned. "Maybe," she said, the possibility seeming marginally more likely than the first time Daphne had made the suggestion the day before last.

A fter borrowing a laptop from the computer technician, Izzie set up shop temporarily at the desk that had been assigned for her to use. First she logged into her work email account, responded to a few queries about other ongoing investigations from her colleagues in the BAU, then typed up a quick summary of the events of the previous thirty-six hours to send to her supervisor. It was a summary in only the loosest sense of the word, highlighting her interactions with the local authorities since arriving—Lieutenant Tevake and his fellow police officers, the chief medical examiner, and so on—a brief rundown of her interview with Professor Kono at the university, and a cursory account of the drug raid the day before. Nothing about the more outlandish theories that she and Patrick had suggested, or about the directions that their investigation into the Fuller evidence seemed to be heading. Just the facts regarding interactions and events that were likely to show up in other official records—police reports, visitor's logs, and the like.

It wasn't that she intended to conceal the true extent of the investigation from the Bureau, or that she would not be reporting her findings once she and Patrick were able to reach some useful conclusion. But she wanted her findings to be completely airtight before she shared them. Things would be difficult enough to explain as it was, without there being questions left hanging that she was not equipped to answer.

Of course, just thinking about how she would ultimately account for all of this in her official report brought to mind the aspects of the investigation that hinted at possible connections, but so far remained tantalizingly isolated. The origins of the Recondito Mining Guild, for example, and the particular spot where the university's Undersight experiment had been carried out. On a whim, Izzie closed the email program, brought up a browser window, and went to an online search engine.

She did a Boolean search using the terms "Recondito," "hills," "mine shaft," and "underground."

The top results were, unsurprisingly, related to mining—principally historical sites or archival documents related to the brief gold mining boom in Recondito in the mid-nineteenth century—or to ongoing mining concerns elsewhere in the United States or overseas that had financial connections to Recondito-based companies. There were several reviews of a now defunct gay bar in Oceanview called "The Mine Shaft," in the days of house and underground music, where patrons allegedly partook of "hills" worth of cocaine. There was a synopsis of an installment of *Behind the Lines,* the sitcom set in Recondito that Izzie had watched back in high school, a bottle episode in which the cartoonist protagonist Trent and his longtime rival Miles were trapped in a cave during an earthquake, and learned to overcome their differences by remembering moments they had shared before, conveniently selected from previously aired episodes. Then a smattering of mineralogical and metallurgical surveys of the Recondito hills and surrounding areas, marking out past mining operations. On the third page of results she finally found a few accounts of the origins of the Guildhall, and popular science accounts of the Undersight experiments, and then . . .

Izzie had expected that there might be some connection between the Recondito Mining Guild and their Guildhall and the university's Undersight project, which was why she had initiated the search. But she hadn't anticipated that there might be connections between them and yet another moment of local interest in the city.

"KILLER CULT HIDES DEEP SECRET," read the headline from an article originally published in the pages of the *Recondito Clarion* in the mid-seventies.

Izzie clicked the link and began to scan the article, which was all about the Eschaton Center for Emanant Truth. Sometimes called ECET for short, the article helpfully explained, it was once a popular spiritual retreat and self-help center in the Recondito hills that had been one of the cornerstones of the counter-culture human potential movement in the sixties and seventies. Those who spent time at the Eschaton Center included rock musicians, movie stars, filmmakers, novelists, scientists, and poets, and by the early years of the 1970s it was poised to have a greater cultural impact and reach than the better-known Esalen Institute down in Big Sur. With increasing regularity, Jeremiah Standfast Parrish, the charismatic founder of the Eschaton Center, was appearing on morning chat programs and late night talk shows, delivering his message of universal love and a new mode of understanding reality to an often bewildered general audience, but he piqued the interest of enough new converts that the ranks of the faithful were always increasing. But then a dark shadow fell over the Center when families came forward with dark rumors about the strange practices that were carried out behind closed doors, where only the faithful were permitted. Charges that ECET was nothing but a cult, brainwashing the gullible and misguided, duped into the service of the egomaniacal Parrish. A Recondito-based private investigator called George W. Jett, who specialized in "deprogramming" young people who had been indoctrinated by cults, was hired by several of the families to "rescue" their loved ones from the Center. He infiltrated the Eschaton Center, and what he found there prompted him to leave and come back with the police. But by the time the authorities arrived, the Center had been turned into a killing field, as dozens of the faithful had been brutally murdered, either by each other or at their own hands.

Izzie knew some of the history from the made-for-TV movie she'd seen years before, and from case studies of mass psychosis she had read while studying for her masters in psychology. But the article from the *Recondito Clarion* that she was reading now, which had been written soon after the tragedy, contained an element of the case that she hadn't encountered before. George W. Jett had managed to bring two young people with him when he had left to get help from the authorities, a young man and woman. The article that Izzie was reading contained an interview with the young woman, in which she recounted some of the things she had witnessed while staying at the Eschaton Center. Most of it echoed what Izzie had learned elsewhere, but there was one detail in particular that had previously escaped her notice. She knew that Parrish had vast subterranean sublevels excavated beneath the buildings that housed the Eschaton Center, and that many of the most secretive activities of the cult were carried out down there, far from the prying eyes of the public. But the article quoted the young woman who had been rescued by Jett as saying that some of the sublevels actually connected to older underground spaces, which the author of the piece speculated might be naturally occurring caves, or perhaps abandoned mine shafts.

It was this detail that had snared the article in the online search that Izzie had run, otherwise she might have missed it entirely. And certainly, the fact that the secret rituals of the Eschaton Center might well have been carried out in abandoned mine shafts was not something that Izzie recalled seeing mentioned in any of the other accounts that she'd encountered over the years. But seeing it now, with the benefit of hindsight, it stood out to her like a waving red flag.

She looked up the former location of the Eschaton Center on a map. She would have to ask Patrick for verification, but it certainly seemed possible to her that the mine shaft in question could be the same one dug by the founders of the Recondito Mining Guild, the same mine shaft that had so obsessed Nicholas Fuller.

And there had been a copy of Jeremiah Standfast Parrish's self-help book in Fuller's effects, hadn't there? Izzie recalled seeing it in the evidence piled up in the community room of the 10th Precinct station house.

So was this another instance of mass murder associated with that same hole in the ground? It certainly seemed likely.

But what was down there? What had happened to all of those people, many of whom had evidently taken their own lives?

Izzie's phone beeped insistently in her pocket, and she pulled it out and tapped the screen. Patrick was texting her repeatedly, asking whether everything was okay, and when would she be arriving.

She texted a quick response, then slid the phone back into her pocket. Before shutting down the laptop, she emailed a link to the *Recondito Clarion* article to herself, satisfied when she heard the ping of it arriving at her phone. Then she pushed back from the table and shouldered into her jacket.

"I'm heading out," she said while walking past Daphne's desk.

Daphne smiled. "Be careful. And don't forget about that drink."

Izzie nodded. The way things were heading, it looked like she might need another stiff drink before too much longer.

CHAPTER SIXTEEN

Izzie's phone rang right before she climbed into the taxi that had pulled up to the curb at her hail. It was Patrick.

"Where are you?"

"Getting into a cab," she answered, her hand on the door handle. "Just left the R.A. offices."

"Don't bother," Patrick said, and from the background noise it sounded as though he were in a car. "I'm on my way to you."

Izzie sighed and mouthed an apology to the cab driver as she stepped back. The driver scowled, gesturing angrily at her through the window's glass, muttering something she couldn't hear but that she was sure wasn't complimentary. The cab pulled away from the curb and back into traffic with squealing tires.

"What's up?" Izzie held the phone to her ear with one hand, her other hand resting on a cocked hip. "When you texted just a minute ago I thought I was meeting you at the station house."

"Change of plans," Patrick answered. "You're still in front of the Resident Agency?"

"Yeah."

"Stay put, I should be there in a minute or two. I'll explain when I get there."

When he hung up, she slid the phone back into her pocket with a sigh.

"Great," she muttered to herself. She glanced around at the surrounding buildings, her stomach growling. Now that her hangover had mostly receded, her appetite had come back with a vengeance. She hoped that Patrick was rushing over to take her somewhere for lunch. Knowing him, there was a better than even chance that he was, actually.

True to his word, it was just a little over two minutes later that Patrick's car pulled to a stop at the curb. He popped the locks, and she slid in the passenger seat.

"Why the change of plans?" she asked, buckling up.

"Joyce called the station and said that she was almost done with the autopsy reports for Malcolm Price and the three bodies we pulled out of his basement. Harrison and Chavez got a warrant to search the apartments of the man and woman we arrested in his kitchen, so I volunteered to go down to the morgue to pick up the reports."

"Damn." Izzie smirked. "I was hoping you were rushing to take me to lunch. I'm starving."

Patrick smiled. "Well, I did say that Joyce was *almost* done with the autopsy reports, right? We've got more than enough time to stop for a bite to eat on the way. And there's a barbeque joint not far from the Hall of Justice that would fit the bill perfectly."

"I never should have doubted you." Izzie chuckled, glancing sidelong at him. "If the whole cop thing doesn't pan out for you, or you ever decide to try another line of work, you should consider being some kind of culinary tour guide. You've certainly put in the legwork."

"Hey, I live in Recondito. There's no excuse to ever settle for a mediocre meal in this town."

Izzie could believe it. She could also easily believe that she would weigh an extra hundred pounds by the time she left, if this kept up. It would have to be nothing but salads for her once she got back to Virginia.

The barbeque joint was clearly a favorite of city employees, nestled as it was in a modest building midway between City Hall on the one side and the Hall of Justice on the other. There were picnic tables set up on the sidewalk out front, where the hardiest of diners braved the elements to enjoy their charred meats, but with the chill in the air most of the patrons preferred to eat inside. The structure itself had clearly been an auto body shop or garage at some point in its past, judging from the concrete walls and the big rolling metal doors on the street front, but now the space was crowded with long banquet-style tables that were arranged in tight rows, covered in red and white checked tablecloths.

It was counter service only, and Patrick and Izzie joined the queue of bureaucrats, clerks, and police officers who were lined up out the door, above which buzzed a neon sign spelling out the name "MOON & SON." On the walls inside the door were hung dozens of framed magazine articles and news-paper reviews, reader's choice awards, and signed photos of various celebrities and other local notables taken at the restau-rant. There was a bleached longhorn skull mounted on the back wall, a lone star flag of Texas, and a bottle of the restau-rant's signature barbeque sauce in a glass case with a hammer hanging from a chain, on which was stenciled "IN CASE OF EMERGENCY BREAK GLASS."

"Rustic," Izzie said as they slowly advanced towards the counter. She scanned one of the framed articles, the headline reading "TEXAS EX BRINGS LONE STAR FLAVOR TO RECONDITO." She glanced over at Patrick. "You can take the redneck out of Texas, but you can't take the Texas out of the redneck, I guess?"

"Maybe," Patrick said, and pointed at a frame photo over-head. "Except *that's* the redneck in question."

Izzie turned to look. The photo showed a diminutive Korean-American woman in her late forties, holding a bottle of beer up in one hand and a bottle of Moon & Son barbeque sauce in the other.

"That's Janet Moon," Patrick explained. "Ran a restaurant in Austin with her dad before the rents there got too high, then relocated to Recondito a few years back. She was a material witness in a homicide that I worked before moving over to Vice, and I got to know her a bit."

Izzie glanced around at the décor, the menu, the longhorn skull, and lone star flag. "Doesn't seem like a Korean joint to me."

"Careful, Izzie," Patrick said with a scolding grin, "that's edging a little too close to racist. But no, the restaurant that Janet and her dad ran back in Texas *did* serve Korean food, and when she moved out here her original plan was to use the same menu. But the way she explained it to me, what she found was that she missed the barbeque that she used to get back home in Austin more than she missed the kimchi and noodles that she used to serve, so she decided to change her plans."

"Huh." Izzie nodded. "Is it any good? The barbeque, I mean?"

Patrick gestured at the long queue they were in, the tables packed with patrons contentedly devouring giant piles of meat. "What do you think?"

"I guess we'll see." Izzie found herself wondering if Daphne had ever tried the place, and how it stacked up to the food that she'd eaten when she was stationed in San Antonio, if she had. Maybe Izzie would bring Daphne here sometime, if she hadn't? And then she chided herself for thinking along those lines, reminding herself that she wasn't getting involved. Even if some part of her really wanted to. . . .

Thankfully, they arrived at the counter before she had gone too far down a hole of self-recrimination.

Patrick opted for pork ribs and sausage, while Izzie ordered brisket and a side of beans. Behind the counter men and women in T-shirts and aprons pulled hunks of meat out of the grill and sliced the cuts to the patron's specifications, joking with one another as they did. Trays with meat piled atop butcher paper were slid across the counter to them, along with plastic tumblers of sweet tea, and after Izzie and Patrick settled the bill, they moved off to find a place to sit.

They were angling for an open spot at one of the banquet tables when a voice called out from behind them. "Howdy, Cop Rock!"

Izzie glanced back as Patrick turned and smiled. "Hey, Janet."

Patrick set his tray down on the table as a woman wearing an apron over a denim shirt came sauntering over. She was just as diminutive in real life as she looked in the photo hung on the wall, but she seemed to take up more space in person than her size might suggest. It was as though her personality occupied more room than her body did.

"How's it hanging, Cop Rock?" Janet Moon said, punching Patrick playfully in the shoulder.

Patrick smirked. "I'm doing okay. Busy, as always."

"Cop rock?" Izzie said, putting her tray down across the table from Patrick's.

"Don't ask," Patrick said, rolling his eyes. "Long story. Bad joke."

"What's the matter," Janet said with a mischievous grin, "you don't like your friends knowing about your sordid past?"

Patrick sighed, and glanced over at Izzie. "I was in a band. A long time ago." He gestured to Janet. "And I made the mistake of letting this harpy listen to one of our old demos one time and . . . well."

"You were good, damn it." Janet shoved him again. "I mean, your band *sucked*, but you were a decent bass player." She turned from Patrick to Izzie, and Izzie felt like she was looking for the best cut of meat. "Who's your friend?"

"This is Izzie Lefevre." She noticed that Patrick introduced her casually, as a friend, and not as an FBI agent working a case. "She's helping me out with something."

"Well go on, sit down." Janet motioned towards their trays. "Food's getting cold."

As Izzie slid onto the bench, Janet nudged her arm.

"Skooch over, sweetie," she said, "I'm joining you."

Izzie obliged, and as the woman sat down beside her, Patrick chuckled.

"Don't you have a restaurant to run?" he said, taking a sip of his sweet tea.

Janet nodded towards the counter. "The kids can handle it for a while. I've been on my feet since before dawn, I deserve a bit of a sit down."

Patrick checked the time on his phone, then put it down on the table beside his drink. He picked up one of the ribs from his tray, glancing around the room. "Seems like business is good."

Janet shrugged. "Yeah, but I'll probably still have to move locations when the lease runs out."

"Really?" Patrick was surprised. "I thought you loved this spot."

"Oh, I do." Janet sighed. "Sure, these cops and lawyers crowd in here every weekday, but nights and weekends this part of town is pretty dead. And with rents going up all over, it's getting harder and harder to make our nut every month."

"I've heard about apartment rents going up," Izzie said, "but I didn't know it was happening to businesses, too." She speared a few slices of brisket with a plastic fork, laid them on a piece of white bread, and drizzled barbeque sauce over them.

"You bet your ass it is," Janet answered. "All these damned tech companies—Parasol, outfits like that—they can afford to pay more, so the folks that own the land start charging more, and on and on. I left Austin when the rents got too high, now I'm dealing with the same nonsense here."

"I'm not worried," Patrick said, blissfully chewing on a bite of pork rib. "If I know you, there'll always be a Moon & Son, one way or another."

"Do you run this place with your son?" Izzie asked, turning to Janet.

The woman snorted. "My wife and I remain happily childless, thank god. No, the 'son' is *me*." She thumped her chest. "My dad opened the original restaurant back in Texas while my mom was still pregnant with me, and he *really* wanted a son." She sighed. "He was a stubborn bastard, and kept the name even after I popped out with the wrong kind of tackle. I think maybe he figured that he'd have another kid eventually, so he kept the name. But mom died when I was little, and he never remarried. I inherited the place when he died, and I kept the name mostly out of spite." She paused, shrugging. "But I kinda like it."

"Well, the food is delicious." Izzie dabbed the corners of her mouth with a paper towel, wiping away bits of barbeque sauce.

"See?" Patrick said. "Told you."

"So what kind of case you two working?" Janet asked him. "Some kind of juicy murder thing again?"

"No, like I keep telling you, I'm in Vice now."

Janet crossed her arms, scowling. "I just keep hoping you'll come to your senses and transfer back. Drug stuff is *boring*, Cop Rock."

"No dice." Patrick shook his head. "You'll have to look elsewhere for gory gossip to share. Besides, even if you *did* want to hear about the drug cases, you know I can't discuss an ongoing investigation."

"Fine, fine, be that way." She waved her hand dismissively. She sighed, and leaned heavily on the table. "Okay, I'll leave you two in peace. If I stay away too long, the kiddos back there get a mite nervous." She stood up, and nodded to Izzie.

"Pleasure to meet you." Then she turned to Patrick. "Stay out of trouble, Cop Rock."

She patted Patrick's shoulder as she walked by, and headed back towards the counter.

"Colorful character," Izzie said, when she had gone.

Patrick glanced over at the counter, then turned back to Izzie. "Yeah. I suppose she is. It'd be a shame if she had to move locations, but I hope to god she stays in town." He picked up one of the picked-clean bones and shook it, emphatically. "I need my rib fix."

Izzie took a bite of beans, then washed it down with tea. "One of the agents at the R.A. was complaining about rising rents. Is that a recent thing, or did I just not hear about it last time I was in town?"

"A little of both, maybe?" Patrick was thoughtful. "Prices have gone up *some* since I was a kid, but it's really been in the last few years that things have accelerated. Like I mentioned yesterday, when the local economy shifted to tech and telecom from fishing and shipping, that changed the whole ball game. Software companies have a lot of capital to spend."

"Companies like Parasol?" Izzie asked. "Janet mentioned them."

"I think she did, yeah."

"I keep running into that name. Learning interesting little facts." She gave Patrick a meaningful glance. "Such as the little detail that everyone who works at the Pinnacle Tower is a Parasol employee."

"Like our two friends in lockup back at the station house, for example?" Patrick dropped the rib bone on the small pile he'd amassed on the tray, stripped clean.

"Perfect examples, in fact," Izzie answered. "Was Harrison able to get anything out of them?"

Patrick wiped his hand on a paper towel, sucking rib meat from between his teeth before answering. "A little. Not much." He pulled his notepad from an inner pocket of his suit coat, and flipped it open. "Ibrahim Fayed and Marissa Keizer. Both of them moved to town in the last year, Fayed from the UK by way of Boston, Keizer from Orlando. Until recently they were working at Parasol, as a software engineer and accountant respectively, but both of them stopped showing up to work in the last month, or so the HR department at Parasol informs us. Which is weird, since both of them were recruited from out of state to work there, and were making hefty salaries."

"That is weird. Anything more?"

"Like I said, not much. We confirmed their identities and located their residences, but they're refusing to talk about their involvement with Malcolm Price, or what they know about the Ink trade. They claim . . . hang on, I've got it here." He turned a page in the notepad, and then read out loud, "'We didn't know that guy. We just stopped in to ask for directions.' End quote." He flipped the notepad shut and slid it back into his pocket. "Harrison and Chavez are checking out their apartments to see if they can find anything useful."

"So presumably they left the good-paying jobs that they moved to Recondito for, and decided that they'd be . . . what? Drug runners? Cooks in a lab? The pay for that kind of work couldn't be *that* great, could it?"

Patrick shrugged. "You can make a *lot* of money selling drugs, actually, but these two didn't have any priors at all. And nothing in their records that would suggest they would be the type to drop everything to take up a life of crime."

"Maybe they had debts off the books? Gambling or something like that. Needed money fast." Izzie chewed her lower lip, thoughtfully. "Are they a couple? I mean, romantically? People do stupid stuff when they're in love."

"I don't know." Patrick blinked, then rushed to add, "About their relationship status, I mean. Not about being in love."

"Um, okay," she said, giving him a quizzical look.

"But you said that you kept running into the Parasol name, in that kind of 'This is an important pile of mashed potatoes' tone that you sometimes use. Was it something to do with Fuller's obsession with Undersight and that mine shaft?"

"No, but that reminds me." Izzie pulled out her phone, brought up her email app, then clicked the link to the article she'd been reading earlier. "I *did* find another connection to the mine shaft, I think."

She slid the phone over to Patrick, who looked down at it and began scanning through the article.

"I'm guessing that you know all about the Eschaton Center murders," she said.

Patrick glanced up at her from under his eyebrows, giving her a look that made clear that was a stupid question to ask. "Obviously."

Izzie reached over and pointed at the screen of her phone.

"Did you know that they did secret stuff in a mine shaft that connected to the Center's subbasements?"

Patrick straightened up, the smug look on his face vanishing. He swiped down through the article, eyes narrowed, reading more carefully.

"I'll be damned," he muttered under his breath.

"I'm guessing that's a no, then." Izzie tried not to sound superior, but knew she wasn't entirely successful.

Patrick met her gaze as he slid the phone back across the red-and-white checked tablecloth to her. "I've been hearing about that case my entire life—growing up here, it's hard to *avoid* it—but I never ran into that particular detail before." He rubbed his jaw, thinking. "Can you forward that to me?"

He picked up his phone and waggled it.

"Sure." Izzie copied the link and then pasted it into a text message.

Patrick's phone chimed, indicating a new message. "Thanks."

Izzie looked up from her phone. "You're welcome, but I haven't sent it yet." She turned and showed the compose message screen.

"Then what . . . ?" Patrick tapped the screen. "Oh, damn." He looked up. "It's Joyce asking where the hell we are. She's been waiting half an hour for us to show up. We gotta go."

As he jumped to his feet and stacked their trash on the trays, Izzie smirked. "It was *your* idea to get lunch at the place with the crazy long line, you know."

"Well, yeah," he said, dumping the trash in a bin and putting the trays on top. "But come on, those ribs? It was totally worth it."

As they exited the place, Izzie was grateful that her stomach wasn't still growling. But she hoped that she wouldn't be getting a second look at her meal when they got to the morgue. She hadn't thrown up yet at the smell of rotting corpses, but there was always a first time.

CHAPTER SEVENTEEN

The scalpels and bone saws on the autopsy table were vibrating in time with the ear-shatteringly loud beat of ABBA's "Dancing Queen" blaring from the medical examiner's office as they stepped off the elevator into the cavernous morgue.

"See!" Patrick shouted to be heard over the din. "I told you so!"

Izzie followed as he crossed the cold tile floor to the open office door.

"You poseur!" Patrick pointed at Joyce Nguyen, who was sitting in a swivel chair at her desk, bobbing her head in time with the music and swaying her shoulders as she rhythmically hit the keys of her computer's keyboard.

She looked up at the sound of his voice, a startled expression on her face. Then with a look of annoyance, she grabbed the wireless mouse, swerved it on the desk, and with a click the music stopped.

"Some goth *you* are." Patrick folded his arms, shoulder resting against the door frame. "I *knew* it was all an act."

Joyce leaned her elbows on the desk and rested her chin on her folded hands. "First, I never said I was a 'goth.' I'm an adult woman, not a member of some teenage fan club. Second, it *is* entirely possible to enjoy more than one kind of music, you know, depending on your mood. And third, stop trying to police my engagement with media, jerk. I like what I like." From her tone and expression it was clear that she wasn't really mad, but playfully annoyed. "And besides, ABBA is awesome."

"Well, I *am* a police officer. If I can't police your media consumption, who can?" Patrick said with a grin. He looked over at Izzie. "And ABBA is most definitely *not* awesome, right Izzie?"

Izzie held up her hands in a gesture of surrender. "Hey, guys, I'm Switzerland in this. Completely neutral."

"Traitor." Patrick feigned mock offense, then turned back to Joyce. "So, what do you have for us?"

The medical examiner grabbed the cane that was leaning against her desk, and used it to help lever herself up out of the chair and onto the thick soles of her impressive boots.

"You guys sent me some real winners this time, I'll give you that." Joyce's cane thudded against the area rug that was spread under the desk, then tonked against the tile floor as she stepped through the door past Patrick and Izzie and out into the main space of the morgue beyond.

"You can thank Chavez and Harrison for this one," Patrick answered, trailing after her. "This is their show, I'm just pitching in."

"Harrison is an ass, but you can tell that cutie Chavez that he's welcome to drop by anytime." She gave him a sly look as she glanced back over her shoulder. "Maybe he'd show a little more respect for my musical choices than *some* philistines do."

There was a body wrapped in a single sheet on one of the autopsy tables. Joyce continued past it to the refrigerator doors that lined the back wall.

"We'll tackle the easy ones first." The doors were about two-and-a-half feet square, and Joyce grabbed the handle of one, yanking it open. "Give me a hand with this," she said.

Izzie stepped forward to help pull out the body tray carriage. It slid out easily, coasting over ball bearing rollers, but before it was halfway extended out the door the putrid smell hit her nostrils, and seeing her lunch a second time became a very real possibility. She recoiled, hand over her mouth, fighting the urge to vomit.

"Here, this might help." Joyce pulled a small jar of Vicks VapoRub from the pocket of her lab coat. "You get used to it in time, but a bit of this under your nose might get you through." She twisted the lid off, and held the open jar out to Izzie.

Izzie dabbed a bit above her upper lip, and her nostrils stung with the mentholated smell. But it was better than the stench of putrescence wafting off the decaying body on the tray.

"I'll take some," Patrick said, face screwed up in distaste. He skimmed a fingertip around the inner rim of the jar. "I thought they smelled bad yesterday."

"They were in a fairly advanced state of decomposition," Joyce said as she screwed the cap back on and dropped the jar into her pocket. "But cutting them open releases a lot of gas and liquid that's built up inside, so . . . yeah, they pretty much reek."

"I think I preferred the ABBA." Patrick dabbed the mentholated cream under his nostrils.

"Philistine." Joyce shook her head sadly, then looked down at the body on the tray. "We're still working on IDing them from dental records, but this first John Doe was the farthest along of the three. Taking into the account the environmental conditions of the basement where you found them—relatively cool and dry—the rate of decay was much slower than it would have been in a warmer, more humid setting, but based on the degree of tissue liquefaction I'd estimate that our friend here has been deceased for at least a month, possibly as much as eight weeks. The skin has already begun to rupture, and there's been some loss of mass due to maggot feeding and decompositional fluids being purged. Hair and nails are loose and easily dislodged."

"Were you able to determine anything about cause of death?" Patrick asked.

"This one's skin and soft tissues were far enough gone that it was difficult to get a complete picture, but there is some evidence of an entry wound at the back of the skull." She shoved the tray back into the cooler, shouldered the door shut, and then yanked open the next door. She nodded to Izzie, who helped pull the tray out.

"Urk." Izzie gagged at the smell. The mentholated rub was helping, but some of the stench was still getting through.

"This woman was a little fresher," Joyce went on, "maybe a week or two post-mortem, and she had the same indicators at the back of the skull. Something had been inserted there. I thought at first it was a stab wound, perhaps with something like an ice pick. Otherwise no signs of trauma, though her body does show indications of malnourishment, and her digestive tract was completely empty, as if she hadn't eaten in some time before she died."

She nudged the tray with her hip, sliding it back into the cooler, then opened the next door down.

"This one was the freshest. Maybe as little as seventy-two hours post-mortem. Malnourished, though with traces of his last meal still in his system. And in addition to the entry wound on the back of the head, I found this." She reached into another pocket of her lab coat and pulled out a small clear plastic evidence bag. There was a small plastic and metal object inside, which looked almost like a dart with only two wings.

"What is it?" Patrick asked.

"It's a ventriculoperitoneal shunt. It's like a cerebral catheter, typically used to drain excess fluid from the cranium in patients suffering from hydrocephalus. This one was entering the subject's brain near the pineal gland, behind the third ventricle." She tilted her head, looking down at the cadaver on the tray. "Pretty inexpertly inserted. Could *not* have been very pleasant for him."

"So he had some kind of meningitis, maybe? Or head trauma?" Izzie asked, thinking of potential causes for hydrocephalus.

Joyce shook her head. "Nope. But I thought I'd run an MRI on the brain once I removed it from the cranium, see what I could find out. Know what I found?"

She looked from Izzie to Patrick and back again, like a comedian waiting for a punch line to land with her audience.

"No," Patrick finally said, a trace of annoyance in his voice. "What?"

Joyce turned and tonked across the tile floors to an autopsy table, atop which rested a folder. She picked it up, and pulled a print from inside. "Take a look."

Patrick took the print from her hand and held it for Izzie to see. It was a color photograph looking down at the top of the dead man's head with the cap of the skull removed. It was gruesome, just bits and pieces still adhering to the inside of the cranium.

"So what?" Patrick glanced up from the photo at the medical examiner. "Empty skull after you removed the brain. What am I supposed to be seeing?"

Joyce shook her head, a macabre smile on her face. "I hadn't removed anything. That's what I found when I cracked the skull open."

Izzie looked back at the photo. "But . . . had it already decomposed?"

"No chance," Joyce answered. "Not this soon after death. And there *is* some brain tissue in there." She pulled another print from the folder, this one obviously a printout of an MRI scan. "Just not very much."

On the MRI printout, they could see the general outline of a brain inside the skull, but with huge shadows swallowing the majority of it, leaving only a husk.

"Were they . . ." Patrick struggled to find the right term. "I don't know, were they extracting the brain through that shunt thingee?"

"Fluid, maybe," Joyce answered, "but you couldn't get much gray matter itself through a tube that small."

"It's like the others, isn't it?" Izzie said. "The vacuoles. Like Fuller's victims, and that dead drug dealer."

Joyce nodded, like a teacher proud that a prized student had answered a hard question correctly. "That's my best guess. But clearly, the degradation is *far* more advanced here, with only the medulla remaining largely unaffected. The medulla could have kept the body alive long past the point where it was able to do anything but the most basic of autonomic functions. Total brain death, in layman's terms, followed by the ultimate death of the body itself."

"So what *were* they draining out of their heads," Izzie asked, "assuming that those entry wounds in the other two bodies was caused by the same kind of shunt?"

"I'm not sure," Joyce answered, her voice tinged with excitement.

"Maybe he could have told us?" Patrick turned and nodded towards the sheet-draped body on the autopsy table.

"Perhaps," Joyce said, nudging the tray back into the cooler and closing the door. She started towards the autopsy table. "But honestly, as it is, your friend here raises way more questions than he answers."

"You read Chavez's report on the incident, I'm sure." Patrick's face was closed, his expression guarded.

"Yeah." Joyce glanced back over her shoulder. "He's a cutie, but that was a load of bullshit."

"Bullshit?" Izzie echoed, trying to keep her own expression neutral. She didn't want to betray any of the suspicions she had about Malcolm Price's last moments.

"Yep." Joyce flipped the sheet back, exposing the head, shoulders, and abdomen of Malcolm Price. The head was almost completely severed from the body, the neck just a tattered hunk of skin, crushed bone, and ripped flesh. "Chavez says in his report that this guy bit an officer in the neck, took three shots to the chest, and then dove headfirst through a plate glass window, landing on the pavement twenty-five feet below." She glanced down at the dead man on the table. "All of that checks out with the physical condition of the remains.

Traces of human tissue stuck in his front teeth, glass particles embedded in his epidermis, gunshot residue on the clothing indicating close range firing . . . the broken bones, lacerations, and hemorrhaging are consistent with an impact on a hard surface after a fall from that height. I have no doubt that those aspects of Chavez's incident report are accurate."

"So . . . ?" Patrick asked, suggestively.

Joyce turned to fix him with a stare. "He claims that the subject got *back* up after the fall and attacked Agent Lefevre here, he took additional shotgun blasts at close range, and *then* Officer Carlson and Agent Lefevre took turns trying to knock his head off with a battering ram. Am I getting that right?"

Patrick and Izzie glanced at each other, but didn't rush to answer.

"That is *bullshit*, plain and simple." Joyce slammed the tip of her cane against the floor tiles to punctuate her point. "Chavez's explanation in his report was that the subject was unaware of the extent of his injuries and could not feel the full extent of the pain, due to some unknown narcotic working in his system. But even if he was completely numb to pain, like *entirely* numb to it, there's no way that the broken bones of his legs would be able to support his weight to stand. To say nothing of the damage sustained by his internal organs in the impact. He was dead within seconds of hitting the pavement. Plain and simple."

She leaned heavily on her cane with one hand, the other planted on her hip.

"So what's the real story? Tempers flare after this guy attacks one of your own, so the guys on the tactical team shoot and batter his body once he's already dead on the ground? Just to get a few good kicks in before the body bag is zipped shut?"

She glared at them, waiting for a reply.

"Well?"

Izzie and Patrick looked to one another. "Do we tell her?" he said.

"Tell me what?" Joyce said, growing impatient.

"She might be able to help," Izzie said, chewing her lower lip with uncertainty.

"Seriously, guys, this is getting annoying. What *really* happened last night?"

"What Chavez said," Patrick finally answered, turning back to face Joyce. "The basic events, anyway. But his explanation is all wrong."

Joyce blinked in bewilderment.

"Malcolm Price *did* jump out of the window and hit the pavement after being shot three times," Izzie said. "And I'm convinced that he died on impact, you're right about that much. But he really *did* get up and come after me just a few seconds later."

The medical examiner blinked a few more times, and then shook her head as if trying to shake something loose.

"Wait, I don't get it," Joyce said. "You claim that he died on impact and *then* attacked you. How does *that* work, exactly?"

"Well . . ." Izzie glanced over at Patrick, who shrugged. She continued, "we're not exactly sure."

"The ongoing Ink investigation has some . . ." Patrick searched for the right way of expressing it. "Some *strange* aspects to it. Chavez's explanation was the most . . . how did you put it? The most 'pragmatic' way to frame it."

"Wait." Joyce gave the two of them a hard look. "You're serious, aren't you?"

"I'm afraid so," Izzie answered.

"Look," Patrick began, "I know it sound crazy but . . ."

"Hang on," Joyce interrupted, holding up a hand to silence him. "Let me think this through." She turned and took a few steps away, head down, eyes on the floor, lost in thought. "Maybe . . ." She glanced back over her shoulder at the dead man on the autopsy table. She shook her head. "No, can't be."

"What?" Patrick asked.

"And you guys *swear* this isn't some kind of gag?" Joyce had turned and was walking back towards them. "I once heard about a sheriff's office that managed to convince their county coroner that they had a vampire infestation on their hands. The poor sap never lived it down."

"I'm telling the truth, I swear on my life," Izzie answered. "But there was more, that I bet Chavez didn't include. I don't know if anyone but Patrick and I were in a position to see it."

Joyce raised an eyebrow, quizzically.

"While he was coming after me," Izzie went on, "he started getting these weird black bruises or lesions all over his body."

"Like the kind that Ink users get?" Joyce asked. "What do the cops call them, Patrick? 'Blots'?"

Patrick nodded, a sour expression on his face.

"Right, the same kind." Izzie nodded, remembering the two shamblers the night before last. "Well, they spread in just a matter of seconds, until there was hardly any unaffected skin left. Like he was just one big bruise. But after he died . . . well, after he stayed dead, anyway, after I hit him with the door ram . . . they all completely faded. By the time that Chavez and the others got to the body, it was like they were never there at all."

"And you saw this, too?" Joyce looked to Patrick, who nodded. She put a hand on her chin, mulling it over. "Eyewitness testimony is often unreliable, as I'm sure you both know. But with the event this fresh in memory, and both of you on hand to witness it . . . I mean, it's *possible* that there's some connection, but . . ."

"A connection with what?" Patrick asked.

Joyce sighed. "Come with me." She turned and headed towards her office. "I need to show you something."

Izzie caught Patrick's eye as they followed behind, but could tell that he didn't have any more idea what Joyce intended to show them than she did.

"First, take a look at this," Joyce said as she folded herself into the swivel chair. With one hand she slid a folder across the surface of her desk to them.

Patrick flipped the folder open and found printouts of MRI scans within.

"That's the brain of Malcolm Price. There's evidence of blunt force trauma, either from the impact of the fall or the battering ram, but that's not the interesting bit. See anything familiar?"

Izzie leaned over to look past Patrick's shoulder at the image. There were many of the same shadowy dots that they had seen in the brain of Tyler Campbell, the drug dealer whose death had brought Izzie to Recondito.

"What's interesting is where these are grouped," Joyce explained, while typing on her computer's keyboard. "See, they're all in the frontal lobe." She used her mouse to open a folder on the desktop. "Take a look at these."

A selection of other brain scans filled the computer screen like a tiled mosaic.

"These are the scans of Nicholas Fuller's victims from five years ago. In every one of these, the vacuoles are most highly concentrated in the front lobe, just like in Malcolm Price's brain.

But in *this* one . . ." She brought up a new image. "This is Tyler Campbell's brain, and here they're more evenly distributed."

"So?" Patrick asked.

"Well, the frontal lobe is responsible for a lot of different functions, including conscious thought, voluntary movement, and even our individual personality characteristics. With such extensive degradation to that region, the subject's brain would be incapable of performing those functions."

"They'd stop being themselves, then?" Izzie asked.

"They'd stop being much of anything," Joyce answered. "Their personality would be gone, sure, but they'd be pretty much incapable of independent thought, or of moving of their own volition."

"But they *were* moving around, obviously." Patrick leaned forward, hands on the desk. "They were alive when Fuller killed them. Just like Malcolm Price was alive when he jumped out that window."

"Right," Joyce said, stretching out the word suggestively. "But my point is that from a medical standpoint, *they* couldn't have been the ones making those decisions. They no longer had the biological capacity to do so."

"What are you saying?" Izzie was afraid that she knew.

"What I'm suggesting," Joyce said, reluctantly, "is that maybe someone—or *something*—was making those decisions for them. It's almost as if the subjects were no longer behind the wheels in their own bodies, but that someone else was controlling the steering wheels."

"Like something was riding them." Izzie's voice was scarcely above a whisper.

"Sure, that's an apt analogy, I guess. Riding, driving, either way." Joyce looked back at the screen. "So my point is, maybe it's not crazy that Malcolm Price gets up and walks around after he is most obviously dead. If his nervous system and major muscle groups are still operational, then whoever or whatever is controlling them could still make the body move around. For a while at least."

"Like a puppet on a string." Patrick turned to Izzie. "Or your Haitian zombies."

Izzie could feel a ball of ice growing in the pit of her stomach. "Like they were being ridden . . ."

CHAPTER EIGHTEEN

"You realize all of this sounds totally crazy, right?" Izzie could still smell the mentholated rub in her nostrils, though she'd tried repeatedly to wash it off before they left the morgue.

"You don't have to remind me," Patrick said, sipping his coffee.

"Just because something *sounds* crazy doesn't mean it can't be true." Joyce looked up at the cloudy skies above. "Have you guys ever read much about quantum mechanics, string theory, higher dimensional space? Because *that* stuff sounds crazy, but it's just science."

Izzie turned to look past Patrick at Joyce on the far end of the bench. It had been her idea to get some air, and so the three of them had left the morgue and the Hall of Justice behind, picked up coffee in to-go cups from Holy Grounds—a coffee shop housed in a converted chapel, of course—and parked on a bench at the Founder's Square park. It was chilly out, but not uncomfortably so, and being out in the open under the wide, gray sky was somewhat comforting after being underground with the dead people for so long.

"It's funny you should mention that," Patrick said. "Izzie and I were just talking to a physics professor at Ross University about that kind of stuff yesterday."

Joyce raised an eyebrow, giving him a look of mock astonishment. "Why, Lieutenant Tevake, are you considering a career change? Going to chuck the law enforcement gig to go off and study the mysteries of the universe?"

Izzie chuckled, and Patrick glanced in her direction before answering.

"It's tempting." He smirked. "But then I wouldn't have an excuse to visit Miss Ghoul here in the morgue."

"That's *Doctor* Ghoul to you, buster." Joyce nudged him. "I didn't spend six years in evil medical school to be called 'Miss,' thank you very much."

"But seriously, you're a doctor," Izzie broke in. "You studied science. How can you justify thinking that some unknown agency is manipulating people's brains, and even controlling their bodies after death? That kind of supernatural stuff is just superstitious nonsense." Though her tone was somewhat argumentative, it was really herself that she was trying to convince.

"I think it's a question of Occam's Razor, isn't it," Joyce answered.

"Is that the one that goes, 'When you've eliminated the impossible, what remains, however improbable, must be true'?" Patrick asked.

"That's Sherlock Holmes, actually," Joyce said. "It's from a story written by Arthur Conan Doyle."

"Um, I'm pretty sure it was Spock who said that." Patrick scratched his chin. "I remember it from a Star Trek movie."

"Of course you do." Joyce shook her head, and turned back to Izzie. "But it's the same basic idea. Occam's Razor is the principle that the simplest solution is usually the right one. Or, to put it another way, you shouldn't make more assumptions than is absolutely necessary." She rolled her eyes towards Patrick as she took a sip of her coffee. "That's the basic tenet of detective work, isn't it? The simplest theory that fits the available facts is the right one?"

Patrick shrugged. "Usually. Ninety percent of the time, maybe. But lots of times new evidence comes along that blows the old theories out of the water."

"Sure," Joyce agreed. "And that happens in science, all the time. But even then, whatever new theory you come up with would be the simplest one to fit. The most elegant, you could say."

"Okay, I buy that." Patrick nodded.

"But *magic*?" Izzie pressed on. "How is *that* the simplest solution to *anything*?"

"I didn't say 'magic' exactly," Joyce replied. "But that's just a question of terminology really, right? What is magic except affecting change in the world around us? We don't think it's strange to turn on a television with a remote control, but that's because we have a basic understanding of infrared technology and that kind of stuff. If a primitive person saw you do that, they'd be convinced they were witnessing an act of sorcery."

"Cargo cults." Patrick lowered his cup.

Izzie and Joyce both looked in his direction, curious.

"That's how they got started," Patrick said. "You guys have heard about cargo cults, surely."

He glanced from one woman to the other, seeing blank stares.

"They cropped up all over the South Pacific during the Second World War," he explained. "There was even one on Kensington Island. The US military used the island as a staging ground for operations in the Pacific Theater, and the Te'Maroans watched as sailors talked into little boxes and then 'metal birds' come down out of the sky and unload boxes of food, metals, and supplies. Most of the islanders didn't think too much about it, but there was one guy who was convinced it was all magic, and that the senior officer on the site was some kind of supernatural being. And when the US Navy left after the end of the war and the planes stopped showing up, he cleared trees for 'landing strips,' built 'transmitters' out of bamboo and coconut shells, and tried to call 'Capten Kole' to bring cargo back to the people. He convinced a handful of others to help out in the cause, and by the time he died the Church of Capten Kole, Sky Navigator was still out there in the jungle, trying to call the metal birds to come back."

He shook his head.

"I went to school with a kid whose parents were devout members of the Church of Capten Kole. We all thought he was bonkers, but he was a true believer, man."

"I wouldn't be so quick to judge," Joyce said. "I think that's just human nature. It's just Clarke's Law. 'Any sufficiently advanced technology is indistinguishable from magic.' It's all a question of how advanced the technology is compared to your level of understanding."

"So you're saying that's what we're dealing with here?" Izzie was skeptical. "Some kind of technology?"

"Not necessarily," Joyce answered. "Just that there might be a rational explanation that we don't understand, and so we call it 'magic' or 'supernatural.' And primitive people aren't stupid, remember. Think about ancient astronomers, right? They didn't have the first clue about stellar formation or gravity on a galactic scale or anything like that, but they built incredibly sophisticated models that predicted the movements of the stars across the skies. They might have even believed they were seeing literal gods and monsters and demigods moving around up in the sky, but they still knew just where to look for any given constellation in the heavens at any given time of the year. Their explanations for what was happening might have been totally wrong, but their observations about what they were seeing were spot on."

Izzie thought about the protective sigils that Patrick's great-uncle had inscribed all over the southwestern corner of the Oceanview, and the various rituals that her grandmother used for protection against spiritual threats. Were they like the bamboo transmitters and coconut shell headphones that those islanders used out in the jungle? Except, maybe, sometimes they *worked*?

And were the tohunas of Kensington Island and the mambos of Louisiana—and who knows how many other shamans and priestesses and witch doctors throughout different cultures and times—were all of them like those ancient astronomers? Doing their best to describe something that was really happening, but limited by the terms and concepts they had at their disposal?

When Patrick glanced over in her direction, she could see by the expression on his face that he was wondering much the same thing.

"So what *are* we seeing, do you think?" Izzie asked the medical examiner, pointedly. "You've suggested that something is making up for the loss of brain tissue in these suspects, taking over the faculties that they biologically wouldn't be able to perform anymore. But is that what's causing those parts of their brains to go missing? Or is the causal relation going the other way, and something is taking advantage of a situation that was caused by other factors?"

Now it was Joyce's turn to shrug. "No idea. We still don't understand the pathology behind the vacuoles, or how it's being transmitted. The early subjects all were down in that mine shaft at one point or another, and might have been exposed to something there, but with Tyler Campbell and Malcolm Price . . . ? There's no indication that either of them ever went down there."

"Maybe we should approach this like profilers," Izzie offered. "Looking at what we know to be true, and then extrapolate from there. Forget any possible connections between Fuller's victims five years ago and the two dead men right now. What characteristics or qualities do Campbell and Price share? Maybe that's a better place to start, since they're right in front of us."

"Well, obviously," Joyce answered, "both of them have the vacuoles in their brains, though in Price's brain they're primarily concentrated in the frontal lobe, and in Campbell's they're more dispersed."

"And they both are involved in the Ink trade," Patrick added.

"Is there any reason to rule out the possibility that both men were *users* of Ink, as well?" Izzie asked. "Price at least exhibited the signature lesions on his skin. Could Campbell have taken the drug, too, instead of just selling it?"

"It's possible," Patrick answered.

"Since we don't have any way of testing for the presence of Ink in the body," Joyce said, "we can't prove that it's there. But absence of evidence is not evidence of absence, so yeah, it's definitely a possibility."

"So . . ." Izzie was feeling her way towards something. "Is it also possible that the Ink itself caused the vacuoles to form in their brains?"

"But Fuller's victims died before Ink was even . . ." Patrick began, but Izzie silence him with a quick motion of her hand.

"Forget about five years ago for the moment," she said. "I'm talking about right now. And do we know of any other thing that Campbell and Price shared in common other than the strong possibility that they took Ink?"

Patrick and Joyce exchanged a glance, then he turned back to Izzie, shaking his head. "Not yet, anyway."

"So wouldn't Occam's Razor say that the most likely reason that both of these men had holes in their heads was because they both took the drug?"

Patrick was silent, thinking it over.

"That would make the most sense, yeah," Joyce answered, after a brief moment's consideration. "And if I hadn't known anything about Fuller's victims from before, I'm sure that would have been my immediate conclusion when I scanned Campbell's brain the other day. It's the connection to the earlier subjects that complicates matters."

"Yeah," Patrick said, paradoxically shaking his head while saying so. "There's just no way. Ink didn't start showing up on the street until *way* after Fuller was dead. I can't see that there's any connection between his victims and these two."

"But maybe you're looking in the wrong place for the connection." Izzie scratched the scar on the back of her hand, absently.

"The only thing that Fuller's victims had in common was that they had all worked with the Undersight project down in that mine shaft," Patrick objected.

"Right," Izzie said. "So maybe the connection isn't between these two dead men now and the people that Fuller killed five years ago. Maybe . . ." She leaned forward, lowering her voice. "Maybe the connection is between the drug Ink itself and whatever the hell happened down in that mine shaft."

"But then . . ." Patrick pulled out his phone and gestured at the screen. "That could mean . . ."

Izzie knew that he was referencing the article about the Eschaton Center murders, which had mentioned the mines. "And maybe there are connections we hadn't even thought about before."

"I'm sorry, guys, you lost me," Joyce said, while Izzie and Patrick were sharing a significant glance.

"It's this article that Izzie sent me this morning," Patrick started to explain, turning to Joyce. But before he could continue his phone chimed that a text message had just arrived. He swiped the screen, reading quickly.

"What is it?" Izzie could see the concerned expression on his face.

"We've got to go," he said, getting to his feet. "Chavez says there's something at Fayed's apartment that he wants me to see."

Joyce was using her cane to lever herself up off the bench. "I need to get back, myself. The cadavers get lonely when I'm gone for too long."

Before turning to walk away, she looked over at Patrick and Izzie.

"I'm sure that I haven't heard the end of this discussion."

"I sincerely doubt it," Izzie answered.

"Yeah, we'll pick this back up as soon as we find the time," Patrick said, tossing his empty coffee cup into a nearby bin. "It feels like we're getting close to something."

"Close to *what*, though?" Joyce quirked an eyebrow.

"I'll let you know the second I figure it out, Dr. Ghoul," Patrick said with a grin.

She rolled her eyes at him and headed off.

"Come on, loverboy," Izzie said, nudging his shoulder. "Let's get moving."

Ten minutes later, as they drove west out of the Financial District towards the Kiev neighborhood, the comment was clearly still gnawing at him.

"'Loverboy'?" Patrick glanced at Izzie beside him in the passenger seat, his hands tightly gripping the steering wheel. "What was that crack about?"

"Seriously?" Izzie turned in her seat to look back at him. "You flirt with her *constantly*. Not that she minds, obviously."

A look of genuine bafflement settled onto his features. "I do not!"

"And again, *seriously*?" Izzie said. "Do you not hear yourself when you speak?"

"I joke around with her, so what? I do that with lots of people." He signaled a turn. "Janet, for instance. Same thing, and I *know* she's not interested."

"Yes, because (a) she's married, and (b) she's gay. But even then, it's different. With Janet, it's like you're joking around with one of the guys. But with Joyce . . . There's this different look in your eye, a different tone in your voice."

"No, there isn't." His eyes darted to Izzie, a sheepish expression on his face. "Is there?" He looked back to the road. "It doesn't matter, anyway. I have a rule that I don't date coworkers, and that includes anyone that I work with, cops or otherwise."

"Yeah, I've got that same rule." Izzie's tone was a little wistful.

"What was that?" They'd stopped at a red light, and Patrick turned in his seat, fixing her with a hard stare. "That air of . . . I don't know. Disappointment in your voice? Is there . . . ?"

"Light's green," Izzie interrupted, nodding at the road ahead.

Patrick turned to face ahead and pressed the accelerator. "Is there someone that you'd be interested in . . . you know . . . if you didn't have that rule?"

She looked out the window, and sighed. "I don't know. Maybe."

"Oh, god, is it *me*?"

Izzie's bark of laughter was the only response that Patrick needed to hear, it seemed, as he hunched his shoulders and glowered at the road. But she felt like his question could not pass without comment.

"Oh, Patrick. You poor thing. Adulting must be very difficult for you." She reached over and patted his shoulder, a consoling gesture. "You are a damned fine detective and a really good cop, but I think you might have a blind spot where this kind of thing is concerned."

CHAPTER NINETEEN

When Patrick backed the car into a parallel spot on Odessa Avenue, Izzie was sure that he must have gotten turned around somewhere. The address that he'd said they were going to was in the Kiev, in the northwest corner of Recondito. She'd spent a fair amount of time in the neighborhood five years before, since the task force had operated out of the 12th Precinct station house there. But the streets around them didn't look anything like she remembered.

"This can't be right," she said, as Patrick turned off the car and started to climb out.

"What?" He ducked down and looked at her through the open door, already standing on the pavement. "Come on, they're waiting."

He closed the door and walked around the car to the curb. Exasperated, Izzie unbuckled and got out.

"I said, this can't be right." She gestured at the characterless condos and apartment blocks around them. "I thought you said we were going to the Kiev."

"Yeah?" He put his hands on his hips. "And?"

Izzie turned in place, looking first one way down the street and then the other.

"Where are all the secondhand shops? The vintage record stores? The cute little houses with the pitched roofs, and the cafés, and the Russian tea room? That store that just sold model trains?" She gasped. "Where's the bakery that made that amazing pirozhki?!"

"Oh, that's right." Patrick shook his head, sighing. "I guess a lot *has* changed since you were last here."

"But . . ." Izzie did another turn. Aside from the feature-less apartment buildings, there was hardly anything of note on these streets, with the only business being a chain grocery store specializing in overpriced organic food. "What happened?"

The Kiev was a half-dozen or so square blocks that had been home to Russian immigrants starting in the early years of the twentieth century, and had retained a great deal of that flavor in the decades that followed. By the 1960s, it had become a kind of bohemian enclave, where artists and musicians took advantage of cheap rents and low costs of living to pursue their passions without worrying much about paying the next month's bill. And when Izzie first came to the city, all of that history was still in plain sight. The Slavic street names, the little old ladies in the tea room with their samovars, the old men in the bars with their vodkas, all spoke to the neighborhood's immigrant past, while the aging hippies, vintage clothing stores, and record shops were testament to it being a counter-culture oasis that had weathered the passage of years. But now, all of that seemed to have vanished.

"Come on." Patrick motioned her to follow as he headed across the street. "The short answer is, money happened. The buildings in the Kiev were never in the best shape, even when they were first built. Cheaply made, and cheaply maintained. That was one of the reasons it was always so inexpensive to live here. But as more and more people started moving to town, space was in greater and greater demand. It was just a matter of time before that hit the Kiev."

"Okay, gentrification, I get that." They had crossed the street, and were angling towards the entrance of one of the apartment blocks. "But why tear down all the buildings?"

"Like I said, the buildings were cheaply made. And all of those single-family homes with those big backyards . . . It wasn't the most efficient use of space, or so the developers argued." There was a uniformed officer waiting inside the glass door of the entry way, and he opened the locked door to let them in. Patrick nodded a thanks to the officer as they walked through, and then continued as he and Izzie approached the elevator. "And there was a fire, which took out the Russian tea room and a few other buildings. . . . Arson was ruled out, but the locals still cried foul. But that sped things along considerably. Then an equity firm bought up entire blocks, and started bulldozing. Within less than a couple of years . . ." He gestured around them as they stepped onto the elevator. "It's still the Kiev, technically, but pretty much in name only."

"That's such a shame," Izzie said as Patrick punched the button for the third floor. "The Oceanview didn't seem to have changed much, so I'm surprised the Kiev has."

Patrick scowled. "Well, I'm hoping that Oceanview is spared that kind of thing, but it might be overly optimistic to say it could never happen." He shook his head, and shrugged. "I'd hate to have to move."

"You know, I don't think you've ever said where it is that you live in town," Izzie said.

"Maybe," Patrick said, glancing over at her with a grin. "But I don't think you've ever asked."

The elevator doors slid open with a ding, and they stepped out to find a couple of uniformed officers standing near an open apartment door a few dozen feet down the hall. Izzie recognized one of them from the drug raid the day before.

"Lieutenant," one of them said with a nod towards Patrick as they approached. "You can go on in, sir. Chavez is expecting you."

Yellow barricade tape with "police line do not cross" printed on it crisscrossed the open doorway, and they had to duck their heads to crabwalk through.

"Tevake," the detective said, glancing up from where he bent over a laptop that lay open on a table on the far side of the room. "Anything interesting from the M.E.?"

"She thinks that you're a cutie," Patrick answered, "but other than that, not much."

"As if." Chavez snorted. "That chick has only got eyes for you, my man."

"What . . . ?" Patrick began to object, but the detective raised a hand to motion for silence. He was wearing blue nitrile gloves, so as not to contaminate the evidence.

"Here, come take a look at this," Chavez went on.

As Patrick crossed the room to join him, Izzie looked around. It was definitely the apartment of a bachelor, and one who was new in town, at that. A few bits of flat-pack furniture inexpertly assembled, a laundry bin filled with several weeks' worth of dirty clothes, a stack of junk mail and take-out menus on the counter in the kitchenette. There were a few partially-unpacked moving boxes lining the wall beneath the bay window, and on the floor beside them a set of dumbells that were gathering dust.

The walls were bare and unadorned, and there were only a handful of framed photos in a small grouping atop the bureau in the single bedroom. The same young man was featured in all of them, sometimes alone, sometimes with small groups of friends, doing the sorts of things that young single people often wanted photos of themselves doing—scuba diving, skiing, rock climbing, singing karaoke. But glancing around the room, Izzie had the strong suspicion that those smiling moments in the sun were the exception, rather than the rule, and that Ibrahim Fayed had spent far more time on his own in this drab little apartment than he did out having adventures with friends. But then, who wanted framed photos of themselves eating dinner alone in their kitchenettes, or sitting on their couches watching reruns in the small hours of the night?

Izzie knew she was hardly one to judge. If a profiler were given the keys to her apartment while she was away, would the assessment of her social life have been any less bleak?

"Excuse me." A CSI photographer stood behind her in the door to the bedroom, an impatient look on her face. "I need to finish up in here."

Mouthing an apology, Izzie slipped past the photographer and back into the small living area of the apartment, where Patrick was pulling on a pair of blue nitrile gloves as he sat down in a chair at the kitchenette table. Chavez was standing beside him, leaning over and tapping the keys of the laptop keyboard.

"Guy left his laptop plugged in and turned on when he left," Chavez was saying, "which was thoughtful of him."

"I'll be sure to thank him when we get back to the station." Patrick laced his fingers together to pull the gloves into place. "So what am I looking at here?"

"Well, it seems that our boy Ibrahim was showing up for work a little more recently than the HR department at Parasol thinks. Or more recently than they lead us to believe, anyway." He tabbed over to an open browser window, displaying a web-based email inbox. "This is logged in to his work account. There are emails in his Sent items from as recently as four days ago, with replies from other members of his team."

"What about?" Izzie asked, leaning over Patrick's other shoulder to look.

Chavez shrugged. "It's all in tech speak, so it's Greek to me. But it seems to be about some kind of new app that they've got in development. Fayed is one of the team leads, or was up until just a few days ago, anyway." He pointed to a particular threaded discussion in the inbox. "Some of the other team members reference our guy being at a meeting in the office last week, but Parasol HR says he stopped showing up to work almost a month ago."

"A mix up in payroll, perhaps?" Patrick suggested. "Or maybe he, I don't know, forgot to clock in or something?"

"Maybe he's got a twin brother, and they take turns showing up to work, *Parent Trap*–style." Izzie thought it was funny, but from the looks the two detectives shot her way, neither of them agreed.

"Okay, so that's a little weird," Patrick said. "But I'm not sure it merited dragging me all the way across town to see it. You could have just sent me a text."

"Right," Chavez answered. "But that's not what I wanted you to see." He tapped a few more keys and brought up another browser window. "This is his personal email account," he explained. "Looks like a lot of the same names from his team at work, but using their personal accounts instead of their work email addresses. And then there's this thread." He pointed to one thread of emails.

Patrick clicked the link to enlarge the thread.

"Third response down, sent by our guy four days ago."

Izzie leaned in as Patrick read aloud. "*'TC was supposed to find us a new host, but didn't make the meeting. Got banged up, I think. Marissa and I are going to meet with MP to arrange a new supply source in a few days.'*"

"Marissa is Marissa Keizer, obviously," Chavez said. "The other one we arrested in Price's place yesterday."

"And 'MP' could be Malcolm Price, then?" Patrick turned to look at the detective.

"That's our guess," Chavez answered. "And TC . . ."

"Tyler Campbell?" Patrick nodded. "But what does he mean, 'banged up'? Like, in a car accident or something? Or beat up?"

"He's originally from the UK, right?" Izzie asked. "Over there it means 'arrested.'"

Patrick turned back to the laptop screen, and then nodded. "That checks out. This was sent the night that we brought Campbell in for questioning."

"But 'host'?" Izzie straightened up, rubbing the back of her neck. "Like, hosting a party?"

"Maybe." Chavez shrugged. "Or maybe Campbell was running some kind of Ink lab, and when he was arrested they needed to find a new place to operate out of, so Price's rental fit the bill. A different kind of party."

"No, that doesn't work," Patrick said, shaking his head. "Price had been in that place for months, doing whatever it was he was doing." He was unable to suppress a shiver. "And those bodies in the basement . . ."

"Anyway, it's pretty clear that this discussion is about Ink, one way or another. And we've got at least five Parasol employees on the string, using their personal accounts."

"Again, still not seeing why I had to be here to see this in person." Patrick leaned back in the chair, crossing his arms over his chest.

"Patience, grasshopper, patience," Chavez chided. "The tech guys from CSI did a first level pass on the laptop. It was open and logged in when we got here, like I said, but it's got some pretty heavy duty encryption on it. And even though he was logged in to all sorts of apps, too, they say the passwords for them aren't stored on the system, and we don't know what they are. So while we can get anything that we want off of the laptop now, unless we can convince Fayed to give up the passwords, as soon as we shut it down . . ."

"You lose access to the apps." Patrick nodded. "Okay, I get it. They could strip the hard drive and get to any data that's stored locally, but we'd lose access to his online stuff. So what is it that we want to know?"

"Well, these are the personal email addresses of his teammates at Parasol who, it seems, are also involved in the Ink trade one way or another, right?"

Patrick and Izzie were silent for a moment, until it was clear that Chavez was waiting for some kind of response. "Right," Patrick said while Izzie nodded.

"And we've got access to his list of personal contacts."
Chavez pointed at the screen. "And Fayed was helpful
enough to leave *this* handy dandy little beauty running in the
background."

He toggled the windows, and brought up an application
that was displaying a map of the city.

"It's one of those 'find my friends' apps," Chavez explained.

Izzie and Patrick exchanged a glance. They'd made extensive use of just such an application five years before, to coordi-
nate their movements in their search for Nicholas Fuller's last
victim, Francis Zhao.

"And those right there?" Chavez indicated a cluster of
dots in the middle of the screen, concentrated in a tight bunch
near the intersection of Gold Street and Northside Boulevard.
"Those are Fayed's friends."

"That's the Pinnacle Tower," Patrick said, studying the
map.

"Which means they're all working at the Parasol offices at
the moment, busy little beavers. But later . . ." Chavez smiled.

"We can track their movements." Patrick's eyes narrowed,
hungrily.

"Bingo." Chavez nodded. "They probably know by now
that Fayed and Keizer got 'banged up,' but chances are they
wouldn't think that he'd be so sloppy as to leave his laptop up
and running when he went out."

"Not exactly a seasoned criminal, this one," Izzie said,
looking around the room.

"Hardly," Chavez agreed. "But if the other people on this
mail string are involved with Ink, there's every reason to
believe that they'll be picking up where Fayed and Keizer left
off, *whatever* it was they were up to. Which could include

meeting with suppliers, making drops, who knows what else."

"So what's the plan?" Patrick pushed back from the table. "Are we going to sit around in this crappy apartment watching this screen until they do something interesting?"

"No, Tevake, because that would be stupid." Chavez shook his head, chuckling. "Our own IT guys are bringing over an uninterruptable power supply to keep the laptop charged, and then they're going to move it over to the 10th station house, taking great pains not to close the lid on the way. And they've got this idea about pointing a web camera at the screen and then streaming a live feed that we can all log in to on our phones, so we can see what's going on with the map from wherever we are."

"That's smart," Izzie said.

"Yeah," Chavez said with a sigh. "Wish I could take credit for that one, but that was totally their idea."

"Well, at least we know it wasn't Harrison's." Patrick stood up. "The only thing that he'd ever think to point at a laptop screen is his gun."

"Come on, man, have a heart." Chavez had a wounded look on his face. "Don't make me stick up for the guy. Bad enough I've got to partner with him on this deal."

Izzie leaned down to look at the city map, and the tight cluster of dots where the Pinnacle Tower stood. "Do you have IDs on these friends of his?" She glanced over her shoulder at Chavez. "Might be worth checking out their records, see if there's any prior convictions."

"We've pulled the names and addresses from his contact list," he answered, "and I've got Harrison seeing what he can find out back at the station house."

"I don't know, you guys." Patrick scratched his chin. "Something about this still doesn't add up. I can see one or two employees at a company getting mixed up in a drug business on the side, but this many? We're looking at something like a half-dozen people, right?"

"At least," Chavez said, shoving his hands in his pockets. "We'll have to keep mining through the email logs, though. There might be more employees involved than we know."

"What are you suggesting, Patrick?" Izzie asked. "You think this is some kind of company sanctioned thing?"

"That'd be a hell of a team-building exercise, right?" Patrick shook his head. "But no, it seems pretty unlikely that Parasol would be involved directly. But maybe there's some rot in the ranks? A manager or high-level employee who's mixed up in some dirty deals, and recruiting runners and muscle from the cubicle farm? Some type of 'I'm a little worried about your quarterly projections, Tom, but if you take this unmarked parcel to this address for me I'll give you a glowing review' kind of thing?"

Izzie had leaned over and was scanning the email thread displayed on the screen.

"It's possible, I suppose, but that's not how these messages sound to me," she said, and pulled on one of the blue nitrile gloves, so as not to leave any prints on the keyboard.

"What do you mean?" Patrick asked.

"Even though they're discussing drug deals on their personal email accounts . . ." Izzie said, hitting the arrow key to page down through the messages. She paused, glancing over at Patrick and Chavez, and added, "Assuming we're reading the situation right, that is." She turned back to the laptop, "Well, these sound more like interoffice memos and project briefings than the kind of chatter you'd get between dealers. I mean, I get that these folks are software engineers and coders and such, but . . . here, listen to this one."

Izzie leaned forward and read aloud.

"*Susan, I know we're approaching the launch date, but I wanted to touch base with you about that latest batch of injectors. Todd tells me that the 7-gauge needles seemed to be addressing the viscosity issues, but with an inner diameter of almost 4 millimeters I wonder if we won't be seeing some phasing issues with the material. Can we try bumping down to 11-gauge needles, instead? That's a difference of a millimeter and a half in the inner diameter, which might still be big enough that the viscosity won't be an issue, but small enough that we won't have to worry about ana/kata leakage.*"

She straightened up, exasperated.

"I mean, seriously, what does that even mean?" she said, throwing her hands up in the air.

Chavez shook his head, slowly. "If I said I knew, I'd be lying."

"Sounds like they're talking about the auto-injectors, though," Patrick said. "Like the ones we found in Price's kitchen. Ink users inject the stuff into themselves with those, like people in anaphylactic shock injecting themselves with an EpiPen." He shrugged. "Or so we think. We've never actually found one with the stuff still in it, just the empties that are left over."

Izzie looked from Patrick back to the laptop. "But if *that's* what they're talking about, this isn't just a few bored tech guys selling drugs on the side to make a little extra money. This is *product development* level stuff." She turned, taking in the modest apartment, the bachelor malaise. "Are these the guys that put Ink on the streets in the *first* place?"

"No chance." Patrick shook his head. "This Fayed character didn't come to town until after I already started working the Ink case. Besides, his email was about dealing with existing problems, so if they were talking about Ink injectors, there were already some in circulation."

Izzie chewed her lower lip, deep in thought.

"He said, 'approaching the launch date,'" Chavez observed. "That sounds like he's talking about a new retail product about to hit the market, not a drug that's already on the street."

"Hey!" Izzie's eyebrows went up. "These are tech guys, right? They release new software applications, sure, but they also release patches and stuff to fix bugs in versions of software that are already out in the world. That's their basic business model. So maybe they're talking about an upgrade?"

"Ink 2.0?" Patrick said, skeptically.

"It makes a certain amount of sense, actually." Chavez nodded slowly. He turned to face Patrick. "She's right, Tevake, that's their business model. That's how they think about these things. Would stand to reason that they'd approach Ink the same way that they do the apps they make and maintain for a living."

Patrick had his hand on his chin, his brow deeply furrowed in thought. "So . . . what? Are we back to this idea that somehow the biggest employer in Recondito, this blue-chip stock technology company, is secretly manufacturing illicit drugs and selling them on the city streets? Because that would be crazy, you guys."

"No, obviously not," Chavez answered. "Why would they need to? They make a million bucks an hour selling games and junk for mobile phones."

"Is that true?" Izzie's eyes widened. "A million dollars an hour?"

"How should I know how much they make?" Chavez rolled his eyes. "They make a *lot*, I know that much, at least. But my point is, sure, there's a lot of money to be made in selling drugs, but nowhere *near* the kind of money that outfit is already making. And completely *legally*, I might add." He took a few steps away, waving his hand dismissively. "No, it might be some manager there or something who's mixed up in this, just like you suggested, Patrick. But the company itself? Parasol? No way."

"Detective Chavez?" a voice said from the direction of the front door.

They turned and saw two civilians with Recondito Police Department IDs on lanyards around their necks, carrying a box of computer equipment. No one had to inform Izzie that they were IT guys.

"Is this the laptop, sir?" one of the IT guys asked, as he and his partner entered the apartment.

"This is it," Chavez answered, stepping to one side and indicating the laptop with a sweep of his arm, like a footman welcoming a princess into a ballroom. "It's all yours."

He started towards the door to speak with the uniforms out in the hallway.

"Shall we get out of here, too?" Patrick said, coming over to stand beside Izzie.

"Yeah," Izzie said a little distractedly, her eyes still on the laptop's screen. "I guess we should."

CHAPTER TWENTY

It was late afternoon by the time they got back to Patrick's car, the last light of day fading in the west. Izzie was still lost in thought as she closed the car door and buckled up, her gaze somewhere in the middle distance.

"Where to?" Patrick asked as he turned the key in the ignition.

Izzie was silent, still staring into space.

"Hello? Anyone home?" He reached over and tapped her on the shoulder.

"Hm?" Izzie blinked a few times, and turned to look in his direction. "Oh, sorry. I'm just trying to . . ." She shook her head, sighing. "It feels like there's an idea trying to come together in my head, and it's just hovering right out of reach, you know what I mean?"

"That's totally understandable, under the circumstances." He glanced at the time displayed on the dashboard clock, then back to her. "I was thinking about heading back to the station house, and looking over the evidence again."

She nodded. "Yeah, that sounds good. I want to take another crack at Fuller's notes. I keep thinking there's something that we're missing."

"Maybe we'll get lucky and something will click this time." Patrick put the car in gear and then nudged the car into the slow-moving rush hour traffic. "God knows we could use an even break."

The community room in the 10th Precinct station house was just as they had left it the day before. After Patrick unlocked the door and ditched his suit coat on a chair, he went to the break room to fetch them a couple of bottles of water, leaving Izzie to survey the landscape of evidence on her own.

Something very strange was happening in the city of Recondito, that much Izzie knew for certain. And strange things had happened there before, it seemed. Were they connected? Or was it just one prolonged episode of strangeness that had never really ended, but simply appeared to go away? She didn't know, but she could not shake the growing suspicion that the key to the mystery lay somewhere in the piles of documents and books and furiously scribbled notes in front of her.

Nicholas Fuller had been a murderous madman with a substance abuse problem, but he was no idiot. He was highly educated and widely read, not just in the scientific disciplines that had been his profession, but in history, religion, philosophy, and more. And it seemed increasingly clear that Fuller had brushed up against the strangeness that had wormed its way into the heart of the city. Like the ancient astronomers that Joyce had talked about, and the cargo cultists that Patrick had mentioned, Fuller had tried to make sense of the strangeness with the terms and the concepts that he had at his disposal.

Of course, by the end Fuller had convinced himself that the only logical course of action to take in response to the strangeness was to murder a dozen of his former colleagues and friends, so his judgement had clearly deteriorated at some point along the way. But the fact remained that investigating what he *thought* was going on might provide necessary clues that would help Izzie and Patrick make sense of whatever it was that they were feeling around the edges of.

The problem lay in deciphering what it was Fuller was attempting to say. The things he had jotted in the margins of books or scribbled in notepads were meant for his own eyes only, it seemed, and even when they weren't written in some kind of code, his notes were full of references that Fuller didn't bother to explain or connections that he failed to spell out in detail. He had known what he was saying, but it was likely that anyone else might find it completely baffling. It was like someone who had just learned to read the English language but who knew nothing about Dublin or the life of James Joyce trying to decipher *Finnegan's Wake*. It was often possible to glean the meaning of individual words and sentences, but the deeper significance of the whole remained completely hidden.

The trick was to start with what they *could* understand, and then hope that they could fill in the gaps.

There was a dry-erase board mounted to the wall of the community room next to the doorway, and by the time Patrick returned with the bottled water, Izzie had already begun to cover it in tightly grouped clusters of words.

"Going old-school, huh?" he said, handing her a bottle of water before opening his own. He slumped down on the nearest chair, looking exhausted, and started to roll up his shirt sleeves to the elbow.

"There's no school like the old-school," Izzie answered, popping the cap back on the dry erase marker. Then she twisted the top off the bottle and took a sip, looking over what she'd written so far. "Okay, what I am missing?"

She had divided the board into two general sections, with "INK" underlined at the top on the left side, and "FULLER" underlined on the other. On the left side she had written the names of the two dead men—"Tyler Campbell" and "Malcolm Price"—and the two suspects who were still in holding cells, "Ibrahim Fayed" and "Marissa Keiser," with small notations under each of them. On the right, she had written "Undersight" with a list of the names of Fuller's twelve victims, "Guildhall/ Recondito Mining Guild," and "Eschaton Center for Emanant Truth," with "mine shaft" in the middle with radiating arrows pointing from it to all three.

"Keizer is spelled with a 'z,'" Patrick pointed out.

Izzie rolled her eyes as she smudged out the 's' and popped the cap off the marker to replace it with the correct letter.

"Anything *significant* that I'm missing?" she asked again.

"Parasol?" Patrick suggested. "There's some connection there, whatever it is."

Izzie nodded, popping the cap off the marker and writing the company name on the left, with solid lines connecting it to confirmed employees Fayed and Keizer, and an arrow with a question mark pointed at Price, who may or may not have worked there at some point.

She connected Price to Keizer and Fayed, noting the address of Price's rental house. Then the marker's tip hovered over Campbell's name for a moment before she put in a dotted line connecting Fayed to him, with "RC?" noted by the dead man's name.

Then she stepped back and turned to the right side of the board. "How about over here? What aspects of Fuller's case am I leaving out?"

She paused, considering.

"Well, I guess I should include Fuller himself," she said, leaning forward and writing his name in the center, "since it all connects to him, obviously."

She thought for a moment.

"And there's that drug that *he* was taking," Izzie went on, and wrote "DMT?" next to Fuller's name.

"What about the old guy that owned the lighthouse?" Patrick said after a moment. "Aguilar?"

"Right." Izzie snapped her fingers. "Ricardo Aguilar. No, *Roberto* Aguilar, Ricardo is the grandson." As she wrote his name on the board and connected it with a line to Fuller's, she added, "Which reminds me, Kono said that Ricardo Aguilar will be back at the university tomorrow. We should check in with him, see if he has any insight to share about his grandfather, specifically what the old guy and Fuller might have been up to."

"Sounds good," Patrick answered. "I'll call in the morning and set up an appointment."

Next to "Eschaton Center for Emanant Truth" she wrote "Jeremiah Standfast Parrish," the organization's founder.

"I'm pretty sure you misspelled 'eminent' there." Patrick pointed at the board.

Izzie turned to look, scrutinizing. "Did I?"

She turned to the table, scanning for the copy of Parrish's self-help book. After a moment she found it, and pulled it from the stack. "No, that's how he spelled it. See?"

She held the book up for Patrick to see the title, *In Search of Emanant Truth.*

"Well, then *that* kook misspelled it," Patrick said, arms crossed.

"Mmm." Izzie opened the book and flipped through a few pages. "No, he spelled it right. But it's not the word you think. He means *emanant* as in emanating or coming from a source, not *eminent* as in famous. Here, listen. *'And it is by following these precepts that the diligent practitioner will come to discover that truth lies not within ourselves but without, and if we surrender our own sullied memories and fears, then wisdom will flow into us from a direction orthogonal to the length and width and breadth which confine our physical forms, emanating to ana from kata out of the higher realms beyond.'*"

"Jesus," Patrick said, rolling his eyes, "that guy sounds crazier than a sack full of cats. Maybe if people had—"

"Hang on." Izzie held up one finger to request a moment's silence, and then closely scanned the page again. "*Emanating to ana from kata,*" she read aloud, then looked back to Patrick. "Wasn't there something about 'ana/kata' in that email of Fayed's that I read?"

Patrick sat up straight, feet on the floor. "I'll be damned, I think there was."

Izzie flipped to the back of the book, searching for an index, but there wasn't one, just a meandering author's note and then an advertisement for the recently-founded Eschaton Center with a post office box address to send off for additional information. Somehow Izzie doubted that anyone was still answering reader mail.

"But what the hell does it mean?" Patrick said.

"I'm not sure," Izzie answered, shaking her head. She turned back to the page from which she'd just been reading aloud. Fuller had written a note in the margin, *"cf. C.H. Hinton"* and just below that had added *"Unlearner = loss of memory and/or personality?"*

As she closed the book and put it back on the table, Patrick stood up and walked to the dry erase board. "But whatever it means, it's a possible connection between that"—he pointed to the left side of the board, with its cobweb of Ink dealers and software engineers—"and that," and pointed to the right side of the board, with the various players in Fuller's manic writings. "So . . ."

He picked up another dry erase marker and wrote "ana/kata" in the middle of the board, then stepped back.

"That's something, at least," he added with a shrug.

"There's the brain stuff, too," she answered. "The vacuoles that Campbell and Price and all of Fuller's victims had. And I guess the three dead bodies in Price's basement, too."

She stepped past Patrick, wrote "vacuoles" below "ana/kata," and then added black dots beside the names of each of the people who were known to have exhibited the condition, and added "3 John/Jane Does" beside Malcolm Price, with a cluster of three black dots beside it.

She glanced from the list of the Reaper's victims to Parrish's self-help book. "Hey, Fuller mentioned the loss of personality and memory. Those are both things that Joyce said could result from damage to the frontal lobe, and his victims all had those holes in their brains, so possibly he was talking about behavior of theirs that he'd observed." She turned to Patrick. "But aren't those also side effects of taking Ink?"

He nodded slowly, his head gradually bobbing more rapidly as a look of discovery bloomed on his face. "Yeah, they absolutely are."

"So there's another connection," Izzie said, writing "personality/memory loss" in the middle of the board below "vacuoles."

Patrick had his hand on his chin, deep in thought. "Don't forget this." He stepped to the left and wrote "No Ink in Little Kovoko" and then "Tohuna symbols of protection?" directly below it.

Then he straightened up, and glanced at the ceiling while searching his memories.

"Hey," he finally said, "when we were retracing the movements of the Reaper's victims five years ago, do you remember if any of them were ever reported to be in the southwest corner of the Oceanview at any point?"

Izzie shook her head. "I don't remember for sure one way or the other, but I don't think so, no." She thought for a minute, then added, "We'd have to check the case files to know for certain, though."

"Just a thought." Patrick scratched his chin. "I mean, like Joyce said, absence of evidence isn't evidence of absence, but it's worth considering."

"I see where you're going with that, though," Izzie said. "We're already seeing all of these points of congruence between the Ink stuff and the things that Fuller raved about, so that's a reasonable assumption to make. We'll flag it for follow-up."

"When we were at Founder's Park with Joyce earlier, you said that you thought there might be a connection between Ink and the Undersight mine shaft itself." He had walked over to the right side of the board and was looking closely at the web of associations surrounding "mine shaft."

"Or whatever happened down there, anyway," Izzie corrected.

"So?" He looked from the board over to her, raising an eyebrow. "What *do* you think happened down there? Did they find something? And if so, is it still down there?"

Izzie chewed her lower lip, then glanced back at the table. She walked over to where the surveys and blueprints were spread, and found the map that Fuller had marked with spirals and jagged shapes and other symbols. She put her finger on the complex geometric figure of angles and jagged lines that marked the location of the Undersight mine. "Is there any way to go down there and find out?"

Patrick was taking a long swig of his water, and wiped his mouth with the back of his hand before answering. "Isn't it still owned by the University?"

Izzie shrugged. "I guess?"

"Maybe Ricardo Aguilar could help us out?" Patrick bobbed his head from side to side while considering the options. "During the Undersight project only team members were allowed to go down there, but Kono said that the whole operation was shut down after Fuller's role in the Reaper killings became public knowledge."

"Could be they still have it under lock and key," Izzie said, nodding, "but maybe we could get someone to unlock it for us?"

"We could always get a warrant if we needed to."

She gave him a sidelong glance. "And what would you tell the judge, exactly? I thought you were trying to avoid a psych eval. You can't very well walk in front of a judge and say, 'Hey,

I think the drug case I'm investigating is tied to some weird, possibly supernatural strangeness buried a few miles underground, can you help me go check it out?' They'd put you under medical supervision before you could blink."

"Okay, okay. Good point." He sighed. "Well, we'll just have to hope that Aguilar can help us, after all. He is still the department head, right?"

"So far as I know, yeah." Izzie rested both hands on the table, looking past the mountains of Fuller's madness at the constellations of names and phrases written on the dry erase board. "Damn, it feels like we're getting close to something, but still missing a few key pieces of the puzzle. Like we can see the edges of it, the corners are filled in, but the bigger picture . . ."

She trailed off, shaking her head wearily.

"Like the idea is hanging just out of reach?" Patrick suggested.

She slumped down into a chair, her head falling back, eyes on the ceiling. "I'll tell you one thing I do know for sure, and it's that I'm *exhausted*."

"Well, you *did* say you had a late night, as I recall." He gave her a sly look. "Just what kind of trouble did you get into after I dropped you off, anyway?"

Izzie sat up, shaking her head. "Nope, nope, you didn't pay to see those cards." She rubbed the inner corners of her eyes with her fingertips, stifling a yawn. "But I really am beat, though. What time is it?"

Patrick checked his phone. "A bit after eight thirty."

"Which is almost midnight, so far as my body's internal clock is concerned. I'm still running on east coast time, I think. Maybe we should call it a day and pick this up again in the morning?"

"I like this plan," Patrick answered, rolling down his shirt sleeves. "Want a lift back to your hotel?"

Izzie managed to push herself up onto her feet with a mild groan. "I hate that you have to keep chauffeuring me around like that. I can just call a cab or . . ."

"No, honestly, it's no trouble." He was putting back on his suit coat. "It's not far out of my way home."

"And where *is* home for you, anyway?" Izzie followed him out the door. "You still haven't told me what part of town you live in."

"Well," he said with a grin as he locked the door shut behind them, "I guess you didn't pay to see those cards, either."

They were driving north on Mission when Izzie yawned so big that it felt like her jaw had practically dislocated.

"You hungry?" Patrick asked without preamble, as they approached the intersection with Prospect Avenue. "We could stop somewhere to get a bite if you want, or . . ."

Izzie held up a hand to silence him. "Please. *Please.* I'm still full from *lunch*, Patrick. I won't need to eat for another week, I'm guessing."

He grinned. "Suit yourself. I'll hit the food carts on the way home, because I *am* hungry."

"Of course you are." She turned and looked out at the buildings as they passed by. "Hey," she said as she glanced back in his direction, "you're not worried about leaving all of that crazy stuff written on the board in that meeting room, are you? What if Chavez or Harrison or somebody wanders in there and sees what we're working on? Isn't that likely to spark questions that you don't really want to answer?"

"Nah, I'm not worried." He leaned to one side and flicked his finger against the ring hanging from the ignition key, setting the other keys on it to jingling and dancing. "This is the only key that's available to check out, so only the captain or the housekeeping staff could get in. And I know the captain won't, because he hates that room—too many meetings with disgruntled community members, too many bad associations— and the housekeeping staff has been told not to clean it while there's evidence in there, and it's not like they're bucking to do any more work than they absolutely have to do, anyway."

Izzie nodded, mostly satisfied. She was still a little concerned about someone stumbling onto what they were *really* working on, but too tired at the moment to argue the point any further.

Patrick turned off Prospect Avenue and onto Hauser, and Izzie's hotel loomed into view just ahead.

"Want to stop in at the Resident Agency again tonight?" he asked, as he pulled towards the curb.

Izzie wondered whether Daphne would still be at work this late, and felt a little thrill at the thought of spending time with her again. But no, there were complications she wanted to avoid, and personal rules to follow.

"No thanks." She shook her head. "I think I'm going to go straight to bed, and hopefully get synced up with west coast time in the morning."

Patrick pulled a U-turn so that he could drop her off on the west side of the street, and brought the car to a stop right in front of the hotel. "You up for breakfast in the morning, maybe?"

Izzie laughed as she opened the door and swung her legs out onto the pavement. "Maybe. I guess. We'll see?"

"It's the most important meal of the day, Izzie."

"Patrick," she was on the curb, and leaned down to look back through the open door, "I'm reasonably sure that you think *every* meal is the most important meal of *every* day."

He smirked. "Could be. Doesn't mean I'm wrong, though."

"Good night, Lieutenant Tevake." She shut the door.

"Good night, Agent Lefevre," he answered with a grin, and then drove away into the night.

Izzie trudged up the pavement to the front door, noted again the red brick façade, and hoped that it would be sufficient protection against bad spirits for her to sleep well.

CHAPTER TWENTY-ONE

Izzie was having a drink in a bar with Daphne, talking about their past relationships, when someone tapped her on the shoulder. It was Trent, the cartoonist from *Behind the Lines*, who was there with his neighbor and long-time rival, Miles. Trent told her that he had something to show her, so Izzie took Daphne's hand and they followed the two cartoonists out of the bar. But as soon as they got outside a man covered in black lesions drove by in a convertible, shouting obscenities at them, and Daphne let go of Izzie's hand and took off running after it, shouting blistering obscenities back at the driver. Izzie almost followed, but Trent grabbed her elbow, and told her not to worry, that Daphne had personal rules that would protect her.

There was an elevator in the middle of the street, and when they got on, Trent pushed the button marked "ALL THE WAY DOWN." As the elevator descended it made rattling sounds like a mine cart rolling over the rails, and the lights grew increasingly dim. Izzie was worried that they wouldn't get there in time, but when she turned Patrick was beside her, and told her it was going to be okay, that he'd called ahead. The darkness was expecting them.

When the elevator doors opened, Izzie got turned around, and then discovered that she was alone, and decided that Patrick and Trent must have gotten off at some other floor along the way.

As she stepped out into the inky blackness, she wished that she still smoked cigarettes, so that maybe she'd have a lighter or a book of matches on her that could shed a little light. Then she remembered that she still had the lighthouse in her pocket from five years before. When she pulled it out, the illumination it cast was feeble and week, though underneath she could hear the rumblings of discordant speed metal, which somehow gave her a sense of comfort. Then she realized that what she was hearing was a speed metal cover of "Dancing Queen," and she wondered if Joyce was in her office.

Then the Grim Reaper came out of the darkness towards her, black cloak draped over his silvery skeleton, with the light from Izzie's lighthouse gleaming on the silver scythe he carried in one skeletal hand.

Izzie wanted to ask the Grim Reaper a question, but though her mouth was moving, she couldn't seem to make any sound.

The Reaper seemed to understand what she meant to say, anyway, and nodded his silver skull once in consent. He turned and pointed into the darkness with the silver scythe.

Then, as Izzie started to walk past him, the Reaper reached out and took the lighthouse from her hands. She would have to continue without it, she understood. Or she wouldn't find what she was looking for.

She kept walking into the inky blackness, a darkness so complete that she could not see her own hands before her. She continued to walk until she could no longer hear "Dancing Queen," until the darkness was so complete that it swallowed up even the sounds of her own footsteps. She wondered if the sound was leaking into other spaces.

Izzie was still only mildly curious when she felt the sharp touch of something on the base of her skull, like a hornet's sting. She didn't raise her hands to swat it away, but kept her arms at her sides, hoping that it would leave her alone. Then she realized that she was no longer alone inside her mind, and that the thoughts that she was thinking were not her own. And then with sick certainty she knew that it was too late. . . .

When she woke suddenly in the heavy-curtained darkness, the room drenched by the noise-cancelling susurration of the white noise app on her phone, Izzie was afraid that she was still trapped down in the dark far below ground. In the puzzling logic between slumber and wakefulness, she had trouble sorting out which was true memory and which she had merely dreamt.

Then the noise that had woken her chimed again.

It was the sound of an incoming text on her phone, the screen pulsing a slight glow as it beeped the notification a second time.

As Izzie fumbled for the phone, she glanced at the clock, and saw that it was almost 9:00 a.m. She'd slept for nearly twelve hours, but felt like she'd just nodded off.

"Damn it, Patrick," she muttered when she saw the preview of the text message on the lock screen: "YOU UP FOR

COFFEE? OR BREAKFAST, EVEN?" Then she saw that it wasn't Patrick who had sent it.

Her pulse quickened, and for a brief instant her memories of the previous night mixed with the half-remembered events of the dream. Had she gone out for drinks last night? Had they held hands . . . ?

Izzie shook her head. No, that had just been in the dream. She hadn't seen Daphne since the previous morning. But when Izzie had left the Resident Agency for the first time the day before that, she had given Daphne her phone number, telling her to text or call if there was ever a need to get in touch.

Which Daphne clearly thought the breakfast invitation merited.

Izzie began to type out a response with her thumbs, a terse but not impolite note declining the invite but thanking her anyway. But as her fingertip hung suspended over the Send button, she began to have second thoughts. She deleted the whole message, started fresh, and thumbed out an enthusiastic acceptance, complete with multiple exclamation marks. But again, before hitting Send she paused. Neither option seemed the right one. She ran the cursor back to the beginning once more, and them typed out a more modulated response.

"JUST GOT UP. NEED TO JUMP IN THE SHOWER. MEET ME OUTSIDE IN 30?"

Izzie bit her lip, reading over it four times before committing. Then she hit Send, and started counting seconds.

Almost immediately the message status went from Delivered to Read, and a balloon appeared with a pulsing ellipsis showing that the person on the other end was composing a response. It winked on and off for a moment before a reply came through.

"SURE"

No punctuation or pleasantry, no comment or clarification, just the one word by itself, stark and alone.

Izzie stared at the screen for a moment. Was Daphne mad at her? Had Izzie's reply given some offense?

Now Izzie was getting offended. She sat up in the bed and slammed the phone down on the side table. What was *her* problem, anyway? "Sure"?

She glanced at the screen again. Izzie had replied with a question, and Daphne had replied with "sure." Daphne was agreeing. There was no tone to the text, and Izzie's first response had been to take offense.

"Would it have killed her to put an exclamation mark?" she muttered as she hauled herself up out of the bed and headed for the shower. It was a good thing she had a rule about not getting involved on the job. She was already a little too invested in this one as it was.

By the time she had showered, dressed, done her personal sign of the cross and taken the elevator down to the street level, Izzie was starting to feel anxious again. She cursed herself inwardly as she walked across the hotel lobby, for fretting like a middle schooler on a first date. She was a grown woman meeting a work colleague for morning coffee. What was the big deal? Besides, she had much bigger concerns to occupy her attention.

But when she saw Daphne on the sidewalk out front of the hotel, she felt a warmth blossom inside, and a broad smile crept across her face.

"Hey, Izzie!" Daphne beamed a smile back at her. She was wearing leggings, a hoodie, and running shoes, and had clearly been out for a morning jog, her hair pulled back in a ponytail and the slightest sheen of sweat on her brow. "I was worried you weren't going to make it." She stopped, looking a little sheepish. "I mean, obviously you were already *here*, it's your hotel after all. I just meant, that you weren't going to be able to make it down . . . to join me for coffee." She shook her head, rolling her eyes at herself. "I'm glad to see you, is what I'm saying."

"It's nice to see you, too," Izzie answered with a grin.

"So?" Daphne clapped her hands together. "Coffee?"

"Sure," Izzie said, without irony. "I can use the boost. Slept like a mummy for twelve hours, but I don't feel very rested."

"You have anywhere in particular in mind?" Daphne tilted her head a little to one side, quizzically.

"Well, I had a decent cup at a place called Holy Grounds yesterday, but I think that it's pretty far away to walk."

"Their coffee is *okay*," Daphne said, her tone suggesting that she was being generous, "but the best in this part of town is probably at Monkeyhaus." She paused, considering. "Do you like cappuccino?"

Izzie nodded, enthusiastically.

"Then Monkeyhaus is the right answer, for sure." She turned and nodded up the street. "It's just a couple of blocks up and over. A little far, but trust me, it's totally worth it."

"Lead on," Izzie said, falling in step with her as they walked up the sidewalk. "I put myself in your hands."

Daphne walked with her hands in the pockets of her hoodie, her elbows tucked in tight, and though Izzie walked a comfortable distance from her side, every so often they were forced to step to one side to let pedestrians walking the other way pass by, or an occasional cyclist who'd hopped on the sidewalk to avoid some snarl in traffic. And when they did, their shoulders would often bump or brush together, and Izzie would suddenly be overly conscious of Daphne's closeness to her.

"So are you having any luck with the investigation?" Daphne asked as they turned off Hauser onto Mayfair. "Did those suspects in the drug case turn out to be Parasol employees, after all?"

Izzie nodded. "A couple of them did, yeah. Current employees or maybe former, we're still trying to work out the timeline. But there's definitely a connection there of some kind. Our working theory is that it's a small group of Parasol programmers and such who are involved in a narcotics ring on the side." She pursed her lips, thinking for a moment. "The theory fits most of the available facts, but there's more to it than that, though."

"So it's a working theory that isn't really working then?" Daphne gave a sly grin.

"Something like that." Izzie glanced her direction as they made their way down the sidewalk. "It's a temporary fix, like duct tape to mend a broken chair. Not the permanent solution."

"Sounds like you might just need to get a new chair, to me." Daphne stepped to one side to let a woman pushing a stroller past, and then side-stepped back. "I've run into cases like that before. I mean, nothing as high profile as the ones *you're* used to working, but on a smaller scale. Sometimes I had to just toss out the almost-but-not-quite-working theory and start over from scratch. Take what I knew to be true and build a new model from the ground up."

"Oh, we're already doing that. Spent the last few hours yesterday charting all of the known data points on a dry erase board at the station house."

Daphne turned, nodding in appreciation. "Nice," she said, stretching and stressing the word. "Much respect, that is old-school investigating."

"That's just what Patrick said, actually." Izzie chuckled. "I don't know, maybe *I'm* the one that's old-school. We have a lot of high tech equipment and computer simulations and behavioral modeling software, but in my experience the biggest breakthroughs in investigations often come from just standing in a room and *thinking*, you know? Making charts by hand and writing down lists and such might sometimes seem a little hokey, I guess, but it helps to focus your thoughts. And helps to visualize the data in a way that's cheap, fast, and easy to manipulate."

"Oh, no judgment, believe me. I can totally respect that." She paused, considering. "I tend to rely on technology a little more than that, I suppose, but maybe it's just the way you were brought up? Were your parents 'old-school' types, too?"

Izzie gave her a sidelong glance, and wondered how much to share.

"I was raised by my grandmother, mostly," she finally said, "and she was 'old-school' like you wouldn't believe." She shook her head. "Like, *really* old-school."

"My folks were pretty white-bread, I'll admit," Daphne said. "Dad was a lawyer, mom was a teacher. I was the middle child of three sisters, and the only one who didn't end up marrying her high school sweetheart and immediately start pumping out kids." A look suddenly flashed across her face, as if she had just realized that she'd inadvertently said something offensive. "Oh, don't get me wrong. I love my nieces and nephews, and I get along great with my sisters. It just . . . ."

"It wasn't for you," Izzie finished for her, nodding in understanding. "I get that. Same here."

Daphne gave her a wan little smile, and it felt as though there were larger things going unsaid, drifting just beneath the surface.

Izzie began to feel the nagging suspicion that larger things might emerge into view if the conversation continued along its current trajectory, and she wasn't comfortable going down that path. Luckily, an out presented itself.

"Is that the place?" Izzie asked, before Daphne could say whatever it was she was about to say.

Daphne looked in the direction that Izzie was pointing, and smiled.

"Welcome to the Monkeyhaus," she said, and gestured for Izzie to follow her inside.

It was a corner storefront with cartoon monkeys cavorting across the big glass windows, and appeared to have been an old-fashioned drugstore and soda fountain once upon a time. Now the marble counter of the soda fountain was all that remained of the original establishment, the rest having been completely remodeled and outfitted with couches, chairs, low tables, and bookshelves. There were people on laptops, others chatting in small groups of twos and threes over steaming cups of coffee, at one table sat an old man and a teenage girl playing chess, and on a long couch along the far wall a group of young women were sitting, all drawing in sketchbooks and happily ignoring one another.

"I don't remember who ended up paying for more rounds the other night, you or me," Izzie said, "but the first cappuccino is definitely on me this morning."

"Oh, trust me, there won't be a second," Daphne said as she sauntered to the counter to place their order. "They brew their espresso *strong* here. Two cups and I wouldn't be able to sleep for a week." She held up her hand. "I'll get the drinks while you grab us a table. Want a scone or anything like that?"

"Sure, that would be great. Whatever looks good."

While Daphne continued on to the counter, Izzie turned in place, looking for a likely spot to sit. She settled on a pair of low-slung upholstered chairs in the corner with a small table wedged in between them.

As she was planting herself in one of the chairs, shifting her belt around slightly so that her holstered gun wouldn't be pressing into her hip, she heard the chime of an incoming text message on her phone.

She pulled the phone out of the pocket of her suede jacket, and was unsurprised to see that the text was from Patrick.

"YOU UP?"

She thumbed a quick response. "YES. GETTING COFFEE WITH AGENT FROM R.A. WHAT'S UP?"

The ellipsis strobed at the bottom of the screen for a moment, and then the response came through.

"TECH GUYS SET UP WEBCAM. SUSPECT'S FIND-MY-FRIEND MAP IS STREAMING AT THIS ADDRESS."

A split second later, a link to a secure webserver came through, followed by log-in credentials.

"THX," Izzie texted back. "WHAT'S THE PLAN?"

"H & C WILL MONITOR MOVEMENT, LET US KNOW WHEN IT'S TIME TO MOVE IN. I'M CONTACTING UNIVERSITY TO SET UP MEET WITH AGUILAR."

"COPY THAT. LET ME KNOW WHEN YOU'RE READY TO ROLL."

A moment later, Patrick texted over a "thumbs up" emoji, followed by a winking face. Izzie rolled her eyes, and clicked the link to the streaming video server.

"Goofball," she muttered under her breath.

She had to copy and paste the username and password several times to get them entered correctly, but by the time Daphne walked over to join her, a plate in either hand, Izzie had the video feed up and running on her phone's screen.

"What's that?" Daphne said as she set the two plates down on the little table. On both of them were pastries, a blueberry scone on one and some kind of currant muffin on the other.

"Daffy?" called out a voice from the counter. "Order's ready."

Daphne rolled her eyes. "I swear to god, if I had a nickel . . ." She straightened up and headed back to the counter. "Hold that thought," she said, glancing over her shoulder at Izzie, "I'll be right back."

The video feed wasn't a perfect solution, but it was a functional one. If Izzie put her phone in landscape mode and zoomed in, she could see where any of the little dots were on the Recondito map, each of them "friends" of Ibrahim Fayed and, more importantly, likely accomplices in the Ink trade.

Daphne came back with two giant mugs of cappuccino. "Here you go," she said, handing one of the mugs to Izzie.

Izzie put the phone down on the table, so she could hold the mug in both hands while taking her first sip. As she brought the mug up to her lips, she noted the little cartoon monkey's face expertly poured into the foam. "Cute. But it seems a shame to ruin it."

Daphne waved one hand airily while taking a sip from her own mug. "Your loss, then."

"Screw it," she answered. "Beauty is fleeting." Izzie took a sip, eyes half-lidded. Daphne was right, it *was* good.

"What's that?" Daphne asked, glancing down at Izzie's phone on the table beside the pastries.

"That's a live stream of an Ink dealer's laptop screen," Izzie explained. "The dots are the locations of suspects believed to be involved in Ink trafficking or manufacture."

"Nice." Daphne nodded slowly, impressed.

Izzie shrugged. "Lucky, more like it. It's strictly amateur hour with this guy."

Daphne gestured to the pastries, inviting her to pick on. Izzie opted for the scone.

"You know, I never even *heard* of Ink before I moved to Recondito," Daphne said, picking up the muffin.

"Nobody had, apparently." Izzie wiped scone crumbs from the corners of her mouth. "It's only hit the streets in the last year, I'm told."

"I mentioned it a few weeks ago to an agent stationed in Boston, a classmate of mine from Quantico, and she said she'd never heard of it, either."

"So far as I know it's only been reported in Recondito so far."

"What? Not in San Francisco, even? Or Portland?"

Izzie shook her head. "Nope. Just here."

"Mmm." Daphne hummed, thoughtfully. "That's weird, right? That it wouldn't have shown up *anywhere* else?"

"It is odd, yeah, now that you mention it," Izzie agreed.

Daphne looked back at the phone, displaying the map of Fayed's friends. "Looks like most of them are . . ." She leaned in close, squinting to reach the street names. "At the Pinnacle Tower." Glancing up, she caught Izzie's eye. "Parasol employees again?"

Izzie nodded.

"Bad enough they keep getting all of the good apartments," Daphne said with a mock scowl, "now you're telling me they're *criminals*, to boot." She shook her head, chuckling.

"No luck with the apartment search?"

"Don't remind me." Daphne sighed into her coffee mug. "I've got an appointment with a rental agent to check out a place on Odessa after work, but I'm not getting my hopes up."

"One of those big apartment blocks?" Izzie remembered the featureless eyesores in the Kiev.

"I think so. At this rate I may be better off biting the bullet and renewing my lease on my old place, even with the bump in rent. It would beat the hassle of searching for apartments that keep getting leased out from under me by somebody else at the last minute."

"Well," Izzie said with a sly grin, "at least all of your stuff is already there."

Daphne chuckled. "So, I was wondering, how long do you think you'll be in town? There's this . . ."

She was interrupted by the ring of an incoming call from Izzie's phone.

"So sorry," Izzie said, and glanced down. It was Patrick. "I've got to take this," she said glancing up at Daphne while she picked up the phone.

Daphne mouthed that it was not a problem, and Izzie felt uncomfortable watching her lips move without hearing any attendant sound coming out.

"What's up?" Izzie said as she held the phone up to her ear.

"I got us an appointment to meet with Aguilar," Patrick answered without preamble, the noise of a car in motion in the background. "Problem is, it's in twenty minutes. The rest of his day is booked after that, and he's leaving town for the weekend tonight. I'm heading there now, but I'm coming from way down in Little Kovoko, and I don't think I'll have time to swing by and pick you up. Can you find your own way there and meet me?"

"Sure, I'll grab a cab and head over right away," Izzie answered, standing up.

"Okay." With a click, the call was ended.

"I'm *so* sorry," Izzie said to Daphne as she slid the phone back into her pocket. "I've got to get to Ross University right away."

"No problem." Daphne smiled, putting down her mug. "I'll give you a lift."

"Oh, I was just planning on taking a cab . . ."

"Nonsense," Daphne interrupted. "My bucar is parked just up the street, and I can get you there sooner than you would be if you had to wait around for a cab."

"Okay, okay," Izzie relented. "I feel bad, though. I didn't arrange for a rental, and now everyone else is stuck chauffeuring me around, when I should just grab a taxi."

"Yeah," Daphne said as they started towards the door, "but that's the one problem with this town: not enough taxis."

"That and the homegrown drug crisis," Izzie said.

"And the occasional serial killer," Daphne shot back, holding the door open for Izzie to walk through. "Can't forget them."

"Nope," Izzie answered, "Even if we wanted to."

Izzie had meant for her tone to be playful and joking, but she couldn't entirely suppress an undercurrent of melancholy beneath her words.

Because if there was ever a memory that she would choose to forget if she could . . .

CHAPTER TWENTY-TWO

"If you're going to be in town for a while," Daphne said as they drove south through Ross Village towards the university, "I'm sure Agent Gutierrez could help line up a bucar for you to use. There's just my car and his assigned to the R.A. at the moment, but we could always requisition something from the motor pool at the Portland field office." She paused, and glanced sidelong at Izzie in the passenger seat. "*Are* you going to be in town for a while, do you think?"

"I don't know yet," Izzie said, sighing. "I sometimes think that we're getting somewhere with this investigation, but then things keep getting more . . . complicated."

"Gotcha." Daphne kept her eyes on the road for a moment before continuing. "The reason I ask . . . well, other than the suggestion about requisitioning a bureau car . . . is that there's this theater troupe in town that does live reenactments of old TV shows. I haven't been, but I hear that it is *hilarious*. Anyway, in a couple of weeks they're doing an episode of that old sitcom *Behind the Lines . . .*" She glanced over at Izzie. "Did you ever watch that show?"

"Are you *kidding*?" Izzie gawped. "I loved that show when I was a kid!"

"Oh my god. Me, too." She sighed, eyes on the road ahead. "It's so, *so* corny, but I *loved* it."

"I think I loved it *because* it was so corny," Izzie said.

"So yeah, anyway . . . if you're still in town, I was wondering if you wanted to go see it with me." She glanced in Izzie's direction, and hastened to add, "Strictly as friends, of course. Not a date kind of thing. Just a going-to-see-a-play-together kind of thing."

"It's okay, I totally get what you mean," Izzie said. "And yeah, that sounds like it would be a lot of fun. If I'm still in town, count me in, definitely."

"Great!" Daphne beamed. "Just don't solve your case too quickly, okay?" She got a pained expression on her face, and shot Izzie a guilty glance. "I'm sorry. I was just kidding, but that sounded funnier in my head than it did out loud. Of course I hope that your investigation goes well."

"Don't worry." Izzie gave her a reassuring smile. "At the rate things are going, it looks like I might be in Recondito for a *while*."

Patrick was waiting for her near the front door of the black bunker that housed the Department of Physics on the Ross University campus. He was dressed more casually than the suit and tie he typically wore when working, instead wearing a T-shirt, jeans, and quilted jacket with a pair of hiking boots.

"What?" Izzie said, looking him up and down, "Is it casual Friday and nobody told me?"

He held his arms out to either side while he looked down at his clothes, a wounded expression on his face. "Hey, I had to get over here at short notice. I was going to stop by my place and change, but that was before Aguilar's secretary told me how tight his schedule was for the day."

"What's the matter? Did you go out and get lucky last night, and this is some kind of morning after walk-of-shame outfit?"

Patrick sneered playfully at her. "If you must know, I volunteer at a school down in the Oceanview on Friday mornings, and I find it puts the kids more at ease if I'm not dressed as incredibly fashionable as I usually am." He jerked a thumb towards the entrance to the building. "Now come on, we don't want to miss our appointment."

As he held the door open and Izzie stepped through, Patrick took the opportunity to give her outfit a once over, as well.

"Besides, with you rocking the jeans and suede jacket every day," he said with a lopsided grin, "I figured I'd slum it a little bit today to put *you* at ease, too."

Izzie slugged him lightly in the shoulder as they entered the foyer.

"What is it with women shoving and hitting me all the time lately?" Patrick said, putting his hand on his shoulder, shamming that he was injured.

"I don't know," Izzie answered, "maybe you really are just that punchable."

"Well *maybe* you are . . ." Patrick began, but was interrupted by the woman sitting behind the reception desk.

"Can I help you?" the receptionist asked, looking up from a crossword puzzle. "Oh, you're those police detectives who were here the other day, right? Are you back to see Dr. Kono again? I think he's in a class at the moment but I can . . ."

"No, thank you," Patrick interrupted, holding up his hand. "We actually have an appointment with Ricardo Aguilar."

"Oh, sure," the receptionist said, seeming relieved that she wasn't required to do anything more strenuous than provide directions. "His office is on the second floor, room 210. You can't miss it."

Patrick nodded thanks, and the receptionist was back to her crossword puzzle before he and Izzie had made it three steps past her desk.

"So you volunteer at a school?" Izzie said while Patrick punched the call button for the elevator. "Let me guess, it's your alma mater?"

"Yeah." Patrick nodded. "Powell Middle School. Why, does that make me a cliché? The cop who gives back to the community?"

"Is that really a cliché? I'd only heard the one about the donuts." Izzie ignored his withering stare. "But what kind of volunteering do you do?"

The elevator doors opened, and a group of grad students bustled their way out. Izzie and Patrick slipped inside, and he punched the button for the second floor.

"It's an elective course," he explained. "I'm teaching them how to play konare at the moment."

"Konare?"

"It's a Te'Maroan game. Some people say it's derived from the Hawaiian game konane, but my great-uncle always insisted that Hawaii got it from *us*. Either way, it's a strategy board game played on a grid with black and white counters."

"Wait . . ." Izzie held up a finger. "Are you the sponsor of the school's *chess club*? Patrick, are you a *nerd*?"

He rolled his eyes. "Says the woman who spends her free time doing jigsaw puzzles and reading books about other people's drug trips."

"Hey, I know that *I'm* a nerd," she said, "but you'd managed to convincingly pass as someone who wasn't."

The elevator chimed that it had arrived at their requested floor, and the doors began to slide open.

"Konare is part of a rich and proud cultural heritage that I'm trying to pass down to the next generation," Patrick said, drawing himself up straight, chest puffed out. "And besides, next semester I'm teaching them Te'Maroan stick fighting, which is *much* cooler."

They stepped off the elevator onto the second floor. This was a nicer part of the building than the hallway that housed Dr. Kono's office, and from the size of his doorway it seemed that Dr. Aguilar's office was considerably nicer, too. Which was only fitting, considering that he was the department head.

Looks were somewhat deceiving, though. The door to room 210 led not directly into Aguilar's office, but to a kind of waiting room, where an assistant fielded calls, scheduled appointments, and dealt with walk-ins.

Just inside the doorway to the left was the assistant's desk, atop which were piled stacks of ungraded papers, towers of doctoral theses, boxes full of research materials, a desk phone, and a computer monitor. Almost hidden behind the mess was a young woman in her late twenties, who when they entered was typing furiously at her computer's keyboard, a pencil clenched between her teeth and a row of Post-it notes stuck to her left forearm. She would twist her head to look down at the notes, turn back to the screen, and type the noted corrections, then search for the next marked passage and start all over again.

Patrick cleared his throat when it began to seem as though she hadn't noticed them yet.

"Yes?" The assistant glanced up at them from the computer monitor, her manner harried but helpful, with a brittle edge to her voice that sounded like she was one crisis away from a complete meltdown, but was for the moment managing to keep the chaos in check. "Can I help you?"

"I'm Lieutenant Tevake with the Recondito Police Department," he answered, then added, "We spoke on the phone?"

There was a momentary pause, as if she were having to process his words, parsing out some hidden meaning. "Oh, right. Of course. I'm sorry." She stood up, the Post-it notes on her arm fluttering like tiny little flags as she swept her arm towards the door at the back of the room. "A million things going on, all at once. You know how it is."

"Believe me, we do," Izzie said sympathetically.

The assistant crossed the floor to the rear door of the room, put her hand on the handle, and then paused for a moment. She glanced back over her shoulder at Patrick and Izzie. "Dr. Aguilar isn't in any kind of trouble, is he?"

"Oh, no, nothing like that," Patrick rushed to answer. "We just have a few questions for him about an old case of ours."

The assistant's eyes widened, her mouth forming a perfect "o."

"Is this about the Reaper?!" She pulled her hand away from the doorknob as if it might burn her, and turned completely to face them.

"I'm afraid I'm not at liberty to discuss the details of our investigation," Patrick replied, as if he were reading from a script.

"It *is*, isn't it?" The assistant took a step towards them, looking from Patrick to Izzie and back again. "Is it true that Dr. Aguilar's grandfather was close to the killer? As in, friends with him?"

"Well, as I said . . ." Patrick began, noncommittally.

"I was a grad student here when that all went down," the assistant pressed on, "and it was *all* anyone could talk about. When we heard that the professor's grandfather had left those houses in his will to the Reaper . . . and all that crazy Mayan stuff? Seriously, it was all *anyone* talked about for ages."

"Houses?" Izzie said. She knew about the lighthouse, but were there others?

"Mayan?" Patrick added.

Before the assistant could say anything further, the door behind her abruptly opened.

"Jessica?" said the man who appeared in the doorway, a stern tone to his words. "I take it this is my ten o'clock?"

Izzie remembered Ricardo Aguilar from their interviews with him five years before, but he seemed to have aged considerably more than that in the intervening years.

"Yes, Dr. Aguilar," the assistant said, spinning on her heels to face him. "I was just showing them in and . . ."

"I'll take it from here," Ricardo said, cutting her off. He nodded curtly towards her desk. "I'm sure you'd like to get back to those edits."

The assistant sighed, and then trudged back to the desk, plucking a couple of the Post-it notes off her arm as she went.

"Come in, please," Ricardo said to them, gesturing to the door, though there was very little that was inviting about his tone or his manner.

Izzie and Patrick filed past him into the office. It was larger than Dr. Kono's, as Izzie had suspected, but not by much. And in every other respect it could not have been more dissimilar. Where Hayao Kono's office had been cozy and comfortable, filled with memories and charm, Ricardo Aguilar's office was characterless, all sterility and function.

"Please, sit," Ricardo said as he stepped inside and closed the door behind them. He gestured to two chairs placed at the front of the desk. The chairs were leather and chrome, the desk a slab of brushed steel atop which were neatly arranged a corded phone, a computer monitor, and a single framed photo of the professor and what appeared to be his wife.

As Izzie and Patrick sat, Ricardo went around to the other side of the desk and lowered himself into a high-backed leather chair that looked like some modernist throne, or like the captain's station from a starship.

"Thanks for taking the time to meet with us, Dr. Aguilar," Patrick said, taking the initiative. "We just had a few questions about your grandfather and his association with Nicholas Fuller."

The temperature in the room seemed to drop several degrees as Ricardo fixed them with an icy stare. He took a deep breath in through his nostrils and held it for a moment, then leaned forward, elbows on the brushed steel surface of the desk, his fingers steepled.

"Yes, well . . ." He began, his jaw tightened. "Kono told me that you'd come by to speak with him, and that I should probably expect a visit. But it was my understanding that you had inquiries to make about the Undersight project."

Patrick glanced at Izzie before replying. She didn't remember Dr. Aguilar being quite so combative when they'd last spoken to him five years before.

"Well, yes, we do have questions about Undersight, as well," Patrick said, his tone conciliatory. "But we're also following up on some leads about Fuller's interactions with your grandfather, and we were hoping that you might be able to provide a little insight."

"I see." Ricardo lowered his hands to the desk, fingers laced together. "But why now, after all this time? I thought the matter was settled and done." He turned to Izzie, glancing at the Bureau credentials hanging from her jacket pocket. "You're that FBI agent I spoke with five years ago, aren't you? You lead me to believe then that when Fuller died the investigation was closed. Has it been reopened?"

"No, not at all," Izzie hastened to answer. "But Lieutenant Tevake here is investigating another matter that appears to have ties to the Fuller case, and so we're revisiting some of the relevant evidence."

"Please understand that I'm not trying to be combative," Ricardo said, sitting back in the chair. "But when it became public knowledge that my late grandfather was associated with the Recondito Reaper, it was . . ." He sighed. "It was a difficult time for my family."

"I can appreciate that." Patrick's tone was supportive.

"Can you?" The professor shot him a hard look. "Some people might crave the notoriety of being closely associated with a serial killer, but I can assure you that my wife and I are *not* those sorts of people. For years after it was all anyone wanted to talk to us about. We stopped going to faculty mixers and social gatherings altogether, tired of being bombarded with endless questions about that gruesome business. It put such a strain on us that it very nearly cost me my marriage."

"I can assure you," Izzie said, "that's not uncommon in these types of cases. The damage that a serial killer can cause is much more far-reaching and widespread than just the immediate harm they inflict on their victims. If your marriage has withstood those kinds of stresses, I think it's a testament to the strength of your relationship."

Ricardo gave her a long look before responding. "Yes, well, thank you for saying so. But you can understand my reluctance to revisit that time in our lives."

"Absolutely," Patrick said. "But please know that anything you share with us today will remain strictly confidential. And that we'll do everything in our power to make sure that you and your wife remain out of the spotlight, should our investigation bring anything new to light."

Ricardo nodded slowly. "Very well. What is it you wish to ask me?"

Patrick reached into an inner pocket of his quilted jacket and pulled out his notebook and pencil. He flipped it open and scanned the page. "Five years ago you informed us that your late grandfather had left the Ivory Point Lighthouse to Nicholas Fuller in his will."

"And it was that information that led to us tracking him down," Izzie added. "But was that not the only property that your grandfather left to Mr. Fuller?"

Ricardo scowled. "No, there was another house in the Kiev, but I understand that the executor of the Fuller estate sold it at auction after he died, and that it has since been torn down."

"That's a lot to bequeath to a casual acquaintance," Izzie said.

"Which is exactly the point we wished to raise, Dr. Aguilar," Patrick went on. "And it was our understanding at the time that before his death your grandfather had gotten to know Nicholas Fuller socially. But when we spoke to Dr. Kono the other day he characterized their relationship as being closer than we had previously understood to be the case. He said that in addition to spending a great deal of time in your grandfather's private library, they often walked around the city together, as though they were 'searching for something or for someone.'" Patrick looked up from the notebook. "Do you know what they might have been looking for, Dr. Aguilar?"

"My grandfather was a very . . ." A pained expression flitted across Ricardo's face. "Complicated man," he finally went on. "One might even characterize him as troubled."

"He served on the City Council before he retired, if I recall correctly," Izzie said.

Ricardo nodded. "He represented the Oceanview District, yes. And he was a lawyer in private practice before that. I don't mean to suggest that he was ever in any kind of *legal* trouble. But he had certain . . . preoccupations. Though 'obsessions' might be a better description for them."

"Such as . . . ?" Patrick trailed off, inquiringly.

Ricardo pushed his chair back fractionally and laid his hands palms down on the surface of the desk, as if needing additional support. "I don't think I fully understood the extent of my grandfather's obsessions until after he died, when I became the executor of his estate. As you know, the lighthouse

that he'd bought back in the fifties passed to Nicholas Fuller
. . . though why my grandfather had ever found it necessary
to purchase a disused lighthouse in the first place, I've never
understood. . . . But the rest of the estate passed into my hands,
including the contents of his private library."

Ricardo took a deep breath, collecting himself.

"I had known since childhood that my grandfather had
an interest in mythology and superstition, of course. And it
was a subject that he and my wife—she is professor of cultural anthropology here at the university—it was a subject
that they discussed often, in particular the belief systems of
Mesoamerica. But it wasn't until I was called upon to handle
the disposition of his estate that I understood just how deeply
his obsession ran. In my grandfather's effects were . . . extensive writings on the subject of the supernatural, that at first I
took to be a layman's attempt at anthropological analysis, but
which on closer examination turned out to be considerably
more . . . involved."

Izzie glanced at Patrick, and could see that he was listening
with the same rapt attention that she was. This was going in a
direction they had not anticipated.

"I discovered that when he was a young man, my grandfather befriended an older gentleman who immigrated to
Recondito from Mexico in the nineteen thirties. From the
Yucatan peninsula, to be precise. My grandfather referred to
him only as 'Don Mateo' in his personal writings, but there is
a black and white photograph of the two of them in the early
fifties, posing in what I was later able to identify as a crypt
in the cemetery of the Church of the Holy Saint Anthony.
This Don Mateo, my grandfather claimed in his journal, was
a priest of Xibalba, an adherent to a secret religious tradition

that traced its origins back to the days of the Maya, though he never referred to him as a priest, as such, but as something like a calendar-keeper or daykeeper?"

"Daykeeper?" Izzie echoed, her eyes widening.

"Yes, something like that," Ricardo said with a moue of distaste. "Apparently, my grandfather was inducted into this 'faith' by the old man, and continued to practice certain rituals and beliefs in secret for the rest of his life." He shook his head. "He always presented himself as a Roman Catholic, though perhaps not a terribly observant one."

Izzie was still remembering the things that Nicholas Fuller had said that night in the lighthouse. *I didn't understand it myself, until the old daykeeper gave me the key.*

"He wrote extensively about the cosmology of this secret belief of his, world-trees and true places, the real and the unreal. I could scarcely make heads or tails of any of it, but my wife thought the whole thing was fascinating. So much so that she asked if she could use the journals in her research. Ultimately she decided not to publish the results, for fear of reigniting interest in our family's connection with the Reaper murders. Just the few people here at the university who heard about her findings were enough to set the rumor mills to grinding again, and we shuddered to think what would happen if her paper were to be published in an academic journal. Which was a shame, since she found a great many references to well-documented Mesoamerican religious traditions in my grandfather's writing."

"Why would publishing her research have reignited interested in that connection, professor?" Patrick asked.

Ricardo pursed his lips. "It might be simpler to show you." He picked up the handset of the desktop phone and punched a few buttons. "Samantha? It's me. Do you have a softcopy of your Xibalba paper that you could email to me? I have someone in my office who I'd like to show it to." He paused, listening. "No, I don't think that . . ." Another pause. "I understand, but . . ." He took a deep breath through his nostrils. This appeared to be a point of contention. "I'll explain in greater detail later, but it is an officer with the Recondito PD and an agent of the FBI, and they've come with questions about the . . . yes, you know that I agree completely." He nodded. "They've assured me that our involvement won't be made public knowledge." A pause, punctuated by a relieved sigh. "Okay, thanks. I'll tell you all about it later."

The professor returned the handset to the cradle, and then slid out a keyboard tray that was mounted to the underside of the desk. He tapped a few keys, scrolled down a few pages, and then swiveled the computer monitor around so that Patrick and Izzie could get a good look at it.

"This is Ah Puch, the Fleshless, the Mayan mythological figure who my grandfather identified as the patron deity of Xibalba." He paused, then added, "My wife would point out that technically this image is identified simply as 'God A' from the lunar eclipse tables in the Dresden Codex, and that the association between Ah Puch and the Mayan underworld as depicted in the *Popol Vuh* is a contentious one, but she is confident that the identification is correct."

There on the screen was a black and white reproduction of a Mayan drawing depicting a skull-faced skeletal figure that was chillingly familiar.

"The Reaper's mask," Patrick said.

Izzie couldn't completely suppress a gasp. "The silver skull."

"Yes." Ricardo nodded. "It would seem that Nicholas Fuller styled his murderous alter ego after the god that my grandfather worshipped in secret for most of his life." He turned the monitor back around and closed the window with a look of disgust on his face. "You can see why we would prefer that this not become common knowledge."

Izzie and Patrick exchanged a look.

"Why didn't you come forward with this earlier?" Izzie asked.

Ricardo chewed the inside of his cheek for a moment before answering. "It wasn't until my wife began to dig deeply into my grandfather's journals that we found the connection ourselves," he finally answered, "and by then the case was long closed. We didn't see that there was anything to be gained from putting ourselves back in the spotlight, especially considering how much greater the scrutiny on us would be if people believed that my grandfather somehow *inspired* the Reaper murders, and wasn't simply tangentially connected to them."

"That's perfectly understandable," Patrick said, though Izzie was feeling a little less generous.

"Dr. Aguilar," she said, sitting forward. "Would it be possible for us to get a copy of your wife's unpublished paper? And possibly to take a look at your grandfather's journals themselves?"

Ricardo squirmed a little uneasily. Izzie could tell that he was tempted to refuse her request, but that he was having difficulty finding the grounds on which to do so.

"I can arrange that," he finally replied, nodding reluctantly. "My wife still has the journals in her office here on campus, so as long as *she* doesn't object, you could pick them up right away."

"Is she *likely* to object?" Izzie asked, recalling the conversation that they'd just overheard, and his comments about the strain that all of this had placed on their relationship.

Ricardo considered the possibilities for a moment before answering. "Possibly. But I think I can convince her. If . . ." He raised a finger for emphasis. "*If* you can guarantee us that our connection to all of this remains confidential."

Patrick and Izzie both assented immediately. "You have our word," he said, speaking for both of them.

"Was there anything else you wished to ask me?"

"Actually," Patrick said, raising a finger, "we were hoping that we might get access to the mine shaft where the Undersight project was housed."

The professor raised an eyebrow, quizzically. "Whatever for?"

Patrick glanced over at Izzie before answering. "Again, just following up on some old evidence, looking for new connections that have recently come to light."

"Well, I'm sorry," Ricardo replied with a cursory shake of his head, "but I'm afraid I won't be able to help you there. The university merely leased the mine shaft and some of the surrounding grounds, but the land itself remained the property of the city of Recondito. At least until it was sold off to a private concern shortly after the university pulled the plug on Undersight."

"Sold?" Izzie said. "To whom?"

Ricardo shrugged. "I don't recall. I remember that it was a matter of considerable debate, since the university had put in a bid to purchase it, but in the end the mayor's office convinced the city council to sell it to some holding company. I'd hoped that we might restart the Undersight project—or something similar—after the furor over the Reaper murders had finally quieted down, but from what I understand the new owners are not willing to entertain any offers to lease the land, for any purposes whatsoever." He frowned. "It's probably for the best, anyway. Scientists are not known to be particularly superstitious, of course, but the fact that nearly everyone who went down into that mine shaft to work on Undersight ended up dead somewhat cast a pall over the whole idea of setting up any new experiments down there."

"Nearly everyone?" Patrick echoed. "I thought that Fuller had targeted the entire team."

"There was a graduate student on the last experiment who either escaped Fuller's attention or else slipped through his net," Ricardo explained. "But so far as I know that was the only member of the Undersight team who survived."

Izzie remembered what Fuller had said about there being "one more," and mentioning "the student" right at the end.

"Well, if there's nothing else . . . ?" Ricardo searched their faces. "Then come on," he said, getting up from his chair. "I'll walk you over to the anthropology department now. Might as well get this out of the way, so we can get on with our lives." He gestured towards the door. "And I hope that this will be an end to our involvement in this, once and for all."

"Dr. Aguilar, we hope so, too," Izzie said, getting to her feet.

He held the door open for them, and as they passed through, he added, "I hope it doesn't offend you to hear that I would rather never speak to either of you about any of this again."

CHAPTER TWENTY-THREE

On their walk across the campus of Ross University to the Department of Anthropology building, Izzie rehearsed in her head all of the logical arguments she could employ to convince Ricardo Aguilar's wife to hand over the materials they'd requested. As it happened, not only did she and Patrick not speak to Samantha Aguilar, but they never even saw her. Ricardo had asked them to wait in the hallway when he went in to speak with his wife, and then had not emerged for nearly a quarter of an hour. Through the closed door they could hear muffled voices, raising in pitch and volume as time went on, but could not make out what was being said. Then, fifteen minutes after he had gone in, Ricardo Aguilar came back out, this time holding a file box not terribly dissimilar to the ones in the community room back in the 10th Precinct station house.

"Here," he said, shoving the box at Patrick. "Take it and go."

As Patrick took the box, Izzie asked, "Shall we return it to you or bring it back to your wife when we're finished?"

"If it were up to me I'd say *burn* it all," Ricardo said, eyes flashing. "But just drop it at the reception desk downstairs when you're through with it. They'll know to get it back to my wife."

He took a deep breath, composing himself.

"Now," he finally went on, "if you'll excuse me, I have a full day scheduled, and then my wife and I will be leaving on a much-needed vacation." He glanced at the box, lip curling in a poorly concealed sneer. "Good luck with all of this"—he looked back up at Patrick and Izzie—"and if there is any luck left over for *me*, I shall never see either of you again."

He nodded curtly, turned on his heel, and walked away.

"I get the impression that he doesn't like us," Patrick said out of the corner of his mouth. "Is it just me?"

"Come on, chess club." Izzie grabbed his elbow and steered him towards the stairs. "Let's get out of here before someone changes their mind."

"**S**o much for the idea of seeing what's down in that mine shaft for ourselves," Patrick said as he steered the car out of the Ross University visitors parking lot. "Not that Aguilar seems like he'd be eager to help us out even if the University *did* own that land."

Izzie had wedged the file box in between her feet on the floorboard underneath the glove compartment, and was leaning forward, rifling through the contents. A stapled printout of Samantha Aguilar's paper was on top, and below that a collection of hardcover journals, not fancy leather-bound numbers

but utilitarian and inexpensive notebooks, like accounting led-
gers purchased at an office supply store. She'd pulled out the top-
most of the journals and was flipping through it, scanning the
pages crammed with solid blocks of neatly handwritten notes.

"Well, maybe we won't need to see it for ourselves," she
said, glancing up from the journal. "Old man Aguilar here
seemed to have a lot to say on the subject, so maybe he can
shed some light on things."

"Yeah?" Patrick glanced in her direction before turning
his attention back to the road ahead. "Find anything interesting so far?"

"This is going to take some time to process, but yeah. I'm
seeing a *lot* of references here that line up with things that
Fuller obsessed over. I've already run across mentions of the
Guildhall *and* the Eschaton Center."

"I thought it was all Mayan mythology stuff?"

"Oh, that's in here, too. Most of the text is about that, actually. Stuff about these 'daykeepers' and their function. Lots
about the disposal of dead bodies, as well. Rendering a corpse
so that . . ."

She stopped short, her breath catching in her throat.

"What?" Patrick said. Then, when she didn't answer
immediately, he repeated a little more emphatically, "What?!
What is it?"

Izzie looked up from the journal. "There's a section here
about the proper method of dismembering a body so that it
is no longer useful as a vessel for, and I quote, 'daimons from
the Unreal.' And it refers to those who are controlled by such
daimons as 'Ridden.'"

Patrick stopped at a red light, and turned in the driver's
seat to face her.

"And?" he said, leadingly.

"That's the same term used to describe someone possessed by a spirit in Haitian Vodou," Izzie explained, a little breathlessly. She turned to look at him. "Nicholas Fuller said that when his victims went down into the dark, the dark came back with them. He said they were 'ridden,' and were carrying 'passengers.' That's when he mentioned that the 'old daykeeper' had given him the key."

She paused, arranging the puzzle pieces in her mind.

"Patrick, I think he mutilated the corpses of his victims because he believed they were being controlled by some outside intelligence. Killing them wouldn't be enough . . ."

"Because they would just get back up and keep on going," Patrick said.

She nodded slowly. "So he did what old man Aguilar describes here. He 'rendered' the remains, so that they were no longer useful as vessels."

The car behind them honked when the light turned green and Patrick failed to move. He took his foot off the brake and accelerated through the intersection, distracted.

"So what are you suggesting?" Patrick finally said, eyes on the road ahead.

"Well, knowing what we know now . . ." Izzie trailed off, remembering Malcolm Price getting up from the pavement, already dead.

She turned to face him.

"What if he was *right*?"

When they arrived at the 10th Precinct station house, the detectives' squad room was a riot of activity. Chavez and Harrison were presiding over the chaos, and it was clear that something big was in the offing.

"What's up?" Patrick said as he walked away from the closing elevator doors, with Izzie lugging the file box and following close behind.

Chavez glanced in their direction as they approached, while continuing to talk to the uniformed officer standing beside him. ". . . and I want them geared up and ready to roll when I give the signal."

The uniformed officer nodded a hasty consent, and then hurried off to take care of whatever it was that Chavez had tasked him with doing.

"What's going on?" Patrick repeated, glancing around the room.

"We think we're onto something with Fayed's 'friends' here," Chavez answered, and turned to indicate the computer monitor on his desk. There was a browser window open showing the same streaming video feed of the laptop that Izzie had seen on her phone.

Patrick leaned down to get a closer look at the screen, while Izzie rested the file box on her hip and leaned to one side to look over Patrick's shoulder. The dots were still mostly congregated at the site of the Pinnacle Tower at the corner of Gold Street and Northside Boulevard, but there were others scattered around the Financial District and City Center either on their own or in groups of twos and threes. Izzie glanced at a clock displayed in the corner of the screen and saw that it was approaching noon. She figured there was a better than average chance that most of the dots that had drifted away from the Pinnacle Tower represented employees on their lunch breaks.

"We've had eyes on them since last night," Chavez went on, "tracking their movements. We managed to identify six of the names from Fayed's contact list that also appeared on the email threads in his personal account that included discussions of Ink, and we've been focusing most of our attention on them. We've got home addresses for each of them." He pointed to a printed map of the city that was tacked to a corkboard mounted to the nearest wall, with six red pushpins marking the residences of each of the suspects, four in the Kiev, one in Ross Village, and one in Hyde Park. "The six suspects spent last night at the addresses that we've got on file, so that much checks out. And each of them was at work at the Pinnacle Tower by 9:30 a.m. this morning. But when we went back through the feed to see *how* they got to work, we spotted something interesting."

He turned to Harrison, who was sitting at the next desk over.

"Can you bring up those snapshots?" Chavez asked.

Harrison grumbled a little, but with a few mouse clicks he brought up a folder on his desktop screen, containing a collection of screen captures of the video feed. He selected six of them and then opened them tiled on the screen, a mosaic of almost identical maps of the city, three images across and two high.

Circles and lines had been digitally drawn on each of the maps, and Izzie guessed it was most likely done by the detectives quickly with a computer mouse and some simple computer graphics program. But while the results might have been inelegant, they served their purposes.

"Each of the six started the morning at their respective apartment or house," Chavez explained, pointing to the red circles that appeared on each of the six maps. "And each of them ended up at the Pinnacle Tower." He pointed to the circles that marked the terminus of each line. "But none of them took the quickest or easiest route to get where they were going."

Izzie leaned in to get a better look. The line that started in Hyde Park veered far to the south as it headed west, past Ross Village and into the northeastern corner of the Oceanview before turning north and finally ending at the Pinnacle Tower. The lines that started in the northwest corner of the city, in the Kiev, traveled south and east *past* the Pinnacle Tower to the eastern side of the Oceanview, before turning north and heading back towards it. And the one that started in Ross Village traveled south *away* from the Tower for a dozen blocks, dipping down into the Oceanview, before turning one hundred and eighty degrees and heading back in the other direction along the same path.

And all six of the lines passed through the same city block in Oceanview, just off of Bayfront Drive not far from the docks.

Patrick and Izzie turned back to Chavez.

"So what are we thinking here?" Patrick asked. "Some kind of drop site?"

Chavez put his hands on his hips. "We're not sure yet. We've had unmarked cars surveilling the area ever since we spotted the pattern, but it's only been a couple of hours and they haven't reported back anything of note yet."

"Have you tried checking the address that they visited?" Izzie shifted the file box on her hip.

"No dice," Harrison answered, shaking his head. "The friends app is only accurate up to a couple of hundred feet, and cellular coverage is pretty spotty out by the docks anyway, so the GPS locations are pretty fuzzy as it is. We know within a city block or so where they went, but not much more than that."

"That's a mostly industrial area," Patrick said, and Izzie knew that he was familiar enough with the neighborhood to take him at his word. "The fish market isn't far from there, and I think there's a cannery or two still in operation. Otherwise it's all warehouses, other than the docks themselves a few blocks east."

"We're checking property records to see who owns the buildings on that block," Chavez added, "but so far as we know, based on what our plainsclothes in the unmarked cars have seen from cruising the area, it's all warehouses and self-storage facilities and things like that, except for one warehouse that's been converted into office space. You know the kind, little shoebox offices with barely enough room for a desk and a phone."

Izzie had been in that sort of converted industrial space before. Cavernous buildings rendered claustrophobic, low suspended ceilings above floors that bounced with every step, thin walls that barely muffled the sound from one tiny room to the next, narrow winding hallways purely utilitarian in design and function. Tiny offices filled with people running Internet businesses, shady accountants, or podcasters who needed a cheap place to record outside of their homes.

"So we're hoping that it's not the office space, I take it?" Patrick said. "Though now that I think about it, door duty in a place like that sounds only marginally worse than the hassle of dealing with a bunch of self-storage bays . . . just getting the search warrants lined up would be a nightmare." He glanced over at Harrison. "I'm glad this is *your* case, guys. I'm happy to just be along for the ride."

"Yeah, well," Chavez jumped in before Harrison could give voice to the sneer that was forming on his face, "don't start celebrating just yet. If we can't narrow things down any further on this end, we're going to need to search *all* of the buildings on that block, and that includes you. Captain's orders. This is an all-hands-on-deck situation."

"Okay, okay, I get it," Patrick said. "And who's responsible for assigning the search details?"

Harrison raised his hand, a smug look on his face.

Patrick rolled his eyes. "Great. Just great."

He turned to Izzie and reached out to take the file box from her hands.

"Come on, let's get this stuff in the community room with the rest of the stuff," he said, starting in that direction.

"Don't get too comfortable, Tevake," Harrison called after him, smoothing down his mustache with thumb and forefinger. "We'll be ready to move out soon. And I'm thinking you'd be a good fit for the office building, so limber up those knocking knuckles of yours."

"What an asshole . . ." Patrick muttered in a voice so low that only Izzie was close enough to hear. But she couldn't disagree with his assessment.

It was only after Patrick had unlocked the community room and he and Izzie were safely inside that they were able to continue their conversation from the ride over.

"You're not really serious, are you?" Patrick said, closing the door behind them. "You think that Nicholas Fuller was *right* to murder all of those people?"

"No, of course not," Izzie answered hastily. "Not really. I mean, it's still *murder*. But my point is that it's possible his delusions weren't entirely delusional, you know? He was pretty far out in the deep end by the time we caught up with him, but maybe his logic when he started out wasn't so crazy, after all."

Patrick put the file box containing Roberto Aguilar's journals and Samantha Aguilar's academic paper down on the table with the Fuller evidence.

"I don't know, Izzie, it sounds an awful lot like you're justifying the actions of a serial killer here."

"No, honestly . . ." Izzie shook her head. "It's just . . . you and I both know that there's more going on here than everyone else realizes. That's why you called me in. But the more that we put the puzzle pieces together, the more it starts to look like there was a method to Fuller's madness. His actions were repellant, obviously, and I wouldn't dream of justifying serial homicide. Far from it. But if we're going to be able to get our heads around what's happening in this town, we need to consider the possibility that the beliefs that lead Fuller down that path might have been . . . well, maybe he wasn't entirely wrong."

Patrick pulled the lid off the file box and set it aside. Then he reached in and pulled out Samantha Aguilar's paper.

"I'm guessing that *this*"—he held one corner of the paper and shook it like a flag in a high wind—"doesn't tell us too much about all *that*, though." He turned and gestured towards the dry erase board with the constellations of names and phrases.

"No, it doesn't," Izzie agreed. "From what I gleaned by skimming through it on the drive here, it looks like she doesn't spend much time dwelling on references to anything other than Mesoamerican supernatural beliefs. And in fairness to her, most of the time that old man Aguilar mentions things like the Guildhall and such, it's without much in the way of explanation, at least based on what I've seen so far. You'd have to already suspect there was a connection there in order to see any significance. Otherwise they just read like non sequiturs."

She stepped over to the box and looked inside.

"If you *do* already suspect that there's a connection, though . . ." She reached in and took out a couple of the hardbound journals, one in either hand. "Well, I think these things might turn out to be *very* interesting reading."

"So where do you think we should go from here?" Patrick asked, leaning against the table.

Izzie tossed one of the journals through the air to him, and Patrick slapped it between his hands, catching it.

"I think we should get to reading," she said, holding aloft the other journal, a sly smile on her lips.

Izzie had barely had a chance to dig into the first of the journals when they were interrupted by a knock at the door. It was a uniformed officer, nodding her head in Patrick's direction as he draped his quilted jacket over the back of a chair.

"Captain wants us all in the briefing room," she said, gesturing for Patrick to follow her. "Said specifically to fetch you."

Patrick closed the journal that he'd been leafing through, and stood up from the table. As he followed the officer out the door, he looked back over his shoulder at Izzie. "You going to be okay in here?"

Izzie pointed her index finger at the open journal laid out on the table in front of her. "I've got enough to keep me occupied," she answered. As Patrick turned to leave, she added, "Could you shut the door on your way out, though?" She was feeling a little self-conscious about delving so deeply into such outré material when a stranger might wander in at any moment.

Patrick nodded, and pulled the door shut behind him as he walked through.

"Now, where were we?" Izzie said out loud to herself, turning her attention back to the journal.

Roberto Aguilar's notes were undated, and so it was impossible to get a precise idea about when they had been written, but it seemed clear that he had composed them over the period of many years. Some contained cultural references that suggested they might have been written as early as the 1950s, while flipping through some of the other journals Izzie had found unambiguous references to contemporary technologies that meant that they had to have been written as recently as the current decade.

Many of the mentions of Mayan and other Mesoamerican beliefs were opaque to Izzie, and she would have had trouble making any sense of them under normal circumstances. But the academic paper that the old man's granddaughter-in-law had written on the subject turned out to be an excellent skeleton key to the whole thing. Extensively footnoted and with a good many marginal glosses and handwritten notations, the paper served as a kind of gazetteer to the more unfamiliar parts of the terrain that the old man's writings traveled across.

As for the writings themselves . . . had Izzie not possessed any grounding in the subjects that the old man discussed at all, had not known anything about the historical context of many of his references, she might easily have taken it for the ramblings of a schizophrenic, at worst, or some inexpert and misguided attempt at a fictionalized autobiography, at best. She was reminded of "outsider artists" like Henry Darger or Opal Whiteley, who spent years crafting immense imaginary worlds for their own amusement, sometimes featuring themselves in prominent roles.

When she was getting her master's degree in psychology, Izzie had encountered a term that described this type of imaginative world building: paracosm. She'd read a case study of a government worker who was convinced that when his coworkers thought he was simply staring off into space or momentarily daydreaming, that he was in fact being transported across the stars to another world, with its own geography and languages and cultures, where he lived an entirely separate life of space opera heroics and derring-do.

Roberto Aguilar's memoirs carried much that same sort of tone, featuring himself in a starring role in a grand story of the struggles between the light and the darkness playing out in the city streets of Recondito. But a grand story that it would be reasonable to believe was carried out entirely in his own imagination. Clearly, based on the occasional passing reference to this aspect of his memoirs in the academic paper, that was the conclusion that Samantha Aguilar had reached. She took the tack of believing that the old man had been in possession of verifiable information about the religious practices and cosmologies of the ancient Maya, but that he had subsequently woven that knowledge into a fiction of his own devising.

But Izzie suspected that she knew better.

She already harbored suspicions that there were connections between such moments in the city's history as the founding of the Recondito Mining Guild, the subsequent destruction of their Guildhall decades later, and the mass murder-suicide at the Eschaton Center for Emanant Truth some two and a half decades later. But when she found each of those historical points and locations mentioned in Roberto Aguilar's memoirs, almost always in connection with the Mesoamerican beliefs that he had practiced in secret for most of his adult life, a more complete picture began to emerge.

Several times as she paged through the journals Izzie wished that she had something on which she could jot down some notes. She had thumbed a few quick lines on her phone's notepad app, but was old-fashioned enough that she preferred to write in longhand whenever possible. She considered trying to squeeze a few quick notes in the corner of the dry erase board, which was already crowded with writing that she was loathe to erase. So when Patrick returned, she breathed a sigh of relief.

"Hey," she said, looking up from the journal she was reading, "do you have a spare notebook or legal pad I could borrow? I want to jot some of this down while it's still fresh in my memory."

"Mmm?" Patrick was distracted, a serious look on his face as he pulled his quilted jacket off the back of the chair. "Probably. But it'll have to wait. We're heading out."

"Where to?" Izzie said, closing the journal.

"That block near the docks," Patrick answered with a labored sigh. "I've been assigned to the search team that's going to be going door-to-door in the office building, see if we can turn up anything interesting." He shrugged into his jacket. "Want to come along?"

Izzie stifled a laugh. "Well, as much *fun* as that sounds, I think I'm getting somewhere with old man Aguilar's journals, so I think I'll stick with this."

Patrick nodded. "Want to stay here while you do?" He paused, scratching his chin. "There's no way of telling how long I'll be."

Izzie climbed to her feet. "No, I think I'll head back to the Resident Agency offices. So long as you don't mind me taking some of these with me?" She gestured to the hardbound journals.

"Be my guest," he answered, heading towards the door. "Just don't tell my captain that you're taking evidence off the premises, okay? Come on, I'll lock up."

She picked up several of the journals and the copy of Samantha Aguilar's academic paper, tucked them under her arm, and followed him to the door.

"Sorry I can't give you a ride this time . . ." Patrick said, trailing off.

"No problem. If I don't take a cab at least *once* when I'm in town, I'll feel like a complete parasite."

Izzie waited in the hallway while Patrick locked the door and then pocketed the key.

"Have fun?" she said, a sympathetic expression on her face.

Patrick rolled his eyes. "Yeah, *right*."

He turned and walked back in the direction of the detectives' squad room.

"And to top it off," he muttered as he went, "I forgot to get *lunch . . .*"

Izzie grinned, and then headed to the elevator. "I guess there's a first time for everything."

CHAPTER TWENTY-FOUR

As the cab carried her north through Ross Village towards City Center, Izzie considered just going back to her hotel to do her reading, instead. But she couldn't recall whether there had been complimentary stationery in her room when she checked in, and besides she never much cared for the way that cheap ballpoint pens flowed across the page, and the lighting in the room wasn't the best . . .

And she realized that she was simply making more justifications to spend time in the Resident Agency offices than she needed, when at the back of her mind lurked a tiny thrill of excitement about spending more time with Daphne. What was it about the human mind, she wondered, that could get so distracted by something as inconsequential as spending time with an attractive person when grappling with such big and difficult to process matters as the ones that currently occupied her attention? Especially since Izzie had already decided that nothing would be happening there.

But *was* something happening there, despite her better judgment?

Izzie pushed such thoughts further to the back of her mind. She had more important things to deal with at the moment.

But maybe when all of this was done . . . ?

"Damn it, girl," she muttered out loud to herself, wrenching that train of thought to a stop, "get your head together."

"What's that?" the cab driver asked, glancing in the rearview mirror.

"Oh, nothing," Izzie said, shrinking into herself, cheeks burning.

But still . . .

Her stomach rumbling, Izzie grabbed a meatball sub and a can of diet soda from a food truck parked out front before heading into the R.A. offices. It was already the middle of the afternoon, and she realized that she hadn't even had a chance to finish the scone that Daphne had bought for her at the coffee shop that morning. It was hardly any wonder that she was starving.

The offices were mostly deserted when she arrived. The computer technician who had been there the day before was updating the operating system on one of the workstations, and a filing clerk was sorting through a big pile of paperwork. Agent Gutierrez's door was closed, and Daphne was nowhere to be seen.

Izzie dropped the journals and her lunch at the desk that had been assigned to her, and then went over to ask the filing clerk where the office supplies were kept. She returned from the storage closet a few moments later with a legal pad and a couple of roller ball pens. She shucked off her suede jacket, draped it over the back of the chair, and then went so far as to unclip the holster from her belt and lay it on the corner of the desk along with her phone. She was settling in for the long haul.

The meatball sub was passable, at best, and the diet soda was scarcely any colder than room temperature, but together they served to quiet the rumbling in her stomach, and let her focus on the task at hand.

Izzie had been skimming through the journals at random back at the 10th Precinct station house, but now she decided that a more organized method was in order. It would be difficult enough to decipher and collate all of the scattered and sometimes cryptic references made by the elder Aguilar without making the work that much more difficult with a random and haphazard approach.

So she selected the journal that, to all indications, seemed to be the oldest of those that she had brought with her, and she began to read.

Less than five minutes later, she realized that she had already filled the first page of the legal pad with copious notes. This was going to take a while.

Some daykeepers had the genius. Others had to use the key. The first humans were truly articulate and perceptive. They could not only speak the language of the gods, but could also see everything under the sky and on the earth. They had only to look from the spot where they stood, and their sight would carry all the way to the limits of space and the limits of time. But then the gods, who had not intended to make and model beings with the potential of becoming their equals, limited human sight to what was obvious and nearby.

Even so, some humans were still born with the genius, able to perceive with their minds things that remained hidden to the eye. Such made natural-born daykeepers, capable of seeing shades and daimons from the unreal, even those who cloak themselves in the flesh of the living and the dead.

In the Dark House of the temples of Xibalba, daykeepers honed their senses in the lightless black for thirteen score days. Running through all the names and numbers of the days, praying, burning incense, letting their own blood, sleeping apart from women, and abstaining not only from meat but from corn products, eating nothing but the fruits of various trees. In this way they turned their attention inwards, sharpening their ability to perceive what was hidden, to See and to Send.

But those who were born without the genius of Sight could still play their part, by taking the *ilbal*. The crystals would take their toll on a body over time, but they were the keys that unlocked that which would otherwise remain hidden. With *ilbal*, one could see the fires through which we walk, and the shadows that lurk unseen all around us.

Izzie looked up from the journals, a little dizzy. Her hand cramped from writing so much, so furiously. She looked at what she had written.

"Ilbal?" she muttered under her breath. Where had she seen that before?

She reached for the copy of Samantha Aguilar's academic paper that lay on the far side of the desk. She flipped through, searching for the reference that she'd seen earlier until . . .

It was defined in a footnote to the main body of Samantha's text.

Ilbal: a Quiche word from the Popol Vuh. *Its literal meaning is a "seeing instrument" or a "place to see," though today ilbal (or ilobal) is a common term for crystals, mirrors, eyeglasses, telescopes, etc.*

What exactly was old man Aguilar describing here? From the context it seemed that this was written when he was a young man, and read as though he were transcribing something that he was being told by someone else, almost like a student taking lecture notes in a college class. With references to ancient Mayan myths and training in the secret temples of Xibalba, the only reasonable conclusion was that Aguilar had been writing down things that had been spoken aloud to him by Don Mateo, the old man from the Yucatan Peninsula. And according to Samantha's academic paper, everything from "Dark House" to "Xibalba" itself, from "ilbal" to "daykeeper," were references that were corroborated by the *Popol Vuh*, the classic Mayan text.

But Izzie couldn't help but remember things that had been said when she was a little girl about her grandmother, that Mawmaw was a "two-headed woman," able to see into the spirit world. That was not a million miles from the "genius" and "sight" that Aguilar had written about. And the ilbal? A key that helped one perceive things that could not be seen with the eye, including the "fires through which we walk"? That sounded like the ayahuasca that the Candomblé priestess who was friends with her grandmother had always talked about.

But it wasn't just a key, was it? It was a *crystal*.

Izzie sat up straight, lowering the pen.

"Wait a second . . ." she said out loud.

The vials of crystalline powder that had been found in Fuller's apartment. The ones that the lab had identified as being similar to DMT.

And what was it that Fuller had said, right at the end?

"I didn't understand it myself, until the old daykeeper gave me the key."

Izzie turned back to the journal that she had been reading. Roberto Aguilar had trained with a "daykeeper" from Mexico, and had carried on in that tradition after his teacher had long since died. He'd become a daykeeper himself, convinced that he was protecting humanity from dark menaces hidden from the view of the rest of the world. And years later, he had come into contact with a distressed young man who was convinced that his colleagues had been fundamentally altered by something they had experienced deep underground, and the old daykeeper had given him a key that helped him understand what was happening.

The drug in the vials *was* that key. That crystalline powder, a DMT-like psychedelic, was the "seeing instrument" that revealed things that were hidden.

"I'll be damned," she muttered to herself.

Fuller had *told* her what was happening, but she didn't understand at the time. He had noticed a change in the behavior of his colleagues on the Undersight team, and Roberto Aguilar had given him a drug that let him see what was responsible for that change. He could perceive for the first time that they were being "Ridden" by something . . . by something . . .

"By what, though?" Izzie muttered.

"Is everything okay?"

She looked up, surprised to see that Daphne was sitting at her desk a short distance away. Izzie had been so engrossed in what she was reading that she hadn't even noticed her coming in. She glanced over and saw that Agent Gutierrez's office door was open, and that he was sitting behind his desk inside. Daphne must have been meeting with him in there when Izzie came in. But how long had it been since she came back out?

"Oh, nothing," Izzie answered, a little sheepishly. "Just talking to myself, I guess."

Daphne bobbed her head back, pointing with her chin at the journals spread over Izzie's borrowed desk. "That's related to your Ink investigation, I take it?"

Izzie chewed her lower lip, considering her answer. "Tangentially, I guess you could say?"

Daphne nodded, seeming satisfied with the answer. "Well, let me know if you need anything," she said, and turned back to her computer.

"Thanks." Izzie returned her attention to the journals.

She figured that at some point Aguilar must have described in greater detail the nature of these "daimons" that he mentioned. And what of the "Unreal" from which they supposedly came?

Izzie kept on reading, intent on finding the answers.

The first time she came across the phrase "true place" in reference to Recondito in the journals, Izzie thought nothing of it. It was a somewhat unusual formulation, an adjective and a noun that, while not often appearing together in casual conversation, did not elicit much in the way of curiosity when encountered once in passing. She assumed that Aguilar had meant that the city was somehow authentic, though expressed somewhat awkwardly.

The next two times that she came across the phrase, she wondered if it was some sort of tic or habit that Aguilar had picked up somewhere along the way, but didn't dwell on it. Her Spanish was rusty, and her Quiche nonexistent. Perhaps "true place" was a direct translation into English of a concept from another language?

The fourth time that she read the phrase, though, she began to suspect that there was a deeper significance that she had missed at first glance. Especially, considering that it revealed that Recondito was not the only "true place," but simply one of many.

Don Mateo, Aguilar wrote, had originally come to Recondito in the 1930s precisely *because* it was a "true place," a region where the walls between the worlds were at their thinnest.

Samantha's academic paper was not of much guidance here. Izzie could only find two times that the old man's granddaughter-in-law had mentioned "true places." The first was an analysis of the phrase itself . . .

The recurrence of the term "true place" might be a reference to the phrase "saqil k'olem, saqil tzij," which appears in the Popol Vuh. *While typically translated into English as "enlightened existence, enlightened words," the Quiche word "k'olem" also carries the meaning "place," while "tzij" can be translated as "certain or true," so that the phrase could be rendered along the lines of "the clarity of the true place."*

The second note, interestingly, was not in reference to the Mayans or the Quiche language or anything to do with Mesoamerica at all, and was instead a mention of a similar concept halfway around the world.

In Tibet, "beyul" are conventionally understood to be hidden valleys in the Himalayas, sacred to the Tibetan Buddhists. But there is a mystical tradition which contends that beyul are in fact places where the worlds of the physical and the spiritual overlap, and it is for this reason that they are not to be found on any map.

Izzie was about to put the academic paper aside when she spotted a handwritten note on the back of one of the pages. It appeared to be a quotation, but it wasn't clear whether this was a revision that Samantha Aguilar intended to make to the paper, or a comment added by her husband or someone else, or something else entirely.

"Kokovoko, an island far away to the West and South. It is not down in any map; true places never are." – Herman Melville, Moby-Dick

That rang a bell with Izzie, and it took a moment before she remembered Patrick telling her about the name for Kensington Island in the native Te'Maroan language. Kovoko something, right? And Kensington Island was certainly far away to the west and south. Was there some other connection there? She would have to bring it up with Patrick when she spoke to him next.

She wondered how the door duty was going in the office building, and felt the slightest pang of sympathy for him being stuck with such an onerous task, which was considerably outweighed by her relief that she wasn't forced to help with it herself.

So, a "true place" was one where the material world intersected with the spiritual one, or something of that sort? And these were hidden away, not included on any map. Izzie could not help but recall the nickname for Recondito, the "Hidden City."

Elsewhere in his journals, the elder Aguilar mentioned that a similar true place had once existed in Central America, and that the order of Mayan daykeepers had arisen in ancient times to help safeguard their fellow men against the dangers inherent in trafficking with the otherworldly. But the dangers arose not only from the "shades" and "daimons" that inhabited that other world themselves, but from those men and women who sought to profit by communing with them, striking dark bargains.

Eventually the Mayan empire fell, and the daykeepers retreated to their secret temples deep in the jungle, still protecting the people as best they could. But centuries later a dark cabal took root amongst the Aztecs, a cabal that used human sacrifice to solicit the aid of the darker denizens of the other spheres, forging alliances with the very same otherworldly powers that the daykeepers had stood guard against.

But, as Aguilar put it in his journal, "the spheres turn in their gyres, and the influences wax and wane." Eventually, the true place situated in Central America was not as potent or reliable as it once had been, and it was as though the walls between the worlds had grown thicker, less permeable. But as that true place waned, another was on the ascendancy, a true place that by the latter days of the nineteenth century threatened to be the most potent, and most *dangerous*, of them all.

Recondito. The Hidden City.

It wasn't simply that strange things happened in the city and a select group of people knew about it. People who knew about such things came to the city *because* strange things happened there. This Don Mateo, certainly, had journeyed from the Yucatan Peninsula to the city in the 1930s because of the weirdness, if Roberto Aguilar's account was to be believed. And what about Patrick's great-uncle, Alfred Tevake? Had he traveled here from Kensington Island for the same reason?

Kensington Island might itself be another "true place," if there was some secret meaning hidden in that quote from *Moby-Dick*.

It all seemed possible. Crazy sounding, and definitely improbable, but not impossible.

But she still had not found any description or explanation in Aguilar's journals that helped bring the "daimons of the Unreal" themselves into clearer focus. And more and more she had begun to suspect that that was precisely the kind of information that would prove useful, if everything else that she had learned was correct.

"I'm going to grab some dinner at the food trucks outside," Daphne said, suddenly appearing beside Izzie's desk. "Want to come with?"

Izzie looked up, a little dazed. She was deep into the second journal now, filling the legal pad with notes, and was so caught up in her reading that she hadn't noticed Daphne's approach.

"Oh," she said, blinking a few times while getting her bearings. "No, that's okay. I had a late lunch." She paused, and then added, "Thanks, though. I just really want to get through this stuff today."

Daphne glanced at the legal pad, half of the pages already filled with notes. "What is all this, exactly?"

Izzie chewed her lower lip. "It's a little hard to explain."

She resisted the urge to cover up the legal pad before Daphne was able to read anything that was written on it, afraid of how that might look. In the end, though, Daphne just shrugged. "I get it," she said airily. "Complicated, right? Well, good luck with it. I'll be back in a while."

As Daphne turned and headed towards the door, Izzie glanced at her phone and saw that it was almost six o'clock. She wondered for a brief moment how Patrick's search was going, but then felt her attention being drawn back to Aguilar's journals like iron filings to a magnet. There were answers hidden there, she was sure of it.

She had been reading a discussion of the "Rattling House," which according to Don Mateo had been the part of Xibalba where a different type of training had been carried out. But Izzie couldn't quite puzzle out the references to "Shifting" and "Shadowing," and she wondered if this was another instance of a Quiche term being awkwardly translated into English. One could master the art of Shifting to other branches on the World Tree, or Shadowing through solid objects and to other places on Earth, by learning to travel freely along each of the four paths that lead from the Crossroads: north and south, east and west, up and down, inward and outward. What could any of that possibly mean?

Samantha Aguilar's academic paper proved to be of little help on this point, only comparing what the old man described in the journal as being somewhat similar to the Sufi concept of *tay al-makan*, or "folding of space," a kind of miracle that the enlightened could accomplish which involved moving instantly to distant locations. There was a handwritten note in the margins, clearly penned by her husband Ricardo.

Samantha, I'm reminded here of the work of the nineteenth century British mathematician Charles H. Hinton, who proposed a fourth spatial dimension in addition to the three dimensions that humans are able to perceive. Might these instances of "inward" and "outward" be equivalent to the terms for movement through the fourth dimension that Hinton coined, moving either ana *(from the Greek for "up toward")* or kata *(from the Greek for "down from")? - RA*

Izzie sat back. Fuller had mentioned Hinton in his note in the margins of the self-help book by the founder of the Eschaton Center, who had described wisdom as *"emanating to ana from kata out of the higher realms beyond."* And in the email thread about the Ink injectors, Ibrahim Fayed had mentioned *"ana/kata leakage."*

And what was it that Fuller had said that night in the light-house? *"Gravity leaks into other spaces, but doors swing both ways."* Professor Kono had explained to them all about the experiment that Fuller had originally planned to conduct with the Undersight equipment, an attempt to prove his theory that the reason that gravity was the weakest of the fundamental forces was because it "leaked" into the higher dimensions. And that Fuller also hoped to prove that our universe is only one of many that orbit through that higher dimensional space, and that sometimes two or more universes can come into contact with each other, with often-dramatic results.

This brought her back to old man Aguilar and his teacher Don Mateo, and their talk of spheres turning in their gyres, influences waxing and waning, and true places where the walls between the worlds were at their thinnest.

Izzie was beginning to feel like one of Patrick's cargo cultists, praying for the metal birds to return, and finding themselves suddenly stumbling across an airport runway.

The only possible conclusion that made sense to her was that all of these people were talking about the same thing, though approaching it from different directions and with wildly different vocabularies. The scientists saw it as a scientific matter, the academics considered it a question of mythology, and the mystics believed it to be a kind of magic, but in the end it was the same reality that they were describing. There were worlds beyond our own, things could move from one world to another, and there were places where that kind of contact or communication . . . or *contamination*? . . . was more likely to occur.

But if doors swung both ways, just what was coming through to this side?

More than halfway through the third journal, Izzie finally found an answer, in a section in which the elder Aguilar described the ways in which he safeguarded the people of Recondito from otherworldly threats.

When he first mentioned putting salt on the ground, Izzie had initially thought that Aguilar was talking about dealing with icy roads in winter. Then she remembered where she was, and how unlikely it was that the roads in Recondito would get icy in the first place. So what was he talking about? She backtracked and reread more carefully.

Salt spread on the ground will serve as a barrier against them, and other crystals can serve a similar purpose. In addition, they are reluctant to pass over running water, fire can keep them at bay, and loud discordant noises can serve to disorient them. But these are only deterrents, and cannot destroy one who is Ridden. Silver can disrupt the connection with the host, whether introduced by bullet or by blade, but unless it remains in the body the disruption will be temporary, and the connection may be restored if the silver is removed while the body is still viable. But the only way to permanently sever the link is to render the body into pieces small enough that they cannot be controlled.

Izzie remembered her grandmother's barrier of red brick dust, protection against spiritual threats. Would the silica contained in the dust be sufficiently crystalline to serve the purpose that Aguilar was describing here? Or was that another instance of cargo cult thinking, aping the form of something without the function?

Which brought to mind the symbols etched by Patrick's great-uncle into the walls of Little Kovoko and filled with white paint mixed with sea salt. Had it been the symbols themselves that safeguarded the southwestern corner of the Oceanview, or the salt in the paint, or both?

Izzie was copying out the passage about deterring and destroying the Ridden in the pages of the legal pad when her phone began to buzz. She glanced over, and saw that it was Patrick calling.

She put the pen down on the legal pad and picked up the phone from where it lay on the corner of the desk, sliding the answer bar and putting it to her ear. "What's up?"

"It's, uh . . ." Patrick began, and faltered. "You should get down here. There's something you need to see."

Izzie sat up a little straighter. Patrick's voice sounded strained, breathless, and perhaps a little scared.

"What is it?" she asked. "What's wrong?"

"I . . ." She could hear him swallowing hard, or possibly gasping for air. "You just need to see for yourself."

As Izzie stood up from the desk, Daphne came in carrying a bottle of Italian soda and a paper bag.

"Okay, I'll be there as quick as I can," Izzie answered. "Where am I going, exactly?"

"What?" Patrick sounded a little dazed, or at least preoccupied.

"Can you send me the address?" Izzie said, speaking slowly and deliberately.

"Oh. Right. Hang on."

A second later, Izzie's phone chimed with an incoming text. She glanced at the screen, seeing a new message from Patrick that was simply a street address in the Oceanview.

"Get down here," Patrick said. "I already talked to Joyce and she's heading here as soon as she cleans up. This is . . . you'll see."

"Okay, I'm on my way," Izzie said, before realizing that Patrick had already hung up.

"Trouble?" Daphne asked, putting the soda and bag down on her desk.

Izzie was already shouldering into her suede jacket. "That police lieutenant I'm working with wants me to see something in the Oceanview. He's been down there knocking on doors, and I guess he turned something up."

"Come on," Daphne said, reaching for her keys. "I can give you a ride down."

"No, that's twice in one day, and I . . ." Izzie began, then trailed off when she saw the look on Daphne's face.

"Seriously, it's no trouble." Daphne gestured to the paperwork on her desk. "It's not like this mess isn't going to be here waiting for me when I get back."

Izzie considered objecting, but then she thought about the urgency that she'd heard in Patrick's voice, the tone that almost sounded like desperation. She needed to get there as quickly as possible.

"Okay, okay," Izzie answered, clipping her holstered pistol back on her belt. She pulled open a drawer on the front of the desk, and slid the journals, academic paper, and legal pad inside. Then she turned and headed towards the door, where

Daphne was already waiting, sipping her Italian soda with one hand and with her keys ready in the other.

"I'll let you drive," Izzie said with a sly grin to Daphne, "but only because you asked so nicely."

CHAPTER TWENTY-FIVE

"Are you sure this is the right place?" Daphne said as she put her car into park by the side of the road.

Izzie double-checked the address that Patrick had texted her, then glanced up at the street sign at the end of the block, and then looked over to the number painted above the entrance of the nearest building.

"Yeah," she said, glancing quickly back at the phone. "This would seem to be the place." She looked up and out the car window. "Not sure what we're supposed to be seeing *here*, though."

As best as she could recall from the GPS maps captured from Ibrahim Fayed's "find friends" app, this was indeed the block that the six suspects had passed through on their way to the Pinnacle Tower that morning. There were self-storage facilities on the east side of the street, and a warehouse converted into office space on the west side, just as Chavez had described. But there was no sign of Patrick, or of any other police presence for that matter.

"Come on," Daphne said, opening the driver side door and swinging her feet out onto the pavement. "Let's look around, maybe they're just inside or something."

Izzie shrugged, unbuckled her seatbelt, and opened the passenger side door.

Even if she hadn't known that they were only a couple of blocks away from the bayside docks, she would have been able to tell in an instant just from smelling the air. Even mixed with the freshwater that flowed into the bay from the Varada River in the east, the briny scent of the seawater that swept past Ivory Point into the estuary from the ocean was almost overpowering.

The sun had set a couple of hours before, but the glare from the streetlamps on either end of the block was nearly as bright as daylight. There were a few cars parked further up the street, but nothing in the immediate vicinity of the address that Patrick had provided.

"Should I call him?" Izzie asked, turning in place to look first one way down the street and then the other. Then she remembered that his number was still in the contact list of her own "find friends" app. She pulled her phone out of her pocket, woke it up, and then tapped the icon to open the app. It took a moment for the GPS to calibrate, and then it swooped and panned until it was centered on the northeast corner of the Oceanview. There was the dot that indicated Izzie's own location, and a moment later the dot labeled with Patrick's name came sliding in from the side as the location data became gradually more granular, eventually coming to a stop only a short distance from her own. Izzie looked up from the phone and glanced around. "We should be right on top of him."

She stepped out into the street, craning her neck to look as far down the block in either direction as possible. It was then that she saw a vintage Volkswagen Beetle come haring around the corner at what was clearly an unsafe speed, windows down and the Dead Milkmen's "Punk Rock Girl" blaring from the car stereo. For a moment Izzie was sure she was about to be run over, leaping to one side just as the Volkswagen screeched to a halt directly behind Daphne's compact hybrid.

"Hey, Izzie!" a voice from the darkened interior of the Volkswagen shouted.

Daphne gave Izzie a look, one eyebrow arched quizzically.

The door swung open, and an impressively buckled-and-strapped thick-soled boot clumped down onto the pavement, followed in short order by a cane and then another boot. Joyce unfolded herself from the diminutive car, and rested heavily on the cane in her hands. She was dressed much like she had been the previous day, only with a black leather jacket on instead of the lab coat she wore down in the morgue.

"Friend of yours?" Daphne asked Izzie.

"Special Agent Daphne Richardson," Izzie answered, looking from her to Joyce, "this is Dr. Joyce Nguyen, Recondito's Chief Medical Examiner." Then, when Joyce raised a finger, about to correct her, Izzie amended, "*only* Medical Examiner, that is."

Keeping one hand on the head of her cane, Joyce extended the other to Daphne. They shook and nodded curtly before Joyce knocked the Volkswagen's door shut with her hip and then started to walk away. She pulled an ID badge on a lanyard out of her pocket and slipped it over her head.

"You two coming?" Joyce asked, calling back over her shoulder as she walked straight past the entrance to the office building with its intercom and security panel, and continued on towards the corner of the block.

"Coming *where*?" Izzie asked, as she and Daphne trailed after.

"Didn't Patrick tell you?" Even using the cane, Joyce could move surprisingly fast. "I was finishing up an autopsy when he called . . . automotive fatality, pedestrian hit in a crosswalk, totally run-of-the-mill stuff . . . anyway, I was closing her up and about to hose down when Patrick called and told me to come running. Said he'd found something while doing a door-to-door that he needed me to look at right away, and that he was calling you next."

"Right," Izzie answered. "Which he did. But all he gave me was an address, and there's no sign of him."

Joyce rolled her eyes. "That goofball. He sucks at giving directions. One time he called me out to the site of a double homicide in the Hyde Park . . . the park itself, not the neighborhood . . . but didn't bother to tell me *where* in the park. I was clomping up and down that damned lawn for an hour before I found him. Well, I've learned my lesson, so I made sure to get *specific* directions." She stopped short, gesturing with her cane like a carnival barker. "And so, *voilà*."

Daphne and Izzie looked around, and then to each other. There was nothing here, no door, no alleyway. Nothing.

Joyce saw the confusion on their faces and grinned, then brought the heel of her cane down hard on the sidewalk, three times in rapid succession. The impact didn't make the thud they might have expected, but something more in line with a *clang*.

Joyce then raised the cane and pressed the tip against the wall of the building, where it pressed a red button on a control panel that Izzie had not noticed before that moment.

"Presto!" Joyce said with a smile, and then stepped to one side as a pair of hinged metal plates on the pavement levered open with the sound of hydraulics hissing somewhere underfoot. A kind of cage clanked up into view, open on two sides and with a curving bar overhead.

"Sidewalk elevator," Joyce explained. "From when this was a working warehouse. They'd use it to load things in and out of the lower levels while the big bays on the ground floor were occupied."

The elevator car clanked to a halt, the metal plates that formed its base now level with the sidewalk's pavement.

"Come on," Joyce went on, pulling the gate open and stepping inside. "We don't want to keep Patrick waiting."

The trip to the bottom of the service elevator's shaft took longer than Izzie had thought possible, and the cage that carried them down had shaken and rattled so noisily along the way that it felt to her as if they had undertaken a long, laborious descent into the underworld, and had not simply gone down two floors to a warehouse subbasement.

The elevator opened onto a dimly lit hallway, with just a sparse few flickering fluorescents up ahead to light their way. The air down here felt cool and damp, but with a strange tinge to it that Izzie found familiar but could not quite place.

"Why ask us to come down *this* way?" Izzie said, looking around.

"Patrick said he was trying to avoid a panic in the office building upstairs," Joyce replied as she stepped out of the elevator cage and onto the concrete floor. "He's hoping to keep this low key until we get a handle on it."

"I didn't realize that buildings in this part of Recondito *had* basements, much less *subbasements*," Daphne said, glancing around. "Especially this close to the water. Isn't this below sea level?"

Joyce shook her head. "No, just above it, actually. With the cliffs on the ocean side and the big hill leading up from the docks, this part of the Oceanview is actually higher above sea level than you'd expect."

The hallway led to the left and right away from the elevator, with closed doors every ten feet or so on either side. There was one open door to their left, though, and as Izzie glanced in that direction she saw a uniformed police officer step out into the hallway, hands over his face.

"Excuse me?" Joyce said, starting to walk in his direction.

The officer lowered his hands and looked towards them, and Izzie recognized him as Officer Carlson, the one who had worked the door ram during the raid on Malcolm Price's home earlier in the week. His expression looked haunted, mouth hanging open, eyes wide and staring.

"What's going on?" Izzie asked. "Is Lieutenant Tevake...?"

Officer Carlson just pointed back through the doorway out of which he'd just stepped. "In there," he said before language seemed to fail him, and he turned away, covering his mouth with his hand as if trying not to gag.

Daphne and Izzie exchanged a glance as Joyce looked back over her shoulder at them. "This looks promising, doesn't it?" the medical examiner said, humorlessly. "Come on, let's go see."

Izzie tasted a familiar foulness on her tongue as she stepped through the door, and nausea roiled in her gut. When she took her first breath after entering the room, her nostrils stung with the same bouquet of ozone and body odor, floral scent and rotten meat that she had first smelled in Malcolm Price's kitchen, only here the smell was much stronger, much more pervasive.

As she looked around the room her eyes began to water, too, as though she were staring into a bright light, though the few bare bulbs burning in the wall sockets were scarcely bright enough to illuminate the cavernous low-ceilinged space they were entering. The room was about the size of Joyce's morgue, and in some ways seemed like a dark mirror version of the sterile order of the medical examiner's domain. There were bodies here too, for example. . . .

Patrick was standing to one side, arms at his sides, staring blankly at the gruesome tableau spread out before them.

"Oh . . ." Joyce said, taking a tentative step towards the nearest of the bodies. "Oh, my . . ."

Izzie approached Patrick, leaving Daphne standing in the open doorway, taking it all in.

"Patrick?" she said, as she drew nearer to where he stood. "What happened here?"

Patrick looked up, a confused expression flitting briefly across his face, as though he didn't recognize her at first, and then recognized her but couldn't remember why she might be there. Only after his features settled back into a more neutral expression of professionalism and comprehension did he answer. "Oh, good. You made it."

Izzie glanced from him to the bodies lying facedown on the benches. She looked closer, and realized that they were massage tables, with headrests on one end for the people being massaged to rest their foreheads, and holes for their faces to fit. Their arms were arranged neatly at their sides, knuckles down and palms facing behind them, their legs close together. There were towels or sheets draped across their midsections covering their buttocks, and if Izzie had slightly worse vision (and no sense of smell) or the lights had been a little more dim, she might have thought they were massage clients waiting patiently for the masseuse to return. But Izzie could see just fine, and the lights were bright enough to see not only the bodies lying peacefully on the massage tables, but the needles and shunts and such that bristled along the backs of their skulls and down their spines, and the large lesion-like dark "blots" that covered their exposed skin. Black plastic tubing snaked from the shunts to either side of the massage tables, draping over the edges and trailing on the ground until they reached a black plastic pump of some kind that sat atop a glass jar. Aside from the massage tables, the tubes, the pump, and the jar, the only other item of note looked like a rolling metal tool chest along the far wall, where the corners of the room were draped in shadows.

Izzie could not shake the sensation that she had been here before, or somewhere very much like this. Then she remembered the dream that she'd had about taking an elevator down from the middle of the street, all the way down into the inky darkness where a silver-skulled grim reaper waited. The reaper had wanted to show her something in the shadows. Was this what she was supposed to have seen?

CHAPTER TWENTY-SIX

"**W**hat the hell is all this, Patrick?" Izzie asked. "And how did you *find* it?"

It took Patrick a moment before he was able to collect himself sufficiently to answer. "I, um . . ." He licked his lips, blinking a few times. "Carlson and I were going door to door upstairs, checking each of the office spaces, seeing if anyone had seen anything unusual. Spent a few hours at it, and by the time we hit the last office we'd come up with nothing. Figured it was time to call it a day and went back outside, and it was then that I noticed the sidewalk elevator. I didn't realize there was a basement in the place before then, but I couldn't get the elevator to work. Turns out it was locked down on this end, but I didn't know that at the time. I figured, we've checked all the offices upstairs, though, so we should probably check out whatever's in the basements before I sign off on the building altogether. So we went back inside and poked around until we found the basement entrance. Somebody had dummied up the original door to the stairway down so that it looked like an electrical closet. They were *trying* to keep people out. So we went down."

Patrick took a deep breath, looking up at the ceiling for a moment before continuing.

"We checked the basement, and there was nothing there. Just a bunch of junk. Old office equipment. Pallets. Nothing of interest. But when we found the sidewalk elevator shaft, the elevator wasn't there. It was one floor *down*. There was a subbasement." He gestured around them, indicating the level where they stood. "We found a way down, and . . ." He nodded a few times. "Well . . . we found this."

There were half a dozen bodies on an equal number of massage tables. Joyce was pulling on a pair of blue nitrile gloves while looking down at the one nearest the door, eyes narrowed, deep in concentration.

"Are they all dead?" Izzie said, looking around.

"Yeah," Patrick answered. "Maybe. I think. I'm not sure." He seemed shaken. "I . . . I don't feel so great."

He seemed really shaken up. More so than Izzie would have expected, even considering how gruesome the scene was. He was acting more like someone who was suffering from a severe fever, or who'd had too many cocktails, too quickly. Disoriented. Out of it.

"Izzie?" Daphne was stepping away from the doorway, coming deeper into the room, eyes on the bodies. "What is this? I thought you were working some kind of drug investigation?"

Patrick seemed to notice Daphne for the first time, eyes widening fractionally with surprise, or perhaps alarm. "You brought someone with you, Izzie?" he asked, his jaw tightening.

"Agent Daphne Richardson," Izzie explained. "She gave me a ride from the Resident Agency offices."

Patrick nodded slowly, as if considering what he thought about having Daphne present for this.

"I haven't called this in yet," he finally said, still looking at Daphne but addressing his remarks to Izzie. "Not officially."

Now it was Izzie's turn to look surprised. "What?! Why not?"

Patrick pointed at Daphne with his chin. "How much does she know, Izzie?"

"About what?"

Patrick turned and met Izzie's gaze. "I'm trying to get a handle on this before I bring in . . . well, before I have to explain it to Chavez and the others. I think this is . . ." He glanced over at the bodies that Joyce was already busy inspecting, and started walking in that direction. "I think that this is some *weirdness* right here."

Izzie followed him across the floor.

"I put a call into Chavez when I found this," Patrick explained. "But I kept it vague. Told him we'd found something, and that I wanted to check it out more before I made a full report, and that he should have our unmarked cars continue to patrol the area in the meantime. I mentioned that there might be something here for the Medical Examiner to check out, but that the scene was sensitive and I didn't want too many people traipsing around in it until we had it fully secure." He glanced back at Izzie, and added, "Which is true, as far as it goes. But the real reason is . . . well, take a look."

They had reached the nearest of the bodies. The smell that she'd noticed when coming into the room—a confusing blend of pleasant and foul, organic and inorganic—was even stronger here, intermingling with the peppery scent of bodies gone long unwashed.

"There." Patrick pointed at a black plastic tube leading from a shunt drilled into the base of the man's skull.

Izzie could hear faint squelching sounds, and there was a low hum from the black plastic pump a short distance across the floor.

"What am I supposed to be seeing?" Izzie said.

Patrick turned to Joyce, who had moved to the next table over. "Do you have a spare glove?"

Joyce pulled a pair of blue nitrile gloves out of her pocket and tossed them to Patrick. He pulled one onto his right hand, and then reached out for the black plastic tube, a few inches from where it connected to the shunt in the man's skull. "Watch," he said, then pinched the plastic tube off between his thumb and forefinger.

As Izzie watched, the black color leeched out of the plastic tube slowly, like molasses being sucked through a straw, starting at the point where Patrick was squeezing it shut with his fingers, and becoming increasingly clear as it traveled towards the black pump.

"And . . ." Patrick said, and released his hold on the tube.

Blackness surged into the tube from the shunt with a loud squelch, gradually filling it with oozing black all the way to the pump again.

"This stuff is being sucked out of their heads," Patrick said. "And that's not all. Take a closer look at the 'blots' on their skin."

Izzie looked down at the man's back. The black marks that marked his skin seemed to be the standard variety lesions associated with prolonged Ink use to her, just like the pair of shamblers that she had passed in Hyde Park a few nights before.

"And if I do *this* . . ." Patrick said, and poked the middle of the man's back with the index finger of his gloved hand.

Izzie jumped back as if a snake had suddenly appeared before her, preparing to strike.

"They moved!" She wheeled on Patrick. "The blots *moved!*"

Izzie turned and looked at the man on the massage table again, narrowing her eyes. Sure enough, the blots were sliding around underneath the man's skin like cockroaches moving around under a sheet, fleeing from the spot that Patrick had just poked with his finger.

"How is that *possible*?" she said.

"I'm working on it," Joyce called over from the next table. "And to answer your earlier question, these people *are* dead." She paused, leaning in to look more closely at the body in front of her, and added, "Well, *mostly* . . ."

"Mostly dead?" Daphne said, coming to stand beside Izzie. "As in *The Princess Bride*, 'mostly dead is slightly alive'?"

Joyce looked up, pursed her lips, and nodded. "Basically, yeah. I don't have all of the diagnostic equipment to make a definitive prognosis, but things just aren't lining up here. None of the bodies that I've checked so far shows any evidence of a pulse, so their hearts don't seem to be beating, but I'm not seeing any evidence of pallor mortis in the Caucasian subjects. And they seem to have been down here a while, and their body temperatures should have been dropping until they reached the ambient temperature of the room, but they're all still right at 98.6 degrees Fahrenheit." She crouched down until she could lean under one of the headrests and look up at the exposed face of one of the bodies. She pulled a penlight out of her pocket, pried open the lids on one eye with one hand, and shined a light into it with the other. "No sign of primary flaccidity, and the pupils are nonresponsive, but the pupils aren't dilated, they're completely constricted."

She switched off the penlight and used her cane to haul herself back to her feet.

"They definitely seem to be no longer among the living, but at the same time, they don't appear to be entirely deceased." Joyce paused for a moment, and then shrugged. "I have *no* idea how that's possible, or what it means."

"And the blots moving around like that?" Izzie said, still a little shaken. The sense of nausea in her gut seemed to be growing stronger. "Like they're *alive*?"

"Honestly?" Joyce shook her head. "That's even harder to explain. If they really were some kind of parasite, maybe, but then we'd possible see . . . But no, even then it wouldn't be manifesting these kinds of symptoms. We're seeing subcutaneous bruising of some kind where those 'blots' appear, and it's not like bruises can *move*. Not like that, anyway. So even if there were something in there that was causing the bruising that *was* capable of moving, it would be leaving some kind of *trail*, right?"

"Izzie?" Daphne was standing right beside her, a mixture of confusion, fear, and annoyance on her face. "What the hell is going on? Is this the kind of 'complication' you were talking about?"

Joyce glanced to Daphne, and then looked to Izzie. "She doesn't know? About the other stuff?"

Daphne's expression grew harder. "What other stuff?"

"The dead man who attacked Izzie the other day," Joyce said, matter-of-factly. "The corpses with the holes in their brains. The connection between the Reaper murders and the Ink trade, whatever it turns out to be. That kind of stuff."

"Lieutenant Tevake?" Carlson was standing in the open doorway. "What the heck is she talking about?"

Joyce turned to Patrick, who had a sour expression on his face. "I guess *he* didn't know, either?" she said, apologetically.

"Don't worry about it, Carlson," Patrick said, glancing over towards the doorway. "I'll explain everything later. You keep watch in the hall and let me know the second you hear anyone coming." He licked his lips again, which seemed to be a nervous tic. "We don't know if Fayed's 'friends' are planning to drop by again tonight, and I don't want to get caught with our pants down."

Carlson nodded, clearly dissatisfied with the answer, but not in any hurry to spend more time in the room with the bodies than he absolutely had to.

When the officer had stepped back out into the hall, Patrick turned back to Joyce. "No," he said, his voice lowered, "I've been keeping this on a need-to-know basis, and so far only you, me, and Agent Lefevre really *needed* to know." He glanced over at Daphne. "And now *you're* in the loop too, I guess."

"Riiight," Daphne said, stretching out the word for effect. "So nice to be clued in. You've been a *big* help." She shook her head and turned back to Izzie. "Look, whatever is going on here . . . it's *crazy*. You realize that, right?"

"It's . . ." Izzie began, then trailed off. "It's complicated?" She couldn't seem to find the right place to begin to explain.

Daphne did not relent, but stepped over to the nearest of the bodies. "Who *did* this to these people? And what are they *doing* to them?" She turned, and pointed at the black plastic pump that all of the tubes seemed to be feeding into. "What *is* that stuff that's being pumped out of them?!"

"That's one of my most pressing questions, too," Joyce said, walking over to where the pump squatted on the concrete like a malevolent toad. She knelt down. "This isn't medical equipment. More like something from a chem lab, or an industrial site." She leaned her head down to get a better look at the jar that the pump was sitting on top of. "Huh. That almost looks like . . ."

She straightened up.

"Patrick, have you taken a good look at this jar?" she asked.

Patrick shook his head, still clearly more than a little disoriented. Izzie couldn't help feeling that she was beginning to lose her bearings as well.

"Well, *do* so," Joyce said. "And tell me that doesn't look like Ink."

Patrick's eyes widened a little, and he crossed the floor to where Joyce knelt.

"I'm feeling a little . . ." Izzie began, then after a pause continued. "A little light-headed."

She glanced over at Daphne, who had a hand over her stomach, and a queasy expression on her face. "Is there some kind of gas leak down here?" Daphne asked.

Izzie sniffed the air. The strange aroma, the odd taste on her tongue, the watering eyes . . . could it all be due to a gas leak?

Or was something *else* leaking in?

"I'll be damned," Patrick said, bending down and looking at the jar. "I've only seen Ink in liquid form a couple of times, but that *does* look just like it." He straightened up, his eyes tracing the path from the pump back to the bodies. "But how is that even possible?"

Izzie walked over to the metal rolling tool chest that stood along the far wall. She took a tissue out of her jacket pocket, and used it to grab on to the handle of the top drawer without interfering with any fingerprints that might be there. Then she tugged the drawer open. Inside she found several unused syringes and a box of surgical gloves. She shoved the drawer shut, and pulled out the next one down.

The second drawer was filled with auto-injector pens like the ones they'd found in Malcolm Price's kitchen. She picked one of them up with the tissue.

"Patrick?" She glanced across the room. "Take a look at this."

The auto-injector seemed to shift in her grip, as if its center of gravity was rolling from one end to the other.

Patrick came over and took the auto-injector pen from her, holding it between his blue-gloved thumb and forefinger.

"Yeah, this is an Ink injector all right. And it seems to be fully charged." He glanced over at the jar filled with viscous black liquid that Joyce was studying, and the tubes leading to the bodies on the massage tables. "So they're extracting Ink *from* these people and then putting it in these injector pens? That doesn't make any sense. Unless . . ."

He was interrupted by a noise from out in the hallway, and from somewhere in the walls or ceiling overhead the sound of hydraulic motors could be heard hissing and grinding.

"Lieutenant?" Carlson stuck his head in the open doorway, a worried tone in his voice. "Someone's coming down the elevator."

Patrick scowled as he tossed the injector pen back into the drawer, and then drew his pistol in one hand, and pulled his radio out of a jacket pocket with the other. "Damn. The unmarked cars on patrol should have spotted something." He pressed a button on the side of the radio and spoke. "Chavez, Tevake here. We've got unknowns entering the facility, and I need backup down here." He paused, letting his finger off the button, but got only static in response. He pressed the button and tried again. "Chavez? Can you hear me?"

Izzie stepped away from the tool chest, unholstered her own pistol, and did her best to shake off whatever it was that had disoriented her. Now was not the time.

"Izzie?" Daphne appeared at her side, a pistol in her hand. "Did you hear that?"

She glanced in Daphne's direction. "Yeah. Someone's coming."

"No," Daphne said, shaking her head and turning away from the door. She gestured with the barrel of her pistol. "*That.*"

Izzie turned to look behind her.

The bodies on the tables might have been mostly dead, but that wasn't stopping them from moving. One of them was raising its head, while another was turning on its side.

"Izzie?!" Daphne raised her voice as her eyebrows shot up. "What the *hell*?!"

"Patrick," Izzie said, turning her head slowly to look at the massage tables that surrounded them. "We've got a problem . . ."

All of the bodies were getting up off the tables and onto their feet, trailing the plastic tubes behind them, like marionettes that no longer needed a puppeteer to guide them. Their eyes were wide and sightless, their mouths moving but without a sound to be heard.

And on their skin the inky blots swirled and swelled as they began to shamble forwards.

CHAPTER TWENTY-SEVEN

"**P**atrick?" Izzie kept her pistol trained on the nearest of the shamblers with one hand, gently taking hold of Daphne's elbow with the other, pulling her back away from them.

"Chavez? Harrison? Dispatch, do you read?" Patrick lowered the radio, his eyes still on the door. "I'm not getting through to anyone."

"Patrick, you might want to turn around," Joyce said, standing near the pump.

He glanced back over his shoulder, and his eyes widened. "Christ!"

Izzie and Daphne had backed up almost all the way to where Joyce was standing. "I tried to tell you," Izzie said.

"Carlson! What are we looking at out there?" Patrick called towards the door.

They could hear the elevator clanking to a halt at the sub-basement level.

"Somebody's getting off . . ." They could just see Carlson in the hallway beyond the door. He drew his service revolver, and stepped out of view, towards the elevator shaft down the hall. "You there! Stay where you are, don't come any closer." There was a pause. "What are you . . . ?"

Carlson stepped back into view, glancing uneasily through the door at Patrick and the others. "Sir? I'm not sure . . ."

Suddenly hands grabbed at Carlson from just out of view, and pulled him away from the doorway.

"What?!" They heard Carlson shout, quickly followed by, "Nooooo!"

Patrick raced for the doorway, with Izzie following close behind. But before they reached it a figure stepped into view, blocking their way.

It was a man, his head titled forward, arms at his sides, wearing only what seemed to be a bedsheet draped over his shoulder and bound at the waist. There seemed to be something wrapped crisscross around the crown of his shaved head, but Izzie couldn't quite make out what it was. Wire, maybe? Or perhaps it was some kind of tattoo?

Patrick raised his pistol, aiming it at the man. "Recondito Police," he said, with as much authority as he could muster.

The bedsheet-clad man ignored him, but took a shambling step forward, entering the room.

"I really think we need to address *that*," Joyce said, nodding towards the six mostly-dead bodies who were standing in a semicircle facing them.

"Guys?" Daphne said. "What the hell is going on here?"

Izzie turned from the door to the six bodies standing behind them, and back again. "Patrick?"

"Hang on," he told her, and then raised his voice to call out, "Carlson? You okay out there?"

The bedsheet-clad man raised his head. His mouth hung open and his eyes were rolled up in their sockets.

His face was instantly familiar, but it took Izzie a moment to place it.

"Tyler Campbell," Joyce said, in a voice that was scarcely above a whisper.

"The drug dealer?" Izzie said, and then remembered where she'd seen that face before—on a body lying under a sheet in the morgue the night she'd arrived in town. The lines on his head weren't wire or tattoos, but were instead stitches, showing where Joyce had cut his scalp, cracked open his skull to remove the brain, and then sewed him up again afterwards.

"It's impossible. He was *dead*." Joyce's eyes were wide, her mouth hanging open. "I removed his *brain*."

"Campbell?" Patrick said, keeping his tone level. "Is there anything of you left in there?"

As if in response, the dead drug dealer took another step forward, and raised both his arms, hands out and grasping.

Behind them, the six mostly-dead bodies took a step forward and raised their arms, too, their movements so precisely timed and in sync that they might have been choreographed.

"Okay, I am *seriously* done with this," Daphne said, hands clenching the handle of her pistol even tighter. "Whatever the hell *this* is."

"I promise I'll explain everything as soon as we get out of here," Izzie said. She didn't feel it necessary to qualify that with an "if." That much went unspoken.

"Patrick?" Joyce said. "Any ideas?"

"I'm thinking," he said quietly, sounding harried. "I'm thinking."

They were being hemmed in by seven bodies that reason would dictate shouldn't be able to move at all.

But reason had left the building some time before.

D aphne was the first to be attacked. The nearest of the mostly-dead things swiped at her, hands grasping.

"Stay back!" Daphne shouted, but the thing kept coming.

Daphne fired two rounds from her pistol, hitting the body squarely in the chest, but it barely flinched. She danced back out of reach just before its hands were able to close around her neck.

"What the hell *is* this?" she shouted.

Joyce clocked another with her cane, but even a solid hit to the side of its head was not enough to slow it down.

They were being surrounded, and their weapons were proving useless.

"We need to get out of here," Izzie said, lowering her pistol. She thought back to what she had read in Aguilar's journals. What deterred these things? Salt, fire, running water, and . . .

"Joyce," she said, turning to the medical examiner. "You've got to have some kind of horrible music on your phone, right? Something loud?"

Joyce blinked absently for a moment, but reached into the pocket of her leather jacket, and took out a phone in a rhinestone-studded case. "I haven't transferred my music library over for a while. I keep most of it on my desktop at work, or in the cloud. I'm sure there's something on here but . . ."

"Doesn't matter," Izzie answered, "as long as it's *loud*."

"What have you got in mind?" Patrick asked.

"Bullets aren't going to work," she answered. "Not unless you've got *silver* bullets on you." She ignored their bewildered looks and pressed on. "Look, I'll explain later, but for the moment, we need to distract or disorient these things long enough for us to get out of here. Loud discordant sounds might do the trick."

Joyce was tabbing through the music library on her phone's screen. "I thought I had Nitzer Ebb or Kraftwerk on here, but I can't find them. Joy Division, maybe? Or . . ."

"Just play something!" Patrick snapped.

"Okay, okay," Joyce shot back. She slid the volume bar to the highest level, and stabbed a finger at the screen.

"*I'VE BEEN CHEATED BY YOU SINCE I DON'T KNOW WHEN*

"*SO I MADE UP MY MIND, IT MUST COME TO AN END . . .*"

The music blaring from the phone's small speaker was surprisingly loud, especially as it echoed off the low ceiling and bare concrete floor of the room.

"How it this supposed to be helping, exactly?" Daphne said, wincing at the sound.

"I'll explain later," Izzie said. "Let's just hope that it *is*." She grabbed Daphne's free hand, and dragged her towards the door. "Come on, Patrick, we're leaving."

"What about *him*?" Joyce said, as she and Patrick edged around the dead drug dealer who was standing a few steps in from the doorway.

"Your phone." Izzie nodded to Joyce, then to the drug dealer. "Put it between you and him."

Joyce did, and Izzie could see that the dead man was clearly affected by the sound. He swayed a little uneasily on his feet, head moving from side to side, as if he were trying to find something in the dark and couldn't quite see it. The other six dead people on the other side of the room were similarly affected, their movements more disorganized, less in sync.

"I guess nobody likes AB—" Patrick began, before Joyce slugged him in the shoulder with her free hand, silencing him.

"Is this *really* the time?" Joyce asked, exasperated.

Izzie was already stepping out into the hall. She could see Officer Carlson on the concrete floor, his head twisted at an unnatural angle. But he was showing no signs of getting up and moving around, unlike all of the other dead people today, it seemed.

Daphne was still holding onto Izzie's free hand, and didn't seem eager to let go. "Where . . .? Where are we going?" She managed, then took a deep breath, centering herself. Between one eyeblink and the next, she went from frightened and confused to being the highly trained and efficient Bureau agent that Izzie knew that she was.

Patrick and Joyce had followed them out into the hallway.

"Which way?" Daphne asked again, releasing her hold on Izzie's hand. She seemed more composed by the second, more in command of herself.

Izzie felt the disorientation that she'd experienced in the room begin to subside as well, and the sense of nausea faded somewhat, still present, but pushed back, less in the forefront.

"The elevator," she said, with more confidence in her voice than she felt.

"You go ahead, check if it's clear," Patrick said. He turned to Joyce, and held out his hand. "Here, give me your phone, you're going with them."

Joyce blinked at him for a moment, working through what he'd said. "But what about you?"

"Don't worry, I'm *right* behind you," Patrick said, easing the phone out of her grasp. "But I don't want these . . . these *whatever* they are following us too closely."

He faced back the way they'd come, and held the phone up in one hand, speaker forward, and his pistol in the other.

"Go," he said.

The thing that had in life been Tyler Campbell was shuffling out the door into the hallway, and the other six were following close behind him.

"Go!" Patrick repeated.

"Come on." Izzie turned and started down the hallway towards the elevator shaft, watching for any signs of movement in the shadows ahead. Daphne followed close behind, her pistol held close to her side, ready for whatever might come.

"Might want to move a little faster," Patrick called from the rear. "It's like they know we're here but can't quite find us."

There were seven dead people jostling in the hallway now, hands out and grasping, as if feeling their way through a darkened room.

"Almost there," Izzie answered without looking back. "Just let me . . ."

She trailed off into silence.

"Izzie?" Patrick called, sounding increasingly anxious.

"Shit," Izzie spat. "The elevator's not here." She leaned into the shaft and looked up into the darkness above. "It must be back up on street level."

"There's the button," Daphne said, and slapped it with her palm. There was no response. She hit it again, and then a third time. "Dead."

"I'd prefer if you didn't use that word just this very moment," Joyce said, shoulders hunched defensively.

"We need another way out," Izzie shouted back to Patrick.

"End of the hallway," he answered, his back bumping against Joyce. The dead people were right behind them now. "There's a stairway behind a fire door. That's how Carlson and I came down."

Izzie turned and looked in that direction. The lights in this section of the hallway were dim, but she could just make out a red metal door at the end of the hall, and there were no obstructions between it and where she stood. "Got it."

She jogged down the hall, eyes shifting left and right on the off chance that any of the closed doors might spring open and some new danger jump out at them. But she reached the fire door without incident, grabbed hold of the handle, and tried to yank it open, but the door was stuck.

"Damn it," she said, tugging harder on the door. She glanced back the way she'd come. Daphne was right behind her, followed closely by Joyce, with Patrick bringing up the rear, the jostling dead people only a short distance behind.

The metronome-like plink and guitar fuzz from Joyce's phone decrescendoed as the song reached its end, and silence filled the hall.

As one, the seven dead people turned and faced Izzie and the others, and started shambling with purpose towards them, arms out.

"Music!" Izzie shouted, yanking harder on the door. "*Noise!*"

The sound of delicate flutes playing spilled out of the phone's speaker. *"CAN YOU HEAR THE DRUMS, FERNANDO..."*

The thing that had been Tyler Campbell and the others were not deterred, but kept on advancing.

"It's not working, it's not working!" Patrick shouted.

Joyce reached over, tapped the left arrow on the phone's screen, and the previous song came blaring out of the speaker again.

The dead people seemed suddenly disoriented, their movements more erratic, less purposeful.

Izzie holstered her pistol, knowing it would be of little use to her against the dead people anyway, and grabbed hold of the handle with both hands. She pulled again, and felt the door begin to give, but it still remained shut.

"Let me help," Daphne said, her own pistol already in its holster. She came to stand beside Izzie, shoulder to shoulder, and grabbed the end of the door handle. "Pull!"

With a scream of metal on metal, the fire door bounced open.

"Inside!" Izzie shouted, holding the door open.

Daphne slipped past her into the stairwell, with Joyce close on her heels. Patrick backed down the hallway towards the door, holding the phone out towards the dead people like it was a crucifix and they were silver-screen vampires.

"Go on, already!" Izzie said, grabbing the back of Patrick's quilted jacket and dragging him through the door.

As soon as they were both inside, Izzie pulled the door shut behind them. It was darker in the stairway than it had been in the hall, and she looked around frantically in the low light cast by Joyce's phone.

"There's no lock," she said, looking the door up and down.

"It's a fire door, Izzie," Patrick said, grabbing her elbow and pulling her towards the stairs. "They don't lock. Now come on!"

Daphne and Joyce were already one flight ahead of them, and as Izzie and Patrick reached the landing and turned to take the next leg, she could see that there was light shining from the next floor up.

"Keep going," Patrick called up the stairwell to them. "The ground level is the next door you'll see."

He and Izzie caught up with them as Daphne was struggling to open the ground floor door. Light was spilling from underneath the door, but it wasn't budging.

"It's dummied up to look like an electrical closet, remember?" Patrick said. "There's a lot of crap piled on the other side. Must have shifted when Carlson and I came through."

Patrick grabbed hold of the door handle, twisted it hard, and then drove his shoulder into the door as hard as he could.

The door slammed open, and light flooded into the stairway. They were on the ground floor level of the converted warehouse space, with a stairway on their left leading up to the floors above, and a foyer to the right that lead to the front glass doors. The ground floor was brightly lit by fluorescent fixtures in the suspended ceiling above, surrounded by acoustic tiles.

"Let's get out of here." Joyce leaned heavily on her cane and started towards the front door.

"It's dark out there," Daphne said, lingering and looking at the glass door, her eyes narrowed warily.

"It's nighttime," Patrick said matter-of-factly as he followed Joyce towards the door.

"Riiight." Daphne was exasperated as she answered. "It was night when we got here, too. But it wasn't *dark*."

She glanced back at Izzie, who realized what she was saying.

Joyce had already opened the door and was stepping outside onto the sidewalk. "Um, guys?"

Patrick followed her out, with Izzie and Daphne hanging back in the doorway.

"The lights are out," Daphne said, looking down the block.

Izzie looked in that direction, and could see that the streetlamps on either end of the block, which had been shining as bright as daylight when they arrived, were dark. Had they been shot out? Or had someone somehow turned them off?

There was noise from behind them, and glancing back over her shoulder Izzie could see the door that lead to the basement stairway being forced open from the other side.

"They're coming," she said, grabbing Daphne's elbow. "We've got to go."

"But the lights . . . ?" Daphne was wary as they stepped out onto the darkened sidewalk.

Joyce and Patrick were already standing by the curb.

"Something's not right," Joyce said, turning in place.

Izzie and Daphne joined them, catching their breath.

"Did you hear that?" Patrick asked, turning and looking up the street.

"What I'd *like* to hear," Daphne answered, exasperated, "is the sound of someone telling me just what the hell is going on here."

"No, look." Patrick pointed towards the north end of the block.

In the low light, Izzie couldn't see what he was pointing at for a moment. The skies overhead were moonless, and the only illumination on the street came from the light spilling out from the glass door of the office building.

Then she spotted it. Something moving in the shadows at the end of the block.

From the office building entrance behind them came a sudden sound, breaking glass and screaming metal, and in the next instant the street was plunged into near total darkness.

"They broke the lights inside, too," Daphne said, looking back towards the office building. Beyond the glass door now was only darkness.

Izzie's eyes adjusted quickly to the lack of light, and she found it was somewhat easier to see the gradations of shadow without the bright lights spilling out of the door behind them.

There were people standing at the end of the block, at least a dozen. Heads tilted forward, arms at their sides, little more than rough silhouettes in the dim. And as Izzie watched, they began to advance, moving in lockstep, perfectly synchronized.

"Recondito PD!" Patrick raised his voice, while pulling a flashlight out of his pocket. He thumbed the switch, and pointed the light at the end of the block. "Please leave the area immediately!"

From the office building came more sounds of shattering glass, as the seven dead people began to smash through the door. In moments they would be outside.

"Patrick," Joyce said, moving closer to his side. "You see that, don't you?"

Izzie and Daphne stepped off the curb and into the street, drawing their pistols.

The beam from Patrick's flashlight played over the people who were approaching from the end of the block, and Izzie and the others could clearly see the massive inky blots that covered the faces, necks, and arms of each of them, all but completely obscuring any distinguishing features. They weren't simply silhouettes in the darkness, they were practically silhouettes in the light, as well.

"Blots," Patrick hissed.

It was a horde of Ink users, all of them pretty far gone, their memories and personalities no doubt completely erased by the drug, who were now shambling with purpose towards them out of the darkness, moving as one.

CHAPTER TWENTY-EIGHT

"**H**ere, take this," Patrick said, handing the flashlight to Joyce. He pulled the radio out of his pocket, thumb on the button. "Dispatch. Chavez. Harrison. Anybody copy?"

When he lifted his thumb, there was only silence in response.

"Why aren't they answering?" Joyce asked.

"I don't know," Patrick answered with a scowl, shoving the radio back into his pocket. "Sounds like there's some kind of interference, maybe. I'm not sure."

"Let's get out of here, already," Daphne urged.

Izzie turned to look towards the south end of the block. "There's more coming from that direction."

She pointed at the dozen or so "blots" who were shambling up the street from the other side towards them. They were being hemmed in on three sides now.

"Well, that's just great," Patrick deadpanned.

It was eerily quiet on the street. The only sound was that of the shambling blots' shuffling feet moving in perfect unison, like fingers on the same hand, closing around them.

"Maybe more music would help?" Joyce held up her phone.

"I doubt it," Izzie answered. "Wouldn't be loud enough out here, too much space to fill with sound."

The thing that had been Tyler Campbell and the other dead people were on the sidewalk now, advancing towards them.

"Come on!" Izzie said, hurrying towards where Daphne's and Joyce's cars were parked a short distance up the street. "Let's get moving."

"Where are they all *coming* from?" Daphne asked, following close behind.

Joyce was panicking, patting the pockets of her leather jacket. "I can't find my keys." She looked up, her expression stricken. "My car keys! I can't find them!"

Patrick put an arm around her shoulders, urging her gently forward as he looked back at the seven dead people approaching from the office building. "Well, we're not going back to look for them."

"Come on," Daphne said, her key ring already in her hand. She pressed a button, and the car alarm on her bucar turned off with a quick pair of beeps. When the others caught up, she was already yanking open the driver's side door. "I'll drive."

Izzie jumped in the front passenger seat, and was slamming the door shut behind her as Patrick and Joyce slid in the backseat.

Daphne turned the key in the ignition.

Nothing happened.

"Daphne?" Izzie said, looking out the window at the shambling hordes who were closing in on three sides, almost within arms' reach.

"It's okay, it's okay, it's okay," Daphne repeated under her breath like a mantra. "You can do it you can do it you can do it . . ."

The engine roared to life.

Daphne shifted the car into gear and took off the parking brake. "Which way?"

"Just drive!" Patrick shouted from the backseat.

The thing that had been Tyler Campbell in life reached the passenger side of the car and grabbed hold of the side-view mirror.

"Okay, okay!" Daphne floored the accelerator and yanked the wheel to the left.

With a screech of tearing metal, the side-view mirror was wrenched off of the car door, but the car kept moving, trailing wires.

The horde of shambling blots from the south was right in front of them, undeterred by the sight of a car speeding towards them.

"Come *on!*" Daphne said, jerking the wheel to the left just in time to avoid plowing into the closest of the shambling figures. "Do they *want* me to run them over?!"

"I don't think *they* want anything," Izzie answered. "They're not the ones calling the shots."

The street they were on curved to the right just ahead before veering back towards the south and merging with Bayfront Drive.

There weren't any other cars out on the street on these industrial blocks, which was hardly surprising given the lateness of the hour. And even when they continued onto Bayfront, the only headlights they saw were blocks and blocks away to the north, or briefly glimpsed up side streets to the west.

"We should head back to City Center," Joyce said. "I want to know how a dead man got up and walked out of my morgue without anyone knowing."

"A morgue filled with dead bodies," Patrick pointed out. "Can you say for certain that the others aren't going to get up and starting moving around, too?"

Joyce started to answer, then closed her mouth, fuming with frustration. "I *saw* it, but I'm still having trouble *believing* it."

"There's another one," Daphne said, nodding in the direction of the sidewalk up ahead on the left, where another person covered in inky blots was shambling towards them from the opposite direction. "They're all over the place."

Izzie turned around in the passenger seat, so she could address both Daphne at the steering wheel and also Patrick and Joyce in the back. "Look, someone is controlling everyone who has taken enough Ink to get the blots on their skin. Both the *living*, and the *dead*. Joyce, you've got too many dead dealers and users down in the morgue for me to feel comfortable about going back there. But there are *living* users all over the city, right?"

Patrick nodded.

"So we need to go somewhere there *aren't* any," Izzie said, giving Patrick a meaningful look.

"Little Kovoko," he answered, nodding slowly. "Assuming that our guess about my great-uncle's wards is correct, then . . ."

"That's what I'm thinking," Izzie said, cutting him off. She turned to Daphne. "Take the next right you come to. We're going to head over a few blocks to Mission and then turn south."

"Got it," Daphne answered, shifting lanes to the right and turning on her signal.

"I don't know that we really need to signal our intent to the undead lurching after us, do we?" Joyce said, hearing the turn signal clicking.

"Sorry." Daphne switched off the signal. "Force of habit. Okay, everyone hold on."

She cut the wheel sharply to the right, about to turn onto Mason. But as soon as they started to round the corner they saw a dozen or more of the blot-covered shamblers blocking the road.

"Damn!" Daphne spun the wheel back to the left, bumping up over the curb and narrowly avoiding running into a stop sign as she veered back onto Bayfront Drive.

One of the shamblers lurched in front of the car, got sideswiped by Daphne's bumper, and was knocked to one side. Those it had impacted with made a sickening crunch. As Izzie looked back she could see that the shambler was already climbing back to its feet, intent on continuing after them.

"Just keep driving," Izzie urged, continuing to look behind. The shamblers were not terribly fast moving, but there were more of them pouring out onto the streets with each passing moment. It was as if they had kicked an anthill by accident, and now a seemingly endless horde of biting insects was swarming up out of the ground to attack them.

The next street up had been torn up for road construction, with barricades blocking traffic from entering. The street after that was swarming with more of the blot-covered shamblers, coming out of dingy apartment buildings. They seemed to be avoiding the most brightly lit blocks, but in this part of the Oceanview, there were more than enough long shadows for them to move around freely on the rest of the streets.

"How many of these guys *are* there?!" Daphne gripped the steering wheel and tensed up.

"Look," Patrick said, leaning forward and pointing ahead through the windshield. "We're almost to Shoreline Boulevard, anyway." Bayfront Drive had begun to curve around to the west as it hugged the edge of the isthmus. If they continued on, they would reach the intersection with Shoreline Boulevard at the southernmost tip of the Oceanview. "We can just double back to the north, and that will take us straight into Little Kovoko. So long as we don't . . ."

He trailed off, his eyes narrowed and his brow furrowed as he glared at the road ahead of them.

There was a city bus parked across all three lanes of traffic ahead, completely blocking their way. A man in a bus driver's uniform was on the ground, unconscious and possibly dead, while a small group of shamblers stood over him, with more still getting off the bus.

"They take public transportation, even?!" Joyce said.

"This is a coordinated effort," Patrick said. "They somehow found out we were down there, and they don't want us getting away."

"But how could they have known so quickly?" Daphne asked.

"I think they're all being driven by the same intelligence." Izzie had her hands pressed together, fingertips on her chin, trying to concentrate. "They really are like a bunch of fingers on the same hand, all trying to close us in. We'll never get to Little Kovoko at this rate . . ."

If the old man's wards couldn't protect them, then what other options were there? "Fire," Izzie muttered out loud. "Discordant noise." She bit her lower lip. "Running water . . ."

She lowered her hands, and her eyes widened.

"Daphne, turn left here!" Izzie pointed towards a paved walkway that continued past the intersection of Shoreline and Bayfront, just before the city bus that blocked their way. "We'll have to hop the curb, but we should be able to make it."

"But there's nothing *down* there," Daphne objected.

Izzie ignored her, and turned around to Patrick and Joyce. "What time does the evening tide come in this time of year?"

Patrick and Joyce exchanged a look.

"Around now, I think," Joyce answered, a little uncertainly.

"Izzie, where do you expect me to *go*?" Daphne was driving up onto the sidewalk, about to turn onto the pedestrian walkway. "I'm telling you, there's nothing down here but boardwalk and . . ."

"Ivory Point," Patrick interrupted from the back seat.

"Exactly." Izzie nodded. She turned back to Daphne. "We might get a little wet, but I think we can make it."

"Wait, you mean to go out *there*?!" Daphne kept her hands on the wheel, but shot a disbelieving glance in Izzie's direction. "But *why*?"

"Because it may be our best shot," Izzie answered. "And just might be our *only* shot, for that matter. We need to put some running water between us and those things. We have to get to that lighthouse."

CHAPTER TWENTY-NINE

Concrete planters dotted the end of the pedestrian walkway, preventing anything but foot traffic from continuing on to the boardwalk.

As Daphne slammed the brakes, her car skidded to a stop just short of the planters. Blot-covered shamblers were already making their way from the intersection down the walkway towards them.

"Come on!" Izzie jumped out of the passenger side door. "Move!"

Joyce and Patrick were unfolding themselves from the backseat.

"I still don't understand," Daphne said, shutting the driver's side door. "Why don't we just call for backup?"

Patrick had his radio in his hand. "It's no good. Still getting some kind of interference."

"And I'm not getting *any* signal," Joyce said, holding up her phone.

"This way!" Izzie was already past the planters and heading down the boardwalk, gesturing urgently for the others to follow.

During warmer months, this stretch of the boardwalk was filled with concession stands, artists with their easels, and buskers with their hats out for coins. But winter was fast approaching, and the wind that blew in from the ocean through the mouth of the bay was biting and cold, so there was hardly anyone about. Just a vagrant searching in trash bins for cans and bottles to redeem, and a couple of teenage hoodlums furtively smoking cigarettes while acting as lookouts for a friend who was tagging the retaining wall with a can of spray paint.

"Get out of here!" Izzie shouted at the homeless man and the teenagers as she ran by. "Trouble's coming!"

The vagrant didn't even look up, and the teenagers just sneered.

"Get moving or you're under arrest!" Patrick shouted, brandishing his pistol and flashing his Recondito PD badge.

The teenagers scattered, and the tagger tossed the can of spray paint off the boardwalk and into the surf, while the vagrant shuffled away, keeping his head down.

Izzie reached the bend in the boardwalk that marked the southernmost point of the Oceanview. At low tide, there was a muddy land bridge that connected this spot to the white rocks of Ivory Point, but the tide was coming in, and only a few spits of mud had yet to be submerged.

"You sure about this?" Daphne said, catching up with her.

Silhouetted against the moonless sky directly across from where they stood, rose the bulk of the Ivory Point Lighthouse.

"I hope so," Izzie answered.

She glanced back as Patrick and Joyce caught up. Joyce was traveling as quickly as she could with her cane, and Patrick had clearly hung back to make sure she wouldn't be left behind.

The blots were already spilling out of the walkway and shambling towards them, the ones from the intersection joined by many of the others, dozens of them in all.

"If we wait much longer the tide will be too high for us to get across," Izzie said, stepping off the boardwalk into the ankle-deep water. She held a hand out to Daphne to help her down. "Come on, we need to get across, *now!*"

Daphne hopped down into the water, while Patrick helped Joyce step down.

"Damn," Joyce muttered, as her feet squelched into the mud. "I *loved* these boots."

"I'll buy you another pair if we make it out of this in one piece," Patrick said, taking Joyce's cane from her hand and putting his arm across her back, helping to steady her.

Joyce put her arm around Patrick's shoulder. "I should wear shoes you could afford on a *cop's* salary? No, thank you."

Izzie had already taken several steps across what remained of the land bridge, and the waters surged higher with each passing moment. She tried to lift her foot to take another step, but suction tugged hard at her shoe and she nearly lost her balance trying to pull it loose.

"I got you," Daphne said, grabbing hold of Izzie's hand. As she helped Izzie regain her balance, a faint smile tugged the corners of her mouth. "I owed you."

Ivory Point was only fifty or so feet away from the board-walk at its closest approach, and by the time they were half-way across that distance the water had already raised to their calves. The salty seawater was bone-chillingly cold, and the tidal surges threatened to sweep them off the land bridge and into the bay.

When Izzie had last been here five years before with Patrick, Agent Henderson, and the others, they had come at high tide on motorboats in the small hours of the morning, hoping to catch Nicholas Fuller before he managed to kill Francis Zhao. They had arrived too late, of course, but had they waited until the land bridge reappeared at low tide they might not have captured Fuller at all.

But now she understood why Fuller had used the lighthouse for his gruesome work, and why he had blared speed metal from speakers at the base of the structure and set out a ring of salt around him at the lantern room at the top. Fuller had been a scientist, and it was as if he had reverse engineered how airplanes functioned by studying the practices of a cargo cult.

Fuller had insisted there was one more before his work was done. He had to find the "student."

Had Izzie and Patrick stopped him too soon? And had they been wrong to stop him in the first place?

All of these thoughts and fears swirled in Izzie's head as they crossed the final few feet to the shores of Ivory Point, and scrambled up onto the white rocks, shivering with the cold, their shoes heavy with mud and their sodden pants legs plastered to their skin.

Only when they were safely standing on the white rocks of Ivory Point's shore did Izzie look back towards the mainland that they'd fled only moments before.

There on the boardwalk stood a mass of bodies, forty or fifty at least, lined up just short of the surging water's edge, facing them. The inky blots that marred their exposed flesh had grown so large that scarcely an inch of unblemished skin could be seen. And front and center stood the thing that had been Tyler Campbell in life and the unclothed forms of the six bodies that they had found in the subbasement of the converted warehouse, all of them as silent and immobile as statues.

"Why didn't they follow us across?" Daphne said, her hands on her knees while she caught her breath. "I don't get it."

"They can't cross running water," Izzie answered. "That's why Nicholas Fuller brought his victims here to dismember, so that the others wouldn't come to stop him."

"Other what?" Daphne asked.

"The Ridden." Patrick had his hands plunged deep into the pockets of his quilted jacket, trying to keep warm. "That's what we're calling them, right?"

Izzie nodded. "Think of it like a kind of possession. They're being controlled by an outside force, but certain things disrupt that connection. Fire, running water, salt. Loud discordant sounds disorient them, which is why the music from Joyce's phone worked back there. And silver cuts off the connection entirely, but only while it remains inside the body."

"This sounds like werewolf rules," Daphne shook her head in disbelief, "or vampire shit. What, are you going to tell me that wooden stakes through the heart will stop them, too?"

"No," Joyce said, "just complete dismemberment. Even removing their brain doesn't seem to be sufficient, if there's enough gray matter left for the nervous system to be tweaked."

Izzie looked towards the medical examiner, a little surprised to hear her talking so matter-of-factly about this.

Joyce noted the look on Izzie's face, and shrugged. "Occam's razor. It fits the available facts."

"I don't know about you three," Patrick said, shivering, "but I am *freezing*."

Izzie turned towards the lighthouse, which loomed above the small residence beside it. "Come on, let's get inside and out of the wind."

The door to the lighthouse was locked, but Patrick thought he could jimmy open the lock without too much trouble.

"So a cop is breaking and entering," Joyce asked. "Are you sure about that?"

"I think we're well past doing this by the book," Patrick answered, his expression grim.

While Patrick worked on the lock, Izzie saw that there was a notice stapled to the wall that stated that the structures and Ivory Point itself were the private property of something called Znth, and that trespassers would be prosecuted.

"Where have I heard that name before . . . ?" she wondered aloud.

"Hmm?" Daphne turned to look in that direction. "Oh, remember, I told you about them. That's Martin Zotovic's private equity firm."

"The same guy that owns Parasol?" Izzie raised an eyebrow. "What would he want with a disused lighthouse?"

Daphne shrugged. "Like I told you, his outfit has been buying up all kinds of property in and around the city. I guess this is one of them."

"Got it." Patrick tone was momentarily triumphant as he stood back and pushed the door to the lighthouse open. Then his enthusiasm flagged a bit as he glanced at the others. "Could be I missed my calling, being a cop. Maybe I would have made a better burglar."

"Get in, already," Joyce said, shoving him towards the door. "You were the one complaining about the cold, remember?"

The ground floor level of the lighthouse was about as Izzie had remembered it. Sealed concrete floor, steel beams supporting concrete walls, a narrow doorway leading to a hall connecting the lighthouse to the modest residence beside it. And dominating the room was a metal staircase that spiraled up into the high ceilinged space to the lantern room above.

"Should we go through to the living area?" Patrick nodded towards the door. "Might be a little warmer in there."

"You can, if you want." Izzie shook her head, and started for the spiral staircase. "I want to go up to the top, see if I can get a better look at the shore from there."

"I'm coming with you," Daphne said, following close behind.

Patrick and Joyce exchanged a glance, shrugged, and then fell in step behind them.

As they ascended several stories' worth of steps, Izzie could not help but recall the first and only time that she had climbed this staircase. The deafening sound of the speed metal blaring from below, the metal railing cold to the touch, the bright lights spilling out into the gloom from the doorway at the top. And the charnel-house stench that grew stronger with each step she climbed. She had known then that they had arrived too late for Francis Zhao, but had refused to give up hope completely.

Izzie tensed instinctively when she reached the top of the stairs, as though her body itself was reluctant to pass through the door and into the lantern room. It was a senseless fear, of course. Nicholas Fuller was long dead, not lurking behind the metal door with sword in hand, ready to attack her. But still, Izzie found that her skin crawled with anxiety, and she had to steel her nerves before continuing on.

She took a deep breath, turned the knob on the door, and walked through the doorway into the lantern room.

It was dark inside, but with the big glass windows that surrounded the room on all sides, enough light eked in that Izzie managed to find her way to the lighting controls mounted on the wall. She pulled a lever, and the bulb in the big lighthouse lamp overhead began to warm up, sending a warm light spilling out in all directions that grew hotter with each passing second.

"I guess the generator is still working," she said aloud as she looked around. "Small favors . . ."

With the light on, Izzie could get a better look at the lantern room itself. The glass window through which Nicholas Fuller had crashed when he fell to his death had been boarded up, and someone had tried as much as possible to scrub off the formulae and symbols that Fuller had scrawled on the remaining windows in black ink. The metal plates that formed the floor of the lantern room had been power washed. Although no trace of the pentagrams, hexagrams, and other sigils that Fuller had painted on the floor remained, faint ghosts of the symbols and characters that Fuller had inscribed on the windows could still be seen, like afterimages that linger in one's vision after the original image has long since faded.

Izzie was turning in place, trying to orient herself, as Daphne and the others stepped out into the lantern room.

"Never figured I'd be coming back *here*," Patrick said, a look of distaste on his face.

"That's north," Izzie said, turning to the right. She crossed the metal floor, and looked out the window. She could see the Oceanview boardwalk across the way, and it seemed that even more of the blot-covered shamblers had joined the others along the shore, staring silently at them. "Must be at least sixty or seventy of them, now."

"But if the only thing keeping them from getting over here is the water," Joyce said, hand on her chin, "what's to stop them when the tide goes out?"

"Sun will be up by then," Patrick answered. "And the Ink makes them . . . what's the word again?"

"Photophobic," Izzie supplied.

"Right." Patrick nodded. "So chances are they'll clear out by sunrise."

"That's weird," Izzie said, rising up on her tiptoes to look past the boardwalk and to the streets beyond. "Looks like there's some kind of broadcast van over there. You know, the kind that news crews use, with a satellite dish on top?"

Patrick came to stand beside her, cupping his hands around his eyes and leaning in close to the glass. "I'm not seeing any markings on it, though. And that doesn't look like the satellite dishes that a news van would have. Looks more like the top of a cell tower. Like a radio transmitter or something."

They both turned to look at each other.

Joyce was looking at her phone. "Still not getting any signal, which is strange, considering how high up we are. I should be getting five bars, easy."

"That thing must be what's blocking our radios and phones," Izzie said. "Like, it's broadcasting some kind of interference that's keeping us from contacting anyone else."

"But who's doing *that*?" Patrick asked. "And what does it have to do with Ink and the Ridden?"

"Okay, *now* will someone explain to me just what the hell is going on?!" Daphne shouted, throwing her hands in the air.

Izzie exchanged a glance with Patrick and Joyce.

"Go ahead," Patrick said, "you seem to have a better handle on this than the rest of us."

Izzie nodded, taking a deep breath before answering.

"The simple truth, Daphne," she said, "is that the world is *much* stranger than you thought it was."

CHAPTER THIRTY

"Ink isn't just a drug," Izzie was explaining. "It is, but it's more than that. It consumes the brains of the people who take it in bits and pieces, leaving behind 'vacuoles,' little pockets of emptiness. And from what we learned tonight, it seems like the Ink is somehow *cultivated* inside of the brains of 'hosts,' and then extracted and sold to new users."

"Wait, so this Ink stuff doesn't just *eat* people's brains," Daphne asked, interrupting Izzie's explanation, "but it *grows* in them, too?"

"That seems to be the case, yeah," Joyce answered. "The pathology isn't like anything I've seen before."

"But where does the Ink *come* from?" Daphne went on.

"The people targeted by Nicholas Fuller exhibited the same condition," Patrick said. "And they were all part of a research team at Ross University that worked on the Undersight project."

"There's an abandoned mine shaft a few miles northeast of town," Izzie added. "And there seem to be other instances of weirdness and possibly possession associated with that same mine shaft going back at least a century or two, so our best guess is that they were exposed to something down there that . . . I guess you could say it *infected* them?" She paused, considering. "I know this will sound crazy, but I sincerely think that whatever force or intelligence it is that's controlling those people out there is coming into our world from somewhere outside our universe, and the place where it's getting through is down in that mine shaft."

"Wait a minute." Daphne held up a hand, faced lined with concentration. "A mine shaft northeast of town . . . You mean the mining claim that Znth bought a couple of years ago?"

"You mean Zotovic's company . . . ?" Izzie began, the implications beginning to take shape in her head.

"Yeah," Daphne answered. "It was one of the properties listed in that article that I read. Zotovic convinced the mayor's office to sell it to his private equity company, in exchange for backing the mayor's re-election campaign. Something about how he'd worked on some kind of research project there before he dropped out of college . . ."

Izzie remembered what Nicholas Fuller had said in that very room, five years before. *"I only have one more to go and my work is finished. The student. I have to find him."* And she recalled what Dr. Kono had said about an undergraduate student who was interviewing to join the Undersight team when Fuller had attacked Alice Thompkins, a "Martin Something-or-other."

"Izzie, you don't think . . . ?" Patrick began.

"Martin Zotovic was with Undersight," Izzie answered, her voice scarcely above a whisper. "The man who now owns Parasol was the last one that Fuller was looking for. The last one to go down into the darkness and bring the darkness back with him."

"How does that even work?" Daphne asked.

"Wait," Joyce put in, "so you think that Zotovic was one of the . . . what did you call them? The *Ridden* that Fuller was hunting?"

Izzie nodded. "It would fit the facts. If Zotovic *was* the student that Fuller was looking for, and he had been down in the mine shaft with Undersight, he was most likely infected with whatever got to the others." She started pacing across the metal floor, scratching the scar on the back of her hand. "But when Fuller died, there was nothing to stop Zotovic from doing . . . well, whatever it was that Fuller was trying to stop him from doing."

"Like dropping out of college and starting a software company?" Daphne's tone was skeptical.

"And introducing a new street drug, apparently," Patrick added. "So it's *not* just a coincidence that a bunch of Parasol employees were part of the Ink manufacturing ring. And it went a lot higher than just a crooked manager or two."

"No, no." Izzie shook her head. "I mean, *yes*, all that sounds plausible, but we're missing something important. This is about a lot more than just the drug. The Ridden are being possessed somehow, even after death. And the Ink in their systems is responsible for eating away at their brains, making that possible. It *replaces* their brain matter with itself, so that it can take control. But we also know that the Ink can *grow* inside of people's brains—hosts—and be extracted to be put into others, right? And all of Fuller's victims had the same kind of vacuoles in their brains, too."

She stopped pacing and faced the others.

"What if the thing that infected the researchers in the mine shaft *was* Ink, only it's not *from* here? Maybe it's something that came through a gap of some kind from a higher dimension, from a higher universe. Maybe that's why you never find traces of the stuff in the users' bodies, because the stuff just goes back to wherever it came from, or it's still there and has just, I don't know, *shifted* into some dimension that we can't perceive."

She thought back to "ana" and "kata," and Aguilar's mention of shifting to different worlds.

"If Zotovic *was* part of the Undersight team and *did* become one of the Ridden, maybe that's why he bought the land that the mine shaft is on, to keep anyone else from going down there." She glanced out the window towards the mainland beyond. "And he'd certainly have the wherewithal to block our radios and phones to keep us from calling for help."

"But where did the Ink we're seeing on the streets come from?" Patrick asked. "Is he just, like, *mining* it down there?"

"I don't think so." Izzie shook her head.

"I agree with Izzie," Joyce said. "If that was the case, then why go to all the trouble of harvesting it from the brains of 'hosts'?"

"But the stuff would have been in Zotovic to begin with, right?" Daphne said. "So maybe *that's* where Ink came from originally?"

Izzie's eyes widened. "He could have harvested it from *himself* and then put it in other people to cultivate more."

"But if it's really something that entered our world from some other dimension or universe or whatever, *and* it's controlling the people who use it, then what *is* it?" Patrick was scowling, frustrated. "And who or what is it that's pulling the strings?"

"The loa," Izzie said.

The others turned and looked to her.

"That's as good a name for it as any," she went on. "In Haitian Vodou, the loa are intermediary spirits from outside our world, who can possess the bodies of the willing. While they're in control, the person is said to be Ridden. When the Ridden move it's because the loa wants them to, and when they speak it's the loa who is speaking."

She looked out the window at the silhouetted figures on the boardwalk, and then back to Patrick and the others.

"I think the Ink is all one thing. It's all part of a single intelligence that exists somewhere out in the higher dimensions. That's why all of those people down there move in sync, and how they all knew right away that we'd found the bodies down in that basement. They're like fingers on the same hand or, I don't know, tentacles on the same squid. Tendrils, I guess, emanating from whatever crack in reality is hidden down in that mine shaft, spreading out into our world."

Patrick and Joyce were thoughtful, but Daphne was plainly frustrated.

"So you're saying . . . what? That this is some kind of voodoo thing? Am I hearing you right? You expect me to believe that voodoo is real?"

"Maybe," Izzie answered. "Or maybe it describes something that *is* real in terms that people back then could understand. Like ancient astronomers and constellations and all that. Nicholas Fuller approached this originally from the science side, until he met an old man who followed an ancient Maya belief system, and then Fuller ended up combining the two approaches. And not just Maya, but stuff from all over the planet, where people have been exposed to this kind of thing before. The old man called them 'true places,' spots where the walls between the worlds are thin, and things can leak from one side to the other. And that's exactly the kind of thing that Fuller's scientific theory predicted." She looked from Daphne to Patrick and Joyce and back again. "So maybe it *is* supernatural *and* scientific, depending on your frame of reference. But either way, we have to deal with it."

"Okay, okay." Daphne nodded. "But deal with it *how*? If you took this to Agent Gutierrez, he'd think you were nuts." She turned to Patrick. "And how are you planning to explain this to *your* superiors?"

"I don't know," Patrick answered, his jaw tightened.

"I *saw* it," Joyce said, "and I'm still having trouble believing it."

"I think this has happened before," Izzie said. "The Guildhall fire back in the forties? The murders at the Eschaton Center in the seventies? I think that was someone *dealing* with previous outbreaks of whatever this is."

"Someone like Fuller's pal Roberto Aguilar?" Patrick suggested.

"Possibly," Izzie answered. "Or the old Mayan guy Don Mateo. He *came* to Recondito because it was a 'true place,' after all, to protect people against things coming through from the other side. And he wasn't the only one, either." She paused, and then added, "I think maybe that's why your great-uncle came here, too."

"That tracks." Patrick nodded slowly. "He always said that he came to Recondito to continue his 'work.' And he clearly knew more about all of this than any of us ever realized."

"So what are you suggesting, Izzie?" Daphne asked. "That we *don't* report this?"

"Not yet, anyway," she answered. "Accusing the richest and most powerful man in the city of not only being behind a burgeoning drug epidemic, but *also* of being possessed by an intelligence from outside our universe? That's not a claim that we can make without *solid* evidence."

"I agree," Patrick said. "But what do we *do*, then?"

Izzie turned and took a few steps away, mulling it over. She glanced at the window, saw the ghosts of mathematical formulae and occult symbols that lingered there, then hung her head. The scars on the back of her hand and on her leg itched, there was a sinking feeling at the pit of her stomach, and she felt suddenly more tired than she had in ages.

"Girl, you best wake up," she could hear her grandmother saying. *"You got work to do."*

Izzie turned back to face the others, her eyes narrowed and jaw set.

"I think we have to pick up where Nicholas Fuller left off. We have to finish what the Recondito Reaper started."

EPILOGUE

Daphne was snoring gently, her head resting on Izzie's shoulder. She'd finally fallen asleep just a couple of hours before, but Izzie was still wide awake. They were slumped side by side on a tarp-covered couch in the living quarters beside the lighthouse, which they'd found after descending from the lantern room sometime after 3:00 a.m.

Izzie and Daphne had spent hours talking in hushed tones on the couch so as not to disturb Patrick and Joyce, who'd gone off to sleep in an adjoining room. With all that had happened the previous day, something seemed to have shifted between them. It was as though a wall had begun to crumble, whether through exhaustion or anxiety or exhilaration or a mix of all three, and there in the darkness the final barrier between them had fallen.

Daphne had agreed to help smooth things over with the Bureau, to keep Gutierrez or Izzie's superiors back at Quantico from asking too many questions about just what was going on in Recondito. They wouldn't be falsifying reports, as such, but covering their tracks for the time being, and justifying the need for Izzie to remain in the city for the time being. They decided that to deal with whatever it was Zotovic was up to, it wasn't going to be quick.

As the small hours of the night wore on, their hushed conversation drifted from pressing matters to more personal ones. They swapped stories of past heartbreaks, hopes and fears for the future, secrets and dreams that they'd never shared with anyone else. It might have been the camaraderie of the foxhole, filters lost and defenses lowered in extreme circumstances, or the smoldering attraction they clearly felt for one another. This was not some casual flirtation anymore. This was something else.

Izzie had been whispering secrets about her childhood in the Ninth Ward when she realized that Daphne was no longer awake. So she sat in silence there in the dark, feeling the comforting weight and warmth of Daphne pressing against her side.

She was exhausted, physically and mentally, and felt emotionally drained, but try as she might Izzie couldn't sleep. She was too keyed up, her thoughts racing a million miles an hour, and no tricks or techniques that she knew were helping to slow them. A few stiff drinks might have done the trick, but she didn't imagine that the previous occupant of the lighthouse had left a fully stocked bar behind.

Finally, Izzie slid her phone out of her jacket pocket, and angled it so that light from the screen wouldn't wake Daphne when she thumbed it on. It was even later than she thought, with only a short time remaining before dawn. There was hardly any point in trying to sleep at this point. They'd need to be up and moving in barely half an hour.

Izzie decided to see what was happening on the shore. Were the ink-blotted shamblers still there waiting for them?

With some difficulty, she managed to maneuver Daphne off her shoulder, gently lowering the sleeping woman's head back onto the couch. Then she slid off the couch and stood up, tucking her phone back into her pocket.

There was a sliver of dim light shining from the door that led to the lighthouse proper, but Izzie still had to feel her way through the darkened room to it. She banged her shin painfully against a stool, but the crack of the impact and the sharp intake of breath that followed apparently weren't loud enough to wake Daphne, judging by the snoring that still sounded faintly from the couch. Izzie managed to reach the door without further mishap, and made her way down the corridor to the lighthouse.

The lights were still shining in the lantern room above, spilling warmly from the open door at the top of the metal staircase. Izzie trudged up the steps, leaning heavily on the handrail. The climb seemed longer than it had the night before, and it felt as though her feet were encased in lead. But finally she reached the top of the stairs, and stepped out into the lantern room.

Her eyes watered as she squinted at the bright light, which seemed to shine even brighter after her hours spent down in the darkness. But when her eyes adjusted, she saw that the lantern room was just as they'd left it a few hours before. Had she expected anything to have changed? She puzzled over the thought as she crossed the metal plates of the floor to the windows on the far side. It did seem that she had the unconscious expectation that something might have changed in their absence. Plunged into the depths of mystery as they were, with

secrets lurking in every shadow, it was as if part of her anticipated that anything might shift or alter as soon as she stopped
looking at it.

What was more troubling was the sneaking suspicion that
she might on some level be right.

Izzie reached the window, and looked out. The waters had
not yet fully receded at low tide, and the first light of dawn was
peeking over the hills to the east of the city. On the Oceanview
boardwalk across the way only a handful of the ink-blotted
shamblers remained, but even as she watched she saw a couple
of them turn and trudge away. By the time the morning sun-
light reached the waterfront, the last of them would be gone.

"How's it looking?"

Izzie spun around and dropped into a defensive posture,
instantly alert.

"Sorry," Patrick said, standing by the open door to the
staircase. "Didn't mean to startle you."

Izzie forced herself to relax. She could hear her pulse
throbbing in her ears.

"Just a little keyed up." She took a deep breath and forced
a weak smile.

Patrick came to stand beside her at the window.

"The last of them are clearing out," Izzie said, looking
down at the boardwalk.

Patrick nodded. "And not a moment too soon. Looks like
the tide is just about all the way out."

Izzie crossed her arms and turned to lean her shoulder
against the window, where faint ghosts of Nicholas Fuller's
formulae could still be seen. "So, are you ready for this?"

Patrick arched an eyebrow.

"For whatever we'll have to do," Izzie clarified. "It's not going to be easy, and it's not going to be nice."

"Yeah." Patrick shoved his hands in his pockets and sighed. "But what choice do we have?"

She chewed her lip, and shrugged. "Daphne's going to help keep the Bureau off our backs while we figure it out."

"Good," he answered with a nod. "Joyce is going to run interference on our side, too. We'll have to report *something* about what happened last night, but she thinks that she can help me keep it vague enough that there won't be any unwanted questions." He shook his head, ruefully. "She's going to have to come up with some kind of explanation for how a dead body went missing from the city morgue, but . . ." He raised his shoulders in a shrug of his own. "We'll figure something out."

Izzie turned and looked back out over the rapidly receding waters, as the muddy land bridge rose once more into view.

"This wasn't what I was expecting, the last time I left Recondito," she said. "Hell, this wasn't what I was expecting when I flew into town the other day. But maybe I'm . . . I don't know, maybe I'm *supposed* to be here?"

"Sounds an awful lot like something that my great-uncle would have said," Patrick answered with a sly smile. "Your grandmother, too, I'm guessing."

"Come on," Izzie rolled her eyes, "I'm already calling into question everything that I thought was true. Don't make me start wondering whether I'm turning into my *grandmother*, to boot."

"Okay, okay." His smile widened fractionally as he turned to look out over the city. "But honestly, whether you were *meant* to be in Recondito or not, I'm just glad you're here."

He turned, and met her gaze. "Because I sure as hell wouldn't want to be facing this on my own."

She glanced back towards the door, indicating the living quarters next door. "Sounds like you *aren't* on your own, though. Or didn't you just spend the night with the queen of the underworld?"

Izzie thought she detected a blush rising in his cheek. "Yeah, well, I seem to recall someone telling me that I had a blind spot where certain matters were concerned. So if you weren't here, I definitely *would* be on my own. In more ways than one."

She punched him in the shoulder, grinning.

"What was that for?" Patrick objected.

"Couldn't help myself," she answered. "There's just something about you that demands to be punched."

He rolled his eyes, feigning outrage unconvincingly.

"Come on." Izzie turned and headed towards the stairs. "Let's wake up the girls and get moving. We've got our work cut out for us."

To be continued in FIREWALKERS